IN THE 1980s WES'
WHEN THE POLIC
INVOLVED, A LOW-LEVEL CRIMINAL WITH
FAMILY PROBLEMS, COLTON PARKER, AND
FELLOW LOW-LIFERS ARE HIRED TO FIND
TWO MURDERERS.

Gamblers, cons, and whores inhabit the night-time bar world
of the early 1980s Odessa, Texas oil boom. Colton Parker—
with a wife, two young boys, and a father-in-law—is a
bouncer for a gambler and loan shark in this dark hidden
world. Danny Fowler cruises this world looking for gay
lovers. When he finds two mean ones, he ends up beaten to
death and dumped on the road to an oil rig. Danny's rich
mother, Mina, doesn't want Danny's night-time life exposed, so
she persuades the police not to investigate. But she hires a
reluctant Colton Parker to track down Danny Fowler's killers.
Colton teams with Bullet Price, a retired whore, climbing up
the bar-world social ladder. With help from a young whore
and a gay tool pusher, Colton tracks down the two oil-field
welders who killed Danny.

Praise for Gambled Dreams

"A brilliant, intense carefully crafted narrative with no feeling
of strain or effort. This is masterwork. The language and
vision match, so the world opens for us as readers without
any waver of authenticity. We are in it and trust what we
are learning. There is always more to understand than we
can, at the moment."—*Mary Hood, author of How Far She
Went and Familiar Heat*

"Jim brings a literary and poetic sensibility to his compelling,
utterly original crime novel, full of edgy, unique characters,
sharp dialogue, and powerful storytelling. Colton Parker, Bullet
Price and Way Low will haunt you long after you've turned
the final page."—*Lee Goldberg, #1 New York Times bestselling
author of Lost Hills, Bone Canyon, True Fiction, and others.*

"Noir-writer Jim Sanderson's tough new novel gives us a two-
generation search for belonging and soul set in the boom-bust

oil town of Odessa, Texas. Sanderson's tortured characters are unexpectedly loyal, and they carry the weight of their own longings..."—*Lisa Sandlin author of Shamus Award winning novels, The Do-Right and The Bird Boys*

"Jim Sanderson is a novelist of exceptional scope and depth. The worlds he creates are sometimes cruel, sometimes beautiful, generally gritty, and always engaging. Jim is one of the best novelists writing in Texas today."—*Dan Williams, editor-in-chief TCU Press.*

Excerpt

"I suppose you heard Danny Fowler got killed last night," Bullet said. "He was beat to death."

"I ain't heard. And why should I care?" Colton said.

"You know Danny Fowler?"

"Can't say as I do."

"You've seen him. He comes in the bars starting around ten. He dresses like some college boy, but he's way older. What he's doing is looking for boys."

Colton pulled his squinted eyes from the line of the horizon and shifted them toward Bullet. "He's queer?"

"He had more problems than that."

"Maybe he deserved it. Maybe he scared some poor country boy, and that boy didn't want Danny Fowler groping around in his underpants, so he took to whaling him and, country boys being country boys, didn't know when to stop."

"Could be. But I figure some smarter boys noticed the cash he carried and robbed him. And then things got out of hand."

"What do you care? Let the police find out."

"The police can't know where he was killed."

Colton turned his bulldog face to her. "I'm guessing he was killed at your whore house motel."

"Like I said, the police can't know that, not yet. But I aim to find those who killed him. But I'm just a woman in a man's town, and I need some muscle, somebody to cover my back. I can pay good. You interested?"

Gambled Dreams

Jim Sanderson

Moonshine Cove Publishing, LLC

Abbeville, South Carolina U.S.A.

First Moonshine Cove edition
March 2021

ISBN: 9781952439049

Library of Congress LCCN: 2021902700

Front cover by The Book Designer, interior design by Moonshine Cove staff

For Liz

About the Author

Jim Sanderson has published seven novels and republished three and an e-book collection of those three novels, and he has published three short story collections, one essay collection, two textbooks, and over eighty articles, essays, and stories. He has become an oxymoron: a literary genre writer. As a  reviewer said, Sanderson writes "Grit Lit." *El Camino del Rio* (novel) won the 1997 Frank Waters Award. *Faded Love* (short fiction), was a finalist for the 2010 Jesse Jones award, sponsored by the Texas Institute of Letters Award. "Bankers," a short story, won the 2012 Kay Cattarulla award, also sponsored by the Texas Institute of letters. *Safe Delivery*, (novel) was a finalist for the 2000 Violet Crown Award. *Semi-Private Rooms* (short fiction) won the 1992 Kenneth Patchen Award. *El Camino del Rio, Safe Delivery, La Mordida*, and *Dolph's Team* form a mystery series. *Nevin's History* is a historical or Western novel. *Nothing to Lose* is a darkly comic mystery novel. *Hill Country Property* is a family saga. *Trashy Behavior* is a collection of crime stories. *Semi-Private Rooms* and *Faded Love* are collections of stories about found and lost love. A *West Texas Soapbox* is a collection of humorous amateur sociologist essays about West Texas.

With forty years of teaching, he is a professor of English and Chair at Lamar University in Beaumont, Texas.

https://www.jimsanderson-writer.com/

Acknowledgment

Excerpts appeared in altered forms in the following:

Trashy Behavior (short story collection). Lamar University Press (Beaumont, TX), 2013.

"Pissed Away." *Shared Voices*, Anthology of South Carolina and Texas Writers with responses. ed. Andrew Geyer. Lamar University Press. 2013.

"Dee Price's Story," *The Book of Villains*. Ed. Josh Wood. Main Street Rag (Charlotte, NC), 2011.

"Playing Scared." *Mystery in the Wind*. Second Wind Publishing, 2010.

Danny Fowler

Part I

Chapter 1

On a Sunday before the sun was up, late in October, after the 1981 Odessa, Texas Oil Show had closed, after all the drinking, whoring, and gambling had ended, Colton Parker stepped out the backdoor of the Cactus Lounge and into an early morning breeze. The sun was just coming up, and it lit a pumpjack. To somebody not from West Texas, a pumpjack would look something like a giant mosquito sucking up blood from the very heart of the earth. The line of orange the rising sun made and the glitter from the new pumpjack almost made the morning pretty, but the cool, kind fall breeze, not a rough West Texas spring wind nor a fall norther, blew tumbleweeds and trash against the pumpjack and a barbed wire fence farther away in the half-light.

Colton Parker squatted on the steps, the way an old farmer would, looked down, and saw crumpled laundry at the bottom of the steps. Raising himself, Colton toed the laundry and heard a grumble and noticed the laundry shifting. One of the drunk gamblers at Snake Popp's game must have come outside to piss in the dark, but he fell and passed out. Best to let him lie, Colton thought, and squatted back down on the step. His head hurt. His eyes still watered from all the smoke inside the Cactus Lounge. He coughed up some goo from his burning throat and lungs. His clothes smelled from the smoke. He had just closed another one of Snake's invitation-only gambling nights. Amarillo Slim himself had once spent the night in the Cactus Lounge, losing big and leaving well before sunrise. Snake had several tables set up and different games went on at each.

Colton was Snake Popp's "assistant." Colton was not tall, but he was a good two hundred and twenty pounds. His was squat like a pulling guard or a bulldog. He was the type of guy that a troublemaker or badass could look at and think he could whip—but wouldn't want to try. Snake hired Colton to keep peace.

All night, with Lionel Dexter, his partner, Colton had watched over the card players. The pros stayed sober and concentrated on the cards. Amateurs faked laughing at their losings or went outside and cried about them. The lump of laundry at Colton's feet was probably a crier. Somebody could have just lost control of his nerves. Somebody could have gotten pissed. So, Colton and Lionel were there, watching and ready. At the end of the night, the way Snake Popp pushed his shoulders back, Colton knew Snake Popp had won big.

Snake Popp was mostly a legitimate businessman. He was not nicknamed Snake because he was as mean as a snake but because, when he was just a kid, he got bitten by a rattler and lost a chunk of skin off his ankle. Snake grew up liking to show that scar to people. He became "Snake," and then he became rich through questionable means, through cashing in on what the good Baptists and Church-of-Christers would call sin.

The backdoor hit Colton in the back. He looked up and saw Bullet Price in the doorframe. Bullet owned the building and the rights to the vending machines. Betty Howard's husband had owned the business, but he died. To support herself, Betty ran the bar. Bullet, being a friend of Snake's and Betty's, arranged for the game after midnight closing. "Almost pretty, isn't it?" Bullet said and sat beside Colton.

Her body was taut. She had lost a breast to cancer and liked to tell people about the operation. She even liked to show them her scar. Her hair was swept back from her face in wings. She was attractive. But a forked scar running down her forehead to her left cheek ruined her face. As with her mastectomy, she liked to tell people about that scar. A broken whiskey bottle gave it to her. Colton looked at the bobbing pumpjack to avoid Bullet because she wanted him to work for her. "Long night," she said.

"It's what Snake pays me for."

"There's better money and shorter hours," Bullet said. "If you want them."

Colton looked at the trash lined up on the fences and watched a tumbleweed catch on the pumpjack and then roll away. Far off in a small pasture, a frisky young horse trotted the length of the fence and then back again, just burning up his pent-up energy. "You're right. It is almost pretty."

The few clouds in the sky had pink undersides. A rooster crowed. The smell of rain was in the wind, though West Texans knew that it would not rain, hardly ever did. And it was as cool as it would be all day. He watched because this truly was as beautiful as it could get in West Odessa, the unincorporated, ill-planned community of trailers, cinderblock buildings, and small bars with tin roofs and gravel parking lots. And in just a split second, as it happened in West Texas, the sun pulled itself above the flat horizon and suddenly the morning was bright yellow light and hot.

The 1981 Oil Show had closed the night before. After the oil show, some of the high-rollers from out of town who wanted to dip their beaks just a little bit longer into the spirit of the show had stayed another night and drifted into the Cactus Lounge for Snake's game. Even some of the locals came, to gape and lose. During the oil show, for those who preferred whoring away from the trailers at Ector County fairgrounds or who couldn't afford the high-priced hotels, Bullet furnished the whores and the locale, the First Quality Motel, out on Second Street. Running whores during the oil shows that ran every other year could make nearly a year's living for Bullet. Running whores was how Bullet got the money to buy the Cactus Lounge from Betty Howard in the first place.

"I suppose you heard Danny Fowler got killed last night," Bullet said. "He was beat to death."

"I ain't heard. And why should I care?" Colton said.

"You know Danny Fowler?"

Colton stared off at the distance. Snake had warned him to stay away from offers from Bullet. "No good can come of working for her," Snake had said. But Colton thought maybe that was just because Snake wanted to keep Colton working for him at what he pays him. "Can't say as I do."

"You've seen him. He comes in the bars starting around nine or ten. He dresses like some college boy, but he's way older. What he's doing is looking for boys. Figures all those loose wild boys come to the oil field to get rich and busting their asses working as worms out on the rigs might be susceptible to his charms. The later it gets, the trashier the bars he goes to."

Colton pulled his squinted eyes from the line of the horizon and shifted them toward Bullet. "He's queer?"

"He had more problems than that."

"Maybe he deserved it. Maybe he scared some poor country boy, and that boy didn't want Danny Fowler groping around in his underpants, so he took to whaling him and, country boys being country boys, didn't know when to stop."

"That could be. But I figure some smarter boys noticed him and the cash he carried and deliberately robbed him. And then things got out of hand."

"What do you care? Let the police find out."

"The police can't know where he was killed. At least not yet."

Colton turned his bulldog face to her. "I'm guessing he was killed at your whore house motel."

"Like I said, the police can't know that, not yet. But I aim to find those who killed him. But I'm just a woman in a man's town, and I need some muscle, somebody to cover my back. I can pay good. You interested?"

Colton pulled his eyes away from Bullet and looked at that frisky pony running for joy within the confines of his corral. Colton thought that, if he looked at Bullet, she would seduce him in a way that didn't have nothing to do with sex but would have him out beating the shit out of people just because of her suspicions. "So why do you care? What's this queer to you?"

"Look at me," Bullet said. Colton obeyed. She balanced her cigarette on her bottom lip and held it in place with her top lip. She slowly slid her denim jacket off one shoulder, then she unbuttoned her blouse, tugged at it to reveal a shoulder. She tugged some more and showed an ugly, twisty pink scar across half her chest. Around her neck was a chain, and dangling from that chain, next to the pink scar, was a casing for a .45 bullet.

Colton had to look, and he wanted to touch the scar and the bullet, but to save himself from Bullet, he said, "Good God, Bullet. Cover that up."

"Danny Fowler bought me that. Saved my life."

"The scar or the casing?"

"The scar, Colton, the goddamn scar. He paid for my surgery. So, you see I owe him big time, and I hurt like hell that I couldn't save his. I'm doing the next best thing and finding who killed him."

"I ain't seen nothing on the news, ain't read nothing. How come you know so much?"

"Like I said, I know where he was killed. And I got something of a witness."

"Shit, Bullet. Well just shit."

The backdoor to the cactus lounge hit Colton in the back again. He looked up. Betty Howard said, "If you can tear yourself away from the view, Colton, Snake wants to see you."

As Colton pushed himself up, Bullet said, "You know with just a little more nerve, you could be making more money than what Snake pays you."

"I ain't gone to jail for what Snake has me do."

"Not yet," Bullet said. "But don't forget about Gervin. And you got to ask yourself, are you making what you should for what you are risking?"

"I'm making due."

21

"You making what you're worth?"

"I figure I am."

"Then hell, you making what you want?"

Colton didn't answer her but walked through the door into the haze of cigarette and cigar smoke in the Cactus Lounge. Betty Howard went behind the bar and started stocking beers in the cooler for the next night. On the other side of the bar, sitting on a barstool, with his head on his folded arms and his snoring rattling the rickety bar and a glass, was Lionel Dexter. Colton walked up to the barstool and lightly kicked it. Lionel didn't budge. Colton kicked it again. Lionel pulled his head up and shook it. "Don't let Snake see you sleeping this soon after working," Colton said. Lionel was much younger than Colton. He was bigger but not as scary. He had a gentle look in his hangdog face and eyes. People might not think he would do what he threatened to do to them. They knew Colton would. But Lionel was quick; he tried hard; and he listened to Colton. He played football for a while, like Colton, a machine with a football some people called him, but as with Colton, a busted knee ruined his football playing. And as some of the old time Odessans used to say, "Without a football under his arm, Lionel was just another nigger," and Lionel knew the score out in West Texas in 1981.

The Cactus Lounge had an office, and Colton entered it without knocking. He sat across from the card table that served as a desk. Snake came out of another door that connected to a small, private restroom. He slapped cologne on his face, trying to wake up. His large silver, gold, and turquoise rings glinted in the early morning light. Snake's silver hair was combed straight back, making him look like that ol' country singer Porter Wagoner. His just-barely-thicker than a pencil-thin white moustache lifted as he smiled. Snake made it a habit, even in hot summer months, to never look hot. He made his living with his big, fancy bar, his bootlegging in dry counties, and his stripper bar. But his passion was gambling. All required that you bluff, but Snake wanted no one to know when he was bluffing, including Colton.

"Job well done," he said to Colton. "Went real smooth tonight. Course there was some weeping and gnashing of teeth, but nobody just lost their shit."

"Bullet's offered me another job again," Colton said.

"Now, Colton," Snake said. "I'm being as fair to you as I can. I ain't got the profits I used to."

"I got a family," Colton said.

"That Mexican family you married into still eating up your money?"

"I got expenses."

"And just what you think you're going to do with your talents other than to work for me? You think that family of yours is going help you climb up the social register? You think you going to join First Baptist and go to church?"

Snake, in his polo shirt with the little alligator where the pocket should be, combed his hair back up over his head, shook his comb, and put it back into his starched cotton slacks' back pocket. "Bullet's talking shit. What can she offer you? Picking up and servicing vending machines? Throwing out drunks?" Snake slid his arms into his new leather jacket.

"This is different. She wants me to help her find out who killed a friend of hers."

Snake stopped pampering himself. "Danny Fowler?"

"How the hell do you know?"

"I hear things."

"How come I don't?"

"Cause you ain't me."

"How about I help her?"

"Goddamn it, Colton. I thought you had better sense. There's police involved. What if the police connect Danny to her, to me, to this place, or to you?"

"So how they gonna do that?"

"You keep out of it."

"She makes it sound like I could help. Sometimes, I feel like I want to know more, be in charge. You know, be more than just help, but help somebody."

Snake pointed. "I know Mina Fowler. Let me call her. But unless and until you get any word from me, you stay out of this." Snake rubbed his hair along the sides of his head. "Aging pretty boy Danny Fowler got killed by butt-fucking queers, and you want to get involved."

"I'm fixing to go home. Like you, I been up all night."

"Bullet and me go back." Snake smiled and flipped up the collar of his leather jacket. He had worked on his suntan by sitting out at his pool two hours a day, even when the weather was cold. He was lean from swimming in that heated pool. His slacks were black with sharp creases. His polo shirt was purple, and he looked as fresh as if he had just gotten up, showered, shaved, and dressed. "I'm just trying to say you got to watch her. She likes you, you got no better friend. But Bullet don't have the same kind of moral bearing as most people."

"But she'll tell you she's still got her soul."

"Listen, let's not get bitchy here. Why don't you come and let me buy you breakfast?" Snake turned around like he was looking for another mirror.

"I got to get home."

"Got or want to get home?"

"My family's going to be in church, and I'm supposed to watch my two boys."

"We can still get breakfast."

"Maybe Lionel'll go."

"This family business is twisting your stomach and your brain in knots. Relax a little." Snake patted Colton's shoulder as he walked out the office door. A year before, Colton and Lionel had driven to El Paso and checked into a Holiday Inn. Then they went to a liquor store just outside of town and started carrying cases out of the store and into their car. It was payment for Snake. A month before, a runty-looking guy said nasty things to one of the strippers at the Stampede. Then he followed her home. That stripper didn't speak English, but the next day she made Snake and Colton understand. So Colton and Lionel waited for the runt out in the parking lot. When that lonely man told Colton and Lionel to fuck off, Colton plowed straight into him, pinning him against the wall, and kneed him in the crotch. While Lionel pounded him, Colton took off the man's thick belt and wrapped it over his knuckles, so his knuckles wouldn't get so battered. After pounding him with that belt, Colton looked at his battered knuckles. The zipper on the inside of that money belt had torn up his knuckles. Colton kept the money folded up inside that belt and gave the belt to Snake. What was that lonely runt to do, press charges and have the police know he was stalking strippers?

Colton stepped back into the Cactus Lounge and the slanting sunbeams filled with the dust falling down from the ceiling and the smoke wafting about. Snake came out behind him and yelled to Lionel, "Hey, Lionel, your partner don't want none, but you interested in breakfast?"

Lionel lit up and looked at Colton, "Boss is buying breakfast and you refuse?" he said to Colton.

"Go on ahead. I got family to tend to." Lionel jumped off his barstool. Smiling, the new morning sun gleaming off his silver hair, Snake steered himself out the Cactus Lounge, and Lionel Dexter, with one last look over his shoulder at Colton, followed Snake into the sunshine.

Colton stepped through several sunbeams when Bullet came in from the backdoor. "That fella got sober enough to stagger down the road. He can't remember where he left his car."

Colton planted his elbows on the bar and worried. Bullet said, "Maybe if you'd studied harder in high school and gone to college, you'd be doing the books for Snake instead of busting heads."

"I was never good with numbers."

"So, you don't know what adds up to what," Bullet said, and Colton smiled. "You want a drink? I'm buying," Bullet said.

"I got to go home," Colton said.

"You know, I got a friend. Ol' Bill Sears. He sells old, beat up cars to illegal Mexicans. He knows they're poor, knows they can't make the payments, but he sells them, collects what he can for several months, takes a loss several months, then repos them. Then Bill sells that car again, and again, and again. Bill is making good money. And now listen to this. When he has a night off and needs cash, your partner, Lionel, rides shotgun for Bill's repo guys. And here's the point. I'm thinking of going into business with Bill Sears. Why not you?"

"Why you so interested in me?"

Bullet poured herself a shot and sipped it. "I don't like to see people sell themselves short. And I could help you. And I plan on lasting longer than Snake Popp. But first you got to help me find out who killed Danny Fowler."

"Why the hell you want me? What I got you need?"

"Reliable people who can provide the type of help you do are hard to come by."

So, Colton went to breakfast with her instead of Snake and Lionel and listened to her schemes and scams. And watched as she fought back tears to tell him all about Danny Fowler.

Chapter 2

Colton lived with his wife and his two sons, Arnie and Mando, in a small house on Adams Street. But to help watch the boys, Elena brought her father into the house, and he stayed. So, Colton lived with Way Low too. The house was old and crumbling, but it was cheap. Colton knew that he should want a family. He knew that a family in place in a house was a part of what he should have and want. A family in your house is social and economic advancement. But he wasn't prepared for a family, a house, or advancement.

On this October Sunday now twenty-nine hours after Danny Fowler was killed, he came home to a nearly empty house. In the kitchen, Way Low sat and listened to a throbbing Norteño song on his transistor radio. It was about bleeding and broken hearts and the women who caused that bleeding and breaking; it was that kind of sentimental crap that sounded better in Spanish. "We have TV," Colton said.

"I like the radio better," Way Low said.

"So, they've already gone to church?" Colton asked.

"Early mass."

"And you?"

"I done fine my whole life without the church. It's for women anyway. Besides, I got a job usually lasts past church."

"Any of that oilfield equipment move?"

Way Low chuckled, "It don't seem to notice me, and I'm getting where I don't notice it. We compromised."

"How's the boys,"

"Look for yourself. They fought over the pan dulce, stuffed themselves. So now, instead of going to church and getting religious, they're sleeping."

Way Low's real name was Raul. He was Colton's father-in-law. Colton's youngest son, Mando, like Colton, had trouble making his mouth say Spanish words. Colton couldn't say and Mando couldn't hear *Amando*, so *Amando* became *Mando*. Mando couldn't hear or say *abuelo*, so Mando and Arnie's grandfather become *Way Low*.

Arnie was eight and stayed to himself, finding things to amuse him instead of finding people. Mando was just six years old, waiting to start school. He did not know words. So Mando was jealous of his older brother. Sometimes at night, instead of going to sleep, Mando would get a flash light under his covers and stare at his picture books and try to say the words that were under the pictures and pretend that he could read. Way Low and his mother and sometimes Colton would read those words to him.

Colton left Way Low to his coffee and music and walked down the hall to the last bedroom. He hesitated at the door, not sure if he should or wanted to look in on his sons or not, not sure if they were asleep or awake, not sure if he should wake them. He forced himself to smile, opened the door, and stepped in.

Mando was smearing deep blue across his coarse coloring book paper with his crayon. Arnie was watching some show about animals on the small TV. They had used sleepiness as a con to get out of going to church. But they were still in their pajamas and fighting sleep.

Arnie looked up at Colton and smiled but turned back to his TV. Mando did not look up from his coloring book, but he stopped coloring, stared at the words under the pictures, and from memory of his mother reading the words to him, tried to recite the word. Colton was interrupting his boy's intensity. He thought to take Way Low's advice—bring home the money—thought he should just leave them to it, but he had sons. "You boys, not going to say 'hello' to your Daddy," Colton said and held his arms open, his smile stuck.

And in unison, his boys said, "Hi, Daddy."

At first Colton did not know what to do, but he remembered and scooped Mando up, got him horizontal between his two hands, and pressed his boy like a dumbbell up in the air until he almost touched the ceiling with him. Then he started to spin, and Mando made his little-boy giggle. Colton felt like he was standing still and the room was spinning around him and his boy. But he kept on twirling, then blew air between his lips to make a humming sound. And Mando made the sound and spread out his arms like he was flying. They called this game "airplane." They wouldn't have too many more years to play it because Mando was growing. Arnie had started school and reading and was almost too big for airplane rides. Besides, he liked watching his TV better than reading, school, or airplane rides. Dizzy, breathing heavy, Colton stopped, curled Mando in his arms, then set him down. He put his hands on his knees to look at the boy eye to eye and wondered what the word *father* meant to Mando, the boy pretending he could read.

* * *

Colton left his sons to their TV, their coloring books, and their words and went into his kitchen. He had already had a breakfast and coffee with Bullet, and though he was tired, he knew that he could not go to sleep. He listened to Way Low's sad songs that he could not understand and stared into his cup.

"Way Low, did Elena say anything when she left for mass?"

"Say about what?"

"About me."

"She says you should go to mass."

"I don't know shit about mass."

"A man's job," Way Low said and waited to point at Colton, "is his job. That is what he should do. So you don't got to worry when you come home."

"I've been offered some extra," Colton said. Way Low twisted in his seat and reached up to turn down the volume of his radio. "There's some things about it that are, are, are not quite right."

"You mean 'legal,'" Way Low said. "I'm a Mexican. I know about these things. You got to figure out the risks. You got to figure what you got to lose."

29

"You tell me. What I got to lose?"

Way Low reached and turned the radio down lower. "What you mean?"

"I don't know nothing about this."

"What's this?"

"This family thing. All that goes on here."

"What's to know? Same as church. The women go. They take care of family. Your job is your job."

"But I don't know what goes on here."

"So don't."

"I got to live here."

"So live here, but don't think so much."

"What if I was to go to jail, or get shot, or something?"

"My father swims a river and pulls me and a raft with our clothes in it after him. Never bitched. You takes your chances when you do what you got to."

Colton stared into his coffee. His nerves danced and tingled. But he knew the coffee and his thinking would keep his brain sizzling. He walked through his house and looked at the crucifixes and paintings of the Virgin Mary, the brightly colored walls that Way Low painted, the bare carpet. He opened the door and smiled again at his boys. They colored and watched, but Mando finally smiled back. He went to his living room, turned on the TV, watched *Meet the Press* until the boring politicians and the political analysts cooled his brain, and he went to sleep.

His own snoring and the hum of many voices speaking Spanish woke him. He rose and went into the kitchen to see children and in-laws coming into his house. The women busied themselves in his kitchen. His sons came running out, still in their pajamas, to play with their cousins. He had no idea of how many people filled his house. He had no idea if he even knew them all. Soon, grease was popping; the smell of garlic filled the air, and the kitchen warmed from heating the dishes that his in-laws had brought over.

Colton drifted and dodged into the backyard, and the in-laws and friends were there too. In one corner, by herself, covered in a blanket, was Colton's mother smoking her Marlboro. It was as though the Mexican people made an empty half circle around this white lady. Colton walked across the half-circle to his mother and sat on the stickers and weeds to be face to face with her. "Thank you for inviting me," Helen Parker said. Even after another husband or two, she never let go of the name that Colton's father gave her. "I don't get the heebies like I used to coming over here. I don't understand most of what they're saying, but anymore I like listening." Helen sucked in on her cigarette, turned her head from Colton, and exhaled the smoke.

"How are you doing, Momma?" Colton asked even though he knew how she was doing.

"I manage," she said.

"What about that nice gentleman you been running with? How is he?"

"Sam? You mean, Sam?"

"Yes, that's it. He seems like a decent sort of fellow."

"He's gone."

His mother retired from her secretarial job too soon. She had nothing to do but hang out in the bars during the day. She met fellow retirees. And Sam was the latest. Colton had hoped that Sam might contribute some of the money that he couldn't. "What happened? You're kind of short on story."

"What's to say. We're two different people." Colton let his mother's statement sit in his mind awhile. His mother exhaled and turned to him. "Colton, I'm not one to say. Lord, I was never one to say. What do I know about successful marriages? But do you fit into all of this?"

"Way Low says my job is to give them the money to have these parties. Somebody must appreciate it."

"You done well for yourself, then."

"You said 'hi' to your grandkids, my boys. That would help."

Helen Parker shrugged. "I was gone most their lives. Now I'm back. They don't really know me or want to. But this is fun." She took a strong pull on her cigarette, then her beer.

"You heard from my Daddy?"

"When your Daddy left, he genuinely left. I have no idea where he is. Last I heard, maybe Arizona."

Colton patted his mother's shoulder. "You want me to go get you a plate? Elena's Mexican food is the real deal."

"No," Helen shook her head. "I grabbed a plate on my way here. I don't want to spoil myself for the cheap Mexican food I get in my neighborhood." Helen looked up at the sky, and Colton followed her gaze. "No clouds, nice day. You got to learn to appreciate things." Colton dropped his head and tried to appreciate things. "You go back in. Mingle with your guests. I'll show myself out directly."

"Come in with me."

Helen hung her empty hand from her wrist and back-waved Colton toward the house. "Scooch on now. Leave me to the coolness and peace in the air."

Colton patted his mother's shoulder once more, then left her to herself. He had dim memories of his father. He had better memories of men coming and going, not that his mother was a whore, just that she had been young and attractive in a town with booms. As Odessans themselves said, "Ain't really nothing to do in Odessa but drinking, fighting, and fucking." He turned to look back at Helen. She seemed to have no regrets, no grudges. She smiled and dropped her hand from wrist to swoosh him back across his backyard to his house.

He finally recognized his wife on the tiny back porch. Elena was small and petite—just over five feet. She could disappear into a crowd, yet when you picked her out in a crowd, you saw her distinct, and your eyes stuck on her. Likewise, her eyes could hold you in place. Colton smiled, and she gave the smile back to him. But behind her smile was a look that said she was happy with her family but disappointed with Colton. He walked to her and kissed her forehead.

"I love you and the boys," Colton said. She flashed that smile that hid something and reached to pat the soft spot on the front of his shoulders.

"Everybody loves you too." She gestured toward the guests. "Everybody here. Who couldn't love my papi?" But activity and all the buzz in the house caught Elena's eye, and she moved away from Colton because she was the host and this was her house.

Colton was by himself in a crowd. He tried to take his mother's advice and appreciate things. But he hazily wished for more and better and waited. What he got was a phone call from Snake Popp. He heard the phone, pushed quickly through the people, and answered it. Snake Popp said, "About that Danny Fowler killing."

"Yeah?" Colton asked.

"I volunteered your services."

"What changed?"

"His momma, Mina Fowler, called me. She's an old friend and too rich to ever die. *She* wants to know who did it, but she doesn't want anybody else to know. Especially the police."

Colton just breathed into the phone. "Colton," Snake said. "You got it in you?"

"What am I supposed to do?"

"Go see Bullet."

Chapter 3

The late Friday night or early Saturday morning that Danny Fowler got killed was the final night of the 1981 Oil Show. The high-rollers from the oil patches across the country came to the International Oil Show in Odessa, Texas every two years. That meant lots of gambling, drinking, and whoring for everybody. During that two week-long show, Odessans said there were more whores in Odessa per capita than any place in the world. The high-rollers running the oil show over at the fairgrounds had their tents, trailers, and hotels rooms. Their parties and their whores were invitation only.

But if you weren't such a high roller, you had Second Street. You pulled off Second Street, and the whores would run out in front of your car, press their cleavage against your windshield, and lick at your side mirror with long, tip-curled tongues. Flashing a badge would keep them off your car. Only telling them you had no money would get them to turn their mini-skirted, oversized asses to you and saunter off to another car. That's how it operated. You drove up and did your whore shopping, and she took you into one of the cheap motels. The Odessa Police and the Ector County Sheriff's Department were not about to stop the party despite what the Baptists and Church of Christers said.

And this was the boomtime. People had come from all over the country to work the oilfields. They'd pushed right out of the city limits into West Odessa, which was just barely-paved streets, gravel parking lots, cinder block or trailer homes (sometimes tents or RVs), and mean bars. At nights, wound up, energized roughnecks with money in their pockets would drive around looking for whores, trouble, or just something to do. Sometimes out of boredom or frustration, they would pull their guns out of their pickups and start shooting up in the air. Besides whores, Odessa had more murders per capita than anyplace else in the country. It even topped drug smuggling Miami. During the boom, during that two-week-long drunken orgy, and during that last closing night, Danny Fowler was out trying to get the kind of love he wanted or needed.

Early in the morning after Danny Fowler was killed, Bullet Price got a phone call from one of her whores. Renee St. Cloud was crying, and she said that she thought that something awful happened in room three of the First Quality Motel. Bullet told Renee to stay where she was but to give her a number. Bullet slung a denim jacket over her shoulders and stepped out of her duplex and into the season's first cold norther. The wind lifted her jacket off her shoulders. Her short hair danced in it. She shivered. The gas stations' hinged signs creaked as the wind lifted them to a nearly steady and level ninety degrees from the ground. But she made it across the parking lot of the First Quality Motel, and she fumbled with the key to open the door to room three. As she flipped on the light, she saw splatters of blood on the sofa, bedspread, carpet, and wall. Bullet went back to her duplex, which is two combined units of the First Quality Motel, called Renee, and told her to get back immediately.

When Renee St. Cloud got to room three and peered in, she pulled her head out of the room, shivered so hard her teeth shook, and looked at Bullet. "You got to believe it wasn't like that when I left." Then she turned her head to puke. "Good God, more to clean up," Bullet said.

"I'm just remembering," Renee said after her last heave.

"Remember later," Bullet said and poked a mop and a roofing crowbar at Renee, "Here."

Renee took the mop but stared at the roofer's crowbar, "What's this?"

"It's what we're going to use to pry up the carpet," Bullet says.

"You gonna ruin that carpet?"

"Don't you think it's ruined as is?"

As best she could, with what little help she could get from Renee, Bullet tore at the carpet, sliced at it with a razor blade carton opener, and rolled it into cylinders. "Hope those ain't your good clothes," Bullet said. And as Renee stared down at her jeans, Bullet splashed bleach on one wall. They rubbed at the spotted blood and bled the color out of their clothes. Then, they pulled the bedspread and the sheets off the bed and wrapped them in a bundle. Bullet told Renee to take the sheets to the dumpster outside behind the complex and throw them in. While Renee was gone, Bullet worked the sofa to the door. And when Renee got back, the two of them got the sofa outside, doused it with bleach, and then dragged it out in the wind and behind the complex of rooms. Bullet sprayed the dumpster with lighter fluid, then lit it to burn the sheets. The flames shot up and twisted and snapped in the wind so that Bullet had to lower the dumpster's lid to keep the wind from carrying a fire to her motel.

In her office, protected from the cold and the wind, Bullet sat behind her desk and sucked in for breath while Renee sat in front of the desk and shivered and whimpered like one of those little lap dogs. "Wow," Renee finally said as she looked around.

Bullet's desk was right in front of the door in the living room. On either side of the desk were golden lamps shaped like naked ladies holding up the shades. The carpet was thick red and black shag. Behind her desk was a rock wall. Next to the rock wall were two golden arches stretching over the entrance to the dining room, which had a chandelier stretching over a chrome and glass table and two long mirrors on the empty walls. Behind the wall next to the dining room was her kitchen.

From behind her desk, which immediately gave Bullet some power over whoever walked in, Bullet looked at Renee St. Cloud, sitting where a customer should be, to see how she was packaging what she was selling. Renee had on a mini-skirt that barely covered her butt. But then it was hardly a butt at all. Same with her chest. Just two mosquito bites, as they said. She had slipped on those wool dancing leggings that some

West Texas girls wore even over boots. She had on a loose-knit sweater with the loose knits letting in the cold wind. She had dirty blonde hair hanging in a couple of strings over her face. And she had pulled those skinny legs up to her chest and hugged them, and those skinny legs shook all of her. She was mostly a little girl trying real hard to play older and sexier. Bullet said, "You're not in trouble, yet."

Renee's teeth chattered as she nodded. Renee St. Cloud's real name was Jennifer Peveto. She was a plain little girl with no particular savvy or looks or money from Seminole, Texas. She wandered to Odessa to see what she could find. She wanted fast and easy money. She found fast and easy but not much money. All she had going for her was Bullet's management.

"I'm scared."

"Of course, you're scared. But you got to calm down and think." Renee shook her head and searched for some answers or comfort from Bullet, who had become as close to a mother as Renee now had. "Now you're going to tell me what happened, and then, we're going to rehearse what you're going to say to any cop."

Renee nodded, sucked in for breath. "You drink?" Renee nodded. Bullet got up and came back with two scotches on ice.

"So now you tell me what happened," Bullet said. Renee squeezed her knees to expose her panties and her ass. She could say nothing. "Go on, now," Bullet said.

"What can I say. I'm doing my job. I'm walking down Second Street with the rest of the girls. Getting what I can. And everybody is gone, and I'm thinking to myself I should just go home, ain't no one else coming by because it's cold, and this bright red car comes by . . ."

Bullet froze. "What kind of bright red car?"

"A red one."

Bullet tried to control her voice. "What kind of red one? What make? A model?"

"A fancy one."

"A Mustang?"

"Maybe." A slow shiver worked through Bullet, but Bullet stopped. But then it started shaking her again.

"Who is in it?"

"This fella driving is dressed nice, like with the preppy kind of clothes. He has those kind of shoes they used to put pennies in."

"Is he wearing a tie? A coat?"

"He has this tan sport coat." Spreading her knees and twisting her glass in between them, Renee raised her glass to her nose, sniffed it, tasted it, then coughed.

"A camelhair coat? Is that what it is?"

"What's camelhair?"

"Tan and fuzzy and soft."

"Maybe," Renee said and tried another sip. Renee shivered.

But the shiver inside of Bullet was not because she was cold. It started because she was thinking of Danny Fowler. "And now you tell me some more. You ain't through yet with just shoes and coat."

Renee made a child's face, that grimace, like when she tasted Bullet's scotch for the first time. "This is nasty. You have something to put in it?"

"Your story?"

"And there's a guy in the passenger's side, and he has on a white Western shirt, the kind with the snaps, and a cowboy hat. And in the back is another guy, leaning up from the back of the red car, between them, and yelling at me."

"And the guy with the camelhair coat is driving?"

"Yeah, right. And this sharp-dressed fella, he pays me. And sos I take them to number three."

Because she hesitated, Bullet said, "What happened inside."

"It was kind of weird. They was in a partying mood. They all drank. Then, we got to doing it. First the guy in the backseat, then the guy with the cowboy hat."

Bullet felt the shiver become a bile-like surge and worked its way up her throat. But she swallowed it. "What about the sharp dresser?"

"He was having none of me." Renee sniffed at the scotch and then smiled at Bullet. "And like you said, no freebies. They both paid. Or rather, the sharp-dressed fella, he paid."

"Did they act like they knew each other?"

"The two boys, the young ones. Did I mention that they was younger than the fancy dresser? They knew each other. They talked about going to The Tank and eating steaks and drinking good liquor. Seems like they must've met the dresser there."

Bullet closed her eyes and asked with them closed. "Anything else they talk about?"

"Work."

"Where was work?"

"They said something about a rig out toward Andrews. Something, somebody's crew?"

Bullet pulled her eyes open. "Who is somebody?"

"I don't remember?"

"Remember, goddamn it."

Renee choked on some of the liquor and lifted her eyes to look at Bullet with soft puppy eyes. "Rafe, Ralph, Raven, Rafters." She sucked in for some air, "I can't remember."

"How did they act around that fancy dresser?"

"Friendly like. And he was real friendly to them."

"How's that?"

"He'd whisper stuff to them. He'd pat their backs."

"Did they do anything to him?"

"After a couple of hours I left. It was cold, and the wind was blowing trash and tumbleweeds down the street, but I figure there's always more money to be made, like you told me. . . . Am I in trouble?"

"I don't know. You think that you can lie to the police?"

"I guess I could." Renee smiled. "Yeah, I can."

"No, you listen to what I mean. I mean can you lie to them and not show what you are saying to be a lie."

She sipped, managed not to shake, looked like she would cry. "I never tried. I never been in a thing like this."

"Well then don't lie. If the police come, you tell them what you told me."

"Thanks, Miss Bullet." Bullet squeezed her whole body in a tight knot of worry, but it wasn't until that afternoon that she knew that the blood was Danny Fowler's.

* * *

When Justan Brady walked into her office, Bullet knew that the powers in town weren't interested in what happened in room three. If it had been a real investigation, a detective from the Odessa Police Department would have stepped onto her red and black shag carpet and eyed her rock wall, golden arches, and naked lady lamps. Instead an Ector County Deputy Sheriff stepped on to her carpet, and this kid toed the ground and stared around with a slack jaw. "Deputy Sheriff Justan Brady," he said, shook her hand, chewed his gum, and removed his hat.

"This is my home. I live here," Bullet said as she opened the door. "You just woke me up from a nap. Can I help you?" She walked around her desk in her bare feet and purposefully swung her still shapely butt for Justan Brady to notice. She sat. He stood, looking at his boot toes and the carpet. Bullet swung her bare feet up on her desk so that Justan had to look at the soles of her feet. "You can sit down if you want."

Justan Brady lowered himself into the chair across from her desk and repeated himself. "My name is Deputy Justan Brady. I'm with the Ector County Sheriff's Department."

"You said that already."

Justan Brady cocked his head and twisted his neck to see around Bullet's feet. "I want to ask a few questions about what I am supposing took place in one of your rooms."

"My name is Bullet Price. I sort of manage this place. I've been in this town several years. That's all I know."

"We thought maybe you might have some ideas about what went on in your room early this morning."

"How do you know it was my room?"

"We found a murder victim, and in his hand was a motel key to your motel." Bullet's mind raced and scolded her for not asking Renee what had become of the key, then her mind jumped back to the words, *murder victim.*

"Who was murdered?" Bullet asked but did not want to know.

"We don't want to release any names yet . . ." Justan leaned toward one shoulder then the other to see around Bullet's feet. And when he moved his head, she tilted her stacked feet in that direction.

"Why not?"

"The next of kin." Bullet squirmed in her chair. "We found a body out on the edge of Ector County, just this side of Crane County, outside of city limits. This roughneck was reporting to his rig for work, and he sees this body in a ditch." Justan hesitated. "Mam, could you move your feet to one side or the other or put them in front of you?" Bullet slid her feet off her desk and under her and leaned toward Justan on her elbows. "Now, what do you know about what went on in your motel last night?"

"I know nothing about what goes on in my rooms. I don't ask."

"Why did he have a key, room three, to your motel?"

"Why don't you tell me why?"

Justan Brady leaned forward and put his forehead in the palm of his hand. He was trying to grow a moustache, but he couldn't quite grow a full one. "Cause we figure . . ."

"Who is 'we'?"

"Me and Senior Deputy, Bobby Cooksey."

"So how much 'senior' you got?" Bullet pushed her face farther out over her resting elbows and raised, folded hands.

"Six months." Justan Brady pulled his hand away from his face and pulled away from Bullet. "My experience is got nothing to do with this case."

"To hell it hasn't. Why are they sending you? Where are the Odessa Police?"

"The crime occurred outside city limits."

"Then where's the sheriff?"

"They sent me."

Bullet's brain bubbled. She was afraid it could explode. "I'm telling you I don't know what happened, but I'm asking you who did you find?"

"I ain't at liberty to say who I found. But he was all beat to shit something terrible. And we suspect maybe it was because he was queer." Justan Brady stopped because he knew he had said too much. But then he went on, "They stole his car."

"Don't stop there. I got a feeling I know who you're talking about. What was he wearing?" Bullet leaned back into her high-back office chair and stared at Justan.

"I ain't at liberty to say."

Bullet thought that at least this Justan Brady had balls and some inkling of what he was doing. "You tell me some more, and I'll tell you if I know who you are talking about."

Justan Brady glanced over his shoulder as if to see if the sheriff himself was watching. "He was missing one Bass Weejun shoe. And his sport coat was curled around his body. And I crawled down in that ditch where they dumped him, and there was a tumbleweed rolled into the ditch and on his face. I'm just thinking that is no way to die, even if you are queer."

Bullet's shiver shakes her until her shoulders and neck quiver. "Did he have a red Mustang convertible?"

Justan put his elbows on his knees and dropped his head so that Bullet had to look at the crown of his cowboy hat. From the way his shoulders moved, she could see this slow boy think. "We found no car, just a body, and a motel key." Justan pulled his head up. "We know there's whores bringing johns into these motel rooms."

"Who doesn't know that?" Bullet said. Bullet felt her teeth grit. She would not cry.

"I'm just saying you should cooperate."

"I am cooperating. I'm telling you I know nothing."

"But you should know something. How could you not know?"

"Where'd you get your investigation training?"

"What?"

"You don't seem particularly good at this."

"Still, mam, you ought to help me."

"Why the hell should I help you, goddamn it."

"Because I'm the police."

"That's why I don't want to help *you*." Bullet breathed in, stood, and turned her back to Justan Brady. She turned back around to face him, wishing to hurt him, thinking she ought to scare him, hoping she wouldn't say nothing stupid. "Look at me," she said. "Look at this." She pointed to the scar on her face. She undid the button to her blouse and held the right side open. "Look. Don't look away." She wore no bra. When Justan Brady raised his head to look, she looked with him. "I'm just thirty-eight years old, but I've got these two scars. The first one an ex-husband gave me when he tried to break a whiskey bottle over my head. They don't break. That's just on TV. And just this last year, at the county's expense, I had a mastectomy. I keep my hair short now. It kind of fits my altered gender image." She lied about the ex-husband.

"I'm sorry for your illness. Your hair-do looks nice. And I like your bullet necklace. I get the connection."

"I'm just telling you that I can take trouble, but I don't want it. Second, I'm telling you that I will fight back. So why don't you look somewhere else?"

"Cause we both know he was here."

"Is this investigation of yours going to be just a murder case?"

"What do you mean? That's what it is."

Bullet dropped her eyes. She was disappointed in him. "It's not going to turn into a vice case is it?"

"We don't have a vice squad at Ector County Sheriff's Department."

"You make me want a cigarette and a drink," Bullet said and rubbed her palm over her short hair. "Are some Odessa cops going to come in here looking for crimes other than murder?"

"I work for the county."

"Justan, it's the oil show. There's whores come in here. It's ironic, ain't it? I sell femininity. And whores have illegal habits. After the oil show is over, I'm going to be real quiet. In the meantime are you going to leave this a murder investigation and not bust me?"

Justan's tongue got thick. "Yes," he said.

"Then tell me for sure who got killed." Justan said nothing. "Was it Danny Fowler?" Justan nodded like his neck hurt, and Bullet watched the crown of his cowboy hat go up and down.

Bullet raised both her hands to cover her face.

"Ms. Price?" Justan scooted to the edge of his chair and reached toward Bullet.

"Danny Fowler's the best friend I got . . . so I'm going to help you."

"What happened in that room?"

"That's what I aim to find out."

"Don't you know?"

"It wasn't me in there with him."

Justan stood. He unsnapped his western shirt pocket and fumbled inside of it. He pulled out a card and handed it to Bullet.

She turned it over in her hand. "This don't even have your name on it."

"I borrowed it from Deputy Sheriff Bobby Cooksey."

"Justan, you said, right?" Bullet sucked in to keep her head clear and to keep from crying. "Go home. Forget all about this."

"I want to find out who did this."

"So do I. And if I can, I'll let you know."

"But I'm the police here."

"Go home, Justan." And as he was told, Justan slowly backed out of her apartment. And within minutes the phone rang and shook Bullet's brains. She forced herself to answer it, and Mina Fowler, Danny's mother, was on the other end, and she said, "Danny's been murdered. Just like we always feared. No one must know what happened. But *we* must know. We have to talk."

"Not yet. I got business yet to do."

Bullet stayed alone in her bedroom and smoked until she choked. Then she showered and dressed to meet Snake and Barbara Howard for the gambling marathon at the Cactus Lounge.

* * *

Bullet Price came to Odessa with the scar on her face but not the one on her chest. Bullet had started out as a stripper and sometime whore, but she put money in CDs and stocks, and then she drifted with oil booms and oil shows to Odessa, where she made friends quick. On a strict schedule she made out herself, she visited all the bars and met those folks who worked with bars, whores, or titty joints. It was after 1971 when Texas left its dark age behind and voted in liquor by the drink at county option. So, Texans left their bottles and the paper bags they wrapped them in at home. Now, if the Baptist and Church of Christ didn't completely take over the county, you could pay a bartender in a restaurant or bar with a liquor license to mix you a drink. But most the owners out in West Odessa and the bars that Bullet frequented couldn't afford the liquor license, so they still sold set ups and beers and passed out paper bags.

During the start of the late seventies boom, Bullet recruited girls and customers. And for two hours a day, late in the afternoon, she would sit in one bar and take calls from gentlemen and arrange for a date. She changed the bars, and so she changed the numbers. That way she avoided the police and got to know all the Odessa bar, whore, and gambling folks.

She saw the country girls who drifted in, saw their desperation in the way they stood, like they had realized they weren't going to find some upstanding, well-to-do Christian man. She recruited them. And she would counsel them. She would tell them they could make good, quick money, but she would caution them about losing their souls or their looks if they stayed in too long or used their money for drugs or booze instead of investments.

And when the big International Oil Shows were held every other year, Bullet made contacts with corporate executives and got dates for them. Then she bought a duplex right in the middle of The First Quality Motel, which was just off Second Street. During the oil show young whores from all over the country, some from Mexico and Asia, roamed the street parallel to Second. But Bullet was there ahead of them—organizing, advising, taking a cut. She and her whores made enough to live comfortable for a whole year during the two-week long oil shows. And all the while, Bullet had investments growing. She was popular, liked to tell stories, was welcomed in bars all across town. What she didn't tell was how she really got that scar, back in San Antonio, before ever she got to Odessa by way of Oklahoma City.

And in the late seventies after an Oil Show, to celebrate, Bullet was sitting in the Tank—an upscale restaurant and bar, which was really a holding tank, bored out on the inside with some windows and doors added and turned into a restaurant and bar, when a handsome man in a silk sport coat, tropical wool dress slacks, and Bass Weejuns loafers asked if he could sit down with her. Bullet of course thought this was the usual ploy. "I'm not working," she said.

"Neither am I," the man said. "You're alone. I'm alone. You look interesting." He shrugged and held up his hands.

"You mean the scar?" Bullet said.

"I mean all of you."

"Don't bullshit me. I got that scar from a whiskey bottle, and I got a bullet round my neck."

"Don't get pissed off at me. I didn't swing the bottle at you."

"You can imagine what I did to that guy."

"All I'm doing is sitting down."

Bullet liked this conversation no matter where it was leading because it was different from the others she got from men. She let this man buy her drink, then another, and another.

Then they ate. They gorged on steaks. Because the Oil Show was over and the visitors gone and most locals just tired out, the place emptied out. Bullet and this lively fella went to other bars, seedier bars, real Odessa bars, with gravel parking lots, no liquor license, ugly strippers, and maybe a whore down for the Oil Show still stuck in town. Everyone knew Bullet, and everyone knew the gentleman with her. Patrons whispered to each other about this odd couple. In the parking lot of one such bar, Bullet climbed into this man's convertible Mustang, leaned across the console and kissed him. After they went to Bullet's place and had some clumsy, fumbling sex, Danny Fowler told Bullet he was gay.

Of course, most of Odessa knew Danny Fowler was queer. That's what Odessans whispered with each other when they saw him and Bullet out together. They knew that he would cruise around in that convertible, spending his Momma's money, looking for a young, wayward oil field worker who didn't quite fit in, wasn't quite sure of himself, was hiding a secret too. But they mostly liked him, and so did Bullet. They became fast friends.

But trouble, like the cause of that scar on her face, had a way of catching up with Bullet. She was just marked for it. After a shower, she felt a lump. So then there was the trip to the doctor, the diagnosis, the choices, the mastectomy, and then the chemo and radiation. But she had no insurance. Women who run whores don't qualify for group rates. She figured she was healthy, figured that insurance was the one thing that she could omit, so she didn't bother. The bills stacked up. She opted not to get cosmetic surgery to fake what had been cut out of her.

Danny Fowler took her to a nice meal at the Tank with his mother. Bullet and Mina Fowler, daughter of old ranch money made into real wealth by oil, just eyed each other. And some witnesses claimed Bullet risked everything by asking, "Well, we going to fuck or fight?"

Mina came right back, "Maybe both."

"Well, this will be one hell of a party, then."

"I thought this was about money, not fucking or fighting."

But somehow the two tough women sized each other up and liked what they saw. Mina probably saw that, for whatever reason, Bullet made Danny happy, so Danny got his mother to pay for the rest of Bullet's treatment.

Like those in the bars, Bullet knew Danny liked to "cruise" around town looking for what he shouldn't find. Bullet knew that urge. Male or female it started in the same place, to Bullet, somewhere between your stomach and groin. And she knew that urge was pointing Danny in the wrong direction at the wrong gender, especially for a place like Odessa. Bullet and Mina saw Danny make several trips to jail and suffer through several ass kickings. Bullet knew it was just a matter of time before Danny's urge to do what he just couldn't help from doing would get him hurt. But she didn't think he'd be dead in a dirt road bar ditch, missing a Weejun, with his camelhair sport coat wrapped around him.

Chapter 4

Colton looked down the row of rooms at the First Quality motel. He shook his head to clear away the fuzz inside it, and when he did, he saw the Pancake House. He figured to have a cup of coffee to wake him up before he talked to Bullet Price. So he sat at the bar and looked out the window at the row of motel rooms with the tumbleweeds shaking in the wind as they grabbed what they could to keep from rolling on into oblivion or disintegration or where ever they go or whatever becomes of them.

As he swallowed, he felt a pat on his back. He turned to see a man with a swollen face. "Colton Parker?" the swollen face asked. "Whatever become of you?" The swelling in the man's face was from fat, and the fat made swells all the way down his body, his chin, neck, chest, and belly. And these rolls were supported by short, spindly legs. He wore a frayed and faded Odessa High jacket. Colton remembered him. He had played football with the guy for the Odessa High Bronchos. Like everybody else, Colton never realized his team's mascot was misspelled until he got out of high school and learned a few things. "You were a star." The man lightly punched Colton. "Come on. You remember me. Jake Raven? Weak side linebacker." Jake Raven held out his arms. "I grew some." Colton nodded. "So, what become of you."

Colton tried to smile, shrugged, tried to get through this story fast. "I went to Sul Ross and tried to play, but I was slow and too small, so now I'm . . . in security."

"I thought you was going to be somebody famous, as tough as you was.

"You never know," Colton said.

"Well, you know, I just never got that college scholarship, so I stuck around. Took over my Daddy's welding business." Jake pulled himself up on the barstool beside Colton, "Here, here, let me give you a card." He pulled out his wallet and dug in it to give Colton a card. *Raven Welding* it said. Then Jake sat down, "Man, we ought to meet up for some beers, you know. Catch up." Colton shook his head, trying to say he had business to tend to. Jake went on, "Man ain't this boom something. Who'd've figured it, but I got employees. I got a couple of youngsters working for me live out in West Odessa in an RV. Those crazy fuckers know a little about electricity, so they climb up an electrical pole and are stealing the city's electricity to fridgerate their beers. A friend of mine owns several vacant lots out in West Odessa, so he got him a loan, bought some RVs, and rents them out. Most the new folks have to live someplace like that." Jake back-handed slapped at Colton. Colton smiled but got up and left a dollar. "But they're lucky. They got friends living in tents." Colton remembered Jake, and he remembered that Jake always talked too much. Colton put the card in his shirt pocket.

He nodded and walked out the door, remembering football. What he remembered was sticker burrs. In Odessa's backyards and on the practice fields, the stickers burrs and goat heads took over in the summer when the sun killed the grass. So, from the time he was six to eighteen, Colton's hands, fingers, knees, and elbows were filled with the festering sores from sticker burr splinters. Colton held up his hands to look at his battered knuckles. Then he turned them over to look at his soft palms. At least, he no longer had festering stickers in his hands.

Colton's father left before Colton ever got to high school. Once he got away and tried playing football at Sul Ross, his mother kind of left too. Then he found her, or they found each other even though they were living close to each other. He paid for her cheap rental house, and he called her once a week and invited her over once in a while. As with his job, he felt like he should keep his past family separate from his present family.

As he walked, Colton looked down at the rounded toes of his Roper boots, one toe then the other. Justin Boots called them Ropers because calf ropers could stick them in a stirrup but pull them out quick and run after the calf. They gave Colton some heft if he wanted to kick somebody, but he could run too. Lionel wore jogging shoes. He was quicker to run. Lionel had been a running back.

Looking at his boot toes, Colton thought about the round-toed cleats he wore when he played football. Mostly, he remembered sliding across baked and cracked nearly grassless fields on those hard, long cleats. Only twice in his career had he played in rain. Then he slid and tore out gullies with those cleats. If he had had some jogging shoes like Lionel's in those days, he might have been a better player. He looked ahead and then over at the rows of rooms for the First Quality Motel. He spotted number three.

When Colton played football, he was an old-style monster man. That's sort of like a strong safety. His job was to crouch in the backfield and wait for the run. And when he saw them coming, he was to run into the blocking and make the tackle. He had a talent of throwing himself into them. But as the running play was starting, as he saw the guards pulling, even as he was getting excited, he got scared, and he had to make himself run into what was stronger and faster and coming. When the play was over, if nothing on him was broke, he'd get excited.

Playing scared like that got Colton a chance at college, at Sul Ross State University, where he didn't have his fingers festering from sticker burrs. But on the last game of his sophomore year, in the middle of the third quarter with Hardin-Simmons University beating Sul Ross by twenty-one points, Colton saw the guards and running backs chugging around the end. He should've stayed where he was, giving them the yards that no longer made no difference. Everybody else on his team was just standing still, but he ran up into those that were bigger and faster and stronger and just buckled. It was a time before arthroscopic surgery, so he was finished with his sophomore year by the time his knee healed. But it did not heal good enough to play more football.

Colton thought he could play through scaredness all the way to a degree. But now all he had was a busted knee and no half scholarship and no part-time job bar backing. So, he went back to Odessa and met Snake Popp. What Snake saw in Colton was that, scared or not, he would finish the play. Colton got used to playing scared.

Colton walked past the First Quality Motel rooms to Bullet's duplex, knocked, and stepped onto her red and black shag carpet. He had to look around at red and black shag carpet, the brick wall, and the golden naked lady lamps. "Ain't you ever seen class?" Bullet asked from around the corner of her kitchen. "You need a drink?"

"I'm on the job."

Bullet walked to her desk with a bottle of bourbon in her hand. She filled two little Dixie paper, mouthwash-sized cups with bourbon and handed one to Colton. "So have a drink on the job. It'll relax you."

"It might put me to sleep."

"I'm working toward forty hours without sleeping," Bullet said. Colton shrugged and downed his bourbon and felt the cheap bourbon burn its way down his throat. Bullet filled up his little cup with another drink. "Well, turns out one way or another you're working for me."

"That's my orders."

"Can you take my orders?"

"Like you said, I'm working for you."

"Some men have trouble taking orders from a woman. You one of them?"

"No, mam."

"Now that also means I'm giving the orders, not you."

"I'm the bouncer, the muscle, the monster man."

"Monster man?"

"It's an old football term. I throw myself into the line and get beat up a lot."

"First off, we're gonna throw ourselves at Mina Fowler. You ready?"

"I wasn't born ready, and I'm not ready now. But what choice I got?" Colton said, and they both downed their whiskey and winced as it burned down their throats.

"The whiskey's cheap," Bullet said.

"I could tell," Colton said.

* * *

Bullet's pickup kicked up a high wake of dust as she pointed its nose down the straight gravel road to Mina Fowler's house. At bars she had heard people who knew Danny or saw his routine wonder out loud why Danny stayed, why he didn't go somewhere else where people might have had more practice at looking the other way. Maybe, whatever his urges, he was a part of West Texas too. And he knew it.

Bullet steered around a wayward ornamental cow standing in the road bawling for food. She looked over at Colton, his hands in his lap, stoic, quiet, taking it all in. Bullet wasn't sure about him. She didn't know him really, wasn't sure he could really do what he might have to do. But he looked the part, and that male look might be all she needed to protect herself in manly West Texas. "You gonna like this," she said to Colton as her pickup bounced past the cows, the tumbleweeds, and the rocky land that long ago lost most of its cattle-supporting grass.

"I seen rich," he said.

"Not Mina rich."

Mina Fowler lived just across the county line in a near sixty-year-old two-story ranch house. She was Ector and Crane County nobility—if either could even consider anybody in them to be noble. Her grandfather had come to the area in a wagon, bought rangy cows, and made himself a herd. Then he bought more land, and that land had oil under it. And Mina Fowler's daddy and then she became rich. For old time's sake, she kept some decorative cattle on the place roaming in between the rigs and pumpjacks. In the same way, she collected husbands, but she kicked them off the ranch when she got tired of them. They were mainly worthless anyway—husbands and cattle. So, she lived without husbands but tolerated the cattle. She had a daughter's husband running the family business and making her richer. Now she had dead Danny.

Inside Mina Fowler's ranch house, Bullet just couldn't help calculating how much she would have to make to live like her social betters. The good thing about Odessa was that you could buy into better society. Colton sniffed. Bullet was scared that, like most men, he might hike a leg and piss on some of the furniture. Like servants, they waited by the front door while Mina staggered away from them to the wrought iron and glass table and filled three glasses with imported vodka. They both watched as she sloshed by the red leather sofa and matching recliner and the white throw rugs over the hand-cut wooden floor slats. The stuffed heads of cows, deer, moose, and horses looked down at them. A painting of Granddaddy, a large portrait of her Daddy and Momma, a few smaller portraits of ex-husbands, and smaller yet photos of Danny and her sister watched Mina, wearing tight jeans, red roper boots, and red satin blouse, slosh to Bullet and Colton. Mina gave them each a jostled martini glass of vodka. Then she turned and, with her swaying butt, commanded them to follow her to the sofa. In between the portraits were blue-bonnet and wagon wheel paintings and photos, sometimes called cactus and cow shit art, which Bullet had seen all her life and hated. She would sooner have her golden arches and naked ladies. Her art and tastes, tacky as they were, still had a relation to modern reality.

Mina stopped quick and motioned toward the recliner, spilled vodka, and said, "Big man, have a seat." Then with knees together, like she just came back from the cotillion, she lowered herself into one side of the sofa. Bullet sat at the other.

"We meet again," Mina said to Bullet. "And you, sir?" she said to Colton.

"Colton Parker." Colton rose to shake her hand.

"Don't get up," she said and nodded to sit him back down.

Bullet didn't wait, "So you know me and what I do."

"I even know where you do it, The First Quality Motel."

"The point is I'm used to being on both sides of the law. So far, I've been paddling in mid-river, and I'm hoping you can help me decide what to do."

"You want money?"

"I wouldn't turn it down," Bullet said.

"Good God," Colton said. And both ladies turned to look at him. "I mean he's dead. That's an awful thing. Let's talk about him a little first." Bullet thought better of Colton. He had balls and heart.

"Thirty-six hours or so ago, I got the call," Mina says. "They tell me later that he was probably dead when they dumped him in a ditch on a road to a holding tank. Somewhere along the line they dropped one of his shoes, a slip on. And they must have just wrapped that camel-hair coat that he liked so much—hell, he had three of them—around him and just dumped him." Mina dropped her head to look in her glass, sipped, then sipped again, said, "What the hell," and took a good long gulp.

"How long you been drinking?" Colton asked.

"Forever."

Bullet squirmed and feared that Colton may lead this to the wrong place. "So why don't you tell the cops and let them find who done this?"

Mina smiled. "I am not oil rich. I am cattle rich. But oil has made me wealthy. I stay here because the wealth gives me some power. My money makes people listen. I don't want an investigation. I've told the Odessa Chief of Police and the Ector County Sheriff to leave the case exactly where it is: Danny's dead. That's all people need to know."

"Hell, who knows how much they'd find out anyway?" Bullet said.

"What are we doing here?" Colton asked.

Mina laughed. "I told you how he was dressed. That was his uniform. He'd put on an expensive camel hair coat and cruise. You know what I'm saying?"

"He'd drive around?"

"So to speak." Mina's brows knitted together. "The Odessa police have picked Danny up several times now, dressed just as was, knocked out, drunk, bloodied or all three because he'd grabbed some cowboy or roughneck's crotch. Maybe somewhere, maybe once in a while, maybe just often enough to give him hope, a cowboy or roughneck returned the favor. But mostly, they beat the shit out of him. I don't want anybody else to know that." She looked at Colton to see if he got it. Bullet, of course, got it.

When Mina was too busy or out of town, Bullet bailed Danny out and told him get out of town, go somewhere where they wouldn't beat the shit out of him for being queer. "Like you did?" Danny had asked her.

Mina's shoulders shook as she looked into her glass. "Danny was just a regular boy before he became queer. That normal little boy was a part of him too. If he dies like this, if someone is prosecuted, he'll die and be remembered as just queer." Mina noticed that her drink was near empty, and she stirred the melting ice with her pinkie.

"People in law enforcement are friends of mine and cases are unsolved. That's how Danny will die." Mina stood and wobbled, but she made her way to the vodka and the bucket of ice and refuels. She said, with her back to Bullet and Colton, "That's why you are here. You are going to find out what exactly happened and why and who did it."

"What about that red convertible? Where's that," Colton asked. Mina turned back around and stared at him. "Sure, somebody somewhere may be looking. But that car is probably nothing but parts spread all over Texas chop shops. Are you sure you're cut out for this line of business?."

"Maybe, they didn't know what to do."

Mina pointed at Colton, "They knew what to do. They planned it. Knew what to do with the car, everything."

Bullet said, "As I was saying," she turned to Colton to tell him to shut up with her eyes. "Jennifer Peveto came here from Seminole, Texas with the sole intention of getting money. I cleaned her up as best

I could and taught her the trade. She still has a lot to learn. She calls herself 'Renee St. Cloud.' But the last time we can know for sure Danny was alive, he was in his convertible with two other boys, and Danny bought those two boys a good time, which was Jennifer Peveto. She took them to one of the First Quality Motel rooms. She left them. The next morning, the room is splattered with blood, and an Ector County Sheriff Deputy by the name of Justan Brady tells me some mud tester found his body in a ditch." Bullet watched as Mina squirmed.

"What happened to the car?" Colton asked.

"The police can't find it. They say it's probably in a chop shop in El Paso by now." Mina paced and sipped, "Justan Brady came by here. He's out of line. I told the sheriff and police chief to do nothing. Brady is snooping around."

"The little incompetent shit," Bullet said.

"The cops?" Colton said. "Cop are in on this? Wait a minute."

"If anybody gave a shit, some newbie like Justan Brady wouldn't be looking into it. He's looking just for show."

"Well, get him not to show," Colton said toward Mina.

Bullet got up to pace with Mina. "Listen now, Mina. You listen. You know what Danny meant to me. Hell, you even mean something. You want me to show you scars to show you what he means? I want to fix this so as to make it up to both of you. So as we are even. So I can sleep at night. So I can do something for Danny. And what I got is Renee St. Cloud."

"Who?" Mina asks.

"Jennifer Peveto. I told you. She still has a lot to learn. It's the name she uses."

"Is she all you got?" Mina turned to square up with Bullet. Out of the corner of her eye, Bullet caught Colton getting up and walking to the Vodka.

"Where the hell you going? You need to listen." Bullet said to Colton.

"I need a drink." Colton said.

Bullet swung her attention toward the wobbling Mina. "What else you got?" Mina asked.

"Like you, I know his routine. I know where he was prior to picking up those two boys."

"There were two?"

"Renee's reliable enough to count." Bullet shouted, "You listening, Colton? This is important."

"It's nothing I can't figure out on my own."

"What's he doing here?" Mina asked.

"He's the muscle. He's supposed to protect me."

Mina turned to look at Colton. "You're what Snake sent? You're Snake Popp's contribution?"

Colton turned, smiled, and gentlemanly as was possible for him to look, bowed his head. "You called him."

"Look, Mina, you pay Colton if you want, but you owe me nothing. I'm doing this for Danny."

Mina was exhausted from the liquor and the worry. She plopped down on the couch. "It will be worth your while."

Bullet sat beside Mina, slowly put her arm around Mina's shoulders and looked up at Colton. As she patted Mina's shoulder and Mina started just little bit of a whimper, she scolded Colton, "Colton, you listening?"

Colton stepped up to them, cocked his head as though he was looking at some unnatural act. "My guess is, if they found his billfold, he had no money." Bullet squeezed Mina's shoulder.

Mina pulled her head up. "They found no billfold."

"The car is gone," Colton said.

Bullet smiled at him and nodded her head. "Most of the time he gets the shit beat out of him is because they find out he is queer after they meet him. But what if these two—I repeat, *two* guys—know he is queer and play along."

"So they set him up. Steal his money," Mina said.

"You got a dim view of humanity," Colton said.

"Sons of bitches," Mina said.

"You still want the police out of this? They got judges and prison sentences. I got nothing like that."

"I want you two to find them."

* * *

On the way into Snake's stripper bar, Colton thought that he wasn't going to like working for a woman, especially if that woman was Bullet or Mina. He thought about his family. He thought that his family was better off with him butting heads and roughing up drunks who deserved it and knew they deserved it so they would never report it, than with him looking for crime and daring people to find him. He wondered what Way Low would say. Then he thought that maybe he just didn't have the stomach for what Mina and Bullet might ask him to do. As he stepped out of Bullet's truck and followed her into the Stampede, he thought that he should ask Snake for his old job back.

Their eyes hurt as they stepped into the dark of Snake's third-rate titty bar. Snake sat next to the center stage and watched a dark-skinned girl in cut-off blue jeans, a man's T-shirt, and very high heels dancing next to the pole. There was no music. She was an awful dancer.

As Bullet and Colton sat on either side of him, Snake smoothed his hair back along the sides of his head and watched the auditioning woman. "I don't know if I even want to hear about it. You two are on Mina's case and payroll."

"Snake," Colton said. "I don't like this." Bullet leaned on her elbows and looked past Snake to Colton. Colton returned her glance. "I mean, Snake. This is just dangerous. There's cops involved."

Bullet said clear and slow, "Pussy."

"Goddamn it," Snake said and broke his attention from the dancer. She stopped, and a voice said, *"Tú duras,* not yet, keep going." Colton looked for the voice and saw a small Mexican man in the shadows on the other side of the stage. "Mina wants this. Like everybody else in this town with things to hide, I owe Mina. So you help her."

"But Snake—"

59

"No 'but Snake's.' If Mina says she can protect you, she can."

"But she never said that."

"She wants us to find Danny's murderers," Bullet said.

Snake turned to look at Bullet. As he did, the dancer resumed and strutted toward them, but she misplaced her foot, the old stage creaked, and she lost her balance. Bullet, Snake, and Colton watched as the clumsy dancer fell. Her arms splayed out in front of her and her legs behind her. "Holly shit," Snake said. Snake motioned with his hand. "Go on. Go on." The woman pushed herself to her knees and stared at Snake. "Alberto, tell her to go on."

"Juan, my name is Juan," the Mexican man in the shadows said.

"Juan, then. Make her move."

"Tú, bailas."

The woman started to gyrate again. "You know, I could work with her," Bullet said. Colton looked around Snake and at Bullet. "I was pretty good. Men watched, even with this scar," Bullet said and pointed to the scar. "At times, the way you absolutely control them, the whole audience, I miss it."

"Okay, stop, stop," Snake said. Then he said, "Let's see your tits." The woman stopped her dance and looked dumbfounded. *"Su chichis,"* Snake said.

The woman looked toward Juan. *"Tu chi-chis,"* he said.

Even Colton could see that this woman hurt. She tentatively reached down to grab the hem of her T-Shirt, and slowly, not teasing but hesitating, wondering, she pulled it to her shoulders, then over her head. She stood perfectly still.

"Oh God, Snake," Bullet said. "She's a child. You don't want her."

"She's eighteen. So she's of legal age. But she's from Columbia. So she's not legal citizen-wise. What else is she going to do?"

"She could work for me," Bullet said.

Colton stared at the child, wondered what he felt, if it was disgust, some evil excitement, or some wish that he had stayed in the oil field and was supporting his family by breaking his back in that way. "Move. Dance," Snake said.

Bullet said, "So we're on it. You tell Mina we're on it."

Colton said, "You gonna give me any kind of a choice?"

"Go find those killers," Snake said and dropped his head. Colton hung his head. "Okay, get Lionel to help you. You and him are partners anyway. Y'all probably don't even think separate." Colton felt his heart twist. He knew what to think about his new order.

Bullet said, "Come on," and Colton followed her out into the screaming sunshine, and their eyes hurt even worse.

* * *

At the sunlit asphalt parking lot of The Tank, Bullet saw herself stripping in Oklahoma City, in one of the titty bars by the airport, just off I-40. Oklahoma City was midway across the southern part of the country, truckers and long-haul drivers all over the place, so Oklahoma City was the capital of titty bar America. Then she saw farther back to dancing in a cage in Bwana Dik's, just above that first section of the river walk in San Antonio, before she got the scar across her face, but also the reason she got the scar across her face. She was never like the girl auditioning for Snake; she was always smarter than the men she danced for—the ones that watcher her and the ones that hired her. And the tease and the grind and the smile and mean look in stripping were the same games she played when she was whoring. And still, even in whoring, she was smarter than the men. Bullet knew that. She looked at Colton. He did not know what Bullet did.

Above the hollowed out first floor of the old holding tank was a second floor with the center cut out, so a customer could look down at the first floor. You could get a good steak and good liquor and drop a lot of oil field money at The Tank. Light was still out, so Bullet and Colton were all there was of a crowd. She led Colton to the round bar, and Larry, the bearded bartender, came up to them. He gave a nod to each one and said, "Bullet," then "Colton."

"Larry," Bullet said. "This ain't social."

"I take it you are here to see about Danny Fowler."

"How do you know?" Colton asked.

"Word gets around."

"Word can't travel that fast." Then, Colton added, "shit."

And Bullet, to calm him, patted his forearm and said, "Word will surprise you." Larry sliced lemons. "So, what is the word?"

"Word is you're looking for what happened to Danny."

"Word is fast."

"Word is beyond believable fast," Colton said. Bullet knew that he was talking to her and himself, not to Larry.

"Sounds like you know what I want to hear."

Larry looked at Colton. "Colton, I didn't expect to see you."

"I didn't expect to see me here either."

"Larry," Bullet said.

"Danny was in here. As usual, only this time, he goes to a couple of boys, and they invite him to sit down."

"And what you figure?" Bullet asked.

"I figure he don't give himself away. And they leave with him."

"You think he could have invited them to go whoring with him?"

"I guess that would be it, given how things turned out."

"You think Danny maybe tried something with one of them, maybe propositioned one, so they beat the shit out of a queer?"

"It looks that way. I bet tonight you'll hear people saying exactly that."

"What did these two look like?" Colton asked.

"One had a hat."

"You got to give me more than that," Colton said.

"I got no more than that. I'm not in the habit of checking out every customer on a crowded night."

"Got names?" Colton asked.

"They paid cash."

"What else you got?"

"I'm a bartender. I don't talk unless people pay me. I don't listen unless they pay me or plant themselves at this bar. Those boys didn't pay and didn't want no one listening."

"What else?"

"One had a hat."

Bullet reached and patted Colton's arm. "What if I splashed some bills in front of you?" she asked Larry.

"Bullet, I like you," Larry said and looked at Colton. Colton put on his mean look. "Cash or not, the story would be the same."

Bullet started to think her way to an ending. What she saw was that the boys were careful to set this all up.

"Suppose you watch for these fellas," Colton said. "Snake Popp would appreciate it."

"I ain't seen no appreciation yet," Larry said. "Especially from that county deputy sheriff come by here."

Bullet stiffened, "What county deputy sheriff?"

"Justan Brady. He's been here and done gone."

"How the hell did he know to ask around here?" Colton asked.

"He said he asked around. People know Danny's habits."

"What did you tell him?"

"Same I told you."

"Jesus," Colton said and swiveled in his bar chair away from Larry.

"Suppose, Justan Brady comes back, how much you going to tell him?" Bullet asked.

"As much as I know."

"How much would it take to keep you dumb?"

Colton swiveled to look at Bullet. "It's Mina's money," she said.

"Mina Fowler has deep pockets."

"Reach on in."

"He asks, then I'll get dumb and bill you."

Bullet nodded, then pulled Colton toward the door.

"You ever smelled a turd?" Colton asked.

"Why would you want to?" Bullet asked.

"You never want to smell it. It just hits you."

"Go home, Colton, and wake up thinking and not sniffing for turds."

* * *

Colton did go home. But he started thinking before sleeping. He thought too much. He wandered through his house. He went into his living room to see his two boys laying on the floor in front of the TV. In his mind, he snapped a camera to take a photo of the boys. He went into his kitchen to see his wife. He went to her and wrapped his arms around her, and she shrugged out from his grasp as she scrapped food from a dish into the sink and the garbage disposal that Colton just bought for her.

"Honey," Colton said.

"Where you been?" his honey, his wife, said.

"I been out. Work."

"I don't know I like this work you got."

"It pays for what we have."

"So would other work."

"I ain't got other work."

"You could try." Elena smiled. She looked up and kissed him on the cheek.

He was glad that this time Elena smiled and kissed him. But Colton still felt hurt, defeated, over-matched. He suspected that he might be able to keep up with just one of them, but Elena, Snake, Bullet, Mina, and Larry the bartender were just too much. Too much had been visiting him too often. He smelled turds. And he couldn't get the smell out of his nose. He placed himself in the doorway between the kitchen and the living room and looked at what he had, his wife and his boys. The other that he had was Bullet and Snake.

Colton grabbed a beer from the refrigerator, popped the top, and went into his backyard. He saw Way Low with his transistor radio and his own beer. Way Low smiled and raised up from his reclining lawn chair. "I don't want to talk now," Colton said. "Maybe later."

And Way Low eased himself down into the chair. "You act like a woman at that time of the month."

Colton went to another lawn chair and sat in it and leaned back. It had warmed, but the night was tinged with wind and coolness. It surrounded him and made him shiver and made him want to stop drinking his beer. Then, from out of the dark, Colton's youngest appeared before him. Mando had a beer. The boy had gone to the refrigerator and pulled out a beer for his father.

Colton sat his beer down and took the beer from Mando, then scrunched to one side of the lawn chair and patted the narrow space beside him. Mando wriggled in beside Colton. And after a couple of sips, Colton hoisted his youngest into his lap and held him tight and said, "You my boy, Mando. You my boy. I gave you that name, you know."

"*Mando,*" Mando said.

"And not *Amando*. Cause I can't say it right."

And Way Low raised himself up in his lawn chair to watch the father and his son. "Mando, can you say, *"su padre?"*

"Super ray," Mando said.

"Tu padre?"

"Tupper ray."

"Mi padre."

"My pod ray."

"I give up on you, Amando. You stay Anglo. Don't look like you going to get no more Mexican." Smiling at his boy and at Way Low, Colton emptied one beer then the next as Mando drifted asleep.

That night, Colton interrupted Elena from going in to talk to the boys as she usually did and asked if he could say goodnight. "You don't know what you get into," Elena said and slapped slightly on Colton's chest. He grabbed that hand, held it. She smiled. Then Colton stepped into his boys' room.

Over in his bed, Arnie swooshed and dived his new plastic model airplane and blew his lips to make the whirring airplane sound that

Colton made when he played airplane with Mando. Arnie had just gotten interested in gluing those planes together, but he was not very good with glue, patience, or reading directions. His fighter plane had globs of dried glue, one wing angling up and the other down, and a missing canopy. Still, with this plane and his own whirring, he didn't need his father to play airplane.

"You going to sing us a song?" Mando asked.

"That's what your momma does. I don't sing so good."

"That's okay," Mando said. "I don't understand the words." Mando started kicking the bed with his right leg, the covers rising then falling. Colton asked him, "What's wrong with you, Mando? You got the heebies?"

"He's weird," Arnie said.

Mando slammed his leg on the bed. "I want to go to school with Arnie."

"He's too dumb to go to school," Arnie said.

"Way Low and your Momma told you. You got to wait until next year."

"A year!"

"But you get to stay home with Way Low."

"Way Low mostly sleeps."

"Be thankful for Way Low."

"I am. But who's my daddy?"

"I told you he was stupid," Arnie said and strafed the bed with his model airplane.

"You know who your Daddy is," Colton said and tapped his chest with his thumb.

"But what if you can't always be Daddy?"

"It don't work that way. Whoever is your daddy stays your daddy."

"But Way Low is mostly here. Like a daddy."

Colton looked toward Arnie. "Do you tell him these things?" he asked Arnie. "Where do you get this? Your Daddy is your Daddy and will stay your Daddy."

"He's dumb," Arnie said.

"Am not," Mando said.

"Just in case, can Way Low be my Daddy too?"

"No," Colton said too loudly. "Way Low is your mother's father. He can't be your Daddy."

Mando wriggled and squirmed on his butt to square away to look at him. "But look, look, my real Daddy has me and Arnie. So why can't Way Low have two kids too?"

"It just don't work that way."

Arnie put down his airplane and said to his father, "See, I told you Mando is stupid." To make his point, he jumped out of bed and ran to Mando's bed and punched him in the chest.

"Arnie, you don't do that. We told you . . ." Colton said as Mando took a swing at Arnie and missed. "Stop that. Fighting and hitting don't fix nothing."

"But, Daddy, I want you to be my daddy. And I want Way Low to be my daddy, and I want to go to school."

"Oh, Mando," Colton said and put his arm around him. "You're not stupid like your brother says. You're smart. But you get yourself so confused."

After he said good night to his boys, Colton wandered into his own bedroom, took off his clothes, and in his underwear, slid into bed next to the lump that was his wife. He rolled toward her. Elena's back was to him. Colton hooked his chin over Elena's shoulder and kissed her on the cheek. She didn't budge, so he kissed her again. This time, Elena rolled toward him and the tips of their noses touched, and they both pulled back to adjust their eyes on the out-of-focus, dim stare that locked them. Colton's closed his eyes to unlock the stare and kissed her. He felt the firm pressure of a real kiss, but then felt her lips tighten and withdraw from him. "I'm home early. Since I am, I just thought..."

"But I have an early day . . . "

"Well, you know, it's just been awhile."

Colton felt the mattress shift as Elena rolled away from him. And he heard, "Tired. Later." He rolled to his side of the bed and thought about Snake's new stripper trying to stand and dance at the same time.

Chapter 5

Most people like a clear, sunny day. The light makes things shine. But in Odessa there's not much to shine. So the light turns harsh. By early summer all the grass is gone; the landscape is sand and scraggly mesquite, not even deserving to be called *a tree*, and dotted with pumpjacks and rigs. The city is concrete, asphalt, and burnt grass and trash and sand lined curbs. There are no sewer drains. What's to drain? Just natural washes to carry away flood and rainwater. The nights cool down fast. You can at least feel the nights. The night soothes, hides, covers up. Bullet and Colton lived in this nighttime world. They both felt exposed in daylight. So unlike Snake Popp, their skin was pasty, not golden. But Colton and Bullet went into the late afternoon sun to start looking for Danny Fowler's killers. Though it was fall and the days had a pleasant tinge of cool in the air, the bright sun spotlighted them.

The only plan that Bullet and Colton really had was to cruise the bars as Danny did with Renee in tow and hope that she could spot the two men who hired her that night. Bullet suggested that they split up to cover more ground. Bullet suggested that she and Renee start at The Tank or one or two of the other better places in town and that, meantime, Colton should drive through West Odessa bars where Danny ended up when he had no luck, which was quite often, and ask questions. When Colton said that he wanted Bullet and Renee to have protection, and Bullet said that she could protect herself, Colton decided that protecting the women would be Lionel's job. Colton, on this job, was the brains. He would lead. Lionel was still muscle; he would follow.

On their second night in the Tank, sitting at the bar, looking over the crowd, Bullet and Renee drank Larry the bartender's special top shelf Margaritas. Bullet had coached Renee. She was to dress less whorish. So tonight, she wore a longer mini-skirt and cowboy boots. She was to look at faces and try to recognize one of the men who came to her that night. Larry said, "So what are you up to, Bullet?"

"I'm up to having a good time."

"You seem like the type to never have a good time." Bullet checked over her shoulder to see Lionel come in, catch her eye, then move off to a table by himself. As Colton told her, this was what Lionel was good at. The only bad thing was that people noticed a black man in Odessa.

Renee hit the bottom of her frozen margarita and sucked in air and bits of ice. Bullet didn't know how long they could do this. It was incredibly boring—and costly. Renee was especially antsy and was drinking and eating up a big chunk of Mina's money.

"Now tell me," Bullet said to Renee. "What were those fellas like, the ones who were with Danny?"

"I can tell you," Larry said.

"You go away," Bullet said.

"They were oil field trash. Been here about a year, I'd guess. When the oil field busts, like it always does, they'll be out chasing some other fast bucks and spending it someplace else."

"I thought bartenders were supposed to mind their own business."

"It's my bar."

"Last time I was here you didn't know nothing."

"I remembered some."

"Well, remember on the other side of the bar. I'll talk to you later." Larry turned his ass to them, but Bullet knew that he had grown talkative because of Renee. Renee was spindly, but she had this look that said she could do wonders for the man who could just clean her up a little. That's what men bought when they bought Renee, promise. That was Renee's job on this job—to offer promise.

Bullet scooted closer to Renee, "What were they like. Were they mean? Funny? Smelly?"

"One was bigger—and uglier—and he seemed to give the orders. Just is he didn't say much. Just sort of looks and sizes up." She returned to her empty Margarita and sucked just air through her straw.

"And the other one?" Bullet asked.

"He did the talking, the bragging. You know how they do, talking about their equipment and all. He was like that, and he had on the cowboy hat."

"Okay, if you see them, you point them out. If they see you, you know what to do."

"Do I have to?"

"It's your job."

"I don't like this job."

"Nobody likes this job." Bullet looked hard at Renee. "But we like justice." When Renee scrunched her face up like she just didn't understand, Bullet said, "And we liked Danny more than justice."

As Bullet fidgeted and watched and told Renee to keep her eyes open, the bar filled. The Tank was like bars she had known, the Bwana Dik on the old San Antonio River Walk and some of the Oklahoma City bars in particular, but it was not like the bars she now had grown into and lived in out in Odessa. In West Odessa, out Andrews Highway, Bullet owned bars that were mom and pop bars, mostly beer bars without a liquor license, some with no heat or air. They lost money, changed hands, had few but loyal patrons. For Bullet's renters, running a bar seemed like a dream compared to labor. But dreams weren't real for these people; labor was. So, Bullet profited. And sometimes, in these boom times, they had an ass kicking or a shooting out in the parking lot. Not inside, in the temple. And ass kickings and shootings were bad for business too.

The Tank was different. It had polished brass, a shiny wood bar and floor, new padded barstools. All the tables and chairs and booths matched. It hadn't had a shooting in the parking lot or an ass kicking inside, but its customers weren't loyal, and just like her bars, the Tank would probably lose money once the boom busted or the unloyal customers found someplace else to go.

And as Bullet watched the Tank fill with the unloyal customers, she saw Justan Brady drift in. He stepped in, took his cowboy hat off, rested his hands on his hips, and like Renee did when she walked in, kind of sniffed the air. He seemed to catch a scent of Bullet and Renee. His head followed his scent right toward them. Bullet looked, caught Lionel's eye, and then smiled sweetly as Justan Brady walked up to them. "Miss Price?" he said to her and extended his hand without the cowboy hat

"Deputy Brady," Bullet said as she shook his hand. "Good to see you."

Renee's head swung toward Bullet, and her eyes pleaded for advice. Bullet checked over her shoulder. Lionel ducked. "Is this Renee St. Cloud?" Justan asked. Renee's eyes stayed on Bullet, who considered and considered again, even while she said empty, pleasant words. "I really doubt you think it's good to see me, Miss Price, but is this Miss St. Cloud?"

"Yes," Bullet said. "Why?"

"I asked around. Some other . . . lady said she saw Miss St. Cloud get into a Red Mustang Convertible. I figure she might be able to answer some questions."

Renee's mouth slowly started to drop. "I'm a good girl. I ain't done nothing."

"No one says you have," Bullet said to Renee but kept her eyes on Justan.

He lowered his eyes. "I didn't' figure you knew her."

"Small world, huh?"

"Miss St. Cloud, could I have a word with you?"

"Justan, I can tell you anything that she can."

"I'd like to hear it from her."

Bullet put her palm against Renee's back and gently pushed her up. Justan stepped out of her way and said, "Let's go to one of those booths." Bullet watched Renee's exaggerated, imitation runway model walk as she floated and wobbled toward the booth. She tried to look over her shoulder for advice from Bullet, but Justan's face got in the way of her glance. Bullet looked behind her. Lionel stared at his table. "Lately, he's been in here as much as you," Larry said.

"The balls of that guy," Bullet said.

Renee sat on one side of a booth, and Justan slid in on the other side. They were not that far apart in age, and from Bullet's position, they looked like youngsters out for a date. And Renee fidgeted and put a fake smile on and drummed the table with her fingers, just like Bullet drummed the bar with hers and watched. Renee's fingers rose and fluttered, and Bullet could almost hear her voice waver. They should have rehearsed this too. And Bullet hoped that Renee was smart enough to know that she was not smart enough to lie. She would get trapped in it.

After a while, after a coy smile, Renee leaned toward Justan and looked like she was begging. Justan dug in his pocket and pulled out a cigarette. He held his hand over the table, and she took the cigarette, and like a gentleman, he pulled a match off the table, struck it, and lit the cigarette. Renee looked at the cigarette and started to talk. Just like a girl, she flopped her wrist back to dangle the cigarette away from her. And she stared at it, and she looked back at Justan. Only now she didn't twitch and fidget, and her eyes didn't try to look back at Bullet. The cigarette, Bullet hoped, was a prop, and it might have given her a way to concentrate.

In a while she was back, and she sat down next to Bullet, and Justan came around to sit on the other side of Bullet. And Lionel stood. Bullet couldn't fake nice anymore. She said, "You not supposed to be looking into this."

"How do you know that?" Justan swung his head toward her.

"I know Mina Fowler."

"Then you changed your mind about helping me?" Justan's eyes smiled.

"You got Renee. What do you need me for?"

"Sympathy."

"I could almost like you."

Justan dropped his head then raised it and smiled with one corner of his mouth. "My temperament, talent, and predisposition don't suit me being a police officer. My talent, temperament, and predisposition don't really suit much of anything. I tried college, but that didn't work out so good, so I knew somebody who knew somebody and became a deputy sheriff."

"You want to keep that job?"

"I do as I'm told. Chief Deputy Bobby Cooksey said he was too old to piss off Mina Fowler. But he said it just pains a cop to let a crime sit. I guess I'm something of a cop."

"You better watch your cock," Bullet said, and Justan pulled back from her. But then he just nodded. He stood.

"You better be careful," Renee just let loose. Bullet thought that she could almost like him. If things had been different, if he had walked into the Cactus Lounge one night . . .

"Where you going to go now?"

"Looking for somebody who knows something, then home. I got a marriage I need to tend to." He turned to go, but he twisted back to look at Bullet. "They found parts of the red Mustang convertible in a chop shop in El Paso. They say 'there goes the case.' But I just got this itch," he said and looked at Renee. "I just want to know more." He turned back toward Bullet, shrugged, and walked toward the door.

As he left, Lionel sat down, and Bullet turned to Renee. "I didn't know you smoked."

"I don't. I just thought if I could put something in my hands and concentrate on it, I wouldn't get so nervous and fuck up."

"Did you fuck up?"

"I just told him exactly what I told you. Word for word."

Bullet started to nod, and she reached across the table to pat Renee's arms. She thought that Renee might someday make a good whore.

And then Lionel said, "Who was that fucker? Was that one of them?"

"That's the only cop working with us."

Lionel said, "We ain't working with no cops."

"Like I said, he's working with us." Bullet cocked her head to think. She said out loud, "Renee, what were those two boys like in bed?"

"Good God, I don't want to hear white ladies talk about this shit," Lionel said. "In the old days they'd lynch a black man for hearing such stuff."

"Some men, black or otherwise, might pay to hear this," Bullet said. Renee shrugged. "Think," Bullet said.

"Sometimes, I just make my mind go someplace else."

"So that's what it's like being a whore?" Lionel asked.

"Don't get ugly," Bullet said.

"If I got to listen, I get to ask."

Bullet hushed him with her eyes and then looked at Renee. "The little one, the one that talked. It was like he was antsy, wanted moving, talking, dancing, touching."

"Any fucking in there?" Lionel asked.

"The big one. It was like he had a job to do and meant to get it done."

"Jesus, you making me excited," Lionel said.

* * *

As the last sunbeams came in through the cracks in the aluminum walls of the Blue Lantern, Curly took his gimme cap off to loosen his tightly coiled curly red hair and rubbed his beard. He was bigger than Colton and even more prone to throw the first punch to get an even bigger advantage. Colton had sized him up before and so, just to be prepared, sized him up this late evening. Colton knew it would be a tough fight but believed he could take Curly, but there would be missing teeth and broken limbs, noses, cheeks, or digits. Colton figured he had to risk it. Bar world gossip would now probably be about Danny Fowler. And Curly was the best source of that gossip.

"Colton Parker, you old son of a bitch," Curly said as he waved his mug of beer in front of him and sloshed it on the table. "What you want?"

"I want to know about Danny Fowler."

"I heard there's some kind of county sheriff's deputy asking about him too."

"You talk to him?"

"I just hear he's been making the rounds."

"What about Danny? You know he's been beat to death."

Curly's smile disappeared, and he shook his wooly head and face. "Problem with some of them *worms* he was always chasing after, huh?" Curly chuckled at his own joke. Colton had heard it before. "Well, hell, they wouldn't have got me. Course if they got Danny, they probably wouldn't of had me in the first place. Course I'd of got them good. Fucking or fighting, either one. I'd of got them." He brought his fist down hard on the table and shook it. He chuckled some more, "I'm a tool pusher, and I'm looking for worms."

"I don't think these was just worms," Colton said trying to keep Curly on track. "They had decent jobs. They were full roughnecks or better, not just starting out."

"Well then, shit. Why would Danny want them? It's that young ass, huh?" Curly laughed some more, and Colton thought that it might be worth the fight to shut him up.

"What do you know?"

"I know Danny pissed me off." His chuckling stopped, his wooly head grew still, and he stopped banging the table. "He had airs. He was better than everybody. Hell, I'm queer, but he was a homo."

"So, you think he deserved an ass kicking to death just on account he is 'homo?'"

Curly pointed at Colton, "I can say he's homo, not you." Curly looked like he was sizing Colton up, not for fucking but for fighting. And Colton wondered if he should go ahead and throw the punch just to get it started. That old feeling of being a monster man came back, of playing scared, of holding back but getting ready to throw himself into it. Quickness and commitment was how you played monster man, was how you at least broke even in a fight.

"You going to talk to me or pencil dick around?" Colton asked.

"I like you, Colton. You ain't queer are you?"

"No." Colton's stomach and fists tightened.

"Like to learn?"

Colton's legs sprung him up. But Curly held up his hands, "Goddamn, now come on. I'm playing with you. Pulling your pud there. That's all." Colton barely stopped himself. He was just short of committing to the act.

"Okay, if we're just dancing around here and groping each other, then I got better things to do," Colton said.

Curly picked his gimme cap from the table and squshed it over his mop-like head, making an explosion of curls come out from under it. "You're a touchy bastard, Colton, but that's okay." He pulled his mug up to his face and downed his beer. He started his story. "There's this guy comes in here just before you get here. And he's drinking and trying to talk to somebody, but there ain't nobody here. Not that anybody would listen to the little prick in the first place. You know the sort, just talking shit, wearing a cowboy hat like he was something special. And he starts in on queers." Curly jerked his head toward the bar, "Marlene, the bartender there, she's tolerating him, making a show like she's listening. But I'm thinking he's talking to me. And I am taking offense." Before he can go on, Marlene put another full mug of beer in front of him. "Thanks, sweetheart."

"Your story have a point?" Colton asked.

"You're just trying to piss me off. You jealous or you want a go at me?" Curly chuckled.

"I apologize." Colton felt safer because he knew that Curly was not thinking. Colton was practicing thinking ahead. He was trying to make a habit of seeing past his act to the end. Detective work was a hard way to make a living.

"So, the little prick describes a guy. This guy sounds like Danny. And he says this guy made a pass at him, offered him money. And then this little prick says, 'and then I showed him.'" Curly got a mean look in his eyes. "So, I showed him. I'm sitting here. So I step to the bar and cold cock him from behind. I tattooed the fucker. Corner of his left eye has a print of my knuckles. I marked him for you."

"Didn't he call the cops, jump back at you?"

"He lays there sucking air like a fish. He knows better than to tangle with me. And Marlene starts cussing him and telling him to get out cause he ought to know better than to come in the bar and talk shit. Marlene likes me," Curly said.

"My guess is he's down West University at the Snug Harbor talking shit down there. It's the next closest bar. My guess is he'll be there for a while." As Colton got up, Curly added, "Now don't get me wrong, I'd go down there and kick his ass myself, but I like it here."

* * *

The Snug Harbor had several themes over the years, but now, for no reason, it had a finished and polished oak trunk jammed in between the floor and the ceiling. It was on the dance floor, so when the drunks tried to maneuver their women around the dance floor, they had to scooch past the oak tree trunk. As Colton stepped into the darkness, he waited to adjust his eyes, then spotted three cowboy hats at the bar. He spotted Curly's knuckles tattoo under the brim of one hat and picked a spot next to this hat. The face under the hat nodded to Colton and then returned the brim down toward the beer. "I guess the other guy is in worse shape?" Colton asked.

"He's in worse shape whether I hit him or not. He's an asshole."

"Can I buy you a beer? I know the guy. My apologies for him."

The man nodded. Colton motioned to the bartender. And Colton tried to think, tried to plan against fucking up. "So why would you want to fuck with Curly?"

"Cause I'm upset is why. I just got laid off." The short man under the hat stared into the opening of his bottle of beer.

"What happened?"

"Got drunk, got laid, showed up late. You know, the whole nine yards."

"What do you do?"

"I'm a welder."

Colton's mind started working good, clicking right along with memory. He pulled his wallet out of his back pocket and found Jake Raven's business card. He handed it to the man in the hat. "Tell him that I sent you." The man pocketed the card, a good sign. "You live around here?"

"You writing a book?"

"Just asking"

"Colton Parker." Colton was not good at making friends or using pleasantries. He extended his hand. The man shook it.

"Mitch," the man said.

"Just 'Mitch'? You got a last name?"

"Look, if you are writing a book, then leave the chapter about me out."

"I'm just trying to be cordial."

Before Mitch could say anything, the shaved-head bartender was leaning on his elbows between then. "Colton," the bartender said. "Y'all are getting kind of loud."

"Get us another beer each," Colton said.

"Put mine in the hole," Mitch said. "I ain't finished this one."

Colton and Mitch planted their elbows and stared in front of them. With a beer in front of him, Colton relaxed, counted to himself, and when he reached twenty, he said, "You know Danny Fowler?"

"Goddamn, you know everybody? Who the fuck is Danny Fowler?"

"Just a guy. But I hear you and a friend was out drinking with him."

"Who you heard this from?"

"The fella that put his knuckles upside your head."

"Are you a faggot too?" The little man squared around. "I mean, is everybody in this town a faggot? Nothing but butt fucking and dick sucking going on here?" The other cowboy hats were moving toward Mitch. Two middle-aged ladies, out for a beer, stood and moved toward the door. This was Colton's game. Now he was the "security" Snake trained him for. He could let instinct take over, but he was proud because he was thinking. Mitch was too quick to start yelling "faggot" at the mention of Danny's name. Colton should try to get him to say more, not beat the shit out of him.

"All I'm saying is I heard you were out with Danny Fowler. So I figure you know him, so I figure you know what come of him."

"You asking me what come of him like I know where he's at or something?

"I'm asking if you know what happened to him."

"I truly don't give a shit."

"He got killed." Three men creeping up behind Mitch stopped and stared at Colton because they had not heard. Colton turned around to elbow the bar and plant his right foot on the bar rail. "I don't mean nothing by it," he mumbled, and Mitch checked over his shoulder then elbowed the bar just to the left of Colton.

As when he was playing ball and as when he was becoming security for Snake, Colton was not *always* playing scared. Sometimes, as with any male of any species, his testosterone just bubbled up because he ran into somebody whose ass just needed whipping, and he knew he could do a fine job of it. At times, on the football field, he saw a weaker boy or just another player in the wrong, exposed position, and he had to unload, just as he got unloaded upon and broke his knee. There was no thought in this, just quickness and movement and momentum and something between anger, meanness, and aggression. Colton felt that now—and so stopped thinking to see ahead. Colton pushed himself up from the bar rail with his right foot to an upward angle and, with his weaker left fist, punched down and out, not even with all his strength, to send Mitch crumpling to the floor.

Mitch's stiff-brimmed hat rolled three feet down the dirty floor of the Snug Harbor, and Mitch's mouth worked like a fish out of water. And he was rubbing the knuckle tattoo on his right side to match the one Curly made on his left side. Colton's squared stance over him told him not to get up. But then the shaved-head man tapped the bar, and Colton turned to see that what he was doing the tapping with was a sawed-off shotgun. "Colton, none of us want to go down this road. And I'm sure nobody wants to go to jail."

Mitch was suddenly on his feet with the other two cowboy hats about to grab him and said, "Yeah, you fucker. You faggot."

"You get out," the shaved-head man said.

"What?" Mitch yelled.

"I started it. I'm gone," Colton said.

"You stay," the shaved-head man said to Colton.

"You're talking shit and starting shit, you leave," the shaved-head bartender said to Mitch.

"Goddamned then if you ever see me or any of my money," Mitch said to the shaved-head man.

"I'll leave too," Colton said, knowing that he wanted to see Mitch's car or wanted to try to follow him to his home.

"You stay here," the shaved-head man said. "I don't want nobody beat to shit, stabbed, or shot in my parking lot."

"You go home," he said to Mitch. "But I don't care if I see you or your money again."

Mitch stomped quickly to his hat, swiped at it to pick it up by the brim, then stomped out of the bar.

Colton made a move toward the door, "You stay."

Colton turned to the bartender. "I'm sorry I don't remember your name. And I'm sorry I fucked up your night. And I'll pay damages.

And I'm not gonna stab, shoot, or beat that fucker. But I am going out the door."

"Colton," the shaved-head man said. "Colton, Colton. Oh shit, Colton." And Colton backed toward the door then stepped out into the newly dark night. He saw two high beam lights pushing toward him through the new dark. He stepped back, and the pickup passed him by, and Mitch was hanging out the window shooting the finger.

Colton made it to his Honda Civic, jerked open his unlocked door, fumbled his keys, but pulled out the parking lot and churned up gravel along the side of West University Drive. Checking behind him, he pulled into the lane and saw tail lights ahead of him. He passed by that car to see the tail lights of the Chevy truck. Pounding his skull with the inside of his brain, he tried to memorize the license plate.

Then the truck pulled off, and Colton followed. He slowed, watched the truck take another right, then speed up to take the right himself. Ahead of him, the truck stopped. Mitch got out and went to a cyclone fence and opened the gate. Colton drove by, but then stopped, got out and ran back toward the fence.

Inside the fence was a double-wide and a whole bunch of RVs. Around them all was an eight-foot cyclone fence to keep out thieves and drunks. Whoever owned the place rented out the spaces to workers living in RVs, just like Jake Raven said. On his knees peering through the fence, he watched the Chevy pull up to an RV, and he pushed the license number to one spot in his mind to fill another slot up with a map to this RV. He watched Mitch go in.

Back on West University, Colton pulled into a service station and started plugging a pay phone full of quarters, calling all the bars on their routes, trying to find Bullet and Lionel.

* * *

Back at the Blue Lantern, Colton sat with Lionel and stared back at him. Their beers sat warming in front of them. He did not look at Bullet. And he just didn't want to see Renee. Bullet repeated, "You hit him. You fucking hit him. Can't you think at all? How is that going to solve anything? What were you thinking?"

"That's right. I wasn't thinking. That happens. But now he's not gonna fuck with me."

"And what good does that do? What good is it that he's not going to trust you?"

"I know where he lives," Colton said, looked at the others, then smiled. "What do you know?"

"Try that on," Lionel said. "An ass whupping loosens tongues and minds."

"I know we still need Renee to identify him. You may have the wrong guy." Bullet then tried a different strategy. "You got a name?"

"Mitch."

"Mitch is all?"

Colton finally looked at Renee. Her head drifted around the bar. "They got food here?" she asked.

As Colton shook his head, Bullet couldn't hide her disgust but tried to be gentle. "Now Colton . . ." There it was, "Now, Colton." It was what a West Texan heard when he fucked up. Worse, it wasn't fussing; it was scolding, demeaning. Without listening anymore, Colton heard Bullet say, "We just all got to try harder. We got to think."

That was better than "now, Colton." But Bullet's fake gentle just pissed Colton off, so he said, "Define *we*."

"What? I means *us*," Bullet said.

"*Us* is all *us*, but *we* means everybody but you. Don't it?"

"Yeah, you good, Colton," Lionel said.

Now Bullet was pissed. Colton, Lionel, and Bullet could see that progress just stopped. Renee said, "I'm hungry."

Colton, Bullet, and Lionel stared a little longer at each other. "I don't know why I'm included in this pissing contest," Lionel said.

With nowhere to go and nothing to say, Bullet said to Renee, "Come on, let's get a burger." They left. And Colton and Lionel went back to staring into their warming beers and saying nothing. They waited long enough so that they ordered fresh beers from Marlene and waited for them to warm. Colton let his attention wander to a table in the corner and watched as Curly sat down with two other oil-field boys and started talking. Glad, finally, of something—that he escaped way-drunk Curly's attention—Colton went back to staring at his beer. "Well, here we are still working, and she and Renee are in bed snoozing by now," Lionel said.

"Not Bullet. Even if she is snoozing, she's still working."

Lionel took a sip of his beer and winced as he tasted it. "Why ain't *us* working with Snake? Ain't he done good by *us*? Why this? We ain't cut out for this."

"You ain't cut out for this."

"Neither is you. We take orders. Lean on somebody, bust some knuckles. Snake does the thinking."

"It's time you started thinking."

"Well, shit."

"Okay so I hit him. So what? Now he's scared of me. Now I can push him around, get some answers."

The juke box whined with an old country song, and the mood was right for Colton and Lionel to cry in their beers. But as they shifted their stares from each other to their beers, a new worry walked in the door, Justan Brady.

"Oh Jesus," Lionel said. "You know who that is. That is the mother fucking deputy dog been asking about this case."

Colton studied the young man. He saw nothing remarkable that would account for Justan's persistence. In fact, he saw no persistence that he had just heard Bullet talk about.

Just from looking at him, Colton could see that he was not a guy who was used to wearing a deputy sheriff's cowboy hat. It didn't fit him right. He didn't wear it like he knew how to cock it or shove it back on his head. And the brim wasn't curled or tapered in the right way. His boots were too pointy. His jeans weren't Wranglers but some K-Mart or Wal-

Mart off brand. He knew nothing about looking the part, so he probably knew nothing about the part.

Justan made his way to the bar and asked questions of Marlene, then he worked from one drinker to the next until he got to the round table in the far corner—where Curly had cornered two other drinkers. Curly invited him to sit down. He sat as Curly talked. But Colton knew that Curly was in a cloudy haze and that Curly's words were just spilling all over and dripping off the table. Justan wouldn't understand Curly. Curly just couldn't be spilling his guts, telling Justan about Colton and the guy who was in here.

"The son of a bitch," Colton muttered.

"Which one?" Lionel asked.

"Both."

"You not gonna hit one, are you?"

Colton waited. "Let's get out of here before we incriminate ourselves. Right now, it's best he don't know who we are."

"I wish I knew who 'we' was," Lionel said as they pushed themselves and saw Justan Brady turn around to see them as they turned for the door.

* * *

Colton made his way through his dark house on Adams Street. He came into a dark living room and saw Way Low with his transistor earpieces plugged into his ears. Way Low's head was back, and he was snoring. Colton shook him, but he did not wake up. So, Colton pulled an earpiece out of his ear, and Way Low shook his head and came to. "I take it everybody is in bed."

"What it look like?" Way Low said.

"What about you?"

"I get enough sleep. Sometimes I even get confused if I am asleep or not. Like now. You a dream?"

"I wish I was."

"So why you waking me up?"

"Look, you tell Elena, you tell her, you just tell her that I'm trying. That things will be different."

"Why don't you tell her?"

"When do I ever see her?"

Way Low shrugged. "Americans, always worrying instead of just accepting what has to be."

"Hell, I don't think she would want to talk to me."

"Wake her up."

Colton thought that maybe he ought to try that. He tip toed down the hall, peered into the boys' room, and then temptation got him. He opened Way Low's door. He saw a single bed, a trunk, like the army would issue, and a dresser. He saw a small table with a hot plate on it. He didn't t know if he admired or pitied Way Low, so he closed his door and went to next door. He quietly pushed it open, undressed in the dark, and with just his jockeys on, he slid into bed next to Elena. He stroked her arm, then her cheek, and she woke with a start and said, "What time is it?"

Colton said, "Time for some family life."

Elena lived in the daytime world and was tired. Colton came in out of his nighttime world. But she wrapped her arms around his neck and her legs around his belly and back. He could feel her body smile into his. Danny Fowler was great, but Colton, finally, after a long time, felt some promise.

Chapter 6

Colton walked past the rows of pipe and bulkheads and stepped onto the wood slats under the awning of Raven Welding. Inside, a silver-haired lady sat behind a desk, typing, stapling, and talking all at once. Colton stepped up to the counter and rapped his knuckles on the top. The woman kept on with her tasks, paying Colton no mind. He rapped again and cleared his throat, but this time the door behind the woman opened and pot-bellied Jake Raven skipped out. Colton remembered that he was a fellow defensive back, thus spry, spindly, and wiry. He could keep up with fast boys and throw himself into a blocking wall too. Between then and now, Jake Raven had let himself go. But he kept a little grace and quickness in his little legs. "Colton Parker! How you doing?"

Colton looked toward the silver-haired woman. "Oh, she don't do much other than what she does. She's so good at it. I don't disturb her." *She* grunted. "Brenda, this here is Colton Parker, baddest monster man ever in Odessa High's defensive backfield."

Brenda did not look over her shoulder. "Hi, badass," she said.

"See," Jake said. "But damn she's good at the paperwork. You here for lunch?"

"Here for business."

"Why don't we do business while we're doing lunch?"

"I just got a couple of questions."

"Now tell me again, Colton. What is it you do for a living?"

"Security," Colton said.

"What's that entail?"

"Requires me at times to beat the holy shit out of people."

Jake's mouth dropped and his man titties jiggled as he forced himself to laugh. And Colton smiled inside his head when Brenda turned around to look at him. That's right, I'm a badass, his mind said to himself.

"I just come by to ask if you had a couple of boys come by here looking for work and using my name to get it."

"Matter of fact, there was," Jake said and came around to the side of the counter to pat Colton on the back. "Let's go get us a lunch and a beer."

"No, no. I just want to know about them boys." And before he could say more, Brenda had two applications on the counter in front of Colton. Colton looked down and saw *Mitchell Robinson* and *Harold Egbert* printed on the top of each form. Mitch wrote his name in big loops, like a girl writes. Harold printed. Below them, were phone numbers and addresses. Colton tried to memorize the names and addresses. He looked up, and before he could even ask, Brenda handed him paper and a pencil.

"I'm not even going to ask why you want these names," Brenda said.

"Old friends is all," Colton said.

"Just like us," Jake said. "Remember when we was playing San Angelo and that stud black boy comes around our strong side and you just unloaded on him? And there he lays just twitching and kicking and convulsing there on the field."

"Don't remember," Colton said, but he thought back about that time and remembered he even scared himself when he saw that star/stud running back all set up to be unloaded on, so Colton did the unloading. And when the San Angelo coach pulled off that boy's helmet, there were two trickles of blood coming out of either side of his mouth and his nose. That kid was going to play scared from then on.

"Where is Mitch and Harold?"

"Hell, I figured if they was your friends and you'd recommend them, even though I didn't really ask you on account I didn't know where you was to ask you, then I'd hire them."

"I recommend them," Colton said.

"Well, besides, there's more work than I got men to do. They're out repairing pipe on a holding tank."

"Where?"

"Right out toward Andrews."

Brenda pulled the paper and pencil from Colton and drew a map, then filled in Mitch and Harold's names, addresses, and phone numbers.

* * *

Bullet and Colton bounced over a rutted dirt road in Bullet's pickup, skidded to a stop, got out of her pickup truck, and rolled their ankles as they walked over the caliche and rock and through the dust her pickup kicked up, toward the two figures working on the pipe. Bullet knew why men come to her bars and bought her whores. It was cool; the dry air felt good, but the dust was up. Even with long streaks of clouds in the sky, the sun was still pushing down on them. All they could see was rocks, pumpjacks, and sand. This time of year, with what few leaves there were falling off, and those bare mesquites or fried grasses shaking at you from the wind, West Texas looked to be only black and white, like an old movie. As one whore once told Bullet, as she was coming back from a weekend with a high roller in Dallas and saw the late-winter hinged gas station signs and weeds and brushy trees shaking in the wind, this trip back was the closest she ever come to suicide. Off at a distance and up high was a hawk, looking down, disgusted, and yelping about it. And Bullet saw a less disgusted buzzard floating on the wind currents looking for the faint whiff of something dead or dying. You're a man. You work in this all day, so you want some of Bullet's beer or whores all night long, even if all you get of company and civilization was a dusty, crumbling bar and a woman slowly losing her soul because you got her price. That beer and that woman were worth indulging yourself. You do it all night long and get fired from the very job that gave you the money to buy the beer and the woman. Up ahead were Mitch and Harold.

Bullet was glad that she worked in the nighttime Odessa world of garish lights that don't ever light up the dark, dingy bars. There is too much light in daytime Odessa.

"You got it down?" Bullet muttered to Colton.

"I kiss ass."

"Do you realize how goddamn lucky we got?" Bullet asked.

"I thought that was the way the police solve stuff, getting lucky?"

As they got closer, one tin-coated head stuck up over the pipeline, then another one. The two tin heads rose and pulled bodies up after them. With the welder's masks on, the two figures looked like the old armored knights. One visor of a welder's mask folded up and then the other one. "What the hell do you want now? I got to get another ass-kicking?" Mitch asked. Next to him, Harold held his still-lit welder's torch up.

They got closer. Bullet saw Mitch smiling. "You got a hell of a lot of nerve," Mitch said.

Colton went through the lines he rehearsed with Bullet, "I'm sorry. I got a problem with my temper. I'm going to these anger management classes."

"Maybe, you ought not go into bars."

"Look, I got you and your buddy a job, didn't I? I can't be all bad."

"Well, I don't know."

Then Mitch turned his attention to Bullet. "Who is this? Your sister? Your momma?"

"I'm the woman is gonna do you two a favor."

Mitch turned his welder's torch off. Harold waited just a second longer. "So must be interesting work," Colton said.

"Hell, you squat all day with a fire in front of your face, see how you like it," Harold said. Then he returned his look to Bullet. "We don't want nor need no favors." He pulled his mask completely off his head. Mitch looked over, saw Harold, then pulled his own mask off his head. Mitch's hair was styled. He had spent money on a barber. Harold's was pulled back into a ponytail.

"You'll like this favor. Colton and I go way back, and I'm helping him with anger management. He told me. I told him we ought to buy you fellas some beers after you get off work."

"We pay for our own," Harold said.

"Well, yeah, he does," Mitch said. "But now me, my favorite brand is free." Harold turned to stare at Mitch, not some quick glance, but an honest-to-god "fuck you" stare. Bullet could see, from all she had known of men, from years of making it a habit of knowing men, in the same way she sized up Colton and knew his strengths—and mostly his weaknesses—that Harold was the mean one. Mitch was just talk.

"I invited a surprise," Bullet said, and mustering up left over performances when she was a stripper and a hooker, she made her eyelid slow down so as to give a long, slow wink, and said, "If you know what I mean."

"We don't want it," Harold said.

"You don't want it? Faggot," Mitch said. Harold's stare told Mitch to shut up.

"What you got to lose?" Bullet asked. "Your virginity?"

"What exactly is you to him?" Mitch said and jerked his chin toward her.

"We go way back," Bullet said.

"I can feel the smoke going up my ass," Harold said.

"Look, Colton works for me, 'security.' But business is slow now that the oil show is over."

"What business?" Harold asked.

"I bet I can guess, faggot," Mitch said to Harold.

"Show up at the Blue Lantern and find out." Bullet turned to Mitch. "You know where it is."

Mitch pushed Harold. Harold looked at him, then at Bullet. "We got work," he said, pulled his mask back on, and pulled his visor down. It had a plastic cover for his eyes but none for his mouth. It was like he had muted himself. Talking was over. Mitch looked, said, "Hell, I want to learn more about your business," and he put his mask on and pulled his visor down.

Bullet turned away from them and Colton followed her. As her feet slid in the caliche, rock, and sand, she hoped she didn't twist an ankle or break a heel. The shoes were expensive. "You done that good," Colton said from behind her. "I couldn't of done it like that," he said.

Bullet stopped walking and turned to look at Colton, "See there, despite your fuck ups, we are a good team."

"My fuck ups?" Colton said.

"Come on, get a sense of humor. We both done good. Renee is gonna I.D. one or both of them. And we're gonna collect our money." Bullet tried another two steps and twisted her ankles. "Why the hell didn't I wear boots."

* * *

Colton should have figured, and he should have warned Bullet, but he didn't. Add it to his fuck ups. Curly was at the Blue Lantern. Why wouldn't he be?

First, as Lionel and Colton waited, Curly was bothering them. Then Mitch and Harold stepped in, and as Colton tried to maneuver them toward a table, Curly stepped up to them. He cocked his head back and forth in front of Mitch to stare at his face, "You the guy I tattooed the other night." He continued examining Mitch's face. "See you got a second tattoo."

"That was your friend here."

"Who is this fucker?" Harold asked.

"Who are you?" Curly asked. As Colton tugged on Mitch's arm, Lionel placed a hand behind Curly's back and tried to steer him.

"Let me buy you a beer," Lionel said as he pushed on Curly.

"I don't want your beer. I don't want to talk to you." Then Curly straightened and slapped both hands on Lionel's chest. He shook his curly head. "And it ain't cause you're a black. I ain't prejudice." Then he side-stepped Lionel and headed back to Colton.

Colton squared in front of Curly. "Remember, we almost had a tough time the other night."

Curly took off his hat and shook his curls. "Bring it on," Curly said. And Colton handed him a beer. With Curly staring at the beer in his hand, Lionel was able to get him back to a table.

Mitch and Harold sat on either side of a table, and Colton sat between them. "Who is that fucker?" Harold asked.

"The other guy who hit me," Mitch said.

"You should keep your mouth shut," Harold said.

"Let's get some more beers," Colton said, and he made his way through the sunbeams filtering in through the windows and the cracks and bellied up to the bar. Before Marlene could give him supplies for Mitch and Harold, a shift in the air caused him to turn to see Renee step in, followed by Bullet. With two beers in one hand and another in his left, Colton steered himself toward Mitch and Harold, just as Bullet and Renee stepped up.

"I'll be goddamn," Mitch said. "Ain't you pretty?"

Renee's face went blank and then it swiveled looking for some help. It found Bullet. Colton could see there was something these women were saying to each other in some sort of physical language that he just couldn't understand. And then, like a nervous tic you couldn't even pick up if you weren't staring at her, Renee gave this tiny little nod of her hand. Colton guessed that they had the right guys.

"This is your surprise," Bullet said and motioned toward Renee.

To this point, Colton had not even noticed Renee's very short skirt and very high heels. He wondered, with the heels, how she even got across the parking lot. And she had what she had in the way of tits pushed up in some strapless bustier or some such stripper attire. Bullet, for her part, had on a tight pair of jeans and high heels, but she had changed into a flowing blouse. "Hi, boys," Renee said. The three men at the bar stared. Curly stared. Lionel stared.

"So, you remember me, Darling?" Mitch asked.

"Shut the fuck up," Harold said.

Renee looked at Colton, and he knew that she really looked for Bullet. Renee's eyes found and locked on Bullet. "Don't look over at her," Mitch said. "Look at me. Don't you remember?"

Harold looked at Mitch as if he was just plain stupefied and shocked. Bullet sat down. And Renee followed her example. Colton sat between Mitch and Renee and stared at Bullet, trying to study her, to learn something.

Bullet's hand fell back on her wrist. She smiled too widely, like Colton had never seen her smile before, and she looked at Harold. "You wanted to party with me and Renee?"

Harold looked at Bullet. "What are you?"

"I procure entertainment," Bullet said. "And it's half-price night."

"We ain't got paid yet." Colton was trying to shake his head so that Bullet could see him. He wondered if he should start swinging now to stop the way Bullet was playing this. All they needed was an I.D., not this danger.

"You recognize her, do you?" Bullet leaned across the table on her elbows to look at Mitch. "Have y'all had a date?"

"I think so," Mitch said. Harold glared at him.

"I don't know what you people are talking about," Colton said. "I thought we were gonna just have some beers and make some introductions."

"Okay," Harold said. He dug in his wallet and pulled out a hundred. "I want you," he said and pointed to Renee. Mitch laughed, slapped his hands together, then rubbed them.

"We ain't doing nothing," Colton said.

"Shut up, friend," Harold said and turned to look at Bullet. "I got me a date. That's what you want, right?"

"What about me?" Mitch said.

"You get her," Harold said and pointed at Bullet.

"She's mine," Colton said.

"What's your job?" Harold asked.

Bullet said, "There's the present, two for one."

Colton stood, thought he should start swinging, checked the impulse, the crash into the line. He looked around and saw Lionel stand and then Curly. "I don't think so," he said.

Harold slowly pushed himself up, "You got to figure out who you are." He reached and grabbed Bullet's hand. He gently pulled her up. "You ain't bad looking, except for that scar," he said.

Mitch jumped up. "Trade you."

Finding words, Renee said, "I remember now. I like you."

"But you got us both," Mitch said.

"Now come on," Harold said.

Colton found Bullet's eyes and tried to communicate in female. He saw a sign and could not decipher it. Then, she leaned across the table to hug Colton and as she did, she whispered in his ear, "Room 3. Watch it." Then she reached across the table to take Harold's hand and led him toward the parking lot.

"Holy fuck," Mitch said and grabbed Renee's hand. As they left, Renee looked back over her shoulder at Colton. She looked scared. And Colton shifted his gaze to Bullet, holding Harold's hand, and he watched Harold's swinging ponytail.

As they left, Lionel was by his side. "I couldn't tell what you wanted me to do."

"I didn't know what the fuck to do."

Then Curly was beside them, "Was those two women whores?"

* * *

Harold sat on the bed in Room 3, Renee beside him, and pointed his finger at Bullet, "So you two got nothing going on here. You just happen to know this Colton. And you just happen to run whores. And one of your whores is her. And he points to Renee." His pony tail with the thick, stretchy coil holding the braid in, fell over one shoulder, making him look less mean, but Bullet told herself not to let his girly ponytail fool anybody.

"The town ain't that big," Bullet said. "And what do you think we have going on? Hell, I thought something else was going to go on."

"Me too," Mitch said. He sat beside Bullet on the couch that Harold dragged to the foot of the bed.

"So where is that other fella y'all was with the other night?" Bullet had told Renee to ask that question, but now was not the right time. You could almost suck in the silence. It was like the silence on the way over, Renee with Harold in his truck, Bullet with Mitch in his, and she checking in the rearview mirror hoping to see Colton's Civic behind them.

"He was just a guy," Harold said.

"If it was Danny Fowler, he's a friend of mine and lots of other people," Bullet said.

"He was a faggot," Harold said. Bullet was sure now. He used past tense too quick and too sure.

"I'll talk to him about that," Bullet said. There was silence. She looked around at faces. Renee looked bland. Mitch looked stupid. Harold looked wild-eyed and mean. His look told her to shut the fuck up.

"We done enough talking," Harold wrapped an arm around Renee and pulled her too suddenly back. Bullet rose ready to bash Harold with anything, saw his hand working up Renee's thigh, Renee writhing like she liked it—or tolerated it. Bullet waited for something from Renee to see if she could see what Renee was thinking. Then, Renee pulled her hand up Harold's inner thigh, and Bullet relaxed.

"I guess that leaves me and you," Mitch said and looked almost like he was a gentleman, and he stood. Bullet caught his breath in her face, and then his dirty hands started unbuttoning her blouse. She could not keep herself from pulling away from him. He had come home from work, taken a bath, brushed his teeth, gargled, but still his hands were not clean and his breath smelled like the oniony hamburger he ate for lunch, only coated in strong peppermint.

Bullet slowly started to unbutton her blouse, and from somewhere way back in the 60s a song came to mind. She couldn't place it, but it was a song from Bwana Dik's on the San Antonio Riverwalk, and her body grinded and twisted to it, and his fingers stopped unbuttoning halfway down her blouse. She didn't hum or sing along, but she listened.

Harold sat up and worked on Renee's blouse. He had it open and off Renee's shoulders. Renee, now with her breasts out of her bra, puppy-noses sticking straight out, like a little girl's, sat too and watched and smiled and noted. "Goddamn, yeah," Harold said. Renee forced a smile for Bullet.

Bullet slid one high heel off with the toe of her other high-heel; then she used her bare toes to pry that other high heel off. She twirled around and had her jeans' fly down. With a short push she wriggled out of her jeans and let them fall around her ankles. Then she stepped up to Mitch.

While Renee and Harold strained to watch, Mitch unbuttoned the rest of her blouse. Bullet shrugged her shoulders and let the blouse fall. Mitch's bared-tooth dog smile turned into a closed mouth grimace when he looked at Bullet's chest. "What done that?" he asked.

The music in her head went silent. "Cancer," she said. "I kicked its ass, but it left the scar."

Mitch reached back and pulled Bullet's hair away from her face. "And that?"

"A trick's whisky bottle."

Then Mitch pinched her .45 casing in between his two stubby fingers. "And that's a fucking bullet."

"Which one of you got the biggest balls?" Harold asked and laughed. "I figure she's tougher than you are, Mitch."

Bullet turned to look at Harold. His smile taunted her. "Show us yours," Bullet said.

Harold bare-chested now jumped up and was out of his jeans and underwear in a flash. With only his socks on, he held his hands up to parade his equipment in front of Bullet, and then he smiled wicked-like, like he knew more than he should about Bullet, and cuddled up with Renee. "I like them younger," he said. "And softer, and prettier. And not so carved up."

When she turned back, Mitch said, "Don't scare me none," and he started unbuttoning his shirt. He shrugged his shoulders and his shirt fell off. He pulled off his boots, one after the other, hopping on one foot as he tugged at the boot on the other leg. And then he stepped out of the crumpled laundry he had made of his pants and underwear. He left his socks on.

Bullet walked to the light switch and flicked it so that the two lamps on either side of the bed went off. But some wayward, lost light still made it into the room.

Bullet went to Mitch, reached for his crotch, rubbed, felt only mush. "Wait, wait," Mitch said. "I don't want to look at it." Light from street lamps sifted inside. Bullet made herself nuzzle him. She stroked his chest and lowered her hand. "Wait, wait," Mitch said. He sat down on the sofa. "Now, you turn around." Bullet turned. "Okay, lower yourself on down."

As she turned her back and backed up to him, Bullet wished that she would find a whiskey dick. She knew that whatever she found she could find herself just as dead. But as she lowered herself, she felt that he was full of life. And after a bounce or two, she felt too. She was not dead, just numb, but growing fuller herself. She looked at the bed at Harold on top of Renee and saw Renee's face bouncing over Harold's shoulder, him making that mattress and its frame shake with his violent thrusting. His groaning rumbled through the motel room. And while the look and sound of his animal meanness filled up the room, Renee's eyes got some liveliness in them—and some deadness, like she was right in between. Like her soul was draining out of her. And Bullet's silly thought was that your soul drains out your soles, so men kept their socks on, so they can keep their souls inside and then go home to their mommas or wives.

As time ticked slowly by, Bullet's pleasure turned to just a tickle. And as she watched Renee's soul leak out of her, Bullet's tickle turned to a thought. Mitch and Harold had made their ways inside of Renee and her. That's why this was dangerous. That was why whores lose their souls.

When Mitch turned into a puddle of exhausted flesh underneath her, Bullet pulled herself up and crossed through the near-dark to the bathroom. She saw Harold's pants. He had greater stamina than Mitch did or did not want it to end, so he was busy grunting over Renee. Bullet grabbed the pants, looked over her shoulder at the crumpled Mitch and went naked into the bathroom. She turned on the water in the sink and the shower. She flushed the toilet. And she went through Harold's wallet. Remember, remember she told herself. She looked for a pen, a pencil, anything. His driver's license had a Dallas address and the number. She memorized the address. He had a pink slip from a Twin Cities Welding Company. He had the picture of a woman. In what was obviously his own rough hand writing, he had scrawled, *Darla*. He had three one-hundred-dollar bills. Danny often carried as many as ten hundred-dollar-bills. He had several credit cards, and in between two of them, was Danny Fowler's American Express.

Bullet's hands trembled. She stuck her head into the shower, not caring about her hair or make up. She pulled her head out and toweled off as best she could and wished that somewhere on her naked body she had a knife or a gun.

With what she could memorize, she stuffed the wallet back in the jeans, turned off the water, stepped out, and saw Harold's bare ass bounding above Renee. Once in a while, he pushed at the sliding bedspread with his sock covered feet.

"I tell you what, you still got it there, Missus Bullet," Mitch said.

"Who said I lost it," she said and stared at Harold's ass and his churning feet. The bedspread finally fell out from under him and Renee.

As Harold finished and Renee inhaled deeply, after a little more rest, like school children, they wordlessly gathered their clothes and got dressed in the half-light.

All dressed, Renee, as rehearsed, said, "Why don't you fellas call me when you get lonely."

Bullet un-gritted her teeth and said, "Cut rate for friends." The two boys started to move in the half-light, searching for clothes and getting dressed.

Harold flipped on the light and stared at her for too long. He was waiting for her to say something. "Well, you two boys proved you weren't faggots. Now run along," she said. "We'll get a ride home, but we need to freshen up for our next boyfriends."

Mitch gave some kind of football yell, like he has just sacked the quarterback, and flew out the door. Harold stayed long enough to say, "I'll be in touch."

When the door shut behind him, Renee's face crumpled. She was crying. Bullet pulled her to the sofa and sat with her arm around her. "It wasn't like the other night. It was like he wanted to hurt me. All I could feel was meanness. He meant me harm."

"I could see that," Bullet said.

Renee pulled herself together and sniffled, "I want a shower."

"That doesn't help. It'll wear off, but not with water."

As Renee got up, the door swung open, Renee gasped, and Colton nearly jumped into the room. Behind him, Lionel stepped into the room. Since Renee was standing, she went to Lionel and wrapped her arms around him, holding on to him like he was the only steady thing in the room. "You okay?" Colton asked Bullet.

"What do you think?"

"Look, I was sitting out there watching. The whole time. Just like you said. And ask Lionel, several times, we nearly busted the goddamn door down."

"That's right," Lionel said with arms now around Renee.

"Well, we sure as hell ain't gonna do this no more," Colton said.

"The mean one with the shine to Renee has Danny's credit card."

Bullet saw Colton think and was scared at the time it took. But he did smile when he got. it. Then his smile dropped, "The sons of bitches."

"They're mean, Colton. Even Mitch." Renee nodded her head.

"We done pretty good," Bullet said. "All of us."

* * *

Late that night in her duplex with the red shag carpet, the gold arches, the rock wall, and the golden naked ladies holding up the lampshades, Bullet had to give it all some thought. Her assortment of liquor sat in her freezer with her frozen microwave dinners. She stored her liquor like the hard-drinking oil field equipment salesmen she knew, in the freezer, ready any time for a cool sip, no ice. Coming home late, you just want a pick-me-up quick. And once you're picked up, you want to get thrown down in the bed. Cold shots work best for both.

She turned on every light as though to light up what was left of the night. She still felt like she kicked ass and took names, but as she rubbed the scar on her cheek and then let her hand glide down her blouse to rub the scar on her chest, she thought she would feel sad. But she didn't. She remembered that, for a while there, in between the planning, the concentration, and the disgust, she actually enjoyed Mitch being inside her. What her scars reminded her was that the only men who would likely be inside her were men like Harold. She started remembering and counting the bumps in the road and the swerves that got her to where she was. But she didn't wish or hope. With an apartment decorated for fucking, Bullet sat alone, sipped her chilled liquor—like a roughneck—and made herself content with what was.

Chapter 7

Colton sat on Mina Fowler's red sofa with his hands resting on his spread knees. He couldn't bring his knees together. He had thick thighs and the gristle and bulge inside his crotch just wouldn't let him sit mannerly. With the bull heads, deer heads, cow heads, and other stuffed heads watching him, he looked like a clumsy and dumb schoolboy not able to pick up on the lesson, even if he had a grown-up's second beer sitting in front of him.

He was listening while Bullet and Mina discussed what ought to be done to Mitch and Harold. Together, Colton and Bullet had presented their detective work. Said what Justan said. Spread it all out before Mina so the facts were obvious. But that devil was still in the details. And those details were what bothered Colton. He wasn't good at interpretation, and from their fuming, Bullet and Mina were leading themselves into some fearful interpretations.

Mina crossed her living room back and forth and again, with her martini glass full, spilling her vodka on the rug and the hard wood floors. And like a dancer, Bullet twisted and gyrated as she followed Mina and confirmed what was starting in Mina's head and coming out her mouth. And when Bullet stopped dancing to listen, she spilled vodka from her glass.

Mina pulled up and turned, and Bullet halted in front of her. Mina raised her vodka glass and tried to point, of course vodka staining her white rug even more. "My grandfather would have just shot them down right in the street. And he would have shot some innocent bystanders just for looking at him funny. And he would have done it because he would have known he would have gotten away with it. No jury in Texas would've convicted him."

"Ah, the good old days," Bullet said.

"You mocking me?"

"A little. You were thinking good. Now you're wishing."

"I'm wishing they were dead."

Colton got some kind of gumption from somewhere. "I thought you wanted to know. That was all. That's done. Now you know."

"Do you think justice is done?"

"When's it ever done?" Bullet answered for Colton. "Question is, what you want?"

"I want justice."

"Well, then you should of gone to the cops in first damn place," Colton said and found himself rising, and he found that he had brought his second bottle of beer with him. "Left alone, to hisself, that Justan Brady would've found them. We just got lucky and beat him. And Justan Brady has the full force of the law behind him."

"So, you think the cops and then trial is justice?"

"I know how that works," Bullet said.

Colton stepped toward Bullet, pointed the neck of his beer at her, sloshing some out, that white carpet getting a slight shower of Vodka and beer. "What you got if you ain't at least got a trial?"

"You got Gervin," Bullet said. That hurt Colton, so he pulled his beer back from Bullet, just as she raised her martini glass of vodka to point at Colton and to spill some more on the rug. "And grow up, Colton. Gervin is the way the world works, not the police, the courts, trials."

"Hey, you two," Mina said. "You got the balls?"

Colton turned around, knew what he would hear, wanted not to hear it, thought he should leave now and be shed of it all.

"Balls for what?" Bullet asked and sashayed toward Mina.

"I'll give you double what I did for finding out who."

"Goddamn it. Danny got fucked, but it was an accident. He tries kissing one of them. Imagine that."

Colton walked toward the two of them, waving his beer, spilling, taking a sip, thinking that sip would calm him, make him think better.

"Danny grabs one fella's crotch, kisses him." Mina squirms. "That's right," Colton said and stepped toward her. "It's disgusting. Think what it would do to a guy like Harold. Think about that. Harold is mean. He'd just start swinging. And he wouldn't stop."

Mina said, "He kills him."

"Manslaughter, second degree. But no premeditation. They didn't plan it. You think Mitch could plan his ass into anything other than a bar?"

"Still they killed Danny," Bullet said. Beer and vodka were flying.

Colton said, "But you ain't thinking right. They don't deserve it."

"They don't deserve to be out drinking and all but gloating about killing a 'faggot'."

"The law wouldn't convict them," Colton said. "You get crossways with the law. You're on your own without the law. Snake knows that. I learned a little."

"That's why there's us," Bullet said.

Colton heard something shatter and was afraid he had dropped his beer bottle. He checked his hand to see he still held it. Mina growled. Off to her left, under a cow's head, was her spilled drink, and soaking in that wet spot was her broken glass. "Kind of dramatic, huh?" Mina said. "I'll have to hire somebody to clean that. You two seem to be arguing with the air. You ain't been listening. Why do you think I hired you? What good is just knowing? Pre-meditated, accident, bullshit." Mina's hard face broke into a smile. Bullet smiled back. "I want them dead."

"Me too," Bullet said.

"So shit," Colton said. "Like a bounty? You want to see a pair of ears, a head, teeth?"

"I just want to know that I'm not living in the same world as those two."

"Double?" Bullet asked.

"You let me know if I can help," Colton said.

"Oh," Bullet said. "I think you need to be involved. Fair is fair."

"I'm paying," Mina said.

"And that part is fair. But I'd like a little more fair," Bullet said.

Mina smiled and extended her hand to Bullet, "What did you and Danny have?"

"We were both kind of soiled goods. We are both way outside in a small town that only allows so much outside. What we had was respect for each other." Bullet shook Mina's hand.

"Wait a minute. What the fuck about me?" Colton asked. "You go down this road, you give up the protection of the law. You can't turn back."

"Who says we ain't been down this road before," Bullet said.

"Ever woman I ever known contemplated this road," Mina said. "Preach somewhere else."

"What about what's right and wrong?" Colton asked.

"You didn't fuck either of those two guys," Bullet said.

"You didn't have a son killed," Mina said.

Colton went into the kitchen uninvited and got another beer. He sipped and listened as Mina and Bullet plotted, screamed, and preached. He let them go. And later, outside sitting in the passenger side of Bullet's small truck, Colton knew that this was what Bullet wanted all along. Danny was her best friend, so she wanted whoever killed him, for whatever reason, dead. And she had even figured out a way to get paid for it. Colton thought that she was the really dangerous one. "You bitch," he said under his breath. Bullet glanced over from her steering wheel to give him a quick gaze and a smile. "See why I wanted to hire you? You can be pretty cold yourself. You got a talent for this."

* * *

Even with just a couple of customers, the Stampede was filling with smoke. It clung to Bullet, just like it clung to the dancers, and Bullet remembered the feel of smoke on her naked body while she danced at Bwana Dik's and then sliding down the hierarchy of titty bars in Oklahoma City. Then she remembered the smoke on her when she got off work. And she remembered the feel of smoke on her and the men who paid her to fake pleasure, excitement, and even sometimes love. It was that feel that bothered her even more than the smell or taste of cigarettes. Still, for years, she smoked, just to have some of that smoke inside her, making her remember and relate to those dancing and those watching. She needed to know them, now more than ever, to make something right for Danny Fowler.

Up on stage was that clumsy, new Mexican dancer, the one who couldn't stand up on her heels, and tripped and stumbled as she tried to grind and tease. Part of being a stripper was to know how to advertise, to just know how men's attention got caught up by the way you moved and bounced your stuff. But this poor girl didn't have it. If she had been real desperate, then maybe Bullet could take this teenager to one side and teach her. But Bullet was not desperate. She had quit that. She was more Snake's partner than trainer or coach.

Behind her walked Colton, who had shown some sort of moral streak, with that same indignation that comes with the streak. She guessed he had lost it. Colton had his face shoved into his life enough to know better. Worse, she wondered if she could trust him. Yes, she could trust him—because there was that moral streak, which included loyalty to her, to Snake. But she was not sure she could trust his competency, his will to do what he was going to have to do. He would have to do what was required of him if he was to advance in this business and feed his family. But she wondered if he had it now. As the men slapping the tables and yelling at the poor Mexican dancer would say, could he grow a pair?

Snake stuck his head out of his office door and smoothed the gray wings of hair down the sides of his head. As Bullet approached, he stepped back, looked around for someone to save him, saw nobody, so stepped back toward his office. But Bullet was up to him, and before she could start, she saw that he had trimmed his moustache into a pencil thin one. "What did you do with your moustache?" Colton asked from behind her.

"My wife got a hold of it. Thought I'd look better less bushy. Now I look like Gilbert Roland or some old timey movie star." Snake cocked his head for them to see his new moustache.

"We need to talk. We got more important things to discuss than the hair growing above your lip," Bullet said.

Snake curled, rolled, and twisted his shoulders to point himself back into his office. Snake kept it dark in his office, so Bullet squinted to try to see. He had a desk and lamp on it. On the desk were stacks of papers. She strained some more to see that the papers were mostly forms, invoices and bills and time sheets. "Somebody has to figure this shit out," Snake said. "You don't see a secetary, do you?" Bullet and Colton remained standing as Snake sat. "Well sit," Snake said.

Bullet stepped to one side and said, "Sit, Colton. I want to be able to move."

Colton sat. Snake slid both arms, in a slick move, out of the arms of his sport coat. As usual, he had on a polo shirt, and this one had a little alligator sitting on Snake's chest. Snake pulled his eyes away from Bullet to look at Colton, "Colton, what is this?"

Bullet planted her left hip on the side of his desk and said, "Tell him, Colton."

"You talked to Mina Fowler lately?" Colton asked.

"No, not since I got y'all two together to investigate Danny Fowler's murder. What? Y'all found out something?"

"We know who killed him," Colton said.

"Well, good, job well done. Now, I got a business to see after," Snake said and started to rise.

"But wait," Bullet said. "Colton, tell him."

"Hold on, Colton. You sure I should hear this?"

"Why? You already know what Colton is going to say."

"I can guess."

Colton turned to look at Bullet. "So, I guess I'm the stupid one for not guessing. Seems everybody knew all along. Well, just hell," Colton said.

"I don't need to know. The less the better," Snake said.

"No, Snake. You're in on this."

"In on what? I don't know shit. So right now I can't tell nobody shit. I know nothing. I'd keep it that way if I was you two."

"You ain't gonna help?" Colton looked at Snake and his eyes dropped. "You get to get out of this? And I'm fucking stuck. You got me into this, Snake."

"And I'm leaving. Best if I don't know." Snake, same as he got out of it, slid both his arms into his sport coat at the same time. He jumped up, shrugged his shoulders and took a step from around his desk.

Bullet pulled her hip off his desk and pressed her flat palm against Snake's chest. She had suspected this. Snake had known Mina too long not to know where she would want to take this. And now, he was showing that he was no match for Mina or someone who might want a chunk of his business. "You're wrong," Bullet said and slid her palm up and over the alligator on Snake's chest. "You're playing this all wrong. You are involved. You got to be involved. No out."

"I was never a part of this."

"Snake? Snake? Snake?" Colton asked with this hurt look in his voice and face. "You told me to do this."

Snake held his palm to his forehead, and Bullet pulled her hand away. "You are wrong. In cases like this, you need everybody involved at the start, involved at the end. It is best if you do know. You got to know. Because if you do, you know what's at stake if you talk. You know that you'll go down too."

Colton stood, paced, and Bullet watched his shoulders as they rose up and down, like he was trying to think, but just couldn't get the thoughts worked through his whole body, as a man like Colton had to do. "Colton?" Bullet asked.

With his back to Snake, Colton asked, "What if the police came asking about Gervin?"

"That's just it. I knew nothing," Snake said.

Colton turned around. "You knew everything. You sent me to Gervin. And I told you everything. Now what would you of done?"

Snake stepped from behind his desk, and Bullet stepped out of his way because he waved her away from him and stepped toward Colton. "The police didn't ask."

"But what if they do?" Colton asked.

Snake turned to look at Bullet. "You and Lionel got to contribute, got to help, and got to know."

Colton's brows wrinkled. "Renee?" Bullet nodded. "Renee knows. Renee's seen them. She's got to know?"

"Renee is going to help me," Bullet said and was proud of Colton for working the thinking through his body and putting the conspiracy together.

"I'm out of here," Snake said and stepped past Bullet.

Colton side-stepped in front of Snake and said, "No, you got to stay." And Bullet thought that, my god, Colton had grown a pair. He'd work out just fine. "You got to know that Mina wants us to kill those two boys."

Snake turned his back to Colton to look at Bullet. She saw his worry pulling his face tight and stretching that thin little moustache the length of face. Snake was smiling, but that smile showed no joy. He looked back toward Colton, then swung back to Bullet, deciding that she was the one to hear. "I'm not a murderer. I'm not a criminal. I'm a gambler. And the reason I gamble is cause I like it. I mean with the cards, dice, the wheel, you can figure odds, you can prepare. You can study people. You can figure out what they're like." Snake held up his hands. "You can reduce your losing through your own hard working and thinking. But there is always luck. And you never know how that's gonna go. And that finally is why I gamble. That luck. Those odds. Your nuts in that vice. It squeezing." Snake looked at the two of them. "But that's it. Gambling is as far as I'm willing to push my luck."

Bullet thought of Charlie Brodsky from Bwana Dik's. She was with him again. Colton standing there, backing her up, and not backing down from Snake. "Your balls hurting, Snake?"

"Yes," Snake said without embarrassment.

"Maybe you ought to make them harder."

"All right, no excuses. No explanations. You two are on your own. I'm not participating. I'm out of it. I won't do it . . . I can't do it."

Colton's voice quivered, "Snake, you the one done this to me. Now you doing this other thing to me."

Bullet walked up to Colton but said toward Snake, "Go on, then."

Snake crossed to his door, pulled it open, said, "Good luck," and left them to themselves.

Colton walked to the chair that he just left empty. He sat, put his elbows on his knees, and then put his head in his hands. Bullet followed Colton to the chair. "Like he said, we ain't got to do this. Not this deliberate," Colton said. He pulled his head out of his hands. "Bullet, goddamn it, you listening to me?"

Bullet patted Colton's shoulder. "We got planning to do."

"I need some time to take this home and wrestle with it."

Bullet thought she needed better help. "We ain't got the time. And we are all we got." She patted Colton's shoulder again, then squeezed it.

Chapter 8

Colton and Bullet dared not go much beyond the Cactus Lounge and Barbara Howard's indifferent ears. In the Blue Lantern was Curly and his loud mouth and Marlene's memory. In the Snug Harbor were the shaved-head bartender and several eye-witnesses to Colton's decking Mitch Robinson. And the Cactus Lounge was quiet. Even though it was still the boom, no one much came in, so the Cactus Lounge would soon go broke, Barbra Howard wouldn't make the rent, so Bullet would have to put her out and sign a lease with the next bar manager with a mixture of hope and desperation.

Colton sat and stared at his beer while Bullet argued how easy a killing would be. Colton argued the other side. He reminded her of Gervin. He said that he still suffered from that and couldn't get it out of his mind.

During this argument, Justan Brady walked in from out of the sun and into the dark bar. He spotted Bullet and walked to them. Colton stiffened and looked at Bullet for an order. Colton was afraid that he would have to unleash on Justan. And that fear must have twisted up his looks and his stare because Justan held up his hands and said, "I come to tell you I'm off the case. I come to compare some notes."

"What case you referring to?" Bullet said.

"The one you're looking into."

Colton looked from one to the other, made himself relax, and extended his hand, "My name is Colton Parker."

"I figured."

"What else is it you figure you know?" Colton asked.

"Mind if I sit," he said.

Bullet gave him the okay, and Colton wished Bullet was not there. He could just sit and ignore Justan. Bullet couldn't. So as Colton sat,

Justan said, "The sheriff himself tells me I'm off the case." Justan folded his hands in front of him. "He don't want it out in the open. But I been asking questions anyway, right up until now. And a lot of questions got your two names in the answers."

"You might want to back off of that line of reasoning," Colton said.

Justan shook his head. "No, no." Colton stiffened. "Now just wait. I know you could whip my ass if you wanted to. Ain't no question about that. But now you just hear me out cause I'm off the case. Sheriff told me cause the police chief told him. And besides that, when I'm at home, dinnertime, my wife, eating her Fruit Loops or whatever it is cause she's too tired to cook, she says I've lost interest in her, says all I talk about is this case, says I'm obsessed, says for me to get over it. So, my marriage is in trouble too. I'm quitting. But I want somebody to hear what I got to say. I figure it's you two. If you will do me the courtesy."

"Go on," Colton said and thought that maybe he was the one who should leave because it was him, not Bullet, who was talking.

"Your girl told me those two boys worked for a casing crew," Justan said, and Colton wrinkled his brows because he was thinking *welders* and then the light behind his brain went off. Renee lied to Justan. Colton smiled to himself and wanted to pat Renee on the back.

"I not only been to bars. I been going to casing crew offices, asking who had left, begging for names, addresses, phone numbers of men who quit during the oil show, men who just hadn't showed for work. Driving by the addresses I did get. Talking to wives. Talking to pissed off men. Talking to more casing crews, mostly boys my age. Standing in the cold, three a.m. in the morning talking, sipping the cold coffee that my hand didn't shake out of the Styrofoam cup, while those boys poured cement down a hole. Nobody knew nothing. Meanwhile, Michelle, that's my wife, is at home, and she stops talking to me. But I remember finding that body."

Colton listened and felt blood pumping through him as he listened. What Justan told about was that night when the mud tester found the body and called 911. As Justan said, the important point for him was that that body was still in Ector County. Ector County sent a senior deputy, Bobby Cooksey—and him, Justan Brady. The Crane County Sheriff, Travis Ashton, pulled up in one of that county's cars. They all hunched their shoulders to the wind and cold that that first big norther of the season left the night before. They looked down into a newly-dug pipeline ditch and saw the body. And Justan told them, as he shook his beer in his hand and raised it to his mouth, that a tumble weed blew into the ditch, hung for a while on Danny's face, tried to make it up the other side of the ditch, but then rolled back and settled back on Danny's face.

Colton, Justan, and Bullet looked at each other, just like Justan, Cooksey, and Ashton must have looked at each other back then. And Justan, while looking at Colton and Bullet, looked like he was seeing it again.

He told them that Bobby Cooksey dipped his foot into the ditch and scooted the tumbleweed off Danny's face with the pointed toe of one of his boots. Bullet brought her head up to stop Justan's story, said, "So you all just looked? Didn't clean him up?" And Colton saw that her anger could push her into saying something wrong. Then he wondered just how mad he could get at Justan's story and where that anger could push him.

"We did what we had to do," Justan said. "We slid into that ditch and looked at the body. There wasn't no blood, no puncture wound, just lots of bruises on his face and chest. His shirt was ripped open. His camel hair sport coat was wrapped around one arm. He was missing one of his Bass Weejuns shoes. 'Lookie here,' Bobby Cooksey says, stood, and walked a little way toward the direction Danny's head was pointing. He bent over and picked up a key with a long red motel key fob attached to it. He held it up for me and Ashton to see. We climbed back out of the ditch. 'I think that ditch and the angle of his body puts him in Ector County,' Travis Ashton said."

Neither Bullet nor Colton could talk. "You started your story," Bullet said. "Finish."

"Lots to remember, but not much to finish. Cooksey and Ashton knew right away who he was, what had happened, and what his momma would say. So Bobby Cooksey tells me I'm in charge of the investigation."

Bullet had to interrupt—and to rub her boot toe into Justan's wound. "You're investigating because everybody knows you won't find much."

Justan slumped in his chair and nodded. "Cooksey tells me to look, starting with Mina, but not to look too hard."

"What about that red Mustang? You told us you found parts in a chop shop in El Paso." Bullet asked.

"So what? What's to know? What's to see? That car is now nothing but parts spread between here and Mexico. We gonna buy all the parts and reassemble it?" Colton watched while Bullet hung her head.

Justan sipped his beer and looked without seeing Bullet. Bullet clenched her teeth and clamped her fingernails into the edge of the table. She said, "So why you talking to us? I need some whys."

Justan made himself think. "My job is mainly arresting drunks, making them pour out the beer or booze in their cars, and then asking them to drive on home, and telling them don't stop for another one. Sometimes, out in West Odessa, I'll stop a bar fight, clean up after one, or get in one while it is going on and I'm trying to arrest somebody. Then I will go home and tell my wife about police work. But here was a chance to really detect something. I wasn't ready. And now my wife is pissed."

Colton fumbled Justan's words around in his mind and thought about his wife and knew that, had he made one or two different choices, he would have been Justan. Justan started again. "I slid back into the ditch, squatted by the body, and looked into Danny Fowler's open eyes. Danny Fowler must've hurt. He must've been all battered up inside. When I stood up, I felt like I had to help him even though he was dead. I felt like telling this to Travis Ashton and Bobby

114

Cooksey, but they were walking back toward their cars. And there I was holding that key and fob in my hand. Something ought to be done."

Colton didn't trust himself enough to trust Justan, so he turned to Bullet and with his eyes asked her for help. "You really through and out?" Bullet asked.

"My wife is a doctor's secretary, and she makes more than me. She lets me know that fact real often. She'll slump her shoulders or cock her head and lean on one hip to let me know, without saying nothing, I had ought get a better job. What I don't tell her is I had probably peter-principled myself right to the very top of what I could do. But I thought if I could find Danny Fowler's killer, maybe I could prove to myself and my new wife that I could stretch my limitations a little farther and become a constructive part of the community with smart and handsome kids making good grades in good schools.

"But my marriage can't stand that kind of thinking. My wife is sitting at home right now watching HBO and probably eating a peanut butter and jelly sandwich for dinner. And I can't stand to be thinking of this no more. I'm gonna quit and take my chances in the oil field. But I just want something done. Something known. I want to tell you what I know. But I want you to tell me what you know."

Colton pushed himself up to buy some time. Again, he thought that he should just walk out. But Bullet kept her eyes on him. He tried to tell her that this was just too tough, that they weren't smart enough. But Bullet said more to Colton than to Justan, "Well let's just see if we can work out what happened to Danny."

So they worked on the story together, imagined it straight through. Bullet started by saying there's these two guys, Mel and Randy, and they work for a casing crew, and they meet Danny at the Tank. So then Justan went to work. And Bullet added to it because she knew Danny's routine. But she didn't tell her suspicions, like she had told Colton. And Colton got confused. Then lost. He couldn't keep the real names different from the fake names. But with Colton listening, Justan and Bullet made a bare-bones story for them all, to set something firm to believe. What they came up with just had to be as true as they could get.

* * *

On the last night that he was alive, Danny Fowler was in the condominium his mother bought for him, and he eyed himself in his full-length mirror. He admired his Bass Weejuns, his pressed wool slacks, and his camel hair sport coat. His hair went over the tops of his ears and in the front in wings. He was a good-looking man, knew he was, and admired himself. He was ready to go out.

It was a windy evening with cold blowing in, and Danny drove his red convertible Mustang around town with the top down and turned up the collar of his camel hair sport coat and wrapped his wool throat warmer scarf around his neck. He checked out Busby's, a small bar downtown. He drove by Graham Central Station, the large Country-Western disco out Grandview. He drove out to West Odessa, out near to Bullet's Cactus Lounge, and looked at several small, mom-and-pop bars. Nothing there would do for the way he was dressed and what he wanted. He went to The Tank.

At the Tank, he leaned his back against the bar—a cigarette dangling out from his knuckles, one foot cocked behind his other leg, a wave of hair falling down on his forehead—and looked for something. It was not exactly sex he was looking for. It was something else too. It was some amusement, some story, something colorful, something relieving him of having to be him stuck in Odessa, Texas. Larry the bartender came up to him and said, "These are dangerous waters for you to be trolling in." Danny nodded to agree with Larry, and he saw these two boys sitting at a table, finishing off their steaks and drinking single malt scotch to celebrate their luck in the oilfield. It was pay day for them. They were starting to get loud. He walked toward their table, reached in his pocket, pulled out two business cards proclaiming him to be in real estate, introduced himself to the boys, gave them his cards, said, "But real estate is not my real line of business."

The two boys did not tell him to fuck off and mind his own business—as some had told Danny. Instead, they listened. And they acted like they knew about Danny. And Danny said, "For my real business, my main business, I manage strippers—and whores."

The two boys had seen the laughing groups of men surrounded by girls in slinky black, green, and red dresses hugging the forms of their bodies. The two boys saw those girls squeezing those exaggerated bodies into the laps of those laughing men. And the two boys figured that those girls got to those men somehow. Danny hoped that the two boys figured he was how. And Danny smiling, dressing like he was from college, acting all smooth-like, his cigarette dangling from his lip, his movie star looks, his business cards, all guaranteed those two boys that he was their man.

Danny bought them some more scotch. Then he recommended one of his favorite scotches. Soon the boys were banging the table with the flats of their hands yelling for pussy.

Justan, Bullet, and Colton called the two boys Randy and Mel (but Colton and Bullet knew their names were Mitch Robinson and Harold Egbert). They were younger than Justan, maybe three or four years out of high school—old enough to have learned a little and hardened some. When they got out of high school there was an oil boom, and the legal age for drinking was eighteen, so they became roughnecks. They worked hard, partied harder, got on a casing crew (though Colton and Bullet knew they were welders), had money to burn if they wanted. They yearned bad for the pussy that they yelled for. And they wanted to believe Danny.

Randy was tall and made to look like he was a body builder by the hard work he had done. He was the quiet one—or he was just scared. Or he was shy, or mean, but it was hard to tell. He said nothing about Danny's offer, just eyed the business cards and Danny's sharp figure. The hard work had made short Mel lean like a cowboy. He liked the way he looked, so he had bought him a new silver belly cowboy hat. It sat proper, crown down, on the seat of the chair next to him. "Where's these whores and strippers?" he asked after more scotch.

Randy mumbled, "Shut up. This guy ain't no pimp."

"You're right," Danny said. "I'm a friend. I know the bartender. Let's get some beers and paper bags and go find some of my ladies."

Mel gave a whoop. Randy just watched. They got into Danny's red convertible Mustang. Randy scrunched himself up and sat in back. Mel got in the front passenger side. Randy was silent. Danny had the top down now. Mel whooped more as they drove to Second Street and splashed his beer in Danny's red convertible Mustang.

Danny found Renee St. Cloud trying to stand still in the blowing cold, hugging herself, trying to keep her short skirt pulled over her freezing ass. She looked like some Greek goddess to Randy and Mel. They went to room number three at the First Quality Motel.

At this point in the story Justan, Colton, and Bullet relied on their memories of Renee's memory. They were careful to remember exactly what Renee had told each of them—and to add just a little from their own imaginations.

Renee and the two boys and Danny stepped into motel room number three, feeling like the wind was still blowing through their hair and clothes, so they rubbed the wind out of their hair and clothes as people were prone to do in West Texas. They drank some more. They eyed each other. Randy had his turn with Renee. And Mel and Danny watched.

Then Mel, a little scared, a lot drunk, had his turn with Renee. "You could act like it was a pleasure," Renee said when Mel rolled off her. When Danny paid her and refused his turn, they started poking him with their elbows and laughing at him. Danny blamed it on the liquor. Danny had more scotch, more beer, and Renee, feeling some relief from being stuck in Odessa and doing what she had just done for a living, drank with them.

But nobody could stop being them, so Renee stumbled out after several drinks, thinking she could find some more customers, but she found she had to puke.

Justan stopped talking. And Colton and Bullet stopped adding their points. They knew that to go farther would be just imagining. They knew that they each had a way they'd like the story to go. So, they settled for the barest and easiest of facts, to keep themselves in check, for after all, the conversation started with Bullet and Colton as an argument. They talked their story into being.

Inside the room, Danny sat beside Mel, told him that they don't really need no more women. Mel wondered for a moment what Danny was talking about, "Well, hell yes we do. Let's get us another one. I still got lead in my pencil." It was Randy who figured out what Danny was asking. And Danny, to let them know for sure, slid his palm inside Randy's thigh and then up.

That same high school urge that made Colton want to try playing football, made him head into the oncoming line of blockers, and even made him kind of enjoy the knocking heads, even if he was scared, made Randy hit Danny on the corner of his head. Mel said, "Goddamn, Queer," and hit Danny too.

Danny held on to his head, smiled, said, "Boys. A boy has to try. Why do you blame me?" He looked at them like he was begging them.

One or the other, by himself, Mel or Randy would've quit hitting Danny and left. But together they whaled on him. They screamed, "Fucking A. Fucker" and "Faggot." They were excited, like they were winning a football game. They high-fived each other when they felt they'd tired themselves out. Then they noticed that Danny wasn't moving. There was a growing puddle of blood on the carpet.

Though they were drunk, they kept drinking. They tried to think. They figured what the hell and pulled all of Danny's money and his credit card out of his wallet. Then they pulled Danny out to his car and stuffed him in the back. They both got in the Mustang. They dumped Danny's body off just outside the city limits. This was a boom time, so they knew a guy who moved stolen cars. Randy delivered it. Mel picked him up.

* * *

They all imagined the same story because that story happened several times before with different Randys and Mels, and probably with different Danny's, and not just in Odessas but all over West Texas.

So Justan Brady went on imagining, to make things right. "The story needs to end. I want to make me smarter, and so I find an address. I go to an apartment, ask around, get a name, find a car registration, check some chop shops, and find Danny's car in say an El Paso chop shop. And a guy there gives me a description. Say of Mel. I find Mel's parents, say in Jal, New Mexico. They give me a phone number. I call it, then trace it Dallas. I arrest him. And he gets convicted of say manslaughter."

"Goddamn, you should quit being deputy and start being a writer."

"It's just imagining."

"And that's all it can be," Bullet said. "That's not how these stories end."

"We can't know. Can we?" Justan said. His eyes grew watery. "To find that out, the law—not us, not you two, not Mina Fowler—but the law should find those two boys and give them lawyers and sit them in front of a judge and let them see was it premeditated or not."

"Well that ain't gonna happen," Colton said. "You've given up. You got to save your marriage. Remember?" Then, knowing that he was on his way to becoming what he must, Colton said, "And who's to say the law is right? Who's to say any of us is right? All we got is what we just made, stories. And who has the right one?"

Bullet looked at Colton like she was proud of him. "Danny Fowler could say," Bullet said.

"And those two boys," Justan said.

Colton said, "Only Danny Fowler is dead, and I expect those boys would lie," and he looked at Bullet. "Best to get used to it. We just can't know about some things. Maybe the things we want most to know, we can't. All we got is stories."

"Y'all got some good points," Justan said. "And I ain't too bright and got no power. I'm just here to say. . . what I said." Justan nodded to Colton then to Bullet in a polite way, then turned his back to them and walked out the Cactus Lounge and into the West Texas brightness.

After Justan left, Bullet looked at Colton and asked, "Well?"

"We got nothing to say. We don't know that it was premeditated. It might have been like Gervin," Colton said but without conviction, like he was finally just resigned to what he has to do.

Bullet sipped at her beer. "So what difference is premeditated to Don and Lula Smiley? What difference is it to Danny?"

"This is something for a trial."

"I thought you were against a trial?"

"No, a trial don't necessarily get the true story, but it can sure as hell relieve us from doing what we're talking about."

Bullet slapped the table, "Like it or not, we are the trial."

Colton hesitated, rotated his beer in his hand, heard trumpets, the strings of a guitar, some quick toll that his life had changed. "I want Harold."

"He's the mean and tough one."

"I want him."

"I'll take Mitch."

* * *

Sometimes, Way Low made himself stay awake or postponed his sleeping to take Mando to his favorite place. They would drive to the UTPB, the University of Texas of the Permian Basin, a tiny branch of the University of Texas. What should UT expect? Odessa wasn't much on education.

In the middle of this loop sat the one building and outside the loop were jogging trails and brush, mostly mesquite and cactus, hiding jack rabbits and quail and sometimes skunks and snakes. But this recreation area also had some ponds with swans and ducks. Mando liked the water birds.

After Colton and Bullet had planned, while Arnie was in school, Colton took Mando out to UTPB, and they walked along the trail and stopped at a duck pond. Mando threw tortilla crumbs to the ducks and watched them swim for the crumbs or waddle up to him. Then a swan came out of the water and stomped with that stiff-legged goose step up to Mando and barked. Mando got scared and threw a whole tortilla to the bird. The swan grabbed it and shook it side to side. And before Mando or Colton could move or think, another big swan was out of the pond and rammed into the first Swan. They became a tangle of soft white, and feathers flew, and Mando ran from them. Colton ran to catch Mando, grabbed him, whisked him up and turned him around, so he could see the two swans. What Colton and Mando saw was their necks wrapped together and bulging and stretching thin in different places as the swans pulled against one another. Then they unraveled and started pecking each other until one backed away with a bloody spot staining his white chest. The other one ran away with the tortilla. The hurt one stood, breathed heavy, and watched Mando and Colton. Colton threw him his own tortilla and gently pulled Mando away from the Swans. Mando cried.

Colton took his son's hand and pulled him to a bench. Mando sat on Colton's lap as he wiped the tears out of his eyes.

"Don't be scared. And don't cry. Start practicing being a big boy. Don't cry."

Mando sucked in to stop his droopy, quivering chin. "Why were they mean like that?"

Colton tried to clear the fog that was forming in his mind. "Mando, I'm gonna tell you something they're gonna tell you ain't true in school. They gonna say that man is the only creature kills his own. But that ain't true. All creatures fight, and sometimes, one gets killed or bloody. They sometimes just got to do it. That's something you got to learn. You lucky you got me here to tell you now."

"Arnie hits me sometimes."

"That ain't the same."

"I want to go to school, so I can read."

"You got time."

"Arnie got in trouble. He got kicked out of school."

"How come I don't know about that?"

"Momma said not to tell you. And he really isn't kicked out. He just has to go and sit in a big room and not bother anybody."

"What did he do?"

"He hit a boy."

Colton shook his head. He didn't want to hear anymore. But he asked, "What happened?"

Mando had forgotten about the swans now and was concentrating on telling the story about Arnie. "Some boy was teasing him. Arnie came up behind the boy and pushed him down and then jumped on him and then hit him on the back with his fist."

Now Colton, not his son, was thinking about the swans. Maybe they did it when they had to, but maybe, like men, they fought just because they wanted to, because they liked it. "When you get to school, you pay good attention. Don't be like Arnie. I don't think he's too smart. You're smarter."

Mando's chest puffed out, "Daddy, nobody but you says I'm smart. Are you sure you're right?"

"You just wait, Mando."

Chapter 9

Bullet told Colton to order Lionel to help, said Lionel owed them all that much. But in something like this, Colton thought he should *ask* Lionel to help. Bullet asked Colton how he expected to do it himself if Lionel just walked out on them. But Colton also wanted to give him that luxury. "What are you going to do without backup?" Bullet asked.

"Who you got?" Colton asked.

"You," Bullet answered and then said to give them a laugh, "or Renee."

The next night, Colton sat with Lionel at the Cactus Lounge. It was late morning, well before they were both usually up, so they yawned in the growing warmth of an early fall morning. And Colton spread the plan out before Lionel. Lionel hung his head and then shook it. "You don't know what you asking."

"I know I want your help."

"You really gonna do it?

"I really got to do it."

"You ain't listening, Colton," Lionel pleaded with his hands, palms up and out. "You just gonna kill somebody. Hit man style, kill somebody."

"Nobody is gonna know."

"That's just half the point. We'd know.

"What was Gervin?"

"Gervin was an accident. We didn't plan it that way. And we got lucky."

"We did good."

"But we do this, we in a whole nother league." Lionel pressed his thumb down on the table. "We security, bouncers, muscle. We may even break some legs. And we will tote firearms if we think we got to. But we ain't going out and killing people."

"Like I said, we already killed people."

"Like I said, Gervin don't count."

* * *

Several years before, Snake Popp sent Colton and Lionel to collect some money. In Lionel's truck, they drove to Don Smiley's bar out in Gervin, which was not so much a place as a leftover bootlegger's bar way out across Crane County line. Don Smiley bought it and sold beers to those few who came in, but mostly he sold illegal Mexican drugs out of the crumbling pile of sticks.

Colton and Lionel walked into the bar on a Monday afternoon. Colton had a gat in his jeans pockets. Because it was summer and too hot for a jacket, Lionel had his shirttail out so as to cover the 9mm. stuck in the back of his pants. This was dangerous. A black man with a gun in West Texas was usually automatically arrested. But, as Snake and Colton knew, a black man with a gun was scary to most West Texans.

They had their usual plan. First they would talk, then Colton would ram into somebody. After getting pinned up against a wall, the man owing Snake usually found some earnest money. If not, Lionel waved the 9mm. They had yet to actually use it.

So inside Smiley's bar, Lionel and Colton stood on the customer side of the bar with Don Smiley on the other side. Don had a trimmed beard and round glasses, like a scholar. He knew who they were. "Fellas, look, this don't have to get ugly. I got the money. I really do. It's just tied up right now."

Don pulled two beers up and placed them in front of Lionel and Colton. "On the house," he said.

"Hell, I'd hope it's on the house," Lionel said, and Colton shook his head like his heart was broke with disappointment. "Oh, look how you upset Colton," Lionel said. "Think what Snake is feeling."

"Look, I've been knowing Snake Popp for fifteen years now. You just go back and tell him I'm good for it. He'll tell you."

"Who you think sent us? Why you think he sent us," Lionel asked.

"What's in the cash register?" Colton asked.

"That's for my family. That's how I make my living," Smiley said.

Colton reached across the bar, knocking his beer bottle over, grabbed Don by his shirt front, and yanked him over the bar. As Don cleared the bar, Colton jerked up, but Don's shirt ripped, and Don fell to the ground on Colton's side of the bar. Quickly, Lionel kicked Don in the head and the side. "Fuck you're 'good for it,'" Lionel said. "Snake wants you to say 'now.'"

Colton bent over and grabbed knotted shreds of Don's shirt in his fists and jerked him back up. "Now is there any need for us to do this?" Colton asked in a sincere voice.

"I say we kick the shit out of him," Lionel said.

"You got to show some earnest money," Colton said. "That's just the way it works."

"I'll show you 'earnest'," Don said. "Look behind you." Lionel jumped to one side, and Colton slowly turned around to see Don's wife, Lula, holding a .38 pistol at her arm's length, pointed at his chest.

"You two get out of here," she said. While Lula kept both arms straight and stiff with both hands wrapped around the butt and poked the gun at Colton's chest, Lionel slid one foot to the other to get around beside her. And when Don grabbed a beer bottle and beaned Colton, spraying beer and glass across the bar, Colton slid to the floor. Before Colton hit the floor, Lionel got his 9mm out but, for whatever reason, maybe because his talk was cheap and he was scared of all this, Lionel couldn't shoot. Lula squeezed the trigger and sent a bullet into Lionel.

From down on the floor with beer, glass, and his blood blocking his vision, Colton committed himself to action, to throwing himself into the on-rushing line, and came up with Lula in his arms. He clobbered her with one fist, then pulled the pistol away with his other hand. Lula was on the ground and groaning along with Lionel, a duet of pain and embarrassment. Don advanced toward Lula, and Colton was not sure what Don intended. "You settle down," he said to Don, but Don, with a shattered beer bottle in his hand kept advancing. So, Colton committed, not with thought but with will and feeling, and shot Don with Don's wife's revolver.

As Don crumpled, Lula grabbed Colton's ankle, and Colton felt a knife or razor blade cutting at the back of his calf, as though Lula was trying to sever in Achilles tendon. Not flinching, aiming carefully so as to not hit his own foot, Colton shot Lula.

Colton squinted through the blood and tasted it. It was running down his face from the crack on top of his head. Lionel had a strained look on his face that begged Colton, along with his moaning. Colton knew his options. He could drag Lionel out, get him to Snake, and then hide out. That would work best if Lula and Don were dead, but he was not sure, and he didn't feel like putting more bullets into them. He could call for an ambulance and just leave town, but he was not yet that desperate. Or he could call the police and plead self-defense. He looked at Lionel, who shook his head and pleaded with his eyes.

Colton went to Lionel, grabbed him, and dragged him out the door. Colton got the shoulder of his pullover shirt bloody when he stood Lionel up, pushed a shoulder into him, and then leaned him up against the passenger side door of the truck. He opened the door and stuffed groaning Lionel into the truck.

He limped back into the Smileys' bar. Neither husband nor wife moved, and Colton thought that surely they were dead. He found Lionel's gun and stuck it in his belt.

He found the Smiley's gun and wiped all his prints off it with a bar towel, for good measure, not sure why, he poured a beer over it. Then with the same bar towel, he tried to wipe up some of the blood. He tried to sop up his and Lionel's blood. But mostly he just mixed the blood up, but that was okay too. Because that way, the ballistics experts—if Odessa had any—couldn't tell who killed who from what direction. The police had to figure out that the Smileys were both killed by their own gun, so he decided to leave it. He thought some more, felt good in knowing that he was thinking his way through this and not just charging. He went to the cash register, opened it, and pulled out the money. The police, he hoped, would think that it was small-time robbery or that the couple just started shooting each other over lack of money.

He got another bar towel, wrapped it around his calf, and noticed, the blood seeping into his shoes and the sting in his leg. He looked in the bar mirror and saw his blood-wet hair and the trail of dried blood down his forehead. He limped back out to the truck. He drove to Lionel's apartment, pulled screaming Lionel out of the truck, opened the door and pushed him into the apartment. "Bleed some," Colton says. Lionel screamed, "What the fuck? Don't you think I already bled enough?"

Colton grabbed him and said, "Hold on to our little gun." Then Colton dragged him back out to the truck, stuffed him in again, and drove him to the hospital. Colton stopped the truck and parked it just short of the Emergency Room. "Lionel, can you hear me?" Colton yelled. Lionel opened his eyes to stare at Colton, didn't nod his head, but his eyes said he could listen and remember, so Colton said, "You were fucking around with your gun, and it went off."

Lionel's eye's fluttered. "But it ain't my gun shot me," Lionel screamed.

"I'm hoping the bullet in you is all fragmented so they ain't going to be sure whose gun it came from. But you tell them it was a revolver. And listen, now you listen, Lionel Dexter. This is your truck. Hard as it was, much as it hurt, you drove yourself here. You got it? You ain't seen me." Then as much as it hurt, Colton ran, and then he walked, and then he called Snake.

By early afternoon, he sat in the Cactus Lounge with Snake and Bullet. The stitches on his leg felt stiff; the ones on his head felt tight; he was light-headed from the pain pills; and he was afraid, as the nurse at the minor emergency clinic told him, that he might have had a

128

tendon damaged and needed to go to a hospital. But Snake did not drive him to a hospital but to the Cactus Lounge.

Snake Popp sat with his head in his hands and muttered, "Oh Christ, what we going to do? I can't think." He was so busy pushing his hands through his silver hair that he could not take the cigarette out of his mouth and flick the ashes off.

"Nothing," Bullet said. "You ought to be proud of Colton and Lionel. They did just as they should of. It's not going to be a clear case."

"What is going to happen?" Colton asked.

"They could shut me down," Snake said and rubbed his head.

Bullet started to give Colton the lecture. "They could piece together a bunch of things, and you could do some jail time. But it's clearly self-defense. All you've done is fail to report what happened."

"What if Lionel talks?" Colton asked.

"Oh shit," Snake said.

"Then you definitely do some time. But if he knows what's good for him, he won't say nothing."

"Oh, Jesus," Snake said.

Bullet turned to him, her hard eyes focusing on him, "Snake, you ever figure you ought to get out of the gambling business?"

"I'm gone," Snake said. "You two figure it out."

"Snake," Bullet shouted after him. "You can play this one of several ways. We discussed the best way. We keep our stories straight."

"I got it," Snake said.

They watched him go, and Colton, working through the fuzz in his head, noted just how hard Bullet's eyes were and wondered how they got that way. And Bullet turned her hard eyes that did give away her hard times to Colton. "I been through this before. It's best if you just clear out and forget who you are for a while."

"I can't just leave," Colton says.

"I got a friend in Dallas could use a guy like you."

"I could work for you? You know, picking up and delivering. Hell, mopping floors."

"You did real good today from your story. My friend could use a guy skilled in those areas."

Colton could note and wonder but not think, so he drank most of his bottle of beer. As long as he was in this blur, he figured he might as well plunge in. "I got a family," Colton said.

"My friend pays very well for the skills he needs. He needs a man can come out on the winning side of a barroom gun fight."

Colton reached toward his ankle and felt the bandage, felt the slight moisture where the blood was soaking through, considered taking another Darvon. "But my family needs more from me than money."

Bullet chuckled, "And just what is that? And what is it you figure you're giving them?"

Colton tried to get his mind to see through the fog in his head, tried to get his mouth to make the right words, but nothing came to him.

"You probably heard me say that, if you look at a whore real close, you can see she ain't got no soul. That's only part of the story. They aren't born without souls. Somewhere along the way they lose them. I know. I used to run whores. I used to be a whore."

"I'm not a whore."

Bullet didn't even laugh. "I had people help me. I tried to repay them. So now, I'm helping you."

"I got two boys."

"So now make money. The sad fact is all you got left to give your family is money."

"Goddamn it, shut up."

"Goddamn it, listen."

"I got a choice."

Bullet said, "Ain't no choice in something like this. You're beyond choice. You just got to have the smarts and the balls to recognize the obvious."

Still later, after a few hours of sleep in Bullet's office, Colton stumbled through his small house on Adams Street. He made his way into the living room where he heard a voice. Way Low was in front of the TV in a recliner sleeping. His snoring mixed with the chatter from the late-night TV show.

Colton made his way down the hall to his wife's room, slowly opened their door so as not to wake her, looked at her sleeping, and looked at the side of the bed that should be his. For a long time, most of what he and Elena did in that bed was sleep.

He backed out of the bedroom and went to one farther down the hall. He opened the door to look in. His sons were sleeping there in their bunk bed. He wished he could be a better father. But he doubted it. Still, he decided that he would stay in this dark house, in his nighttime Odessa world, and try to become a father. Lionel never talked, so Colton got to stay and work on what was left of being a father.

* * *

Colton owed Lionel. And as Lionel's eyes blinked in front of him as they sat across from each other at the Cactus Lounge, Colton felt guilty again. "You shouldn't of told me," Lionel said. "Last time, I was grunting through pain. Now, I got no grunts to hide behind."

"Want me to shoot you?"

Lionel smiled, but then dropped that smile. "I ain't gonna do it, Colton."

"Come on," Colton says. "It's more money."

"I got a wad of bills in my pocket now. And I'm letting that wad of bills take me to Dallas or Houston and finding me some job cleaning after white people. I'm going legit."

"What? Don't help. But you ain't got to leave."

"I ain't gonna do nigger time. And in a town like this, I get caught, I'm doing way hard nigger time."

"You ain't gonna get caught."

"Suppose you get caught?"

"I ain't gonna get caught."

"That don't matter. I do this, I change. It's just not my line of work. It's what I think of me and what I think I am. And I don't want to go there."

"No reason to leave. You can still work for Snake."

"No, I can't work for Snake because you told me. You should never of told me. So now I know. After Gervin and I'm grunting and groaning in that hospital and getting skinny afterward cause I got a good portion of my stomach shot away, I know I can't do it. I can't live it like that. You told me. Now it's best if I never know what you done. Just get away. This town was over for me when I stopped playing football. Now it for real over." Colton looked at that small-looking black man that was once referred to as a machine with a football. As did Colton, Lionel dropped his football.

"Come on. Don't be a pussy."

Lionel smiled. "You know it ain't that."

"You just gonna walk away from everything?"

"What I got to walk away from?"

Lionel shook Colton's hand and left him to finish his beer and his life in Odessa without backup.

* * *

Colton walked into *his* sun-filled house. Way Low had opened the blinds and raised the windows to let the dry air in and freshen the place. Colton sniffed, looked—toys, some flowers (Elena's or a relative's doing), a few dirty dishes scattered from the kitchen table to the coffee table, open magazines. It looked like a home, but Colton wondered if it looked like *his* home. He wondered what *his home* would look like.

He yelled for Elena but got no answer. He made his way through the living room, the hall, and then the kitchen. He looked out the kitchen window to see Mando and Way Low in the backyard. Way Low sat in a lawn chair and watched Mando as he ran barefooted around in the yard. And when Mando got thick, hard stickers in his feet, like the stickers in Colton's football playing hands, he whimpered and limped back to Way Low. And with Mando in his lap, Way Low pulled several

132

stickers out of Mando's feet. No pre-school or kindergarten for Mando. Such stuff was a luxury, just another expense. Colton's boy would start first grade blank. So Mando stayed home to play by himself or with Way Low, who just woke up, ordered and cleaned the house, then played with his grandson before he started his job watching for oil field equipment thieves.

Colton stepped out the backdoor and said, "Mando, come here." Mando jumped out of Way Low's lap and ran to Colton, but on the way, he picked up another sticker, danced a little, and then toughed it out to run to Colton. And Colton picked him up and whirled him around by his arms and hummed like an airplane. Then Colton carried his son back to Way Low, sat down in a chair beside Way Low with Mando in his lap, and looked at Mando's feet. "Lookie there, you got a big one." And he pulled a hard one out of Mando's tough heel. "You gonna be a football player."

"I'm gonna be small. That's what Way Low says."

"I wasn't that big," Colton said.

"But Momma's small and Way Low is small."

"Abuelo may be small, but he's tough," Way Low said, not getting up. He smiled up at Colton. "As tough as your daddy."

"Tougher," Colton said. Mando squirmed in Colton's lap and looked at the punctures and thorns in his feet. After a while, Colton said, "Get up now. I got to talk to your grandpa. Go play with your brother."

"But my brother's in school. That's why I got to play with Way Low."

"I forget. Then go play with one of those millions of toys you got in the house."

"I want to talk with you and Way Low."

"This is man business."

"I want to talk man business," Mando said. But with a flick of his wrist, Way Low sent Mando skippin on tip toes across the backyard.

"Couldn't you make him wear some shoes?" Colton said to Way Low.

"He's getting tough feet. Tough feet is good."

"Feel it," Way Low said. "Feel it. The dry, the temperature. It's just about as good a feeling on the skin as the weather can be. Now if there was just something to look at."

Colton leaned his back against the cool back of the steel chair. "Yeah, it is nice. Too bad we don't work in it."

"We can sit in it."

"What time is work?"

"Dark," Way Low said. "Wish I didn't have to stay sober. Otherwise, I would be out here drinking all your beer."

"I need to be sober, too."

Way Low squirmed and got this look that he got, like he already knew what you were going to say and was just humoring you so as to let you say it yourself. "You got something to say?"

"They're asking me to kill a man."

Way Low didn't change his expression but squirmed just a little. Colton thought that he could go no further, for he had never made his mind up as to whether or not he could trust Way Low. Way Low was pleasant. Way Low helped. But in something like this, Colton was not sure. "You going to do it?"

"I need help. But I got no help."

They both paused as the dry air crackled between them. "You asking me?"

Colton tried to think but then gave up. "Would you be of any use?"

"When an illegal Mexican gets to this country, he has three years. In those three years, he has to learn the language, get him a job digging ditches or shoveling shit or some kind of manual thing, but then he has to get a better job, to become useful. He doesn't, he goes back to Mexico, breaks his back working for nothing and then dying too soon, or he ends up a criminal."

"So, you did good in three years?"

Way Low smiled and shook his head. "Took me six years."

"What you saying?"

"I'm saying I done some tough things."

"Can you kill a man?"

"Can you?"

"He really needs killing."

"Because *he* needs it or you and your friends need it?" Way Low leaned back in his chair and rested his elbows on the arms. "Makes a difference in what you become. Whether he needs to be dead or you want him dead. Can you do it?"

"I need backup." Colton hesitated before he said what he really meant, "And I need advice."

"What type?"

"First, should I do it? Then how."

"Sounds like the *how* is the easy part."

"It is."

"I'm a Mexican. I know how these things sometimes work in Mexico. And maybe, I been across the law's line more than you. You let me think about this. And you need to think too. You want him dead?"

"I think so."

"You just think."

Colton pushed himself up. "All I been doing is thinking. And I want to stop thinking and do something. So, you think—in a Mexican way. But hurry."

Way Low nodded. And Colton left Way Low to go into his house, looking for Mando. He found Mando in front of the TV set, staring at a blank screen. "What are you doing? That set ain't on."

"I'm imagining it," Mando said.

"Mando, ain't you something? Bad feet, but a good mind. You just keep imagining."

"Daddy?" And when Colton paused to look at him, Mando said, "Why ain't you here at night? Where do you go?"

"I'm out earning us a living. Trying to get enough money to buy you shoes so you don't get the sticker burrs in your feet."

Mando jumped and ran barefooted toward the back door. "Where you going?" Colton asked.

"I left my shoes outside."

Colton watched Mando turn his ass to him and run on tip-toes in the soothing dry air and the brown and barren yard looking for a pair of nylon sneakers. Colton decided to buy Mando a new pair of sneakers, maybe those high-dollar running shoes, only for tykes, as soon as he could.

Chapter 10

Bullet Price always said that the curious thing about johns, no matter how rich or poor, cleaned up or trashy, was that most kept their socks on. Maybe they wanted to be able to grab their shoes or boots, slip them on, and run out the window or the backdoor in case a cop or a wife was coming. Their pants didn't seem to matter as much. Then she'd tell you that if you looked close into a whore's eyes, you could see if she had lost her soul or not. Most, she said, had—or would.

Bullet could comment from experience. She first got that experience in San Antonio when she was young and teeth-itching good looking.

By the time she got to Odessa, Texas she was running whores, as Texans say, but not whoring herself. After several years in Odessa, she diversified from whoring and got well-off. She bought low-down, failing buildings with bad plumbing, mostly out in West Odessa, and rented them out as bars, nasty video shops, or mom and pop restaurants. But she retained the vending machines and the rights to their profits. So that way, while her renters' businesses were failing, she made money. Whether running whores or buildings and vending machines, Bullet Price was good at coping with the rotating labor pool while making money. In the nighttime Odessa world, Bullet Price was a success.

* * *

Christina Price was never *only* a whore. In the mid-sixties, young and pretty, with a body that curved in the right ways to meet the fashions of the time, always adapting, Christina Price started out as an exotic dancer in San Antonio. It was still the dark ages in Texas, the time before 1971, when liquor by the drink was legalized. Until then, liquor drinkers brought a bottle in a brown paper bag into a bar, sat it on the table, and ordered set-ups, cokes and ice. Of course, a few places claimed to be private clubs and charged a dollar membership so they could sell you an overpriced bottle themselves.

Christina eventually worked her way to a job as a go-go dancer in a bamboo cage at Bwana Dik's on the San Antonio River Walk. Bwana Dik's was just a bit sleazy but was also new and hip and swinging in the sixties. Both men and women drank while girls in bikinis shook their assess while in cages. Some cages lowered right down from the ceiling. Bwana Dik's was downtown and catered to the high rollers who came off the street. On the backside it faced the river. By the mid-sixties in preparation for San Antonio's "Hemisfair," the fashionable and safe parts of the river walk had spread beyond Casa Rio and under Bwana Dik's balcony. On hot summer nights, Christina liked to go out onto the small balcony in her bikini, have a smoke, and cool off in the night air. She knew that airmen on leave from Lackland Air Force Base and teenage boys gathered on this edge of the nice and slightly dangerous part of the river and gazed up at Bwana Dik's balcony aching for the prizes in Bwana Dik's cages. When she stood out on the balcony on these hot San Antonio summer nights, Christina, one of Bwana's Dik's best dancers—not because of her dancing or even her body but because of the way she looked at the customers—would squirm or flex and look directly at those Air Force or high school kids and make promises with her eyes, her smile, and her body. She was always advertising. So sometimes, the airmen or high schoolers would pull out their fake I.D.s, or the doorman would look the other way, and they would come into Bwana Dik's and spend all of what little money they had watching Christina and the other dancers.

Bwana Dik's had an ex-semi-pro football player, six-foot-six Charlie Brodsky, as a bouncer. Charlie could take somebody down or out with a tackle, a fist, a knife, or a gun. Charlie had been to prison once, looked it, and wasn't afraid to go back. If a patron really needed a girl, really wanted to see all of what he saw dancing in the bamboo cage, then he could screw his courage into himself and ask Charlie. If Charlie saw no danger for the girl, he would collect an appropriate amount from the gentleman, take out a cut for himself, save the rest for the girl, and then introduce the gentleman to the girl in the cage. Charlie would then call a special number at the Lee or Bluebonnet Hotels, inexpensive hotels but not yet gone to seed. The girl would sit with the gentleman, or gentlemen, during her break, and then after she got off work, the gentleman or gentlemen would escort her to a reserved room at the Bluebonnet or Lee Hotels. If a girl had any problems, the gentleman or gentlemen answered to Charlie. Christina was one of the most popular dates.

On a summer evening with no date after work, after showing off the curves of her body to the high school boys and the airmen, Christina was sitting by the bar rubbing her bare feet after wearing high heels when she danced. She was already a veteran at Bwana Dik's, was smart, and knew the way Bwana Dik's and the rest of the world at that time worked. Charlie Brodsky came to Christina and asked her if she really trusted him. Christina said she did. Charlie studied her. "Just how tough are you?" he asked her. "You act tough."

"You checking me out or what?" Christina asked.

"Twister Adams wants to talk to you," Charlie said.

Twister Adams was really Loren Adams, but he got his new name when he got a lot of money and twisted into and out of trouble. Twister had controlling interest in Bwana Dik's and a lot of other places. So, Charlie escorted Christina up the stairs of Bwana Dik's to the third floor office. He knocked; another big guy let them in. This was Twister's gambling room, high rollers, hot shots, people who couldn't afford to lose but did anyway. Charlie sometimes collected. And Charlie and Christina made their way across the gambling floor with its poker games, roulette wheels, and craps table—all illegal in Texas, along with the liquor by the drink Twister served—to a door on the opposite wall. Charlie knocked, a voice sounded, and Charlie escorted Christina into the next part of her life.

With a drinker's explosion of veins in his nose and cheeks, Twister looked pink. He had on a powder blue polyester suit, white shirt, and pink tie. He had on white shoes and matching white belt. He escorted Charlie and Christina to his desk and then walked around it to sit behind it. They all stared at each other, and then Twister got down to business. "Christina, Charlie here tells me you're a bright girl. I want you to answer me straight up."

"I don't plan to do anything but," Christina said.

Twister's face dropped into a frown, then he managed to push his mouth into a smile while his eyes still frowned. "What plans you got?"

"What do you mean?"

"I mean, you not thirty yet, but you close, right? What you going to do at the end of your dancing days? What you going to do if the men don't want to pay top dollar for the pleasure of your favors?"

"Try something else, I guess," Christina said. Charlie looked at her like he was trying to tell her to watch her mouth.

"Well, I can help with that something else," Twister said. "Now you listen for a while before you talk. Then you think real hard for a minute or two and then you talk. Now, what I'm offering you, what I'm about to say, I never said. But I got a business associate down in Monterrey in Nuevo León, Mexico. He's sending a negotiator of sorts to see me. I want to entertain the negotiator, but I don't want to see him."

Christina, of course, a smart girl, could guess where this was going, but she was still young, had a few options in her life, and so she screwed her butt into the seat of her chair and lightly bit the side of her tongue. Twister continued, "I asked Charlie to take care of this negotiator in order to send a message to my associate in Mexico. He's got a plan, but it involves you." Twister cleared his throat and looked down. He was the one tongued tied, but Christina dared not speak yet.

"She's tough enough," Charlie said. "Just is she willing?"

Christina didn't know who to answer to, Charlie or Twister. "Can you kill a man?" Twister asked.

Christina started to answer, but Twister was too quick for her to get any words out of her mouth, "Now you think, then think some more before you say something. What's at the end of this deal is a good job

140

working for me or a big ol' lump of money for you to use as you wish. Hell, go to college and become a cheerleader, stay drunk for a year or two. But you take the money, I don't know you. You're gone. Now have you thought?"

He held up his index finger. On it was an over-sized diamond ring. "One, you going to do this or no?"

Christina knew enough of the world she was in to know that she could not say, "no." She already knew too much. Christina said, "Yes."

"You going to take the job or the money?"

Christina figured she had a choice here, and she knew if there was any room to wiggle in Twister's offer, this was the place. "The money. But I'd like to see some up front."

Charlie turned his head away from Christina. Twister looked at her with his forced smile. "Okay then. This is all I want to see of you. You and Charlie plan this out and get it done. Charlie'll bring you some money in a day or two, and when I read about things in the paper or, better yet, hear about them, then you'll get the rest of the money."

Christina fidgeted before she left. When Charlie motioned for her to go, she stood, but she asked, "What kind of job would it have been?"

Twister looked bored now. "A suitable one."

Christina nodded. "I thought so," under her breath, then followed Charlie back through the gambling.

* * *

Charlie told Christina, "A gun has problems. Even with a silencer, someone might hear something. It's bulky. Then you might drop a casing somewhere. Someone finds it. A knife is bloody and messy, but easier to hide, and you don't leave as much evidence." Christina didn't dare disagree because she had nothing to say because she knew she was in way over her head. Charlie peeled the rind off of a cantaloupe and had Christina slicing into it with a sharp switchblade. He coached her, told her to apply just the right amount of pressure, got her to pull the blade toward herself, to slice, not cut—well, just like a cantaloupe.

Charlie fixed what could be problems. When Christina brought a client to the Lee Hotel, she always gave the night manager at the desk a knowing smile. And he would courteously smile back and take the client's money. But Charlie sweetened the night manager's smile with an envelope filled with a bunch of bills. He told the manager the money was for forgetting things if the police or anyone asked about what might happen. And he told the manager that he would call soon and ask for a particular room on the third floor and that the manager would have that room available no matter what.

He did the same for the maid who cleaned up the third floor. Her money was for her to show up early, clean the room, and not talk. He "bought" the mattress from the maid and wrapped a plastic sheet around it and stuffed a switchblade underneath the mattress.

Charlie took Christina out for a meal at Casa Rio. They sat by the river. Charlie smoked and flicked his cigarette ashes into the river. He looked at Christina almost tender-like and reached to put his fingertips on top of her hand. Instead of jerking her hand away from him, Christina held her hand still while Charlie stroked the top of it. "Now, can you do this?" he asked.

"We've been practicing."

"But I never asked you, can you do it?"

"A little late now," Christina said. She tried to smile. Charlie wouldn't even look at her.

"I'll be at the door listening, my gun ready. And I'm going to have some help with me." Christina nodded and grew more worried.

"I almost wished you'd said 'no' when Twister asked." Charlie pulled his head up to look at Christina. "I don't like to think it of you."

Christina said nothing, but she took her opposite hand and patted Charlie's hand, the one that was feeling the back of her hand. They sat like that for a while, Christina realizing that big, tough Charlie might feel something for her. "Once I got into Twister's office, did I ever really have a choice?"

"I guess not. But I could have covered for you." Christina got a little fond of Charlie, but she also realized that, if she wanted, she could have gotten him to do most anything for her. Of course, maybe he was getting her to do what Twister wanted.

The associate from Mexico's representative was a big man named Saucedo. He wore white dress pants and a short-sleeved, lime-green mock turtleneck pullover with elastic at the bottom. He sat with Charlie while Christina danced on this table. After her dances, Christina sat at their table. Christina felt Saucedo's breath on the side of her face as she leaned over to hug him. And she looked at Charlie's wide eyes when he watched her hug Saucedo. As the night went on, Christina watched Saucedo's eyes grow blurry from the booze that Charlie poured down him. After her last set, she sat with them and coaxed Saucedo to drink even more. The plan went perfect. Christina's service was compliments of Twister. And together Saucedo and Christina walked arm in arm with Christina faking sexiness while Charlie trailed behind in the late-night downtown shadows and alleys. When they got to the lobby of the Lee Hotel, the night clerk gave Christina a knowing smile.

Once in the third-floor room, Christina stepped into the light coming in from the downtown lights. And she took off all of her clothes. Saucedo did the same, except for his socks. In the faint light, Christina saw that his thick whiskers went all the way down. The hair on his shoulders was as curly as, but not as thick as, the hair on his chest. She stepped in that runway-model, playboy-bunny fashion toward him and hugged him. He was sweaty too. And his breath smelled like the combination of liquors he had drunk.

She pulled him on to the bed and on top of her. He entered her—in all kinds of ways. She was tempted to just let her mind go somewhere else, but she needed her concentration for what she had agreed to do. So, she felt every part of him on or in her body. And a chill went through her because she was thinking about what she was going to do. And, as he thrusted and moaned, he said, "Wow, that a way, baby."

She pushed and shoved, but he grunted and was not about to give way. She said, "Let me get on top." He didn't quite understand, so she pushed and poked and shoved until she was straddling him. She bent to him, kissed him just under his ear, reached in between the plastic-lined mattress and the bedsprings, felt the switch blade, and pulled it out.

She pulled herself up away from his face. He was smiling, motioning with just his eyes to do some more. She flicked the blade out, raised the knife, and pushed it through the suddenly thick air toward his throat. But she didn't press in and then pull like she'd done with the cantaloupe, she swiped. And with one great jerk, Saucedo flipped her off him. He got to his feet, holding his throat, gurgling, blood seeping through his fingers.

He lurched toward her like one of those horror movie monsters—Frankenstein or the Mummy—stiff legged, one arm in front of him. But when his feet caught in his pants, he bent over and brought them up. While one hand held the blood in his throat, he groped around on his pants with his other. Finally, he pulled a pint bottle of whisky from his pants. He tried to break it against the bed post, but it wouldn't break. He tried against the lamp stand. Christina heard breaking glass and then saw Saucedo inching toward her with a fist full of glass shards. She swiped and poked. He swiped and poked. Christina felt like he could have grabbed her and poked and twisted the glass shards into her. But he didn't. Maybe he wanted to torture her.

She was cutting his arm. He was cutting hers. And after the girly-style swipes, he got his fist full of glass across Christina's face. She backed up and raised her hands to her face, one still holding the switchblade, not daring to let go. He still held his throat. But he smiled.

Christina heard the door rattling in its frame and then heard Charlie shout her name. "Help, Charlie," she said loud but not screaming.

Saucedo turned from her toward the door in time to see Charlie come stumbling through it. Saucedo raised a bloody fist. Charlie raised his hand. In Charlie's hand was a pistol with a silencer. Charlie shot twice. Saucedo gurgled, fell over backward, and died.

Charlie stepped toward Christina and looked at her face. "Oh Jesus," he said. "Hold on."

Christina tried to hold her face together while Charlie closed the door and flipped on the light. He looked once at Christina and breathed in. Christina pushed harder on her face. Charlie flipped the mattress over and pulled up the plastic sheets. He then folded the plastic sheets around Saucedo and then huffed as he pulled the bloody Saucedo to one side of the room. He went into the bathroom and came out with wet, soapy towels. He began trying to clean up what he could with soap and water.

In the light, with Charlie checking back over his shoulder at her, Christina realized that she was stark naked. A dancer and hooker gets used to having no clothes on so that she sometimes forgets whether she's dressed or not, especially if her face is slashed open. Christina took several steps forward and bent down to grab her clothes. While she was bent over, she saw a few drops of her blood mix with the mess on the carpet.

As she tried to stuff herself into her short skirt and tight blouse, Christina thought she ought to look in the mirror, just to check out the damage. When she got most of her clothes on, she moved toward the mirror, but Charlie said, "Don't do it. Best not to see yet."

Christina backed slowly away from the mirror, feeling her face, like she was checking to see if it was still there. Christina's mind zipped from then until years down the line to what she would do with a ruined face.

When he was satisfied with his cleaning, Charlie turned off the light, opened the door, and checked in the hall. A small, young Mexican boy pushed a rolling food serving cart into the room. Together, Charlie and the boy pushed and tugged the plastic-wrapped Saucedo onto the cart. With parts of him hanging over the sides, they rolled Saucedo to a service elevator, took him out through the kitchen, and threw him into the bed of a pickup. Christina followed behind them the whole way, holding her face. And then Charlie got in the pickup and told her to get in the Mexican boy's car.

Christina climbed into a battered Plymouth Valiant with the boy and watched Charlie drive off with Saucedo's body. The boy began to chatter, "You don't look too good." Christina was afraid to move any part of her face for fear of it becoming all distorted. "So how was it? I mean, like what was you thinking with all that cutting going on?"

Christina just remained silent for those ten blocks to Santa Rosa Hospital's emergency room—where that Mexican boy dropped her off. When she walked in, a pregnant woman said, "Oh, my God. Honey, does it hurt?"

"It stung. Now it stopped."

Christina knew that the doctor and nurses knew what she was and how she got that cut as they stitched her up. After all, they worked late in an emergency room in a downtown. They had seen whores cut up and beaten up before. You just couldn't know when a john was going to get pissed off.

Just as the sun was coming up, Charlie appeared in the emergency room to pick Christina up. He hung his head to keep from looking at her. He couldn't make himself say anymore than, "Goddamn, I'm sorry." Christina asked him where the body was. "Best you don't ask," he said.

"So okay, you've done this before. What do we do now? How safe are we?"

Charlie squinted into the sun. "On the seat there is the rest of Twister's money. Best if you just get out of town and find honest work."

Christina nodded to herself because she didn't really want to stick around anyway. San Antonio, for her, was as dead as Saucedo. Still, Charlie looked like he was going to cry. "It's just that I'm going to really miss you," he said.

That cut on her face turned into a forked scar across her forehead and left cheek. So, she slid a rung or two down the whore ladder. She also did some stripping, and she managed strip joints in Oklahoma

146

City, which of course has the reputation of having the best titty-bars in the country out on West I-40. And Oklahoma City titty bars was where she came by her name. With that scar on her face, she was not about to get a usual stripper name, not *Chastity*, *Mysti*, *Dawn*, *Monique*, or *Renee St. Cloud*. She chose Bullet. And when a patron gave her an empty .45 casing, she put that on a chain and wore it around her neck—as a reminder to herself and a warning to the men watching her.

The whoring and titty bar work was mostly for getting by. She was not about to spend Twister's money on getting by. She invested in savings accounts, stocks, bonds, and certificates of deposit and watched that money grow. When she would tell men about looking into a whore's eyes to see if she had lost her soul, she'd add that the question was really *when* and *how* she'd lost her soul. The *why* was usually obvious. Then she'd smile, point up at the scar on her forehead, say she was not a true whore, just a getting-by whore. She'd smile real big and say she still had her soul. And then she followed her money and her instinct to Odessa.

* * *

So instead of Charlie Brodsky, Bullet conspired with Renee St. Cloud to kill a man. Bullet and Renee made the bars looking for Mitch—or Mitch and Harold. But what they got was a message from Harold on Bullet's message machine at the First Quality Motel. He wanted a "date" with that "pretty Renee girl." This would have to be a conspiracy on the fly. Bullet called all over looking for Colton but couldn't find him, but she did find Snake. "Snake, you got to find Colton, and you got to tell him to be at the First Quality Motel, watching room three, tonight."

She heard nothing. In her mind, Bullet saw Snake there with his phone pressed against his ear, trying to think. "I don't know if I ought to do that," Snake finally said.

"Okay, I don't have time to argue. A total of four words. First Quality Motel, tonight. Write them down. But get those words to Colton."

"Bullet?"

"Goddamn it, Snake, you want me or Renee splayed out or gutted in front of a deputy sheriff?"

"It ain't that."

"Now tell him we're switching. I got Harold. He gets Mitch."

"No, I ain't hearing you."

"You want to get found splayed and gutted by the deputy sheriff?"

"Bullet!"

"Well then, you listen to me. You got friends. And you owe it to us. Now you find Colton, and you tell him to be at the Quality Inn and watching room three." Bullet could almost hear a sucking sound as Snake pulled the phone receiver from his ear.

So then Bullet was with Renee and trying to keep her from crying or from panicking as they waited for Harold at the Snug Harbor. Bullet had made the plan quick but with all the guidance of her past. She couldn't expect Renee to get it right off. But she hoped that Renee could just follow the orders and the order. Renee took a sip from her tequila. "Drink all you want. You don't have to be sober. You just got to remember."

"It's remembering that's bothering me."

"Then stop remembering and just get drunk."

"But you see, I done them, those two boys, who I thought was just boys, and then they done what they done to that friend of yours, despite he was gay, and now I'm in for more bloodletting."

"It could be us."

Renee stopped sipping, and Bullet could see from the way Renee sipped just the right amount of tequila to keep from choking or getting the full flush and burn down her throat that Renee had been drinking a lot of tequila during her young life. She might do just fine. "You are right. It *could* be us." And Bullet was almost proud. The young whore had learned—maybe she was soulless, but smart. Maybe she was better prepared than Christina Price was.

"If it was Mitch, I could go on with this. He's just weird and funny and maybe even cute. But that Harold is mean. I know what he is. I seen it that first night."

"It's Harold. And you gonna do him because he has cash in hand and you're a whore."

Renee pulled back and looked at Bullet over the brim of her tequila glass. "You ain't got to say it like that. I used to be a good girl."

"'Used to be.' And what you got to show for it?"

"If I'd stayed good, I wouldn't be doing this."

"Well, you are doing this."

"I don't know if I am liking your tone."

Bullet shook her head and patted Renee's forearm. "Then think about Danny."

"Oooh. He's dead," Renee said.

"But when you had the three of them, he was the nicest one. He at least had some charm, some sympathy. He didn't make you feel dirty."

"He didn't do me."

Bullet shut her eyes, "Then think about getting even for all of it. For the fact that you had to give up being a good girl because of the likes of those two."

Their conversation could not go on because Harold came into the bar. Taking long, exaggerated steps, his boot heels clicking on the floor, he sat by Renee, flicked his ponytail over his shoulder, put an arm around her, pulled his lit cigarette from his mouth, licked her neck, and said, "Hello sweet meat." While he was licking and squeezing, the shaved-head bartender came up to the inside of the bar across from Bullet and asked, "Is everything okay?"

"Business," Bullet said. The bartender nodded and backed away. But he kept this quizzical look on his face, saying maybe that he could help.

Harold nodded in Bullet's direction. "I guess we figured out how you fit into the situation. So, I guess we won't be needing you no more."

"Who's this 'we' you talking about. Mitch outside?"

"Mitch don't need love as much as I do." Harold reached to his lips pulled his cigarette out and crushed it in the ashtray on the bar. "Mitch and me had a few disagreements."

"I'm gonna need to see some cash," Bullet said.

Harold turned to Renee again. And he stuck his tongue out, real deliberate, and pressed the tip against her neck, right where it joins her shoulder, and pulled it on up to the very bottom of her jaw. "I thought I got to see if the merchandise was worth it. Test it out, so to speak."

"Some up front," Bullet said.

But the shaved-head man was in front of them on the other side of the bar, and he said, "This kind of proposition can't go on right in front of me. You take it outside."

"I'll take it outside, put it in my truck, and take it where I like."

"Where you're going to like is the First Quality Inn. Otherwise, she don't go," Bullet said.

The shaved-head man leaned his head in between Bullet and Harold's heads to say, "What did I just say?"

And Renee, learning and growing, yet losing her soul, leaned over toward Harold, grabbed his face with both her hands to turn it toward her, and kissed him square on the lips, then pulled back to say to the shaved-head bartender, "Me and my sweetie will say what we like, in front of whoever we like, because we got love." She kissed him again. "And muscle," she added.

Bullet watched, yet shifted her head toward the shaved-head bartender, and worried to herself, as Renee took Harold's hand and pulled him toward the door. And on the way out, Renee reached into her purse and pulled out a maroon key fob with number *3* written across the top and shook it for Bullet and anybody worried about her to see. The only one who took note was Bullet. And Colton couldn't be found.

* * *

After pushing her truck to the limit to get there before Harold and Renee, Bullet waited in the closed closet of room number three with the switchblade in her hand. Because the room was empty, Bullet knew that Renee asked Harold to stop to get a coke, to pee, anything to delay them just a little. In the dark Bullet debated just one last time about what she was going to do. She tried to see far enough into the future to know what this act might lead to. But her mind drifted back to Danny and his indignity—and hers. Bullet knew that she was smarter than when she tried to cut Saucedo's jugular. She squeezed the switchblade and waited. She thought. She knew what she would do with the money from Mina. She knew how much she would give Renee. She knew what that money might mean to Renee, and then hoped, but then smothered the hope, that Renee, with money, would quit being a whore and save what she had left of her soul. But Bullet had never seen that happen. And her mind went back to Christina Price's shaking hand and botched slice that turned into a swipe. She hoped that now she did not need a big man at the door. Still, where was Colton?

Bullet heard the door to the motel open, heard the click of a light, saw a band of light at her feet, leaned against the side of the closet and tried not to breathe. Through the barest crack in the closet, Bullet watched.

Renee led Harold in and stood in front of him. Shrugging her shoulders, showing she had learned, Renee shed her shift, her lacy half-assed, loose negligee, and then she undid her jeans and wiggled out of them. Then, she began to dance in nothing but her panties and bra for Harold. Harold stepped up, and like a man, just as Bullet knew he must do, knowing he was going to get all he wanted, unfastened the bra and pulled down Renee's panties. But in the harsh, judging light, Renee kept dancing, naked, for Harold. And maybe, Bullet guessed that, even if he had some plan other than pussy, he had forgotten all but what his groin was telling him. She was skinny, she was not pretty, a country girl with no hopes, but she was learning and working it, just like Christina did at Bwana Diks.

And after Renee stopped the swerving and the gyrating, Bullet heard Renee say if maybe, please, they couldn't turn off the light. Because, she said, she wanted things to be sweet and romantic, because Harold was special, she just knew he was. And the light went off.

After stretched out moments, Bullet heard grunts and groans and Renee screaming with fake delight. And Bullet, surprising herself, thought, what about love? She pushed such thinking from her mind. Then she heard Renee ask if she couldn't please get on top. "What, what," Harold said. "Why you so particular?"

"Ain't you getting your money's worth?" Renee asked.

"That's better," Renee cooed some more. What the fuck indeed about love? And then Bullet slowly pushed the closet door open. She took a tentative step toward the bed and saw Harold's head resting at the foot of the bed and pointed toward her. He slammed his head on the bed so that his braided ponytail flipped up and down as he went into and out of Renee. And then, as Bullet stepped nearer, Harold, not seeing Bullet, went stiff, no bouncing, no pumping or gyrating, no flipping ponytail, and he asked, "So bitch, what is going on? What you and that scarred-up old lady planning?"

The bouncing stopped. The fake ecstasy stopped. But Renee, turning pro, leaking out her soul, but giving it up for Bullet and Danny, ground and wound and swirled and said, "Honey, let me make you happy."

And Harold had his open palm over her mouth and was raising his fist, "What do you and that crazy, titless bitch think you know? What about this faggot? What are y'all planning to do?"

Bullet stepped forward, switchblade in her hand. "Hey, there's somebody in here?" Harold said.

"Baby, Baby, Baby, be sweet" Renee said, moved, and reached up for Harold's cheeks. But Harold pulled away from Renee and lifted his chin and tilted his head back to try to see behind him.

"What the hell," Harold said when Renee froze. And as he tried to flip Renee off him, Bullet flicked the switchblade open, stepped up

152

behind him, grabbed his chin with her left hand, and pulled the switchblade across his throat, just like it was a cantaloupe with the rind peeled away. A neat line of blood spread under his chin and began to trickle. And Bullet, knowing better, said, "Faggot! This is for that other faggot—Danny Fowler!"

Bullet pulled out the plastic sheet she had shoved under the bed and spread it out at the foot of the bed. Renee still straddled Harold and watched. And then in a delayed-like flicker of realization, she stuck her knuckles into her mouth to keep from screaming and jumped off Harold. As Bullet grabbed Harold under the shoulders and pulled him bleeding toward the plastic sheet, Renee hopped up and down and rapidly waved her hands in front of her over the thought of screwing a dead, bleeding man. Harold fell and sent gurgling sounds into the room. Harold's head tilted back some more, making the thin line under his chin wider, and his eyes looked at Bullet. "If you're still alive, then know that this is for Danny Fowler. You shouldn't have set him up," Bullet said. Harold gurgled. Renee jumped up and down.

Renee, naked still, ran to the front door and turned on the light. The slit in his throat had tributaries of blood coming out of it. Bullet looked down Harold's body, his braided ponytail, his hairless chest, his shrinking male equipment—his socks. "Why do they always leave their socks on? Where's he going to run? And from who?" Bullet asked.

And soon the door was booming and pounding in its frame, about to bust open, and Renee pulled it open without Bullet's okay, and there was Colton, breathing heavy and saying, "You all okay?"

Bullet couldn't help but smile. "Superman. Thank God, you didn't bust in here in the middle of things."

"I waited until I saw the light come on. Figured you had a plan." Colton smiled back at Bullet, but when he looked down at Harold, like Renee, he quivered just a little.

Bullet and naked Renee and Colton gathered up Renee and Harold's clothes and threw them on to the sheet on top of naked but sock-wearing Harold. Then they pushed and shoved clothes and arms and legs to bundle up the clothes and Harold inside the plastic sheet. Renee went to the closet and pulled out her small bag and changed into a pair of jeans and a T-Shirt. Colton watched Renee. Bullet was glad that Colton got the message and was there, even if they didn't need him. But she had no time to think about things. She went to the closet and pulled out a plastic and aluminum lawn recliner. And she said to Colton, "You gonna help?"

Bullet and Colton strained to pick up the lump of body and bed clothes wrapped in plastic and lift it on to a plastic and aluminum lawn recliner. Then, as dressed Renee held the door open, they got the lawn recliner to Bullet's pickup. They could barely lift it, but with a heave, they got the load into Bullet's pickup.

"When did you come up with this?" Colton asked Bullet as Renee headed back into the motel.

"To tell the truth, I kind of made it up as I went along."

"Oh shit," Colton said, but he smiled. "Are you okay?"

"Easy money," Bullet said.

"So, you can just cut a man's throat?"

"You were all but there to see. You just missed it."

"Jesus."

"It wasn't the first time. But I done better this time."

Colton toed the asphalt with his Roper and stared down. "You need me? I need to ask? You want me to ask."

Bullet, feeling something she hadn't felt since Charlie Brodsky, reached with one hand to grab Colton's chin to hold his face still, and then leaned forward to kiss him. "You stay here. And then you go get Mitch."

Bullet and Renee, with a tarp over Harold's body, drove out to the Fowler ranch and met Mina. On short notice, with only a quick pay phone call, Mina had had a ranch hand bull doze a ditch that very afternoon. Mina even helped Bullet and Renee pull the evidence into a ditch. They sprinkled gas on it and set it afire. While the fire was roaring, the smell of burning flesh ate at their stomachs, and Bullet

154

showed Harold's billfold to Mina. In it was Danny's credit card. Then she threw it into the fire. "Good riddance you son of a bitch. And I hope you see Danny in heaven or hell or wherever it is, and he can beat the shit out of you," Mina said.

Bullet felt both of Renee's hands wrap around her left arm. "I think maybe you should thank Renee, Mina."

Mina turned to them with the blaze of fire behind her and said, "Thank you, Miss, Miss whatever."

"Me, I don't need no thanks," Bullet said.

"Is that what you want? Thanks?"

"No, I ain't being a smart ass. My thanks is knowing he's dead. I almost want to wait here and watch him burn."

"Oh no," Renee said. "I want to take a shower."

"Like I said, it don't wash off."

"Don't be so soft, Missy," Mina said. "Tomorrow the same obedient hand who dug this hole will cover it up. Now, where is the other guy?"

"He's being taken care of," Bullet said.

* * *

That night, Bullet went into her duplex and stepped into the red shag carpet and looked at her golden figures of naked women holding up the lampshades, the rock arch, and the gold trim. It was decorated to appease men's fantasies, even if those fantasies had no chance of being real. And Bullet knew then that for her whole titty-dancing, whoring, pimping life, she sold fantasies. And she remembered that she had never had a gentleman, a trick, or even a fuck buddy in this duplex decorated for fantasy fucking.

Then she went into her bedroom that was piled with her dirty clothes, jeans, boots, tennis shoes, women's western shirts. She opened drawers and looked for panties. She went to the closet and looked for a dress. She looked for lingerie, something sexy, sheer. She looked for something a man might like. What she found was old stuff she had hauled to Odessa from Oklahoma City or San Antonio. Those clothes had held up well, her sexiness hadn't.

She walked through her house and turned off the lights. She grabbed her liquor out of her freezer and sipped it straight. And she figured that Renee St. Cloud was just not ever going to be the same from the whoring and the killing and the blood. And she wondered what direction, Renee's life might go. And thinking about Renee, she realized what she saw around her was the direction her life went.

And while she wondered if she had anything left that made her like other people, she rubbed the scar on her face and wondered just how disfigured she was. Then she reached into her shirt and felt the vacant spot with the twisting scars and the empty .45 casing. Because Danny Fowler had already paid for the operation, she got the bare, basic operation. She couldn't ask him for the cosmetic part too. And when the cutting started, she thought she wouldn't want a fake tit. But now she thought that they cut something out beside that tumor, and she wished that she could stuff something back in beneath the twisted scar tissue.

Chapter 11

Colton pulled his Civic in front of his mother's rent house. It was in a neighborhood on the southwestern part of the city that had turned bad, but lucky for Colton, out of some neighborly obligation, the Mexicans living in the area kept an eye on his mother. On his way up the sidewalk, the setting sun harshly lighting his way, he looked at his shadow stretching up the front of the house and the loose bricks in the wall. He stopped to look at the pecan tree. The big, ripening pecans were pulling the limbs toward the ground. The place needed work.

Helen Parker answered the door before Colton reached it. She held it open for him, and Colton went in. "So nice to see you again." Colton turned in the middle of the living room. Like his, her furniture was wearing. The TV had rabbit ears. She had dropped cable. The white drapes had the gray stains from her cigarettes. The place smelled of crushed cigarettes and Lysol. "You seen my place before," Helen said.

"You ever thought of moving?"

"Where the hell am I gonna get the money to do that?"

"Maybe a nicer apartment over on the northeast side, next to the mall."

"What would I do there?"

"What do you do here?"

"Get by."

Colton sat on a padded recliner. Some dust rose up around him. When he looked up into the window, he saw beams of dusty light coming through the windows and the walls. "You need to get the walls fixed." Helen didn't answer but went into the kitchen and came out with two cold bottles of beer. Colton took his while his mother sat across from him on the sofa. Colton stared into the opening on his bottle of beer and watched the cool vapor rise.

"You came here to tell me something or ask me something," Helen said. "Or do you want to just drink a beer?"

"Momma, I'm gonna do something bad."

Helen sipped, eyed Colton, and he ducked his gaze from her. "Is it mean?"

"It's just," Colton said toward the toe of his Ropers.

"*Just* what?"

"Just. As in justice. As in people getting what they deserve."

"Then how can it be bad?"

Colton took a quick sip of his beer. He stood. "It's just, but it's mean."

"Geez, Colton, you're confusing you more than you're confusing me."

"Well, it's just that I got to tell you is all. I got to tell you that, if I do it—"

"*If.* I thought you said *was*?"

"I'm gonna do something. But whatever it is, it's gonna change things."

"Things always change, Colton. Do or don't do what you're gonna do, things will change."

Helen got up and went to her purse for a cigarette. As she pulled one out, Colton said, "You should quit."

"Yes, I should. Sometime soon, I will. See, change."

Colton let himself smile and sat down to talk to his mother about quitting smoking. She looked to him to be strong and healthy. Over the years, Colton thought, he had grown older than his mother. For Helen, as with Colton, money and life were hard enough so that you just had to learn reality. But unlike Colton, Helen had some hope. When his beer was empty, Colton walked out of her shabby house through the bright sunshine to deal with Mitch.

* * *

Colton sat behind the wheel of his Civic and watched the light in Mitch's trailer's window. He reached inside his leather jacket and fingered the pint bottle of Rich and Rare Canadian whiskey. He wanted some alcohol encouragement and adrenaline. And he wanted Mitch to get a whiff of liquor. For a probable drunk, Mitch might be even more scared of a drunk Colton, and Colton looked even meaner drunk. And who knew what a mean looking drunk like Colton might do. Colton pulled out the pint, opened the top, and took a sip.

"You drinking now?" he heard from beside him.

Colton held the bottle out to the passenger side. "It's for the effect. I want him thinking I'm drunk."

Way Low took the bottle, took a sip, then handed it back to Colton. "Let's get started," Way Low said. "I'm supposed to be at work watching the rusting oil equipment go nowhere."

Colton shoved open the door of his Civic, shoved his hands into his jacket to feel the grip of the .45. The pistol was big and clumsy and not accurate, usually making a mess of things, but like a drunk waving it around, it was scary. A tiny 9mm would not have the same effect. It was the effect Colton wanted, but in getting it, he was charging right into the line. His knee hurt.

"Wait, not so fast," Way Low said from behind him.

"I want to get this over. I don't want anybody to see."

"Who you think is watching at two in the morning?"

Colton walked up the steps, rehearsing in his head, once again, what he and Way Low had been rehearsing and planning, only with Harold in their minds, not Mitch. Now, with Harold done in by Bullet, less than three hours before, he had altered the plan. Mitch was a different kind of human, and Way Low had agreed. Colton hoped that the changed plan might save his soul.

The door to Mitch's recreational trailer was cheap crap. Colton felt in his pants pocket for the wire. He dug it out and got the hook into the lock. He heard the click, pulled out the wire, and tried to open the door. But the cheap crap door still held. It caught. Colton put a shoulder into the door. Nothing. Then again, and the door swung open and nearly off its hinges.

Colton was inside quick with his pistol in his hand. The first thing he noticed was that the trailer was hot. He immediately started to sweat. He heard some blaring, looked over his shoulder to see an MTV clip. The next thing he noticed was over on the couch—Mitch in his underwear and flailing around because he had just jumped out of his sleep.

"Calm down," Colton said. He held the gun with one hand and reached into his jacket to pull out his pint bottle of Rich and Rare.

"What is it with you? You over here to whip my ass again?" Mitch asked.

"We're here to kill you," Way Low, holding his 9mm., said from behind Colton as he stepped into the trailer and closed the busted door behind him.

Colton got the cap off the bottle and took a drink. He offered the bottle to Way Low, who took the bottle and took a sip.

"Should y'all be drinking in the midst of a killing?" Mitch asked. He got his knees up under his chin and hugged them. "Since y'all are drinking. You mind if I have a snort?" He started to get up, but Way Low was immediately up to him and slapped him backhanded with his hand opposite the one holding the pistol to send Mitch back on the couch.

"Where's your thermometer?" Colton asked and saw it down the hall.

"Why's it so hot?" Way Low asked.

"I get cold," Mitch said. Colton looked around, saw prescription bottles, a bottle of tequila, a bong. Then Colton backed down the hall, keeping his gun on Mitch, to lower the heat. He stepped back in and said, "Where's Harold?"

"Fuck him," Mitch said. "Didn't your buddy tell you? He fired us. Cause of Harold. We show up late, and fucking Harold, who normally don't talk much, starts cussing out your buddy, and then he started telling him how he should weld and run his business. And then he started saying that that titless lady pimp you hang out with and her young whore are spying on us. And he wants to fuck them up. And so I say, 'You do the fucking up yourself.'"

Before he could finish, Way Low stepped up again, and this time he hit Mitch with the butt end of the gun. Colton heard the smack of metal on skull. And Mitch whimpered as he fell to the floor on his knees and held his head. "Who is this little Mexcan fella?

"Sit back down on your couch," Way Low said.

When Mitch said, "Who are you?" Way Low raised his hand like he was going to backhand Mitch again. Mitch raised his hands to cover his face. "Goddamn, is that fat, red-headed, queer tool pusher gonna come in here and whip my ass too?'

"You don't' seem to get it. We don't mean to whip your ass. We mean to kill you."

Mitch stared at Way Low and blinked, then he twisted his head to look at Colton. "You too?"

Colton nodded and said, "You better listen to him."

"Fuck him. If you're going to shoot . . ." But before he could finish, Way Low stuck the muzzle of his gun in Mitch's mouth. Mitch quivered and lifted his eyes up to look at Way Low. He had a chipped tooth and an area around one tooth bled.

"You bite down on that barrel real good. Just like you sucking a dick. Just like you was this Danny Fowler. And you think about what you done."

"What I done?" Mitch slurred from his drinking and from the barrel of the pistol shoved into his mouth.

"Let's not fuck around," Colton said. "Pull the trigger."

"Whoa. It was Harold, man. It was all Harold," Mitch tried to mouth out with his mouth full of pistol barrel. Way Low pulled the pistol out.

"We got to kill you," Way Low said.

"No you don't. No you don't."

"Then you got to pay some way. We could cut something off you."

"What?"

"Say like a toe, a finger, *tú verga,* huh? I think that would be good."

"My what?"

"Your dick," Colton said.

"Goddamn, take a finger."

"How about a hand?"

"Your prick would be good and fair. After you raped and killed Danny."

"Raped? what are you talking about rape?"

"Homosexual rape."

"There was none of that. He was the faggot. He tried this move on me. It is me should be getting the hacked off body parts."

"So, you did kill him."

"I didn't. No, not me. It was Harold."

"How did Harold come to kill him?"

"I ain't saying."

"You said 'fuck Harold.'"

Mitch looked from Way Low to Colton, "We made this pact."

"Harold is dead."

"He's toasting over a fire or stuffed into a grave by now," Way Low said. Way Low chuckled, "Maybe, he's somebody's chili meat."

"Harold is dead?" Mitch was blinking and trying to stand.

"Sit the fuck back down," Colton said and shoved him down onto the couch.

"You fuckers killed him? You fuckers did it?"

"I didn't say 'we' did I?

"But I heard Harold told a friend of mine how you killed Danny," Colton said.

"It was him."

"How you planned it all out. Planned to kill him, just on account of he was a queer," Colton said.

"No, no, it was Harold. And Harold didn't mind killing a queer. That just made it better. But he knew that he would have money."

"So you planned it?"

"Harold comes to me says he knows where we can get some money. It was just like rolling queers. But Harold gets too drunk. When Danny sticks his hand down my pants, Harold started hitting him. Then more and more. And him, Harold, was smiling, and there's blood on his fist and splattering."

"And you had nothing to do with this."

"Nothing."

Way Low stepped up and slammed the butt of his gun into Mitch's face one more time. "Would you fucking stop that?" Mitch scolded.

And Way Low pulled out a knife and asked, "what you want cut off, so we can show good faith."

"I got nothing to cut off."

"Then we going to shoot you."

Colton shoved his pistol toward Mitch. "Wait, wait, wait. Let's see. Let's see. There's my billfold. There's my license. Take my license. Take it. Give it to them."

"Our boss wants to see you dead or see some body parts," Way Low said and swiped at the air with his knife.

"Tell him you killed me. Just tell him. And then, see, you give him my billfold, and then you say you buried me. Body parts still attached."

"And what's to keep you from showing up and making us liars?"

"I'm gone. I'm out of Odessa."

"Out of Texas," Colton said.

"Louisiana. I got friends with oil work in Louisiana. I always wanted to see Arizona."

"Then go."

"What?"

"Right now, go. Get in your truck and drive. Don't even stop until you're at least five hundred miles away."

"Let me get some clothes. Let me pack. Let me get dressed."

"Now," Colton said.

And Way Low looked at Colton. "Let's get at least a finger."

"What about my stuff?"

Way Low looked at Colton, and Colton said, "Two friends, worthless oil field trash, just took off and left everything behind. Happens all the time."

"Okay, okay, okay, I'm out of here."

"Your billfold." Colton pointed his gun down, and Mitch went over to his billfold and handed it to Colton. Colton pulled out credit cards, social security, and license, then gave the wallet back to Mitch.

"I got to have walking around money."

"Rob a liquor store. You get a new license in a new state. And these credit cards disappear, so do their accounts. Get some new ones." Colton looked at Way Low. "Play dead or be dead. Your choice."

"I'm out of here," Mitch said.

When Mitch stood up, looking at him in jockeys made something click in Colton. It was for himself, but also for Bullet, and maybe for Danny Fowler that Colton swung. He was not used to a gun. His job was to use the force of his body. When Mitch got up rubbing the side of his head and saying, "What the fuck?" Colton swung again, and this time he heard the soft whack his left hand made. He kept the gun in his right hand. And as Mitch went down, Colton remembered to pull his finger off the trigger, so he didn't shoot himself or Way Low.

"Whoa, man," Way Low said. "You change your mind. You gonna kill him?"

"Holy fuck. No, you ain't gonna kill me," Mitch said.

And Colton, before he swung for the third time, knew that, with more punches, he could kill Mitch, and he knew he could kill Mitch because he could want to and because he could let himself. He swung the third time. And this time, Colton felt Mitch's face crunch against his knuckles.

"Okay, okay." Mitch said. "So you let me know how much I got to fight back."

Colton bent to crash his bruised left hand knuckles on Mitch's cheek. This swing was not as hard. It only sent Mitch's head in a half-arc. But when Mitch turned back to look at Colton with sorrow and just plain begging in his eyes, Colton saw the busted nose, the spray of blood on Mitch's chest, and the dented in cheek, and Colton knew what Mitch and Harold felt as they beat Danny. He knew how Danny must have looked. And he knew how Mitch and Harold could just have beat the shit out of him and then kept beating him, even though they didn't even plan to go so far as to kill him. It's just what comes of this business. And Colton knew he was beating Mitch not so much because of what Mitch was or what Mitch did but because he wanted to not be here, to not be doing this, and Mitch was the closest son of a bitch to punch. Colton dropped his head because now he had lost the want-to and the will to kill Mitch.

"So what? You finished?" Way Low asked.

"You finished?" Mitch asked.

"You got thirty minutes to pack what you can in your pickup. And don't you even stop at a doctor or an emergency room."

As Mitch got dressed and made several trips back and forth to his truck, with Colton keeping a wary eye on him, Way Low sat down on his sofa and watched Mitch's TV.

Mitch, in jeans and T-shirt, hesitated in the frame of his door, turned around to face Colton and leaned against the frame. "Times up. Get gone," Colton said.

"You not going to shoot me in the back are you?" Mitch asked. Way Low looked at Colton for an answer.

"You know, don't you, that I can never say a thing about this to anybody. And you can never say nothing about this. Only ones ever to know are the three of us. And that's better odds than what Danny Fowler had."

"My story is I fell down."

Slumping, staring at his feet, Colton said, "You say anything. You're gonna be answering questions about Danny. And if I'm anywhere near, I won't shoot you, but I'll just beat the ever-loving shit out of you. For the sheer sake of doing it. Just like you done to Danny."

Mitch stared at Colton and then at Way Low. "I guess I wish things was different." Then he turned back around and walked down the steps to his trailer. Colton got up to watch him drive away.

After he watched Mitch drive off, Colton walked back into the trailer and saw Way Low laughing at some HBO show. "You don't watch TV at home. Why you watching it now?"

"Not as good when you're getting it for nothing."

"Come on, we got to go."

"I thought you was gonna kill him. Point is you could of, no matter what you wanted to do."

"I found out too late."

"All that planning and skipping out of work would have been for nothing."

Way Low pulled a big candle out of his pocket and lit it. "Come on," he said to Colton, and Colton followed him into the kitchen. Way Low turned on the oven burner then blew out the flame to let the butane start to fill the house. "We got to hurry," he said to Colton.

They both ran from the trailer, leaving the lights and the TV on, just like somebody was home, and they got into Colton's Civic, and pulled out of the trailer park slow, watching the trailer as they drove off. As they pulled on to West University, they heard a rumbling and looked over their shoulders to see flames off to the side of the road and in back of them. "This isn't in city limits," Colton said. "But the fire trucks will get here in time to douse the ashes so nobody else's trailer catches fire."

"You think we was mean enough?" Way Low asked.

"You're the one supposed to know."

"I never done this before. I only heard about it."

"Goddamn it, you didn't tell me that."

"I'm Mexican. So, I know. You done really good. You scared me. That's what you're good at, scaring people, not killing them."

* * *

166

Colton rang Mina Fowler's doorbell and waited. He had called from a pay phone and said that he was coming by. The morning was behind him and just creeping up over the straight line of flat earth to the east. He did not want Bullet with him and had called her too, and told her so. This was for him, a reckoning with himself, for himself. Mina answered the door in a plush cotton robe, hair dangling in front of her face, eyes red, swaying from waking up to soon. They stared, and she didn't invite him in, but Colton stepped in, figured he didn't need an invite, even if he never would have just stepped in just two days before.

He walked to the sofa and sat. "You got any coffee?" This too was part of Way Low's plan. Swagger all the way through it, even to the jefe. Don't let anybody see anything in you but meaning what you say. Like you couldn't possibly lie.

"There's a Town and Country convenience store on the way back to town. Stop there; get you some. I plan on going back to sleep as soon as the door closes behind your ass. If you haven't guessed, it's been a busy night for me too."

Colton twisted in his chair as some of his nerve and swagger drained out of him and puddled up under his feet. His tongue caught in his mouth, the way it used to do around Snake, but would no more around him, maybe Bullet no more either. "I got something for you."

He reached in his pocket and threw Mitch's license and credit cards on to the coffee table. Mina crossed one leg right, dead-on in front of the other, the way a fashion model would walk, and one bare thigh after the other sneaked out of the slit in the front of the robe as she walked toward Colton. And Colton imagined the men and the number of them that had seen her like this in the morning. After what they must have done with her the night before, did they feel satisfied, did they run to the bar and brag about the babe they just had the night before, or did they feel like Colton?

Mina picked up the license, held it up, reached into her robe pocket, and pulled out her reading glasses. "This is your proof?"

"Like Bullet said, you want ears?"

"Where is he?"

"Burnt."

"Is he dead?

"Maybe you'll see it on the news," Colton said, felt that puddle, pinched the drain for his nerve, and continued. "His trailer burned down. They probably won't know if a body was even in it or not. But we left him there. He wasn't moving, and he was probably dead. But I ain't sure. But just to be safe, I tied his hands and feet with an electrical cord."

"Did he know why he died?"

"While I was making his head all pulpy, he must have felt what Danny felt. To his credit, he was his smart ass, punk self to the end."

"Danny probably was too."

Mina lifted her eyes from the license and stuffed her glasses back into her robe pocket. "Thank you." She walked to the kitchen counter and grabbed her purse. "Here's a dollar for that cup of coffee. Get a large one. You'll get the rest later. When the money's been properly *adjusted*. If you don't mind, would you show yourself out."

She turned her ass to him and walked back toward her bedroom. Colton rubbed at his imaginary puddle at his feet with the toe of his boot, put his hands in his jeans pockets, and gave a tug up to lift his balls. He left feeling real confidence in his new-found abilities.

* * *

The surprising thing was that Bullet called it just right. Nothing roared or blew. No retribution. There was just one more crack in the dried earth. Unlike Gervin, this affair just simmered a little on Colton's mind, then went away. Lionel should have never walked out on it.

Without worry, Colton concentrated on being in a family. Elena had read that the best thing for a family was to have at least two meals a week together. So, two nights a week, Colton sat with his family for an American meal: roast and potatoes, hamburgers, hot dogs, spaghetti, but no Mexican food. And Elena even said a prayer. She was the only one who would say a prayer.

For their fourth meal together; Arnie, Way Low, Mando, and Colton unfolded their hands and reached for the Church's Fried Chicken. Elena had decided that bought fried chicken or pizza served the same purpose as home-cooked meals.

"We should talk," Elena said.

"What about?" Way Low asked.

And then Arnie, making a sound like a mushy clap, farted. Colton's laugh was tearing up his throat, but he, like everybody, else was silent. Elena couldn't speak, but she stared into Arnie. He wriggled and bowed his head as he should have for the prayer. But then he giggled just like a little boy. And then Way Low started to chuckle. Then Colton let his laugh come up his throat and out of his mouth.

After they started to eat, Elena was silent. Way Low and Arnie talked about what sports Arnie was learning about in school. But Colton studied the strained look on Elena's face. He had seen it before. He had been seeing it more lately. She raised her fork slowly to her mouth, caught Colton looking at her, smiled, but then lost that smile real quick.

After dinner Way Low and Arnie watched TV. And Colton, with Mando standing beside him, watched Elena tote the dishes to the sink, but she did not wash them or stack them in the dishwasher. Instead she walked down the hall to their bedroom and closed the door. Colton walked behind her, and Mando followed him. Colton reached down to pat Mando's head. "Why don't you run to the living room and watch TV with Way Low and Arnie." Mando shook his head. His youngest sensed something about his mother that none of the smarter ones could. Colton kept his attention on Mando, the son he just couldn't understand. "Go on now, Mando. This is adult business. It ain't for you." Mando didn't budge. He just stared at his father and the closed door. "Go on now. I ain't gonna tell you again. You'll just get bored listening to us." This time Mando took two steps backwards, then turned his back to Colton to run down the hall to the living room. Then Colton tried to open the bedroom door. It was locked. He shook the handle, but the door would not budge. He banged harder and said, "Elena." He should never have put a lock on that door.

"Go away," Elena said from behind the door.

"What's wrong?" Colton asked. And looked down to see Mando staring up at him. The boy just couldn't stay away.

"Nothing. Just leave me alone," Elena said.

Colton kicked, but not hard, at the door frame. "Goddamn," he said, forgetting that Mando was beside him. Colton knelt down to be eye-level with his son "Mando, what you doing here?" Mando looked like he had made a new discovery and it was going to make him cry.

"Waiting for Momma."

Colton said, "Come to the living room with me."

Mando shook his head. "I want to see Momma." Colton dropped his head and then walked to the end of the hall and turned to the living room, but he looked around the door frame to spy on his wife and son.

Mando knocked on the door. "Leave me alone," Elena said.

Mando knocked again and said, "Momma."

The bedroom door opened, and Elena stepped out and asked, "What do you want, Mando?"

"To see you. I want to look at you."

"Look at me?"

"Yes, to see the way you look."

Elena stepped up to her son but then pulled back to look at Colton. "Mando, you are different. But please don't stop being my little boy." She scooped him up and hoisted him to her chest. "Oh, mijo, you are still my little boy. You are not yet a big boy." Elena turned into the bedroom and pulled the door closed behind her. Colton turned back into the hall and walked to the door and checked the handle. It was still locked. He shook again. "Go away," he heard Elena say deliberately. Colton dragged himself into the living room, sat, and tried to laugh with Arnie and Way Low at the comedy show on TV.

That night, Colton slept on the couch, and late in that night, he felt something next to him. He started and pushed but saw Mando. "Mando?"

"Daddy," Mando said.

"What are you doing in here?"

"I'm laying with you. I want to lay down next to you before I get too big."

"Mando, what gives you these ideas?"

"I can lay down with Way Low and my Momma. But I don't think I ever lay down with you."

Colton rolled and lifted his boy into the couch so that he was spooning him. "Mando, you a good boy. And one day you are going to be bigger, and you are going to understand more, probably more than Arnie." He squeezed Mando, "So I am going to tell you something, and I want you to remember it."

"Okay."

"I ain't saying anything is gonna happen. But it might be that I might have to leave for a while or for a long time. But I want you to know, even though it ain't likely to happen, that I don't want it that way. And me gone don't make no difference for you. You just go on ahead and go to school and learn the words you always talking about learning and be a big boy.

"Okay," Mando said as his eyes started to close.

"You got to know that I am your father. I ain't giving up on that." And he held Mando, and before too long, Mando was asleep in his arms.

Chapter 12

Bullet heard the whispers in the Blue Lantern as she stood next to Colton and waited for Snake. She had also heard the bar patrons in the Snug Harbor and the Cactus. The locals really said nothing; there was no sound, but a vibrating buzz kind of carried the news through the West Odessa bars. The news was that Colton Parker was a badass.

Bullet was not sure how the whispers got out. In the days since their killings, she had said nothing. Colton would not be so foolish. Besides, him talking about his own exploits would be unseemly, unmanly, not good form. Maybe Snake, but Snake was still cloudy about just what did happen. Maybe Mina. Or maybe one of the conspirators—Mina, Snake, Colton—or Bullet herself—let some little tidbit slip. Or maybe the whispers formed when Mitch's trailer started blazing.

But you could count on Curley. As Bullet listened to the gossip, Curley planted himself at the bar on the other side of Colton. "Goddamn, I'll know better than to tangle with your sorry ass again," he said to Colton.

"You seem determined to start tangling," Colton said. And Bullet thought maybe Colton was turning into a badass.

Curly laughed, "Fucking, drinking, or fighting is what I'm good at, so I don't mind getting it on. But I mean a real badass. Kind of like a heartless mother fucker."

Bullet pushed caution back in her mind and hoped not to scatter any tidbits around. She stepped to the side of the bar so that she could see Curly and asked, "So what makes him such a badass?" Then she couldn't help it. "Why not me?"

Curly chuckled. "You can't be a badass. You're a girl."

"Can a queer be a badass?" Bullet shot back.

"You starting to piss me off,"

"So why am I a badass?" Colton asked.

"We seen you deck that little piece of shit, the one I give the tattoo for talking shit about Danny Fowler. So now the place he is living blows up. You put two and two together."

"You hit him too. Why ain't you the badass?" Bullet asked.

"Hell, I'd of fucked it up. Like I said, I just like fucking and fighting, not burning shit up. I ain't that mean or smart." Curly chuckled, slapped Colton on the back, and said, "Let me buy this man a beer."

"So how you know this guy's place blows up?" Colton asked.

"Hell, I seen the orange glow from my own house."

"So how you know that it was Mitch?"

"Cause I ain't seen him around, and because, that's just what people say."

"Or that's what people want to say," Bullet said. "Me, I ain't seen nothing, and I ain't supposing nothing."

Bullet saw her mistake standing right in front of her. She had not figured on folklore. She had not considered Curly. Colton looked at her as if to ask, "What we gonna do now?"

Curley went on, "I don't know anybody but what would say the little, fake cowboy piece of shit deserved it." Curly took off his gimme cap, and some of the lower halves of his red curls dangled out from under the pasted indentation his cap made on his head. He couldn't keep still, so his curls shook in front of his face.

Curly went on turning the unspoken whispers that Bullet was hearing into a noisy conversation with himself and Colton. Snake walked in. Like Bullet did, Colton looked back over his shoulder to catch Snake's eyes. But then turned his attention back to Curly. Colton might yet have to become a badass and whip the shit out of Curly to shut him up. Curly was Colton's. Snake would be Bullet's problem. Snake walked up to the bar on the other side of Bullet and planted his elbows on it. "You know what I been hearing?" he said.

"Yes, I do," Bullet said.

"What we going to do?"

"Nothing."

Bullet turned to look at him. Snake's bottom lip came up to touch his pencil thin moustache. His eyes were red, like he had been up too long. "Should we even be out like this? Shouldn't we go to the Cactus where things are quieter?"

"Why should we be worried and hiding? We ain't done nothing. Don't put a target on your ass, Snake," Bullet said.

"This whole situation is playing hell with my nerves."

"Be nervous all you want. Just don't say nothing."

Then, Justan Brady walked in.

Bullet's stomach tensed. She pulled her hand up her cheek and over her scar and pushed her hair off her forehead. "Jesus," she heard Snake whisper. Colton looked away from Curly to catch Bullet's eyes. Bullet knew that her eyes twitched in her head as she swung them between Colton and Justan. She made herself think that Justan was a kid, a little shit ass, without the ass or the balls to be any kind of cop. He planted his elbows on the bar next to Snake. And the line of them, at once, on cue—Curly, Colton, Bullet, and Snake—looked at Justan. "Hi, guys," Justan said. "Mind if I pull up a piece of bar?"

Marlene was up to Justan with a bottle of beer. Justan said nothing as he pulled a dollar out of his pocket. And Bullet noticed that on that pocket was an Ector County Deputy Sheriff's badge. "How's your family?" Bullet asked.

"Family's gone to shit."

Colton pulled himself away from Curly and said, "My family's not so good either." Colton and Justan eyeballed each other, and both smiled at the same time.

"I thought you quit. Didn't have the stomach for it."

"Thought I was going to quit. But I didn't. Guess I re-figured my situation. And my stomach and nerves got better. My marriage didn't. You could kinda say it's what I got left."

Curly grumbled to himself just loud enough for everyone to hear. "Can't you have a private conversation?" Snake seemed to be shrinking in on himself, just making himself narrower.

"Well, it's like this," Justan said. "Trailer catches fire out off West University. By the time the truck gets there, it's nothing but smoldering ashes. Person living there may of been in it, may not of. Arson experts done all kind of testing and just don't know if they found burnt pieces of bone or not. Now, this is all outside of city limits, so it's a county matter."

Bullet can't help but interrupt, "So because nobody cares about the case, they give it to you."

"You got it," Justan said. "I'm supposed to see if I can figure anything out."

"What have you figured?" Snake asked, then shrunk back up.

"I figure, whatever it is, it's best not to cost the county much money other than my time."

Justan sipped from his beer, probably for dramatic effect, just to get their attention, just testing them. "But curious thing is, the fella with the burnt trailer worked with and got fired with a fella who just disappeared. He left all his shit in a trailer. And their last known employer, Jake Raven of Raven Welding, says Colton recommended them."

Bullet's stomach dropped. She wanted to stoop down and pick her stomach up. It was probably down by the bar rail, next to Snake's puddle of piss. She glanced over at Colton. His face was firm. Justan started again. "So, I got to ask you, Colton. And I'm glad all of y'all are here to ask you too, 'what you know?'"

"I know Curly knuckle tattooed this one little fucker because he was an annoying homophobe. Ain't that right, Curly?" Colton jumped right in. Bullet wanted to tell him to be careful.

Curly looked over with his curls shaking in front of his eyes and said, "Damn right. He deserved it. He had a nice ass, though. But I wouldn't of done him because of his attitude."

Colton interrupted to get the story over. "Then I hit him too. But I'm more gracious than Curly, so I helped him get a job because I felt guilty."

Justan nodded his head, like it was heavy and he could just barely pick it up. He looked like he was aging right before them. "And funny thing is I did some phoning, and I come up with that one boy's momma. I talked to her, and I left her crying. She ain't heard from him."

Bullet saw Colton stiffen and then he looked at Justan like he wanted to ask, and she knew that he wanted to ask "which boy?" "It's not quite like the ending of that story y'all helped me imagine up about how it would all end. But it might be going that direction."

"You might do good to remember that we were imagining that end. It ain't real," Colton said. And Bullet wished that Colton would just shut up.

Justan smiled at him. "You got me there. Reality is a lot tougher."

Justan stretched up on his tip toes and looked down the line of them. "Where's that other fella? Where's that buddy of yours, that black boy?"

Colton turned to face Justan, said, "He's gone. You want to track him down too? Talk to his momma? I'd like to know where he is myself." Then Colton turned to look past Marlene and into the mirror.

"So y'all know nothing?" Like Justan even had to ask, Bullet thought. "I figured as much. But I figure eventually, either somebody is gonna figure out something or somebody is gonna say something."

Bullet could feel Snake shiver. She felt Colton's stiff muscles. He sucked in some air. "So maybe y'all could listen." Justan paused. They listened. "The law helps us, protects us. You can count on the law to do things that you don't want to do, like dealing with disappearances, and killings, and fires. But if you cross the law, you ain't got the law to protect you no more. I think it's just that simple. I think maybe I'd think it over before I crossed to the other side of the law."

Bullet's stomach and Snake's body were shaking, all because of a piss ant deputy sheriff. It was innocent Curly, who didn't have to be careful, who leaned on his elbows and toed himself up on the bar rail and said, "Oh. I get it. You're in here thinking we had something to do with all these little circumstances. Now I hope you know you're just talking shit."

Colton stared at his large knuckles that had been flattened by jaws and heads and then looked ahead over the bar straight ahead so that Marlene caught his stare and stopped to get an order. Colton spoke for them. "What if the law starts out not protecting you? What if just because of circumstance, you're outside of the law? Let's say you're a wetback or just poor bastard with no choices or a black man like Lionel and living in a mostly white Odessa, then, Justan, where is your theory about the law?"

"I guess you have introduced a good topic for debate," Justan said. "But I ain't here to debate. I'm just still trying to find the whos, whats, hows, and whys. I got the wheres. We'll have to have that debate later."

"I got the price of a beer. You want to debate?" Curly asked.

"But I ain't got the time," Justan said and looked at Bullet. "I got to go home to my empty apartment. But if y'all could help me out any."

As he turned to leave, Colton turned from the rest and said, "Can you smell my ass or something? How is it you always know where I am?"

"It ain't hard to find that baby-shit yellow Honda Civic you drive." Justan started to leave, but he stopped and turned back around to tell them all but mostly Colton, "Colton, you know it's just that the thing is that I can't get Danny Fowler's body out of my mind. He shouldn't of been done like that. There's some more to add to our debate. It's not you I want. I don't want none of you. It got personal. I realized I was, by temperament, a detective. So I need a story. I don't want nobody hurt, but I'm short of story." Justan nodded to them and walked out the door.

After thirty minutes of Curly jabbering while Snake, Colton, and Bullet stared at the back of the bar, Snake said goodnight and headed for the parking lot. Bullet motioned with her chin to Colton. Colton said, "Curly, buy me a beer. I'll be back for it after I talk to Snake and piss." That kept Curly at the bar so that Bullet and Colton could follow Snake outside.

As her boots crunched the gravel, Bullet shivered in the night's coolness and looked at Colton and Snake lit up in the blue from the reflection of the Blue Lantern's portable sign sitting out by the gravel driveway. They looked almost scary. "Holy shit," Snake said. "He's gonna find out."

"Dead men don't talk," Bullet said, and she watched Colton pull himself up rigid against the cold night.

"You mean you want to kill Justan?" Colton asked flat and matter-of-fact.

"Oh, good God, no. Don't even say that shit," Snake said.

Bullet studied Colton's calm face, and while studying, said for him and Snake, "I mean Harold and Mitch don't talk. And neither do we." She shifted her stare to Snake, who stared down at his boots. "Is that agreed?" No answer. "We don't talk, right, Snake?"

"And we got to watch what we say," Colton said.

Snake said, "I'm gonna end up with an ulcer the size of a dinner plate." He toed the gravel. Then, cause he'd left his Lamborghini in his garage, he dared not drive it in nighttime West Odessa, he stepped into his Lincoln. In the distance they heard pistol shots or the banging of equipment, and in the distance, toward the dark horizon, they saw tiny flames from gas runoff or the glow from some pipe, valves, and gauges called Christmas trees. This was boomtime, it was where they lived.

As Snake pulled out, Bullet grabbed Colton as he headed back into the Blue Lantern. "Mitch is dead, ain't he?"

"I said he was."

"We'll have hell to pay if he ain't, and Justan finds him, and he talks."

"That's a lot of *ifs*," Colton said.

"Was that a real question about killing Justan or are you just shitting me?" Bullet asked.

"It's just what come to mind."

"Could you do it?"

"I think I could. I wouldn't want to, but I think I could. We should never have made that story up with him." And Bullet's mind cut back from the hydrogen sulfide-rotten egg smell that covered Odessa to the smell of cigarettes, the spray of hose water on cement, and of gasoline and stagnant water from early morning San Antonio. And her mind left Colton's new-found stern face and voice to Charlie Brodsky's face over a breakfast after a long night of working. Colton, like Charlie, would play out his hand and do what he had to do.

* * *

And then early in the morning, quitting time for a whore, just as Bullet got herself into bed, Bullet got a call from Renee. She was crying, and she mumbled about being confused and wanting to go back to being a good girl and going back home. Bullet asked where Renee was and just got more mumbling. So, she jumped into her pickup and drove in the early morning just before day break in that West Texas rarity, a gentle falling rain. Usually in West Texas, the rain came in bucket-fulls for fifteen or twenty minutes and then went away in this mad, mean outburst against man and nature, as if saying, "so you settled here." But this late-night outburst left some cold mist and fog behind it.

Bullet crept through the flooded downtown streets. Why build drainage when it hardly ever rained? Let the natural draws drain the town. Once in a while, she could see her headlights actually dip below water in a few low spots, but she didn't stall and kept pushing. She closed in on some old two-story apartment buildings in southwest Odessa. She knew Renee lived close by. She splashed and surged through the water to see a skinny kid with streaked blonde hair pasted to her forehead and face and a heavy-with-wet sweater stretching and dripping around her. She pulled up, opened the passenger door, and said, "Get in here." Renee St. Cloud, who stopped being Jennifer Peveto, climbed into the car.

"What are you doing in this rain?"

Renee didn't answer, just looked straight ahead, "I don't know."

"What do you mean, 'you don't know?' You got to know something."

"I got no idea."

Bullet risked taking her eyes from the road long enough to see Renee. Her hands shook. Her shoulders twitched, and the twitch sent a tremor up through her neck and into her head. "How long you been up?"

"I got no idea."

Renee pulled her hands together and put them into her lap, but they still shook. Bullet didn't know what to do but decided to get Renee to her duplex. She drove through the deep water on Second Street and got to the Pancake House just as the first gray streaks for morning showed. She stepped out of the truck and hurried through the rain toward the awning but saw that Renee did not follow her. Renee stayed in the truck. Bullet ran back through the mist to open the door, took Renee's hand, and pulled her through the rain toward the awning. Then, she pulled Renee into the Pancake House and into a booth. Bullet sat on the other side of the booth and watched Renee shiver.

As Bullet tried to think of what to ask, a short man with a giant belly jumped off the stool by the counter and waddled up to them. "Hi, my name is Jake Raven. That name ring a bell?" A bell did ring in Bullet's head, Colton's friend who hired Mitch and Harold. She lifted her head to see a smiling round face with cheeks and chin drooping. "No," Bullet said.

"Well, see, I just thought I recognized you."

"I look like a lot of people."

"Well, see, I just thought you went to Odessa High. What year did you graduate?"

"I didn't. And I didn't go to Odessa High."

By this time the waitress was at the booth and saying, "Jake, leave them alone. Not everybody wants to reminisce about high school." Then Renee slowly lifted her head to look at the waitress and then swiveled her head to look at Jake. And she smiled, as though she had spotted a john. And this look, from this young thing who looked even younger wet, must have scared Jake because he backed up toward his stool and then turned his back to Bullet and Renee. "We want coffee," Bullet said. She looked at dripping Renee. "And we'll split a tall stack of pancakes, with bacon."

When the waitress left, Bullet leaned on her elbows across the table and toward Renee. "Are you okay? Did you take something?"

"This woman lives next door gives me these pills to make me calm. I been taking them since Danny Fowler got killed."

"How many did you take?"

"I mostly just don't stop taking them."

And as the waitress came back with the coffee, Renee sucked in, making herself snort, and just started crying. She tried to breathe in through the crying and gave a whiney howl. That howl brought Jake Raven over, and he asked, "Anything I can do?"

"No," Bullet said.

"Nothing you can do," the waitress said to Jake and eyed Bullet for an answer.

"She'll be all right," Bullet said. "She just needs something to warm her up."

"I think she needs a doctor," Jake said.

"She needs some coffee," Bullet said. But when she slid her forefinger through the coffee mug handle, Renee started shaking and sloshed the coffee around. Renee tried again, and this time, besides the shaking, she couldn't seem to lift the coffee mug.

"You better get her to the emergency room," Jake said.

Bullet got up and pushed herself in front of the waitress and Jake and sat beside Renee. She put an arm around Renee and said, "She's okay. She's okay. She just needs to get warm." The waitress and Jake left, and Bullet worked her outstretched arm up and down Renee's wet back and rubbed the side of her arm and her shoulder. With her other arm, Bullet helped Renee raise the coffee mug to her lips. Renee slurped and gurgled the hot coffee. "Can you eat?"

"I ain't tried," Renee said.

"In how long?"

"Two days. Worse is, I can't sleep. So I just been walking around."

"For how long?"

"I don't know. I think all I been doing is walking around my apartment building."

The waitress brought the stack of pancakes and put them in front of Bullet, and again, she eyed Bullet for an answer. "Just keep Jake, there, occupied," Bullet said.

Bullet took her arm from around Renee, picked up a fork, and cut out a square of dry, syrupless pancakes and held the spongy dough in front of Renee. Renee bit at it and then started mechanically chewing. "What you want to do?"

"I got no idea."

"Think."

Renee stopped chewing. "I think I would like some more of that coffee." So Bullet helped raise the coffee mug to Renee's face. She gurgled some more.

"You got to quit this. You got to get yourself in order," Bullet said.

"I can't."

"Stop that 'ain't,' 'can't,' 'don't know' crap. You got to take control."

"I can't."

"Oh Jesus," Bullet sipped her coffee and said. "Okay, you gonna give me an answer. You may have to think, but you gonna give some kind of answer. So here goes. Best as you can say, what is it is bothering you?" Renee turned to look at Bullet. "Okay, think."

"What you think it is? I mean, I helped kill a man."

"Shit. Shhh," Bullet said and scooted closer and put her arm back around Renee. "I asked, huh?"

182

Renee chewed, and as she did, surprising Bullet that she could even do two things at one time, she said, "I see those boys. And I hear what that Harold said to me. You didn't see his face. It was all twisted and mean. And I swear if you wouldn't of come out from that closet when you did, I swear to God he would of choked me or worse."

In times with pats on her shoulder, Bullet said, "Shh, shh, shh."

"And now why it is I'm taking these pills is that I don't think that I can ever do nothing with no man." She sucked in for some breath and tried to think, but she just couldn't get past the pill fog in her head. "I'm too young. I lost what it is that makes me a woman."

"You just got to be tough. Don't let life do this to you."

"It's done been done."

Bullet hung her head. She tried to clear through the sleep fog in her head. She wanted to retain Renee's services, but Renee was no good to anybody in the shape that she was in. And Bullet knew that she needed to get Renee away from Justan Brady. "What if I took you home?"

"I can't go home like this."

"You got a Momma?"

"Yes."

"Mothers will always take you back."

Bullet got Renee to agree to pack a few things and then come back later and get some rest. In the meantime, Bullet would take her to her mother in Seminole. The two of them packed what they could of Renee's things and stuffed them in the bed of Bullet's truck. And fighting against sleep and the dampness that burned off by the time they got started, Bullet drove Renee to Seminole. And after some driving around town, Renee was able to remember where she lived. Finally, Bullet pulled up to a small wood frame house with all the paint dried by the sun and dragged off by the wind. A swamp cooler stuck out of the roof, and one window was broken.

With Bullet parked at the curb, Renee staggered to the front door and rang the bell. After a few moments, the door opened, and a wide figure stepped into the doorway and hugged Renee, all but pulling her inside the house. Because she was so sleepy, Bullet's head bumped against the steering wheel to wake her up and bring her back to staring at the front door of that shabby house.

Then that large figure came walking toward the truck, and Bullet saw that it was a woman in a bathrobe. The bathrobe could barely cover the woman's girth, and Bullet wondered how this could be the mother of skinny Renee. The woman stopped in front of the truck. Bullet leaned across her seat and rolled down her window. "My name is Gwyn Turk. I'm her foster parent. She's got no real parents. But I raised her through junior high and what she had of high school."

Bullet nodded, "Can you help her?"

"I ain't gonna get paid nothing for this."

"She's in trouble."

"I can see that. She's passed out in there. Just exhausted."

Bullet grabbed her purse, pulled out her wallet, then pulled out a hundred-dollar bill. "I've got this."

"That ain't even gonna be a start."

"Clean her up. Get her a job at the Dairy Queen to pay you back. But she has to get out of Odessa."

The large woman put her forearm up against the frame of the window and peered in through the open window at Bullet. "She wasn't as tough as she thought, huh?"

"She is just a girl. How could she be tough?"

"I take it you know," the woman said. But before Bullet could get angry, the woman said, "Let's unload the truck. What ain't in here, just sell or burn."

Bullet stepped out of the truck and felt a cool chill in the wind that had just picked up. As she and Gwyn got the last of Renee's stuff into the house, Bullet asked into the wind, "What became of her real parents?"

"Father's worthless. Mother's locked up for distributing drugs." And though she wasn't asked, Bullet followed Gwyn into the house and saw

Renee passed out, asleep, exhausted, or all three on the sofa. "I know who you are, or rather, what you are."

Bullet turned, took a step back. "And what is it you think I am?"

"I'm not trying to be rude here. I'm just guessing what she was doing in Odessa. I'm just guessing what you are."

Bullet shrugged, found herself unable to admit what she was, said, "I'm a friend."

"Well, you brung her back. She just turned nineteen, you know. She dropped out of school and left here when she was seventeen." Bullet winced. That meant Renee was working for her as a minor. She didn't want to think about the fines or the prosecution. "You might have saved her soul."

Bullet stared at large Gwyn. She pushed her mind into thinking but couldn't. Finally, with Gwyn looking at her, Bullet said, "You write me down a name and address, and I'll mail a hundred a week until I can't afford it no more." Gwyn came back with a pen and a notepad. As she wrote down her address, Bullet said, "That make what I am any better?"

Bullet showed herself out and left Renee as Jennifer Peveto, another woman's problem, and she followed the wind to Odessa and wondered if Jennifer Peveto could recover her soul from Renee St. Cloud.

Chapter 13

In early fall of 1983, less than two years later, the boom had busted. The bars in West Odessa all had the same sign. It said, "An oilfield prayer: please God, give us another oil boom, and I promise not to piss this one away." New glass office buildings that never housed one executive were deserted and had broken glass and tumbleweeds inside of them. Every other house had a *For Sale* sign, but no one bought. People just walked away from the mortgages and didn't even put a *For Sale* sign up. The R.V.s and mobile homes in the chained off trailer parks were gone—towed off or rotting. Unused pumping machinery and rigs rusted in the vacant storage lots that Way Low used to watch.

With oil crowds gone and Baptist and Church of Christers bitching, cops and Texas Alcohol and Beverage Control busted mom and pop bars—easier to get than the bigger, better bars that catered to the Baptists and Church of Christers. Odessa no longer liked its official slogan, "Odessa is Crude." It wanted a safe, God-respecting, family-safe community. Renee St. Cloud, Bullet heard, got Jesus and went to work at a Dairy Queen in Seminole, Texas. Without Renee St. Cloud and the others, Bullet had to close her operation at the First Quality Inn. She kept her duplex but turned her business completely legit, renting her bars to one bankrupt owner after another but keeping the rights to her real treasures, the vending machines. Barbara Howard lost the Cactus, so Bullet took it over and tried to run a bar and a business office, all but living in the place, working twelve-hour days. Snake Popp lost his illegal dancers and his Lamborghini. The Stampede closed two days a week and few of the high-rolling gamblers ever came to town. Snake's wife stayed with him, for now. So did Colton. And to make some extra money, with Bullet's advice and recommendation, Colton repoed cars for Bill Sears. He got shot at and shot back. Way Low lost his job. He walked with Mando and Arnie to school, and he was there to get the boys and walk them back home. But Way Low developed a limp. During the boys' school hours, he listened to his transistor radio, and at nights, he watched TV shows.

Elena had gotten a job as a secretary for the school system. And she stopped talking to Colton.

And in the midst of the trouble, Lionel showed back up. And Bill Sears put him to work with Colton repoing cars. He took to it well.

Curly had little or no work, so he just stayed at the Blue Lantern. The Tank closed. The Snug Harbor closed. The Oil Show was coming up, but people said the high rollers would be crying in their beers instead of drinking them and whoring. The whores lacked enthusiasm, so Odessa did not plan to increase its per capita ration of whores. Mina Fowler was rich enough to escape any real harm. Mando started the second grade. He made sense of the words and figured them out, but the numbers were tough.

In early fall or late Summer of 1983, just after closing, the sun still burning into roofs and parked cars, Colton sat in the dark coolness of the Stampede Lounge. When the boom left so did the smoke, so the Stampede was comfortable, blocking out the harsh light and heat outside. And Colton sipped his frosty mug of beer and watched the dancer in front of him. Since he first saw her nearly two years before, she had learned to balance on her high heels and even gyrate in a way that a man would like. What spoiled that escape from the heat was that the Stampede couldn't protect Snake or Colton from the bust.

Snake shook his head and said to Colton, "I got nothing. I got a family to feed. My wife's making nearly as much as I do giving school kids pee-pee passes. It ain't right." Snake gestured towards the dance floor. "You see any women you would pay to see naked?"

"She's got better," Colton said.

"Well, evidently, nobody else thinks so. And evidently nobody wants to see any women dance in here naked. So, I got nothing."

Snake kept his silver, pencil thin moustache. And he smoothed the silver wings on the sides of his head before he returned his head to his hands. "Just look at her. She still can't dance a lick," he said.

"No, I been watching. From what I remember, she is better."

"A lot of good her better does me."

"Collections? You got people who owe you. Even without Lionel, I could hurt some people."

Snake pulled his head out of his hands to look at Colton. "Anymore, you kinda like hurting people. You got used to it or what?" Colton didn't answer. Snake said not just to Colton but all of Odessa, "Yeah, people owe me money, but too many to ass whip. And what if I did send you out? You'd whip their asses, and still no money, and still you're broke because then I can't pay you."

"Security?"

"Who can afford to gamble? I can't get a game going. It's like they just pulled the cork and everything that made this town enjoyable and profitable for us just swirled out."

"You mean the oil?"

"It's not just the oil. It's the spirit of people. It's gone. We're beat. We're all pussies now. Might as well pray and ask God to forgive us while we're starving to death."

"What's Bullet say?" Colton had seen less of her. She could no longer afford to hire him away from Snake. She gave him what small jobs she could. But Bill Sears' repos and moving, hauling, and repairing vending machines couldn't feed small boys.

"Bullet says it will all come back. Says to hunker and wait. She might as well be telling us to pray."

Colton felt and heard a whoosh next to him and looked to see from chest down a man pulling out a chair. And when that man sat, Colton saw that he was Justan Brady with a straw cowboy hat making his forehead and eyes dark.

"Shit," Colton said and turned just in time to catch Snake push himself up and say, "Enjoy yourselves."

Colton turned back to Justan, who pulled a wad of bills out of his shirt pocket, and suddenly the clumsy dancer was in front of him pushing her crotch in and out, right in front of Justan's face. "There's plenty of other tables," Colton said.

"I came here to see you."

"You know everywhere I go?"

"You still drive that little yellow Honda Civic. Like I told you, it ain't exactly inconspicuous."

"So how long you made it a habit to follow me around?" Colton looked down at his hand to see a slight tremor shake his beer.

"Relax. I ain't been following you for some time. I come here to talk."

Justan's face went forward then back as the clumsy dancer poked her crotch at him. "Irony is my life got better. I'm an Odessa policeman now. I got a real uniform. I got a pension, and mostly I drive to wrecks and direct traffic and try to stop family disturbances. And I'm engaged now. To a good woman. And she is pregnant. What can I say, we started a little early." Justan shrugged.

Colton thought about his family. Mostly, he didn't see Elena. She came in late, way after her job, and Colton didn't ask himself or Way Low about what she did. And if he didn't have some kind of nickel and dime task from Snake or Bullet, he drank beers until the beer bars closed, and then he might go to the Cactus to talk to Bullet, sometimes until the sun came up, mostly to avoid being at home. "My life got worse," Colton said. "My family still ain't so good. My father-in-law is raising my boys. He might be making a mess of it."

Justan nodded his head. He turned away from the clumsy dancer, and Colton saw her disgusted look as she realized that she was dancing just for herself. "My life is better from that time when I was trying to solve crimes and didn't have the sense to just solve nothing and let just deserts work themselves out. From that time, when I'd come home and find my wife eating a dinner of Fruit Loops because she don't want to cook but does want to cuss at me for giving her no better than Fruit

Loops. But one thing has stayed. It's Danny Fowler. I feel like I should of cared. Somebody should of cared. And somebody should of done something. And then I think of them boys that killed him, the ones I named Mel and Randy, and I wonder what must be going through their heads. And what if they got families, and they are living with some kind of awful guilt that is eating up their livers and their families. And then I figure that those two boys might be dead too."

Justan paused and cocked his head, making a shadow across his face with his cowboy hat. Colton turned away from Justan to watch the poor stripper, but he said, "What do you want from me?"

"I'm off duty. I'm not working. I'm telling you *I* want to know. I got to know something. I want to know there is some principle at work in the world, some kind of design, some kind of justice."

"Thought you believed justice was for the courts and police and betterment of the populace?"

"I'd settle for knowing."

"Maybe you need Jesus?"

"I'd start looking for answers in the church if I thought they was there."

"Sounds like you need some forgiveness and mercy your ownself. Sounds like you ought to be in church howling about forgiveness and mercy instead of looking for justice."

"Not justice, just answers."

Colton turned to look at Justan and to drive home the point. "I got no answers."

Justan turned to look at the dancer, "You know, though, I just want to think, just maybe, those boys I called Randy and Mel, were really named Mitch and Harold. I found that out on my own. I found Mitch's mother. Seems he's still alive. But she don't know where. And I ain't said nothing to nobody."

Colton went to the bars not just to escape his failing family but to forget Mitch. Up to now, Colton had seen Justan in a bar, but Justan was just having a beer and not asking questions about Mitch or anybody else. He once even had a few beers with Justan. But still Mitch haunted Colton. But listening to Justan, Colton realized he could forget Mitch. So, just like that, he did. Justan could keep the burden of worry for himself. But he still felt some meanness toward Justan, and he wanted to give some of that uneasiness and constant liver-gnawing worry to Justan. So, he told Justan. "I never said nothing to you before, but all you ever had was the testimony of a whore. Hell, you probably busted her. And she's the only one ever said it was two boys. For all you know, she could of killed Danny Fowler. And all you got is the coincidence that two boys disappeared right after Danny Fowler. There's probably no relation."

"I'm asking you."

"And I'm saying I got nothing for you."

Colton looked at his beer, just as Justan did, and Colton saw some relief in the reflection of his glass.

"Well, thank you," Justan said. Then he asked, "What is it you do?"

"Whatever I can."

And Justan must have felt mean himself because he said, "I hope you get lucky like me and get a good job and find a family." But more than meanness, Colton felt grateful to Justan for relieving him of Mitch.

* * *

Colton did get lucky. A few nights later, Colton was in front of a beer at the Blue Lantern to ponder and forget. He bought Curly beers because Curly had spent what money he had and was well on his way to passing out at the Blue Lantern. Since he was out of work, he had all day to drink. "Goddamn, Colton, if it turns out you ain't the best friend I got," Curly said as he picked up his latest free beer. What Colton had come to ponder, despite Curly, was what Bullet had just told him.

In her office at the Cactus Lounge, she had given him a number to call. It was the number of a friend of a friend in Fort Worth. This friend heard from a broke, out-of-work former Odessan about this cold-hearted, badass in Odessa, this Colton Parker. And he talked to Bullet. He needed a badass. Someone who was cool, could bust a head, could pull a trigger. There could be a lot of money involved. Now, Colton held this business card between his fore and middle fingers. The card was for a broke and closed-down welding company, but on the back, Bullet had written a dollar sign, the name *Charlie Brodksy*, and a number. Colton felt like he was a monster man diving into the on-coming blockers.

Bullet told him, "I go way back with Charlie. I owe him, and he owes me. Kind of like us."

"We owe each other, all right," Colton said.

"Don't be mean."

"I have a family."

"Do you?"

"Now who's mean?"

"Then do the right thing by them. Get them some money."

Colton sat at a table in a dark corner on one side of the bar with Curly's scratchy, raw voice wearing out on him. He drank until Curly's ragged head fell forward, and his chin caught on his chest, and his gimme cap fell onto the table. The shadows from outside crept into the bar. The juke box played nothing but weepy country western songs. A couple tried to dance, but mostly it was oil field trash, trying to drink away the bust in the oil field and their lives.

As he raised a glass to his lips, he saw a tall man in a cowboy hat step into the bar and hold the door open. And stepping in after him, smiling and patting at the man was Elena. She was in a miniskirt that just did cover her butt; her hair was pushed up to the back of her head; and her high high-heels must have made her struggle to get across the gravel and into the bar, maybe even holding on to her gentleman friend. Colton had never seen her in this skirt; he could not remember a time when she dressed like this for him. He could not remember her dressed like this at all.

Colton started to rise, but his momentum caught in his thighs and then just wore out so that he plopped back down in his chair. He scooted the chair farther into the dark shadow in the dark bar and watched the man and Elena at the bar.

Elena laughed at the man. And before they got through their first beer, she stretched on her tip toes to kiss him. And he pulled his hand slowly down her back until he reached her butt and smoothly yet firmly pulled his open palm over her convex butt. Elena did not brush his hand away but grasped it in her hand to keep it planted on her ass. And anyone watching could have figured how the night would end for those two.

And Colton wondered why he did not get up and pound that man in the cowboy hat with his thick knuckles. Hell, he could have gotten Curly to do it for him. If Gervin and Mitch could happen, then why was this man still standing and patting his wife's butt? But in pondering and forgetting in the Blue Lantern, Colton had put brakes on that surge that made him play scared, that sent him charging into the line. He would charge, would forget all hesitation and thought and go into it without fear or conscience, if he needed to. But now he had learned to contemplate before he got to needing to. What Colton realized was that Elena protected him from wanting women. He had her, though he rarely saw her and hadn't done nothing but lay beside her and snore. He had been wound so tight with worry about his fate, his friends' fates, his family's fate that he had not had time to worry about what he should be getting from his wife. And while he wanted what every man wants from a woman, he was not sure what else he wanted or needed from Elena. But what he realized about her now was that she needed a man. She was still young and pretty enough to make men's teeth itch. And, even if he didn't get what he should naturally want a woman for, she needed that from a man.

Then there was him. When he went to Sul Ross State University as a monster man and played scared, he left his family. He no longer had one. Then he found Elena and got Way Low, Arnie, and Mano. If he left them now, gave up a second family, with what he was and what he'd done, he wouldn't have another family, probably never would.

So, Colton sneaked away from the fuzzy-headed Curly, went around to the other side of the bar, out the backdoor, and then to his car. He drove home, hoping to get there before Elena, so he could talk to Way Low.

* * *

When he got home, Way Low was sitting in the middle of the couch watching the commercials between the *Hill Street Blues* and the ten o'clock news. When Colton stepped in, Arnie took that as a clue to go to bed. Mando lingered to talk to his Daddy. And Colton grabbed him and swung him around and said, "Little Mando."

Then Way Low, who Colton knew was becoming both the boys' father and mother, told Mando to run to bed because it was late. Mando ran down the hall, no doubt on sticker scarred feet, and climbed into bed with his brother.

Colton sat on the couch, and Way Low scooted down to get a good view of him. Colton stammered and cleared his throat and fidgeted. Way Low said, "I can see this ain't good. Why don't you just try saying it out like it is?"

"I got to ask something that might really be disturbing."

"Like you disturbing my shows. What can be so disturbing?"

"I just seen Elena all dressed up. With a man."

Way Low's eyes narrowed, and he shifted his gaze toward the TV. What he saw was the newly-hired attractive and buxom Mexican weather lady giving her report. He got up, limped to the set, and turned it off. He sat back down. "How did Elena look? Was she dressed nice, look all sexy?"

"She looked real nice. I don't remember ever seeing her like that."

"Mexicans expect that the man can run around, chase pretty women, once he gets married. That's just the way it is. Man got this pair of fuzzy little balls making all the decisions for him. Can't help it. But the woman is supposed to stay home and take care of the kids. And doing that she going to turn into a mama and get fat. Can't help it. So with a fat wife taking care of his babies, a man goes looking for a still young, un-mama woman. You get my point?"

"I don't think I ever get your point."

"If she stays slim and pretty, then she's probably not being a mama and is out looking." Way Low shrugged. "You just told me Elena stays pretty."

"Prettier than ever. I wouldn't have guessed."

"I would have. Don't you pay attention? You two don't *see* each other, and I mean with like your eyes *see*."

"We're married" Colton said. Way Low shrugged. "What am I going to do?"

"I wouldn't go beat up no boyfriends or nothing. That leads to more trouble."

"What about them boys?" Colton asked.

"You still the Daddy."

"You're telling me I already lost Elena?"

"How much your boys see you?"

"You're telling me I lost them too." Way Low nodded.

Colton stood up and paced. "I have a chance to take a job. It requires me to beat the shit out of people, maybe kill them. I ain't got all the details. But it'll pay me more. But to take it, I got to leave. Now I got to decide how to best take care of this family. Tell me what you think."

Way Low leaned back in his chair and let the recliner lift his feet off the floor. He stared at the toes of his feet in his socks. He had been complaining that his toes hurt him. Then he thought. Laying back and speaking, he gurgled his words, "Like you said, you lost them. What you think is the best way to take care of your family?"

"That a real question?"

Way Low slid the recliner's leg-rest down and stared at Colton. "No. It ain't. I thought you could figure it out."

"Take the money?"

"What else you got to give them? And second, right now, what's more important than money. Elena don't make none. I got no job. I think I told you once before. First job a man got is his family, then his friends—no not friends, his compadres—then his job—if he got one. He should take care of family, then friends, then job. If he can, in the best way he can."

"And I got only one way." Way Low nodded his head.

Colton paced and Way Low said, "Should I tell you good-bye?"

Colton didn't answer Way Low but rounded the corner from the living room to the hall. And there he saw Mando and Arnie's backs as they quickly tip-toed back toward their bedroom door. "Hey, goddamn it. What are you two doing?" Arnie ran into the bedroom, but Mando turned back around.

Colton's eyes settled on Mando. "What you heard?"

"We wasn't listening," Mando said.

"Go get your brother," Colton said, and Way Low was behind him standing in the doorway with his face hanging down. Mando turned to go into the bedroom. But Arnie appeared at the door to take up for his brother.

"What do you think you heard?" Colton asked them.

"We heard nothing," Arnie said in this defensive way that sounded like he was already practicing denying the crime.

Colton looked at both of them, and Arnie had this cocky smile. Colton turned to look at Mando and told him, "And you heard nothing." He dropped to a knee to look at Mando and Arnie eye to eye. "Well, you may have heard some talking. But you 'heard' nothing. You never say you heard anything, even to yourself." Colton was trying his best to be a father.

And then Way Low was walking down the hall toward them and saying, "Oh shit. You two. You two. When you going to learn to mind? You just lucky, old Way Low is too old and now has got bad toes to whip you."

196

Like he was chasing chickens, Way Low held out his hands and swished Mando and Arnie to their room. There are "good nights," not "good-byes." But before Way Low could turn out the light, Colton grabbed Mando and was making the whirring sound by blowing air through his lips and was twirling him above his head for one last airplane ride. The two brothers ran to their beds. And when Colton took a last look and was satisfied that his two boys were okay and then turned out the light and said, "Now go to sleep," he heard Arnie whisper in the dark from his bed to his brother, "I think Daddy did something bad."

A few minutes later, Colton banged on his mother's door. Helen opened the door and tilted her head to one side when she saw Colton. She opened the door to let him in, but he stayed outside. "I just heard Arnie say that his daddy had done something real bad. I have."

Helen's eyes smiled, and without meanness, she said, "I guessed at that." Then her mouth smiled.

"I'm leaving. I got opportunities."

Helen dropped her head and snorted, probably to keep from crying, brought her smiling eyes back up, clouding with a few tears and said, "Why don't you come in? Have a beer."

"I'm afraid if I do, I won't be able to do what I got to."

Helen started nodding. She reached into her pocket, pulled out a pack of cigarettes, got one in her mouth, and lit. "I got to do something. I got to have my hands filled. How about I go back in and get a beer?"

Colton shook his head. "I got other people to see."

Helen nodded and sucked in on her cigarette. "There is some to that genetics. You, me, your daddy, we always running but just stay stuck." She reached out to touch his face. "You be careful out there doing whatever it is you're fixing to do." Colton raised his hand to put against the back of her hand that was on his face. "And try to be good."

Colton put one foot in back of the other to put some distance between him and his mother, then turned his back to her.

* * *

In Bullet's office at the Cactus Lounge, Colton fidgeted in front of Bullet. Bullet squeezed the card table that served as her desk and eyed him as he told her his story about Elena. She felt this shiver, like indigestion, run up from her stomach and into her throat, and she wanted to let that shiver out with the words, "I knew, but I couldn't bring myself to say, and this is just what happens."

While she was thinking that, Colton said, "I just didn't want to be home at that house when she got home. I been sitting out there drinking for an hour. Now it's closing time. I've made up my mind. I want that job."

Bullet knew that Colton never had a choice, that this was the direction that he had been headed for years, but she had not dared to say what she knew. She knew that she had a place in her heart already scooped out and saved for Colton. It was somewhere next to Charlie's place but not as big.

"We'll miss you," she said. "I'll miss you. I'll tell Snake."

"I can tell him. I'll drop by. I owe him that."

"In matters like this, you ought to just disappear. Just get out of town. Start off new, fresh. Get a new name."

"A name like yours?"

"It's a good name. A sweet name. Mine is *Christina*."

"So that's it?" Colton asked, and Bullet nodded. "And this is it for me in this town."

Bullet's hand trembled just a bit as she thought about her own exile from San Antonio, about Renee's exile from Odessa, only taking her pill habit with her, about Lionel's exile. Now it was Colton's turn. "I wish it was different. And up in Fort Worth, you got to be careful. Like Justan Brady said, you ain't gonna have the law, so you got to protect yourself first."

"Is there like a school you can go to?"

"Don't worry. Charlie Brodsky will teach you."

"Okay, then. I'll disappear," Colton stood. "Can I start tomorrow?"

"You can sleep here tonight, if you want." Colton nodded. Bullet pushed herself into thinking more. "Of course, if you really want, you can sleep at my place, with me." Bullet saw that Colton was thinking, considering her offer, and was flattered. "Consider me a going away present from me." Though she had just offered to be his whore, Bullet felt nothing like a whore. She could feel her soul.

Colton thought, then said, "No, I'll stay here. I better keep it all business. Otherwise, I may get confused. And I may back out. But I'm gonna think about it. And I probably ain't gonna go to sleep."

Bullet stepped from around her desk and threw her arms around Colton and squeezed him. When she pulled away, they were both crying. And Bullet reached up and felt the scar on her cheek because she wanted to look better. And then she remembered the scar on her chest and fought against the droopy chin, but she lost because she was remembering her scars and her aging and her life because she was remembering all that she had lost and was thinking of all that she may yet lose because, like she said, their ways were set.

"Christina," she told Colton. "It was a name my momma liked."

Colton stretched a shaking hand to her scar and slid his hand down the side of her face. And Bullet closed her eyes to feel that hand and shuddered. "Once after my surgery, with the healing scars, Danny Fowler came to see me. And he did just what you are doing."

Bullet shuddered, let her shoulders slump, let tears form for the first time in years, and felt the flat of Colton's hand on her scarred face, Colton said, "I hope we done right by him."

Mando

Part II

Chapter 14

Youthful energy, the idea that they were rough characters, or boredom made Arnie and his friend Henry itch so bad that they barely let the sun go down before they walked into the convenience store to rob it. The summer sun left an orange stripe across the sky in back of the store. And bright yellow outlined Arnie and Henry as they marched through the shimmering heat waves toward that glass capsule of candy, beer, and cigarettes. Their hands were in their pants pockets, which bulged with their 9mm pistols.

Mando, nowhere near grown, sat in Henry's Subaru with his hands squeezing the wheel, his knuckles turning blue, and his neck stiff from jerking it around, so he could see Arnie and Henry making their way into the store. Then the lights for the store buzzed to life, and the world was half-light, half dark.

Mando had watched Arnie grow up to this moment. On his way through school, Arnie got mean or pissed off. He wanted more and slouched around the house bitching about what he wanted or didn't have until Elena finally told him to straighten himself out. The world don't have to care about you, she told him. Don't expect it to. Arnie didn't listen to Elena because neither he nor Mando could account for the blur of cowboy hats and boots that were her boyfriends. But Mando, in a primitive way, could see that his mother was keeping her early-middle-age desires separate from her boys and Way Low. The boots and hats never stayed very long in the house. He told his brother that boyfriends didn't matter. Then Way Low took his turn and told Arnie he better just get used to the world not giving a shit about him. Nobody gave a shit about you, Way Low told Arnie. And Arnie told him that he was going to make the world give a shit.

Arnie, by the time he was fixing to graduate high school, had become the bad boy that other Odessa High parents told their sons and daughters not to talk to. And Henry was another bad boy, more clearly Mexican than Arnie and Mando, poorer even than them, with a bigger pissed-off attitude toward the world than even Arnie. Arnie and Henry got together. And when they decided they would show the world, they would veer off the road toward the shitty low-level, work-a-day lives they were headed to, they told Mando that he would be the driver.

Mando squeezed that steering wheel because he didn't want to be with them. He was happy on that road to a shitty, low-level, work-a-day life. He didn't begrudge the world. He wasn't pissed off at it. He would have liked to have dropped out of the world, but knowing he couldn't escape it, he had decided to hide from it. And he had done a good job. Nobody noticed him. But then Arnie and Henry decided that Mando should be their driver.

Over his shoulder, Mando saw Henry holding his arm straight out in front of him, aiming at a Korean guy behind the counter. Mando couldn't see the pistol, only the barrel, and it looked like Henry was pointing a really long finger at the guy just doing his shitty, work-a-day job, just trying to get by. And this Korean guy crouched, like he was bending for something, and then he straightened up, and because of the counter, Mando couldn't see what his hands were on. Then, like a girl who sticks out her tongue real quick, a yellow flame with a red tip darted out of Henry's pistol barrel, then got sucked back into that barrel. The Korean flinched but kept on straightening. Another tongue darted out. Then the counter exploded. Then another red, blue, and yellow explosion went off in front of the counter. And Henry stepped back, faster and faster, staggering, held his hands up, then fell below Mando's line of sight.

Mando twisted the keys, but the car was still running without his even knowing or remembering. He put it into gear, but remembered Arnie, so he slipped the gear shift back into park. In those seconds, the world got dark, and Arnie came running out of that store with an explosion behind him. He ran flat footed and carried a lone twelve pack of beer. Arnie realized he had the beer and flung the twelve pack away from himself, and when it hit, several cans of cold beer rolled out of the carton and spewed and gyrated on the asphalt. Arnie got in and looked at Mando like he had no way of explaining. Mando hit the gas.

But they went nowhere. The car was still in park. With his foot still on the gas, Mando shifted. Gears ground and the car shot out. "Hurry, hurry," Arnie said.

Mando pressed down with his toes. The little Subaru took off like it was a plane about to lift off the ground. "No, not here. The other way. The way we planned," Arnie said.

"I can't remember."

"Turn."

So, with his toes still on the gas, Mando tried to turn. Or the car turned itself. It shot off the road. Mando tried to steer, but the car paid no attention to him. And out of respect for Arnie, Mando kept his foot on the gas—right up to the time the car hit the telephone pole, and then even after. Mando's foot just kept going, right through the manifold, and Mando could hear the cracking of his toes and then of the bones in his foot, and then he felt a dull, hot throb make its way through his leg. His seatbelt probably kept all of him from going out through the manifold. But still, Mando kept trying to press the gas, but his smashed foot couldn't press, so the car stopped. Mando looked over at Arnie. Arnie's seatbelt had kept him from going through the windshield, but his seat had come detached. Arnie's head pushed against the dashboard. He pushed backward with his head and shoulders. His seat fell back into place and pulled him with it and his head off the dashboard. Blood was running out of a long gash in Arnie's forehead. Mando tried to get out, but he couldn't move his right leg and could do nothing with the foot on the end of it. He looked at Arnie again, and his face folded forward.

Arnie held his face in his hands and then tried to push it back into place. With one hand holding his face together, blood seeping out between his fingers, he opened the passenger door with his other hand. Arnie was out the car door and running into the now dark. Mando wanted to go with his brother, but he couldn't make his foot move. The last Mando could see of Arnie was him holding his face with one hand and pulling a strand of barbed wire with the other hand, and stepping through that barbed wire fence that lined the street, then running off, cross-country, through the brush, into the dark.

Then pain started searing up Mando's leg, into his hips, on up into his chest. Now he couldn't move his leg. He tried shaking it against the pain, and when that didn't work, he tried shaking his whole body. Convulsing and twisting made the pain hotter, and Mando reached the threshold, the end of pain, and his body and mind just got numb. Then he saw faces.

The first was a pimply face of the paramedic who poked and groped Mando with his rubber-gloved hands. The face of another paramedic, a woman with short hair, smiled as she gave him the first shot of pain killers. Then time and space went away. The next face was a woman's too. Mando could tell by the eye-liner, molded lashes, and sculpted eyebrows, not by anything else, because she had a surgical mask stretched across her nose and mouth. Her face was close to Mando's. She said something to him, and he could hear, but he couldn't make sense of words. For the time being, he had lost his fascination in words. And then, feeling himself being shaken and hearing his name, he saw his mother's face way too close to his. She pulled back from him. And there, behind was the last face, Way Low's. His mother's stern look accused him of awful crimes, mostly against her. Way Low's face looked amused.

"What do you think?" Elena asked and straightened herself and turned slightly away from him. As was his habit, Mando said nothing. "You not going to just sit there. You going to tell me about this?"

Way Low hobbled to the side of the bed and sat in a chair. His face was between Mando's mother's face and Mando's sight. "You know what you done to your foot?"

Mando shook my head. This was the first that Mando had been really awake, so how was he to know? "They had to pry it out of the car. It was jammed into nothing. Just a little baby foot. Just toes on a stub."

Mando twisted to see his mother. She was crying—for his foot or for his crime, he didn't know. Way Low went on, "You got tough toes. They okay. But you crushed all kinds of bones in your foot. So they put in pins and plates and wires and make you a new foot. You got metal now instead of bones."

Elena shoved her way in front of Way Low so that her face was now between the two of them. "What are you thinking when you do this? Why did you do this? You think I raise you like this?" Mando began to think about the way he was raised, and mostly it seemed like he wasn't raised. He followed, did as he was told. He listened. He read whatever he could get my hands on—just to understand words. "You think this was right what you did? You think it was smart? It was just dumb. But I want to know what you was thinking."

Way Low pulled on Mando's mother's shoulder, "Elena, come on. Mijo, he don't know what he thinks."

Elena whirled around, "You shut up. You might have given him this idea." Then her face poked back at Mando. Way Low looked hurt.

Arnie had come to Mando and told him that he had this idea and that Mando should help him. And so Mando listened. Unlike Mando, without things to occupy his mind, Arnie got upset. He was raised, but not by their mother, but by where they lived and what they saw and what they wanted and what they watched on the TV that told them what they should want. Arnie always figured that he and Mando were just left out. They were cursed by Colton Parker, or rather, whether they liked it or not, he and Mando were just like Colton. And whether their mother and their teachers or the bright kids with promise liked it or not, Colton was right about himself and about his boys. They were just always short of the line. They couldn't carry a football or shoot roundballs or score high on the achievement tests or dress right or become popular. And such as they were, Arnie argued to his younger brother, no one was there to take care of them, give them a job, make sure they made good. Way Low knew this, Arnie had said. Their mother used her boyfriends to hide from this, Arnie had said.

Arnie had this friend, Henry, and Henry was like them, and so Henry drove around Odessa, thinking and dreaming. And what he thought was how easy it would be to rob this one particular convenience store—because the gas was too high, so nobody ever stopped, because, even though it was on a major interstate, that interstate was out of town and so no cops or people lived close by. And once Arnie and Henry robbed this one, what was to say they couldn't start knocking off more convenience stores and liquor stores and bars closing down late at night. And then, when they graduated or didn't graduate or dropped out, Arnie and Henry could just take off to wherever there was for them, someplace that wasn't oil-field broke Odessa. But they thought they needed a driver or a shotgun to cover them—at least for this first store. So that was where Mando came in.

"Well, you gonna answer me?" Mando's mother asked.

"I didn't think," Mando said. "It was Arnie's idea."

"Well, you better start thinking." Elena started to cry.

"Mando, Arnie's face is gonna be crooked," Way Low said.

Mando remembered. "Did they catch him?"

"Sure they caught him. Where was he going to go? Running across desert out there, bleeding, holding his face together." Way Low waved his hand around to show his disgust. "The county for sure ain't going to fix his face right. And we ain't got the money for no reconstruction surgery. Arnie's going to be ugly."

"What about that Henry boy?"

"He's dead." Way Low looked at his daughter, then at his grandson. "And Arnie is ugly. And you probably going to be crippled."

"That store owner?"

"The doctors pulled some bullets out of him. His left arm might not be much good, but he's still breathing."

"And what's gonna happen to Arnie?"

Elena wailed. Way Low shrugged. "The police are gonna want to see somebody punished. It's going to be Arnie or you or both you."

Way Low pushed himself up and put an arm around Elena, "Why you want to do this?" she asked.

"You supposed to sleep," Way Low said.

"Is it night or day?"

"It's late in the night or early in the morning. I don't remember no more. It's still dark."

Mando looked down at his right leg. There were bandages all round it. "You sleep."

They turned for the door, but Elena turned back around, "You want me to stay with you?"

Mando shook his head. "You go home. I'll sleep." And they turned out the light as they left him in the room.

But Mando couldn't sleep. They had hooked a heart monitor up to him, and it beeped every thirty seconds. And he couldn't get comfortable, so he squirmed and rolled—all night long, until the door squeaked open, and this man stepped into the room and sat in a chair close to his bed. Even though Mando could get no sleep, he was fuzzy from trying to sleep, so he only sensed there was this other body in the room. He was able to reach above him and found and lit this little bed lamp above his head. And half in light and half in shadow, he saw another face. He could tell from the man's red eyes that he was tired. The man took his neat, trim gentleman's style cowboy hat off and laid it in his lap. He wore a white shirt, dark suit, shiny black cowboy boots with pointy toes, and a black string tie. "There's no reason to call me *Daddy*. You can call me *Colton*."

"What are you doing here?"

"Your mother told me. We should talk a little."

Colton's face was rough and looked like it had been made rougher by fights and accidents. Arnie's face would now look like his. Mando felt his face and remembered that what was mangled on him was his foot. "I've seen Arnie. He looks bad. They purposely did a half-ass job on him." Colton got up. He looked down Mando's right foot. "I hope they done right by you."

"What's Arnie say?"

"He's just mad. He can't think clear. Can you think?"

"Didn't you check with nobody to get in here?"

Colton shook his head. He pulled at his shirt sleeve cuffs to get them below the suit jacket cuffs. He sat back down. "Nobody needs to know I'm here."

"So why you here?"

"To see my two boys—who just took a jackhammer to their lives."

"What do you care?"

"What were you thinking?"

Mando went through what he was thinking or not thinking and just doing while he said again, "It was Arnie's idea."

"I figured you were the smart one." Colton eased back in his chair and looked up at the ceiling. "I hear you read all the time. I hear you're kind of a different sort of kid, meaning that you got some smarts you're hiding."

"If I'm so smart, what am I doing in here?"

"That's what I said. Why you hiding your God-given intelligence?"

"God didn't give me smarts. I earned them."

"So then why didn't you think about what you did?"

"I thought." Mando thought that something about Colton, unlike with his mother, made Mando want to talk to him, to keep up with him, to show him that he could say just as mean a things as he could, even meaner, tougher.

"So why didn't you choose the right time?" Colton asked Mando.

Mando let himself lay back on his pillow and looked up at the liquid dripping down a plastic tube and then into his arm so as to put his foot to sleep. "It was Arnie's plan."

"So why didn't you tell him to pull it off in the morning, as the sun was coming up, not as it was going down? Less people around. And really, it's probably better in daylight, at dusk or dawn, actually less people to see than at night, with lighting all around you. Why didn't you put on a mask?"

"We wasn't thinking. I guess."

"See?"

"So why should you care?"

"I'm just here to tell you what is. You choose this sort of life, then you got to be smarter. You will be next time."

"What next time?"

"I figure this ain't going to be enough for you and Arnie. I figure you going to get the itch to get some 'crash and dash money,' more chump change. And after maybe the third time and more smashed body parts, you'll get even smarter. And then you will go on to more lucrative things . . . if you can stay out of hospitals, jails, or morgues." Colton said this all matter-of-fact like, like he was a teacher and Mando was a C student.

"So, this is how you got started in what . . . Well, whatever it is you do?"

"There was this time, see, in Gervin. This mom and pop store. My partner Lionel and me went down there to collect a debt." He stopped. "Turn off that light. I like the dark better. And with the dark, this story might put us both to sleep." So Mando turned off the light, and Colton told him about that hold up and what it cost him, and Mando didn't go to sleep. Neither did Colton. Mando listened as close as he could as he was accustomed to doing. Mando didn't like the story, but he liked the way Colton told it. He used the right words. He would hesitate to find the right word so as not to confuse things with the wrong word, to keep it honest. Colton's way was a good way to tell a story.

And when Colton finished the story-telling part of his visit, he got down to the business part of his visit and pulled an envelope from out of his suit jacket's inside pocket. He threw the envelope on to Mando's lap, and Mando jumped, then winced because he jiggled his leg and the drugs were starting to wear out. Inside the envelope were hundred dollar bills and a sheet of notebook paper with two names written on it and numbers next to the names, *Snake Popp* and *Bullet Price.* "I couldn't get in to see your brother, and I was not about to make an issue of it. I couldn't talk to him. So, it's up to you. You understand me, Son." Mando winced again when Colton said, "son," not "Mando" or "boy," but "son."

"That's for the best lawyer you can find. You want suggestions, you call me and ask. My address is inside. Don't give it to nobody, not even your mother. You need help, you go to Way Low. Or you call those two people. Bullet and Snake owe me. You understand?"

Mando nodded. "Arnie's gonna have to do some time. You too maybe. But you got to try to stay out of jail. You got to be the one to beat the jail time. You got to think of the story that will keep you out of jail. A lawyer can help you with that. Way Low can help you with that. And there's some other names and numbers in there. You understand."

Mando nodded again. "Ever since we played that airplane game, I knew you was gonna be the one to grow up smart and right." Colton rose slowly and took measured steps toward the door. He opened and peeked in at Mando once more. "You remember that airplane game, don't you?"

Mando said yes, then blew air through his lips to make his father's airplane sound. Then Colton added, "You got to be careful if you stay in this sort of life." Those words failed Mando. They were not the right words for him. What life? But Mando held the envelope to his chest, thinking that someone might rob him.

As his father opened the door to step out, "Wait," Mando shouted. Colton looked angry when he turned around. "I want to know. I want to know who is my family. My grandmother, your mother, what happened to her? I don't see her no more."

"She lives with me," Colton said, and with light shining through the open door lighting him, he looked almost like he smiled.

"You live with your Momma?"

210

"And I'm giving you money. It's not like I deserted. It's like I got different duties." Colton threw his shoulders back, said, "Go to sleep," then walked out and shut the door, leaving Mando in the still dark room.

With his money, his mind whirring, the heart monitor beeping, Mando stayed up through the night, and then he went to sleep when the nurse turned off the heart monitor and sunbeams filled the room.

Chapter 15

Arnie became for Mando a figure he saw through a plexiglass screen. His voice was a scratchy whisper and whimper that Mando heard through a telephone headset. A set of tiny metal clamps lined his forehead just above his eyebrows and closed the gash that nearly cut his face off. His nose was almost straighter than before the crash, making him look a little dignified. Instead of looking at Mando, Arnie held his right thumb on the right side of his head and shaded that gash with the rest of his fingers, like he was embarrassed, but not about his looks and not by robbing the store. "Henry was a fuck up," he once said in the phone. "I should of took total charge. If it was up to me, we would of stuck up one of those West Odessa bars, robbed some old lady closing down for the night. Henry was a fuck up."

Waiting for his trial, Mando could see Arnie grow more bitter. The botched robbery was one more proof to Arnie that he was now condemned by his own luck to be on the outside. The inevitable prison sentence was more proof. The lawyer Way Low found and Mando paid with Colton's money tried to coach Arnie to beg, to cry, to moan for forgiveness, but he either stared straight out at the world or spread his fingers across his slow-healing gash. He couldn't fake remorse or sorrow, so rather than look the fool, he just didn't look, and even when staring straight ahead, he saw nothing but his own disgust and bitterness, and no lawyer could teach him otherwise.

Arnie was close enough to an adult to be tried as one, so the State of Texas wanted to keep him in jail, and he got no bail. He said he didn't want it. What did he have to do outside of jail? Go back to high school and get laughed at because he was up for a crime and had a gash across his head? How could he study? He was just as good in jail.

Mando was still a minor. He did as his lawyer told him. The State of Texas didn't want to see Mando ruined, so he got bail. And when he appeared for trial, he got three years of probation, just enough to cover him through high school. Arnie got three years. He got out in a year-and-a-half. He had more scars on his face and new ones on his hands. "Fights," he said. He had a tattoo, one he said he could never show Mando. He learned more about robbery in prison. Arnie left his family to earn a living being a thief. He must have been pretty good at it because Mando hardly ever heard from him, until he was well out of high school. Colton wrote Mando a letter. As good as Colton was in telling a story, he wasn't much good with words in a letter. After a bunch of *this*'s and *that*'s, he finally wrote in his loopy, old-fashioned cursive that Arnie was awaiting trial for grand theft and fencing stolen goods in Fort Worth. Colton offered bail. Arnie refused. Colton wrote again when Arnie got convicted.

* * *

When Mando returned to school, on probation, hobbling on crutches, dragging his cast by his side, he became a different kind of outsider than Arnie. He stayed to himself, even hung his head so he didn't have to look at people. In class, he half listened, but mostly he chased words. He read magazines, books, labels. One time, he even grabbed a telephone book sitting next to a public phone in the long hall and took it to algebra class, thumbed through the yellow pages, and thought about what words businesses got put under. In a way, wondering about why a doctor was a *physician* instead of a *doctor* or *surgeon* was a lot like figuring out algebra. So Mando became a loony, the weird kid that everybody knew would just end up doing something awful.

When his cast came off, Mando held his foot up as high as he could on a stiff leg. "Now, you are going to have to get therapy to work on the muscles," the doctor's assistant, not a *nurse*, said. "But Dr. Maxwell did a fine job." Dr. Maxwell's fine job was a red and pink scrunched up and flattened foot with five normal-sized toes sticking out of it. Mando let his leg down to look at his foot dangling below him off the examination table. He wiggled his toes. They worked. But his right foot looked to be a size smaller than his left foot. "It'll start looking better," the doctor's assistant said.

So Mando hung his head and dragged his foot to school and read the phone book or ads or pages from newspapers he pulled out of the West Texas wind. He hoarded words and stuffed the pages with those words on them into his backpack. And walking home one afternoon, he flexed his toes as he had been doing in rehab. Then he walked faster, and then faster, until he was jogging. A dull thud, like he was running barefoot over rocks, worked from the ball of his misformed foot to his heel. The weight of his backpack, loaded with words, made it hurt worse. Rather than quit, Mando began to jog harder, faster, and kept time with alternating dull thuds. Then it went away. His foot felt good. He felt good.

He was running with the strong afternoon wind. It pushed him. He stopped, turned around, and ran the opposite way into the wind. Dull thud, skip a beat, dull thud again. Then ease, even into the wind. He turned again, ran some more, with the wind, and it carried him home.

Everyday, he ran faster. He timed himself. He brought his lunch, begged for other kids' lunch money, looked for nickels in ditches, begged for money from his mother and Way Low. When he had enough, Way Low drove him to the mall, and he went into the tennis shoe store, looked at the racks of running shoes, tried on every pair, and going only by the feel of the sole of the running shoe on the soft carpet, he bought a pair of running shoes. Running became easier; the dull thuds didn't last as long, the time between pain and floating in the wind got shorter.

On Saturdays, Way Low drove him to the mall bookstore, and he sat at the magazine display and read the running shoe magazines. He would re-read and force himself to memorize what they said. And once, when Way Low came to get him, Mando told him to go ahead home and leave him. Way Low fussed but left Mando. And after he finished reading, Mando ran the eight miles home.

He stood on some notebook paper and traced his two feet. He cut out the shape and sent them to a company that made plastic inserts for running shoes. His right foot came out of the accident pointed inward, pigeon toed, and because nearly everyone *pronates*, a new word, most feet needed correction. Mando's right foot, shrunken as it was but pointed inward, countered his pronating left foot and made his gait a speedy wobble. But that right foot was a hoof. It spread out when he ran. Rather than cushioning it needed a structure. So, this company made a green and yellow orthotic that Mando stuck in his shoe, and the dull thump, but not the wobble, went away.

Then he read more. Runners gobbled spaghetti or other carbohydrates the night before a big race. The carbs quickly turned to sugar and kept on turning to sugar so that the runners would have plenty of energy the next day. Since his mother always had flour tortillas in the refrigerator, Mando tried to gobble two or three a night before he jogged in the morning. Otherwise, he read about calories and energy. He ate fruit, nuts, and vegetables. Except for the tortillas, he tried to avoid breads. He turned himself into a cave man by eating what pre-agricultural people ate. He shrunk. He cinched his pants up with his belt wrapped securely around him. His cheeks and belly became hollowed out.

As the weather began to chill, Mando wore sweat pants to school so he could run home. And, on one of those fine fall days, Indian Summer, 70 degrees and the wind died down, he pulled off his sweats, and in his jean cut offs, he began doing laps around Odessa High's football field. In the middle of the field the football team practiced. As Mando took a lap, then another and got in a quick half-mile, football players looked up from their huddle to watch him. Some pointed. Here was the weird kid running circles, going nowhere, probably lost. One coach broke off from the practice and crossed the track and sat in the bleachers. He had a cap pulled low, coaching shorts pushed to the limit of an expanding gut, and a stop watch in his hand. Mando did a mile, and the coach clicked his stop watch each time Mando passed him.

And by the time, Mando stopped, hunched over, breathed in, and then started his second mile, the coach stood on the track and yelled at Mando to let his hands flap back over his shoulders, let even his fingertips go loose. "Now bear down," the coach yelled.

At the end of the second lap, Coach Gonzalez walked over to Mando while he sucked in breath. With his hands on his knees, staring at his right foot, Mando heard Coach Gonzalez say, "Straighten up. Last as long as you can straight up."

"You have any idea how fast you were going?"

"I don't got a stop watch. I just guess."

"How come you wobble every other stride?"

"One foot's shorter than the other."

"Does it hurt when you hit on it?"

"Just sometimes."

"You training?"

"Yes."

"For what?"

"Just training. I just like running. I might as well see how much I can do it."

"Good God, son. Why don't you go out for track?"

"What do I got to do in track?"

"Run. Is something wrong with you, son?"

"Nothing but my foot," Mando said.

So Mando went out for track that spring and ran the mile and the ten thousand meters. He didn't so much out run people or race; he outlasted them. He ran with himself, not against other runners. It wasn't competition. He ran to school, would go to practice and run, and then run home, and at nights, with Way Low fussing at him and his mother telling him he was crazy, he would soak his puny foot in ice. And once, one of his mother's boyfriends, waiting to take Elena out, stared at Mando soaking his foot. Mando pulled his puny foot out to show the boyfriend. The man under the hat looked at Elena like he was scared of the boy.

And Mando could study words and think about how they worked, and the words became his. And running was like the words. With words, he could stop being him and be with the words, yet always stay him. And with running, he could become a part of the running itself, a part of movement and motion. And yet there he would be, him, experiencing the motion and movement that is a part of the way the world works. He learned about movement and momentum in math and science. What he didn't need was people. He went to the state meet.

With school out, he got what jobs he could to buy running gear, and he would run from his house to Golder, then out Golder, past 42nd, past the mom and pop bars that Colton used to go to. He ran past horses in dirty corals, choking on the dust the other horses kicked up, on and on. Then he would turn around and go back.

And in the fall, he ran cross country. It was even better than running around a track. On one meet, he ran around the rich folks at the Odessa Country Club. The golfers stayed off the course one Wednesday and let the track team run through the course for their cross-country meet. As he passed people by as he closed in on the finish line, he felt himself full of energy, like the air was buoying him up, and he felt proud and happy with himself because he was out in front of everybody, not that he was ahead mattered, just the fact that he was enjoying the movement and had other people to measure his movement.

That finish line came to him. And after he crossed and forced himself to slow, because he did not want to stop running, was not yet spent, he straightened like Coach Gonzalez told him to do, and he breathed in, again and again, but the burning in his gut pulled him over so he could look at his feet. His right foot felt like it was on fire. A few more breaths, he plopped on his ass, pulled off his shoe and looked at his foot. It was scraped and bleeding. The orthotic had slipped. With his special-made green and yellow orthotic in one hand, his shoe in the other, Mando looked up to see Way Low looking down and smiling at him. "Look who I brung," Way Low said.

Standing next to him was Colton, smiling even harder than Way Low. "Damn, son. You running like you scared. What you scared of?"

"I don't know," Mando said. Colton wore a very soft black leather jacket that matched his black jeans and black tennis shoes. He wore one of those gangster-like or news-boy hats, a "cocksucker" hat, Mando's friends would have called it. It was a gray and black plaid. He looked at Mando and folded his arms across his chest, smiling the whole time.

"Well, you stay scared, play scared like I used to. Let it chase you, as long as you can run like that. Just don't let it catch you." Then he stuck an envelope in front of Mando. Mando stuck his orthotic back into the shoe and took the envelope. "That's part of the prize," Colton said.

Inside the envelop was enough money to keep Mando in the best jogging shoes he could mail order, since Odessa didn't have any really good running stores. "You just keep running," Colton said. The sun highlighted his cheeks. But there looked to be dents in his checks, places that were shadowed because the sun couldn't get into those deep dents, and his teeth looked too white and straight to be real.

"Thank you," Mando said because he thought he had to.

"Mando, I don't know what your mother told you about me. But I tried."

"I know."

"No, you don't know. Can you walk with me a bit?" Mando nodded. Colton jerked his head. And they walked away from the coaches and the few people there to watch. "I never knew how to be married. I never knew how to be in a family. What you heard is true, but then it ain't true too." And Colton tried to explain how it was for a man like him, to be running away from something he didn't know was chasing him, only that it was there. It was there in being him married into a family like Elena's. Mando listened. And when Colton stopped his story, he looked at Mando like Mando could have said something to

218

make him feel better about what he had done, but Mando didn't know enough to say anything. "I tried," Colton said. "It wasn't enough, and maybe I could of tried harder. And I was scared. It was like I was playing scared. You understand." Mando couldn't say nothing. "It is like running. Now what's chasing you, Mando?"

"Nothing."

"It's something. You got to figure it out." Then Colton smiled at Mando. "But damn if it can't chase you across the finish line. Know it, but don't lose it."

"Sir," Mando said, not "daddy." And when Colton looked at him, he asked his question. "How is my grandmother?"

"She's sickly. She has spells," Colton said and patted his son's back. "Does your mother still have those boyfriends?"

"Not as many."

Chapter 16

Other than his movement through running, the rest of high school stood still for Mando. Nothing much amused him. The highlight was that he used his father's money and some more cash to buy a seven-year-old car. Driving wasn't as good as running, but he liked driving.

There were some girls, some backseat gropings in Mando's new used car. But the groped girls didn't show much interest in him. And he was glad—because he didn't want the kind of girl that would be attracted to a dope like him. The girls with the red or blue streaks in their jet-black hair, with their black fingernails, tattered jeans, studded tongues or lips tried too hard to be outsiders. Mando didn't like the desperation. And they made him think of Arnie, the real outsider, out there somewhere running away from something. Eventually, the something caught Arnie. And he went to prison again.

All Mando did was run. And read. And he wished that he could come up with a way to do both at once. That would be the greatest escape, to wonder about the words and the things they tried to explain while becoming a part of the very landscape through quick-paced movement, to escape the world and yourself, by being you escaping. Running and reading bent his mind, but the bend felt better than the girls, the underage drinking, or the pot.

When he graduated, Mando didn't have a plan about what to do. So just before classes started, with a loan from Way Low, he enrolled in Odessa College, the local community college. One semester he made three As and two Bs. The next semester, he didn't go to class. He sat in his room.

Elena and Way Low couldn't get too pissed off at him because of Arnie, who was in prison, again, so Mando looked like the good son. But they tried to talk to him. Elena came into his room, the one he used to share with Arnie, but now his, and asked, or rather told him, "What the matter with you? You got no ambition, no wants?"

"I want to be left alone."

"And do what?" Elena squared herself, her feet placed directly below her shoulders, and folded her arms. Mando remembered the fancy gentleman in the black suit and boots who came to see him in the hospital and the rough gentleman in black jeans and tennis shoes who watched him win the cross-country race. His mother and father both stood alike. No wonder they split. They were all tougher than Mando.

"You got to want something. Everybody has to want something." Mando was not sure he even knew what *want* was. Mando wanted *is*.

So Mando said the obvious, "I want to run."

"And so how you going to make a living? Where do you think that money comes from? What you thinking?"

"I just don't know. Maybe something will come to me."

Mando sat on his bed. At this time, in their house, Mando pretty much stayed in his bedroom and wished that the door had a lock so that he could lock them all out. His mother sat in the chair across from him. "Mando, what's going to become of you?"

"I got no idea."

"I'm not asking for an answer, especially no smart one. I want you to think. I want you to prepare yourself for something." Mando said nothing. "What are you going to do?"

"You want me to give an answer now?"

She shot up, stomped her foot, and left Mando to himself.

Then as he listened to a strong late March wind scratch at his window and find ways to blow through the seams of their crumbling house to bring swirling dust into his room, Way Low limped into Mando's room. Way Low was developing diabetes and, though he wouldn't admit it, he was losing feelings in his toes. "Your mother's worried," he said. "And when she worries, she fusses to me. And I'm tired of listening to her fuss."

"She doesn't want me to answer her when she asks me questions."

"Me either, but she still wants me to do something. So, I am doing something. I am asking you what you going to do with yourself."

He waited while Mando said nothing. In some ways, Mando thought that he would like to grow up to be like Way Low. He never seemed angry or upset, unlike Elena. Somehow, he just got by, and Mando thought that might be the best way to get through your life.

"Look, I don't like it, but I was a night watchman; then that company went broke because the oil boom busted and they got no metal to watch. So, then I'm poor again. Now I look at the papers and a computer screen and answer the phone at the Fed Ex office. I don't get paid much, but I don't do much. What about you? You want to be like me?"

He said those words like it was a real question, like he was really asking if he wanted some backyard or backroom job Mando could just disappear in. "I wish I could tell you," Mando said.

Way Low held up his foot and watched the tip of his shoe. He wiggled. "You know, I don't feel shit." Mando could tell that Way Low was scared, thinking about himself, not Mando. *"Tú pendejo* brother at least had a plan. He knew what he wanted. Problem was he just couldn't get it. Especially the way he went to getting what he wanted. But you? You know nothing. I like your brother's way better."

He pushed himself up and stomped his foot on the floor. "Nothing," he said. Then he smiled because of what he was about to say, "I'm going to call your father." He laughed on his way out.

And like the voice of God converted into words and coming from the U.S. postal system, Mando got a letter from Colton. It had two familiar names in it, *Bullet Price* and *Snake Popp.*

* * *

Mando called Snake Popp, and on an early afternoon, he walked out of the wild spring wind and into his new nightclub, the Midnight Rodeo, a cavernous, empty, classy bar. In high school he heard the cool kids whisper about sneaking into this bar. There were teenage fantasies and pleasures in this bar. And those pleasures and fantasies lasted all the way into middle-age for some Odessans. They paid top dollar for Snake Popp's liquor and sometimes even a cover charge to rubber-neck the dancers working their way in a counter-clockwise direction around the Midnight Rodeo's large wooden floor. The rubber and carbon soles of Mando's running shoes stuck on that varnished wooden dance floor. A bartender warily watched him as he walked up to the empty bar. "It's made for boots, not no tennis shoes."

"These shoes are for running."

"Ain't you got a proper pair of boots?"

"These are all I got."

"What you want?"

"I'm here to see Snake Popp."

"See that door?" Not one to waste a movement, he jerked his head to his left. A door said *office*. Mando pulled his jogging shoes across the floor and knocked. A voice from inside told him to come in. He opened the door to silver-haired Snake sitting behind his desk. "So, you're Colton's boy?"

Mando nodded and sat down in front of his desk when Snake motioned. Snake chewed gum in one side of his mouth. He ran one hand through his silver hair. "Why do you suppose Colton sent you to me?"

"To get a job. I'm kind of down on my luck."

"You don't want the kind of jobs I got."

"I don't think I got the right to be picky."

"I got nothing where you do something romantic like bartending."

"I need a job."

Snake pushed himself up from his chair. His silver hair matched his silver slacks. He ran his hands through his hair again and left two indentations right at the top sides of his head. His mouth worked grinding the gum. "You been in many fights?"

Mando didn't dare tell him the truth. He was a runner, not a fighter. "Few."

"Colton, Colton," Snake said and shook his head and looked away from Mando. With his head still hanging, he said, "Look, truth is, I just got nothing." Mando nodded. "No, truth is I got nothing I want to give you." Mando nodded. "You catching my drift?" Mando nodded again.

Snake sat back down in his chair and put his feet on his desk. "Your father should have thought of that."

"I think he did," Mando said to Snake's boot soles

"What do you mean?" He tilted his boots to one side to see Mando.

"Maybe he wants me to have a tough job."

"Did he say that?"

"He doesn't say nothing to me. He wrote my mother and put a letter for me in with hers."

Snake yanked his feet off the bar. "Stand up," he ordered. Mando stood. "There's not much to you. You play football or anything?"

"I run."

"What do you mean?"

"The track team, and now I run, every day, all on my own. Thus, the shoes."

Snake leaned over his desk to look at Mando's jogging shoes. "Those're pretty," he said.

"And I read a lot. Does that help?"

Snake settled back into his chair and worked that piece of gum. "What you want to do with yourself?"

"I been getting asked that a lot."

"So?"

"So maybe Colton—"

"Colton?"

"I have a hard time calling him *my father*. Even harder to call him something like *Daddy*."

"Colton?"

"Colton may want to give me the chance to try something."

"Do you know what Colton's job for me was?"

"No, sir."

"You're too small to scare anybody." Snake's face twisted up like he was trying too hard to think, or like he had gas or heartburn. "No, no. You run on and find someone else willing to give you what you shouldn't have. The old days are gone. If they ever was here. And I'm getting too old for the old days and don't miss them."

"I need a job."

"You ever stock a beer cooler?"

"I could try."

"That'd be less dangerous."

"I'm not scared."

"You say that now."

"I'll say anything now. I need a job."

"Well, you're honest. But a little weird. Let me think." Snake put his elbows on his desk. "Because you're Colton's boy I'm gonna think real hard. But I'm slow-thinking—and getting worse—in the meantime, you go see Bullet Price." He scribbled something on a card and handed it to Mando. He read the words *Bullet Price*, again.

* * *

Mando went to the Cactus Lounge, where Bullet had an office. The bar had beams of sunlight drifting in from the cracks in the aluminum siding. And about half-a-dozen rough, grizzled drinkers gathered at the bar. A woman fast losing her looks was behind the bar. Mando walked through waves of smoke to the edge of the bar and cleared his throat to keep from choking and wondered if the smoke ever found its way out of the Cactus Lounge. "Are you Bullet Price?" Mando asked.

The woman shook her head and said, "Honey, you look around."

A skinny figure at the bar turned its head toward him, and what Mando thought was a man in a gimme cap was a woman. She had lost her looks, but you could see that somewhere, back a long time before, she must have had something. Mando figured that she must have given up on looks once she got the scar that ran across her face. She slipped off the gimme cap to reveal two wings of short, gray hair running along the sides of her head. She shook her head and her hair fluffed up but settled back into place in their wings. "That would be me," she said.

"I'm Mando Parker." Bullet got up and jerked her head to one side. "Come with me," she said. Then she looked at the other drinkers who probably sat there every day drinking their ways toward oblivion. "You boys, excuse me."

As she led Mando toward a door to one side of the bar, he watched her from behind and noted that she did have a trim woman's figure. He followed her through the door. Bullet went to a desk piled with paper and microwave trays and paper cups. She sat down behind the pile of paper trash and shoved it with her hand until it fell over the top front of her desk. "Have a seat."

Mando sat on a chair in front of the desk. "You want a beer?"

"I'm only eighteen."

"You're honest. That's good. You want a beer?"

Mando shook his head. He wanted to concentrate on why he was here, "So you talked with Colton Parker?"

"Off and on. Mostly off. Nobody from the old days talks much to your *father*," she said. "So you need a job."

"How did you know?"

"I talk on and off to Snake Popp. What kind of work are you willing to do?"

"The kind that pays."

"You talk a little like your father."

"I'm nothing like my father."

"You got a little of his look in your eye, but you lost his heft."

"I mean I'm just nothing like him."

"The jobs I got need someone like him."

Mando dropped his head and stared down at the tops of his jogging shoes. "What do you like to do, Mando?" Bullet asked.

Mando brought his head up and felt himself smile, "Run and read."

"What about girls? What about drinking?"

"I'm not too lucky with girls. And I've never drunk that much."

"You're not queer are you? Hell, that would be a riot. Colton Parker's boy turns out to be queer."

"I'm not queer."

"I'm just saying Danny Fowler would be rolling over in his grave laughing if Colton Parker's boy was gay."

"Who's Danny Fowler?"

"Your father ever told you about Danny Fowler?"

"I never see my father."

"You work for me, you got to drink a little. And listen." Bullet pushed herself up, left the office, and came back with two bottles of beer. She set one in front of Mando.

"I'm underage."

"Grow up and grow a pair."

"Danny Fowler was my friend." Bullet said. She told Mando about Danny and his mother and his murder. And that led her back to her stripping days and her scar and her cancer, and another beer for each of them. By the third beer, Mando didn't see any end to the story, and he was having a hard time paying attention what with the beer that was working its way through him. Bullet wound her story back around to Colton. "Oh, everybody knew him. It was different then, and the oil field was special. But it was because of Danny Fowler that your father left."

"How's that? I figured he just left my mother cause. . . well cause.

"Now you're interested."

"I just don't know him. I mean I never grew up with him."

Bullet studied Mando, then said, "There's time yet."

* * *

Bullet invited Mando back. And he had illegal beers with her. And he learned that, if he drank two or more beers before he ran, he couldn't finish his run. And he learned that, if he drank a beer or two after a run, he'd get an instant hangover. So, he'd do his running in the morning, have lunch with Way Low, then drive to Bullet's and drink a beer with her, her treat, just because he was Colton Parker's boy. And he also learned a little about his father. When she felt like it, she would tell Mando about his father when she first met him. But when she would get to the name "Danny Fowler," she would stop her story.

And then she told Mando she had a job for him. He could work repo. "Snake and Bill Sears got to admit that illegal immigration is good for the titty and car businesses," she told Mando with her smile making her scar stretch. "Snake gets strippers for cheap, and Bill Sears sells an illegal a car, repossesses it, and sells it again, sometimes to the same guy. Snake don't want to hire you, but maybe you could get into the car business." She told Mando about Lionel Dexter. "You can never be like your father," she said. "But maybe you can be another Lionel Dexter. She sent Mando to see repo man Lionel Dexter.

* * *

Lionel Dexter sat behind the wheel of the tow truck with some lost lights from a street lamp making parts of his face shine. He had finished telling Mando the story about walking out on Colton. It was dark, so Lionel couldn't see Mando's face, so Mando didn't have to worry what his face showed. This was the first time Mando had gotten this far into the story. And so he was sorting through his mind to see what he wanted to think about his father and his family.

"I went out into the world," Lionel told him. "It was too big, so I come back."

What happened out in the world is that, after he left Colton, with his money, Lionel drove to Dallas, couldn't find a job, robbed a liquor store by waving his 9mm, and got scared. He saw what could become of him. He came back to Odessa, to friends. Those friends just happened to be Snake and Bullet. Colton was already gone, and he told them that he couldn't work in their kind of business no more. So, they introduced him to Bill Sears.

And after he had finished his story, he had started wondering about what would have become of him if he had of stuck with Mando's father. Being a repo man was no kind of life. Or maybe being a repo man wasn't that bad? Especially compared to what Colton might be up to?

And just what kind of future would a black man have in Colton's line of work?

Mando held the barrel of the shotgun, trying to twist this explanation of his father around in his head before he asked anything and interrupted Lionel's out-loud wondering. Lionel glanced in the rearview mirror above him, and Mando glanced into the long, rectangular rearview mirror on the passenger door. The lights to the small house went off. And there in the driveway sat their quarry, a three-year-old Jeep Cherokee. It was time to stop their wonderings and thinking and get on with business. "They gone to sleep now." Lionel said. "Let's give them some time to get all comfy."

They parked a half-block up from the Cherokee and had the tow faced toward the driveway. "Hell, I know a goddamn Cherokee backwards and forwards. Seems only people who can't afford 'em buy 'em. Ignorant mother fuckers."

"You're making me nervous," Mando said.

"All them bugs fluttering around in your belly and up your throat, you get used to 'em. This is just gonna be real simple."

They waited, "But shit, I know them cars. I know 'em. I mean right under the steering column. Snip, snip again, and the alarm is disabled. Then snip, cross some wires, and the car starts."

"What you thinking?"

"I'm thinking nobody pays no attention to a car alarm going off. They go off all the time. And if it stops soon's it starts, then we're good. And I'm thinking I know them cars."

"But we could get a key. Bill Sears says we could get a key."

"Bill Sears don't want to take the time to get a key. He wants his new car back now, sos he can turn right goddamn around and sell it again, sos I can repo it again."

"But I bet the guy inside'll come running if he hears an alarm."

"You thinking good now, son. But let's have some fun."

Mando heard the handle to his door click. "You come on around and get in the driver's seat."

"I don't like this. What you going to do?"

"I'm still that bad ass mother fucker. I'm gonna practice up my repo skills."

"But we're just gonna tow it, right?"

"No, I'm gonna drive it out that driveway, and you gonna pull up behind me."

"This just don't sound good."

"I'm gonna give Colton Parker's boy a lesson in repoing."

"How about we just tow it?"

"Shit, I coulda been just as big a bad ass as Colton Parker. I was the muscle. I was the big man, the football player. I coulda been the high-priced murderer, criminal, ninja fuck assassin or whatever he is now. It coulda been me too."

He was talking himself and Mando into a dangerous area. And Mando's mind flashed back to him sitting in that Subaru in front of the convenience store that Arnie and Henry were fixing to rob. "You better think clearer."

Lionel looked over at Mando and tilted his head, but he wasn't giving himself a pep talk now, he was making an excuse, knew he was making an excuse, but made it anyway, "But you see, in them days, a black man just couldn't hope for the advantages in the big-time crime world, like a man like Colton had."

"Let's just back on up to that Cherokee."

"Do as you're told, Colton's boy."

So Mando eased out, holding the shotgun, (*always hold it*, as Lionel had told him), eased around to the other side of the truck, and gently eased the shotgun past the steering wheel to rest it on the transmission hump and the seat, and then he eased into the driver's seat. "You start that truck and hold on to the shotgun," Lionel said. And from the rearview mirror, Mando saw Lionel skipping toward the Cherokee.

Mando squinted into the rearview mirror, then he turned his head to look. Lionel had his metal slim jim down the driver's side window. He jerked, opened the door, and jumped in as the car horn started. In seconds it stopped. Mando strained his eyes and ears. He couldn't hear the car starting. He did see the brake lights flash on then off. He looked so hard at the Cherokee that he didn't see the short, fat man in a wife-beater tank top step out onto the porch. He took even longer to see the small pistol the man held in his hand and lifted to aim at the Cherokee. Mando almost shouted, "Lionel," but his name came out a whisper. Mando couldn't really see Lionel, but he imagined him inside that car fumbling with the wires.

Mando opened the driver's door, stepped out, and pulled the shotgun out with him. "Hey, what the fuck you doing," the fat man said and pointed the gun at the Cherokee.

"Shoot over their heads," Lionel's voice said in Mando's mind. So Mando got the shotgun pointed at the man, raised slightly, and pulled the trigger. A chunk of the man's porch shredded right over his head, and the fat man jumped to the ground and started shooting his own car, sending sparks flying out of the metal bullet holes he was making in the Cherokee's rear. And out comes Lionel. He ran like the high school football star he used to be, and he yelled, "Shoot, shoot." Then again, "Shoot the mother fucker." The man couldn't spot Mando, and even from the distance, Mando could see he was scared. He put his face down, and his gun still in his hand, he covered the back of his head with his hands. Mando shot off another chunk of his porch.

Lionel got to the passenger side door and leaped in. Mando ran to the driver's side door. "Watch where you pointing that shotgun," Lionel said.

Mando started the truck, then pushed the accelerator to the floor. And then, Mando's smashed foot started to ache, and his leg started to tremble, like it was remembering that crash in front of that convenience store. And then his mind remembered, and then his body stiffened for the crash. "Whoa, shit," Lionel said.

But he didn't crash. He made it around the corner. And then he eased off the gas, and they drove at the speed limit down a dark Odessa street.

"Damn, you done that good," Lionel said. "Shit, you good at this. Cool as shit. Just like your daddy."

"Tell me about my father," Mando said.

"What you want to know?"

"As much as I can stand?"

While they drove to see Bill Sears and admit their defeat, Mando heard Lionel's suppositions about his "high-priced murderer, criminal, ninja fuck assassin" father's life and work.

* * *

Bullet herself complimented Mando, said he had talent. She fed him more beers in the mid-afternoons at the Cactus Lounge. Lionel and Mando did most of their repoing late at night, but sometimes in mid-morning, after he'd run, Mando would go over to the garage where Lionel kept his tow truck, and he would go over the finer parts of repoing with Lionel. And without Mando's asking, Lionel once said to him, "I guess you heard about Gervin?" So Mando learned about Lionel's opinion of his father along with alarms and hot-wiring.

And since Mando liked words, he turned his attention to the words in auto manuals. He'd buy them from auto parts stores and read about the electrical systems and thus the alarms for all sorts of brands. He tried to memorize what he read. Lionel would quiz him, "Damn, you know this. Can you do it?"

So Mando tested himself. To see if he could do what Lionel had failed to do. They had found that Jeep Cherokee and, on their second attempt, they towed it right into Bill Sear's lot. And he sold it again. And then Bill Sears had told them to repo it for a third time. In an Albertson's grocery store parking lot, Mando found that same Jeep Cherokee.

This time was a Saturday afternoon, so the Albertson's parking lot was full. Mando figured, as Lionel told him, on a full lot, this time of day, with this kind of crowd, nobody was going to pay attention to a car alarm. Mando walked up to the Jeep Cherokee and pulled his slimjim from out of the back of his jeans. "What are you doing?" a young woman holding a baby asked as he worked the slimjim down the side of the window and into the door.

"Locked myself out," Mando said. She smiled, Mando yanked, the alarm went off.

Smiling, the shopper stood right behind Mando watching him. "That's impressive," she said.

Mando was inside, feeling down the steering column with his left hand, his shears in his right, and cut the wire. He got the large socket wrench out of his back pocket, twisted the ignition out, stripped and crossed the wires. The Jeep started. In the rearview mirror, he saw the lady standing behind the Jeep. "Mam," he said. "I need to back out." She watched him back out and then drive out to 42nd.

When Mando pulled into Bill Sear's car lot, Lionel and Bill were waiting for him. Lionel opened the door for Mando, and when he stepped out, Lionel inspected the work. Meantime Bill, wearing his black gambler's style hat, patted Mando's back and said, "Slicker than goose shit." Lionel nodded and shook Mando's hand.

Later, Lionel and Mando pulled off what was one of the gutsiest repo tricks. They drove together to a car with late payments. Its soon-to-be ex-owner got off work and walked up to it, climbed in, and started it. Mando hopped out of Lionel's truck, ran to the ex-owner's car, pulled open the door that he hadn't locked, pulled him out of the driver's seat, and drove off with the ignition still intact and the car keys in his hand. So as not to be mean, Bill Sears mailed the car's former owner's other keys back to him.

With his repo money building up, Mando was able to move out of the house. Elena was proud of him for finding something to do with himself. She said that all he needed was a little direction. She told Mando that he was nothing like his father. With Mando gone, she might be wanting to concentrate on more boyfriends.

Mando was glad to be out of the house and renting a small RV parked in gravel lot out in West Odessa. He felt like writing Colton and telling him that he was living in a lonely RV in a gravel and mesquite cleared lot. He was cramped and hot, but he liked his new quarters. He could read. And he had wide-open but dusty West Odessa to jog through.

In the summer that he moved, with Mando's window unit struggling to keep the RV cool, Way Low stopped by to visit Mando. He had a cane and shuffled when he walked. Mando had to help Way Low up the steps into the RV. And Mando nearly had to fold Way Low into a chair by the kitchen table that folded out of a wall. With his left hand, Way Low tugged on the hem of his right pants leg until he got his right foot resting on his left knee. He began to massage his toes underneath the cloth to the top of his tennis shoe. His brown, wrinkled face lifted from his toes to Mando, and his eyes shifted to Mando's feet. "You still wear your fancy tennis shoes."

"I still run. Your feet still hurt?"

"The diabetes, the doctors say." Sweat was beading on his forehead. Mando's too.

"That air-conditioner is too small and don't work too good."

"I been in worse. But the doctors tell me to stay cool, not over exert."

"This is a short visit?"

Way Low nodded. "I hear about you from my friends. They say Mando is a big man. They say if they could make a corrido, they'd sing about Mando the repo man. The song would be something like 'buy your cars from the gringos, but hold your soul 'cause your car is Mando's'"

"I don't worry about that. I done what you told me. Momma is proud of me. I got a career."

"But I'm just saying, 'know your place. Know what you can do.'"

"I'm a good repo man."

"Then that's what I'm saying. Don't be like your father. Don't make his mistake. Know what you are good at. Know your place. Know your limits. Stay in them."

"What did Colton do?"

"He went over his limits."

"You just said that. What do you mean? What was it he did?"

"I'm just saying. know what your limits are. Your father is somebody else."

"Have you talked to my father?"

"That's why I'm here."

"My father's here?"

Way Low hung his head like he was ashamed of what he was going to tell Mando. "Our old house with all its bad electricity and plumbing is just fine for me. But your father, bought *us* a new one. He put down a lot of money, so we don't have much to pay for rent."

"Where's this house?"

Way Low couldn't look at Mando. "It's in Country Club Estates, with the rich people. It's got four bedrooms, one for me, one for your mama, one for you, one for Arnie, if he ever gets back, which ain't never gonna happen. It's got everything."

Mando just started shaking his head. "Where does he get so much money?"

"The point is I'm supposed to tell you to come back and live with us. This house is so big, you don't even see anybody."

"I got this place."

"Your mother and your father want you in the other house."

"No."

"How about you go to the big house, and I move in here?" Way Low chuckled.

"Where does he get the money?"

"You know where he gets the money. He don't hide it from us. He just don't say nothing about it."

"What do you think of all this? What do you think of what he does?"

Way Low said nothing. He just rubbed his foot. Mando could tell that he was getting tired and wanted to go. So Mando helped him down the steps and to his car. He opened his door for Way Low and helped him inside. When Way Low started the motor, he pressed too hard with his right foot and the engine roared. "Can you feel the pedal?" Mando asked.

"Not too good."

Way Low gave Mando his warning, and Mando should have listened better because with his repo skills growing, he found himself in the Cactus Lounge sitting beside Bullet Price while she sized him up. "You done good. You must learn quick." Mando just nodded. Bullet smiled to make her scar even more crooked. She coughed, then again. "Damn, must be a cold." She coughed more. "Yeah, you're smarter than your father. He didn't learn as quick."

"I still don't see that I have much in common with Colton."

"You would say that, but you do have some common traits." Bullet pulled a pack of cigarettes out from behind the bar. "Don't look at me. I quit. But the menthol helps the cough."

"I thought the doctors said to quit."

"I have quit. A lot of times. This is just an exception." She lit the cigarette, breathed in, breathed out smoke, and smiled, like she had wanted that puff for years. She stared at the lit tip of the cigarette, then crushed it out on her own bar, leaving a black smear in the wood. "I want to offer you another job."

"I thought I was doing good at repo."

"But you learn. And you're young." She reached behind the bar and pulled out a small automatic pistol. She reached again and pulled out some 9mm. shells. "Start practicing shooting that." Mando reached toward it very slowly. "It won't bite."

"But I might end up shooting myself or something valuable."

"The idea is mostly that you just have it. And if you ever need to use it, you just point it in the general direction of what you want to hit and keep squeezing the trigger."

"So why am I going to be pointing it at anybody?"

"Cause you're gonna start collecting coins from my vending machines." When Mando felt his eyes raise, Bullet coughed, then explained, "Snake and me own a bunch of these bars. The owners rent the building, then go broke. So just like Bill Sears, we rent the buildings out again, but we retain the vending machine rights. The cigarette, video game, and condom money all goes to us. We even got a few machines that take bills. At night, after the bars close down, somebody has to go get the coins and the bills. We want that somebody to be you. Well, I do. Snake says we shouldn't be hiring you. But what the fuck does he know."

"What's Lionel gonna do?"

"He can still use you. Some nights you work for me. Some nights you work for him." She coughed again. "I guess I should see a doctor." Mando nodded. "You have insurance?" Mando shook his head. "You ought to get some. Don't depend on the emergency room."

Thus Mando went from the repo business to the vending machine business. Like a coyote, he lurked at night, out of sight, in the dark shadows. It was his father's world. If he wasn't stalking a car in South or West Odessa, with stray dogs barking at him, and the night shift neighbors wondering if they ought to pull a gun or make a phone call, then he was going in the back door of a West Odessa bar and gutting a vending machine by flashlight. He kept that 9mm. stuck in the back of his pants, with his shirt tail out to hide it. Sitting with Lionel or in his own truck off and on throughout the night made that hard metal of that 9mm rub a callous on Mando's back. But in the winter on crisp days, with what little humidity there was sucked out by the cold but bright winter light, as he drove with Lionel or by himself in his little pickup, he could see the stirred dust swirling around under the street lights or bar lamps, like nighttime ghosts looking for a drink after hours.

And sometimes some people left from the time when Colton was in this world would buy Mando a beer and call him "Colton's boy." And sometimes the older bartenders would give him a free one, even though he was underage, probably because they figured he was one of them now and because he was Colton's boy. Mando drank their beer anyway.

In the mornings, when he could push himself awake, he would run. And in the winter at sunrise, the dust would swirl in the dry winter light or sandblast the cinder block buildings if the wind was really up. This wasn't powerful, strong circles of light that lit the dark, but a true light. This was not his father's world. He could run and read in this world. But Mando had to find out which world he belonged to. As Way Low said, he had to find his place.

After several months, he stepped out the back door of the Snug Harbor with bags of money dangling over each shoulder. A single light lit the back door and the way to his truck. It gave him a narrow path, almost like one of those pointer lights, instead of a real light. It was mostly in front of him and darkness was around him. But he saw something beside himself, and he felt some kind of a whoosh of movement beside him. He made the mistake of stopping. A bat, a stick, or a tire tool came out of the dark. Mando got his forearm up close to his face. So that long heavy lump knocked his hand into his face. He couldn't help but fall over backwards and follow the back of his head to the ground.

All Mando could see was dark, then red. Then a little light got into his head or mind. And he saw two boys or small men bent over scooping up coins from the busted cloth sack. Instead of gravel, the ground was covered with coins and some dollars that got stuffed in the newer machines. He must have dropped all four bags. He groaned. Then a dull pain worked its way up from the small of his back, like he had fallen on a rock. When one kid raised up to look at him, Mando saw that it was indeed kids who had done this to him. When the one kid raised his arm, and in it was this expandable baton that he must have mailed ordered for, Mando reached toward that dull ache in his back. The 9mm came out easy.

He pointed it at the boy's face. He studied that face. It was pimply, with big whiteheads all over it. The boy was snaggled-tooth. And the boys' eyes were scared. Mando moved his wrist just a bit, toward that baton. And when he saw or thought he saw the boy's wrist flinch, he pulled the trigger. Blood sprayed behind the boy's hand, and the boy dropped the baton. Beside him, Mando felt then caught a glimpse of something solid moving, the other boy running. And that boy with the pimply face and the now shredded right hand started crying. Thinking of him and Arnie in that Subaru, Mando screamed, "Run. Just run. I won't shoot." As the boy ran away, Mando decided that he did not want to live in his father's world.

Chapter 17

Mando did not go to the emergency room. He did not go to a doctor. Bullet and Lionel looked at his forearm and forehead. Both said that they could see nothing wrong, could feel no broke bones. Mando tried to stay up with his jobs, but lugging the coins made his arm pulse, and most worrisome, at night, his vision got blurry. When he ran, on every other footfall, his forearm and then his head seemed about to explode from gushing blood, so he had to slow to a walk even though his crushed foot didn't hurt. Walking in the cold wind, instead of running, he felt humiliated. And once, he stopped running into the wind to bend over to think. Somewhere in Odessa was the boy trying to read his homework and do his street hustling with a goodly portion of his hand shot off. And Mando was the one who did that to him.

Mando went to see Way Low and Elena. She, of course, offered to pay for Mando to see a doctor. Way Low inspected Mando's wounds and pronounced him strong. When Elena stepped away from them, Mando checked over his shoulder to see if she was out of hearing range, and said to Way Low in a whisper, "I shot this boy."

"He dead?"

"No, he ran away. But he's missing some fingers."

"Must've been a good shot."

"Shot his hand before he could hit me with this baton."

"Justified." Mando nodded, and Way Low studied Mando's face. "But you feel bad. Your stomach's churning around 'cause you don't like it that you shot him." Mando nodded. "Pay attention. Your guts are trying to tell you something."

"What're my guts saying?".

"You warning yourself. You either got to get over what you done. Or quit doing what you done. Know your place."

Mando moped around most of that winter. And on a cold day, with the chilly wind outside the Cactus Lounge but with some still finding its way into the bar and some still shaking the walls from the outside, Mando had just dropped off some deposits from coins and was sitting at a table, having a beer, reviewing his life—or what there was of it—when Bullet walked out of the office with a short, mean-looking man. He looked shorter, wider, meaner, and scarier than the last time Mando saw him. "Mando," Bullet said. "Your father."

Bullet turned back to her office, and with the wind whistling through the walls and the frames of the windows, Colton stepped toward Mando, his hands in his jacket, scaring Mando, whose expression seemed to say that Colton might pull those hands out and beat the hell out of him. "Good to see you, again," Colton said. And then a smile cracked his face. "You changed," he said.

He sat down across from Mando. He was short and squat, just like Mando. But he was wide, and even with a jacket and fedora on, he looked like he was muscular. His face was not quite like Mando's, all angles, with scars, and baked to a dark brown. He was Anglo, yet he was darker than Mando was, and Mando was half Mexican. His lids seemed permanently draped over half his eyes. Under his eyes, his cheeks were puffy. He was a man who could do some damage to you. His face said that he wouldn't mind damaging you. Mando saw what he might look like with another baton or tire tool bounding off his head.

"I got a rented Lincoln Continental outside. You want to take a drive around town while I reminisce?"

Mando said, "sure."

Colton's face lit up as he drove around town and passed his old haunts. He told Mando about fights, about who he beat up, about close scraps. He told Mando about Snake, good enough man and tough as they come on the gambling table, but a real "pussy" in an actual fight, which was why he hired Colton and Lionel Dexter. Then he drove by the house on Adams Street followed by the house where his family now lived—in a rich people's suburb next to the Odessa Country Club.

"Who you think bought that house for them?" he asked Mando. Mando didn't have to answer.

Then they drove through the wind and the blowing trash and tumbleweeds and dust back to the Cactus Lounge. Some of the dust, wind, and trash followed them in, and Colton sat at a table and set a pint bottle of bourbon on it, and a young waitress brought them coke and ice. Bullet was gone, and Colton got to the point. "You see what I got. You seen that rental car outside. I own one just like it. In Dallas, I got a nicer house than your Momma, and I live in it alone. You understand me, boy?"

"Yes," he answered, although he didn't understand.

Colton slammed the table with his flat palm. "No, you don't. That was set up, testing your honesty. You don't know shit. Ain't no way I can be a father to you. Not now. I'm just this old guy with some money attached to him. But you looked at my face. Bullet probably told you some things. I explained some things I done. And now I'm telling you, you stick with Bullet, and you can have what I got."

"Yes, sir, I'm working at it."

"You ain't listening, Mando. You think. You want what I got?"

"Yes."

"No."

"All right, 'no.'"

"That's right. I'm just this old guy with some money, someone who will deposit money in an account for you to get your ass back in college and erase the bad mark you left there."

"But I got this."

"But you don't listen." Colton lifted his bottle and took a sip. "You seen that scar on Bullet's face? She shown you that scar on her chest where they cut off a tit?" He didn't wait for Mando to answer, but the answer was that Mando hadn't seen her chest. "She likes to show off that surgery. Makes her think she's tough. Well, she is tough. And she'll make you tough. And tough can be useful to some people with money. And you can be living in a big house by yourself, driving a

Lincoln Continental, and chewing on your own liver because you know all you got is nothing, is just the price somebody paid for you, and now they own your sorry ass. And there's your brother in prison eating his liver because he knows he made his life into total shit. And here you are flunking out of college and pissing away anything you got."

Mando was getting scared. "You ain't going to hit me, are you?"

Colton started laughing. "No, beating you ain't going to do no good. You ain't listening. I'm telling you I'll pay for you to get your ass back in college and then out of it and make less money than me and maybe even end up with less money than you got now and end up with a shitty little house and some screaming kids of your own because you got a job some college asshole can get. And that ain't the place where this job is leading."

"I don't get it."

Colton reached into his jacket and pulled out a check. He put it in front of Mando. "You get one of these a year for three years. You can piss it all away. Or you can invest it by giving yourself a glimpse of a different type a world than this and seeing if you like it better. Bullet will be here awhile."

Mando couldn't believe the amount written on the check. "How did you get this kind of money?"

Colton stuck his forefinger up under the brim of his hat and pushed up, so Mando could see his mangled face. "I had to kill a few people. I beat up some others. If the cops ever get me, I got enough information to plea bargain myself into a lighter sentence. You want to be me?"

"Did Way Low call you and tell you to talk to me?"

"See, you are smart, maybe not college smart. But you can figure stuff." And as he smiled, his face looked like it would crack.

"Does my mother know you're here?"

"She doesn't know I exist."

"So, you and Way Low keep in touch."

"Me and Way Low go back. We got some secrets."

Colton kept smiling. "You just busting to know what Way Low and I done."

"I been guessing for years."

Colton folded his hands and hung his head. The wind outside whistled. A tiny piece of paper skirted across the wood floor. "Now you realize how dangerous me telling you something is?"

"Yes, sir."

"Bullet's told you about Danny Fowler, right?" Mando nodded. Colton lowered his head and shook it, like he was deciding between his own best interest and his blood. And because Mando was blood, he said, "Some people wanted his killers dead. Those people included Bullet. Well, Way Low and me saw to it that one of his killers was dead."

"There's more to the story, ain't there?"

"See, you are smart."

"What's the rest of the story?"

"I think I ought to save it for a time when it can do me and Bullet and Way Low less damage." Mando's eyes asked him when. "That time ain't far off."

"I could of killed a boy."

"But I heard your aim was good," Colton said.

"Did you kill somebody?" Colton looked away from Mando like he was dodging the question.

"Where?"

"Here."

"I told you about Gervin, right?"

"So did Lionel."

"And you ain't told anybody, right?

"I don't talk much. And the people I talk to are the ones who tell me the stories."

"What I do for a living is 'fix things.' Sometimes that involves 'fixing people.'" He started his story, but when he got well into it, to the part where Mando knew what he'd done and how'd he become what he was, Colton stopped. Then he said, "When the time is right, you ask Way Low." Mando stared at him because Colton had short-changed him on history.

"How about some more information?"

"It depends."

"You said you live alone. Where does my grandmother live?"

Colton shook his head to help him think, "She passed." He stared at his son. "It was sudden. Her heart. You got Way Low's and her blood in you. You got to believe in genetics. You go to a doctor?"

"Not much."

"Go."

Mando was sad to hear about his grandmother because, though he was trying to get himself away from his family, he wanted to account for them, to know about them. He started feeling kindly toward his father, so Mando said, "I think my mother quit all her boyfriends."

Colton nodded. "You're a good boy. Your temperament don't match this kind of work." Colton stopped to think, then said, "I knew this guy, Justan Brady. He was bothered by such stuff as you are."

"And?"

"And I got to get back to my life."

* * *

Mando thought that he would return to what he knew, reading and running. But again, there weren't too many job openings. What he ended up doing was to drive down to San Angelo and talking to the track coach. Coach Singletary wanted nothing to do with him, but Mando had on his jogging shoes and convinced Singletary to step outside and walk with him to the track. "Time it," Mando told him. Singletary looked at him like he was some kind of Martian or something, but he raised his wrist to his face. Mando stretched, and then he ran at a fast pace then pushed it. He got in a mile when Singletary yelled for him to stop.

Singletary's squint was carved into his face, probably from years of staring down tracks. He poked that hand carved face at Mando and said, "I got people run a mile faster."

"I didn't know what I was running or why."

Coach Singletary didn't look much different from the West Texans Mando saw in the Cactus and other bars in Odessa, so Mando figured he could talk to him like he was sitting in the Cactus Lounge. "I can go faster if something is chasing me."

The squint lifted. "I got no scholarships."

"I just want to run."

"You run cross-country?"

"My specialty."

"You get your ass accepted and enrolled, and in the fall, I'll chase you."

It was something Mando wouldn't have done before he worked for Bullet and Bill Sears. He didn't have the confidence. But somehow, they gave him some of theirs.

The next fall, he was enrolled at Angelo State University and tried out for the cross-country and track team. Singletary just let him run into or with the familiar West Texas wind, and then he told Mando that, during the winter and spring, he'd train him to be a miler.

Meantime Mando had to figure out something to study. He couldn't major in reading and running, so like the other jocks, he started taking courses in kinesiology. He liked it okay. Reading about the body and figuring it out was sort of like studying the auto manuals to repossess them. But Coach Singletary and some of Mando's jock friends told him that, since he liked reading so much, he ought to major in English because it had lots of reading.

In spring, with wind getting stronger, and his legs and pace getting stronger too, he started taking literature courses. He didn't like them much, but he was going to stick with anything he started.

And sometimes, on his way to the cafeteria, or walking back from the cafeteria in the dark that came early in winter, Mando would end up saying a few, spare words to this tall, muscled up, red-haired volleyball player. She had three inches on him, shoulders wider and more powerful than his, a reach that was nearly as long as one of his legs, and thighs that bulged more than his, even in her baggy sweats. A long jumper on the way back on a cold night said, "Look at her. You'd know you'd want to do her, but she'd probably tear your ass up."

Mando knew words; he just didn't use them much around these younger guys, but he said, "But you'd still probably like it."

She showed up in an anatomy class, and they looked at a dissected fetal pig together. Smelling of formaldehyde, their fingers rubbed together inside the pig while they felt the blue tendons. Mando looked up at her, she down at him, and even with the formaldehyde in the air, Mando could smell her breath—smelling of a decayed tooth. Then he saw that chipped tooth with the brown edge to it. "You're looking at my tooth," she said.

"It's pretty."

"It's getting fixed soon as I got the money."

Come spring time they took walks around campus together. With Daylight Savings Time, they sat outside her dorm. And then at the end of spring, before they left for summer, Mando drove her out to O.C. Fisher Lake, and they looked out over the shallow lake with the cracked clay working back from the waterline and watched the sun set behind a clump of mesquites. Making his way through the smell of that tooth, he kissed her. And she didn't whip his ass. And Mando not only survived the cramped squirming and twisting in the cab of his truck, but he truly enjoyed it.

Dolores was older than most of the students, just like Mando. She had grown up with strict Church of Christers in Abilene, Texas. She grew up liking to play volleyball and doing anything that her parents or the Church of Christers told her not to do. She got drunk. She smoked. She got arrested for marijuana and a little cocaine. She had a baby before she got out of high school, but she gave it up for adoption. She flunked out of Abilene Christian University and Cisco Junior College.

So now she was at Angelo State, not wanting to talk to anybody or start a romance, just wanting to get out. Just like Mando. He didn't have time for her, but Mando spent as much time as he could with her.

And as he was growing to like her more, he was liking literature less. So on through another cross-country season and into a winter, and then into a course in the short story taught by professor doctor Dalrymple. In the first week of real winter, right after thanksgiving but before Christmas, just that time when you know it's going to stay cool, Dr. Dalrymple asked him to come by his office to talk about his paper.

Dr. Dalrymple liked to smoke. He couldn't do it inside, so they went outside into the cold wind. And as Mando grabbed his elbows and raised his shoulders to his ears, Professor Dr. Dalrymple puffed and exhaled smoke into the wind. "Mr. Parker," he said. "You have a way with words. Your writing is good. But you could just go deeper. You could deal more with the questions that the stories bring up."

"That's just it," Mando said. "I got no problems with words. It's the questions I don't like."

Dalrymple shivered as he tapped the ashes off his cigarette, "Literature is about questions. That's the complexity I'm talking about."

"I know."

"But you like the words."

Mando hugged himself and stamped his feet. "It's like the words are there to explain the meaning of things, the way to do things. And that's why I like words, not necessarily 'reading,' but words. Words can make the questions go away."

"The questions are the real point of thinking. That's why you are in school."

"Back when I was repoing cars, I read the auto manuals to learn about alarm systems. I did. I want the words to march in order like that. I want the reading to be like that."

Dalrymple gave Mando this funny look, "I haven't heard that before. That's new. But that's not the way literature works."

"Well, there's too much literature. There's too much we don't know, even with the words helping us."

"So why are you majoring in English?"

"Coach Singletary told me to."

"Let's go get warm," Dalrymple said, and he snuffed out his cigarette, and they went back inside. So Mando took courses in technical writing, teaching writing, and rhetoric. In those courses, the words answered some stuff. But Mando stuck with kinesiology too, because it gave more answers.

* * *

After two years, Mando had some part of a scholarship and a mostly on on-off relationship with Dolores. At a cross-country meet in Austin, running along the Colorado River walkways, seeing actual scenery without stuff blowing in the wind, Mando was running the best and most enjoyable he ever had. It wasn't him so much; the scenery—the water, the trees, the slight humidity became him. His legs were churning, and they were a part of this "it" that he was in and a part of him too, but they weren't really part of a just-him. "It" was all working together, no matter what "it" might be. He wasn't racing. Time didn't exist. He was a part of this scenery, and he would be, from here on out.

And in record time, he saw the finish line ahead of him. Ahead too was Coach Singletary squint smiling at him and Dolores who wanted to come to Austin to party afterwards on 6ᵗʰ Street. Then his right foot, the one he had jammed through a manifold, stopped working. "It" stopped working for him. He felt like he had fallen out of heaven and was back in a strange new earth—or hell. He felt a snapping deep inside of him, not just in his foot, but through his whole body. And then there was not hurting, just that finish line and Mando seeming to go backwards.

He tried slinging that foot with his leg like it was a lump of meat on the end of his leg, but it wouldn't hold him up. He hopped on his other foot, but that just took him so far. Nothing hurt, nothing was that shocking. It was just that he had lost all that he had just felt.

Dolores and Coach Singletary ran to him. He got to his butt and looked up at them to see Coach Singletary's squint and Dolores' red hair making a slim burning halo around her face. Coach Singletary got his shoe off, and there, on the end of his leg, was something that looked more like a formless lump of tan dough than a foot. Coach Singletary gingerly hefted his foot and squeezed. The foot didn't have bones, no structure, just lumpiness.

Three hours later, Mando was in a hospital bed with his foot soaked in ice. He had an I.V. full of salt water and painkiller, neither of which he needed. And while Dolores held his hand and Coach Singletary stood with the doctor at the foot of the bed, the doctor explained. The metal and the screws the Odessa doctors had put in his foot held, but his bones didn't. It was all the pounding that Mando was giving it. And in turn, the pounding created several stress fractures in otherwise good bones. The foot was pulverized. Running was over for Mando.

"Goddamn," said Coach Singletary. "Two years you been running. Didn't it ever hurt?"

"Off and on," Mando said. "But I just gritted my teeth against it. Then I got used to it. I like to run."

Dolores said, "You idiot." Mando just stared at his propped-up foot, like he was going to start cussing it for betraying him.

When he came to from surgery, he was in a dark hospital room. It must have been the middle of the night. A bleeping heart monitor woke him. Now his heart was betraying him, keeping him awake. The door opened, and a thickset figure stepped in. It turned on a lamp. "Doctor?" Mando asked.

The figure sat in a chair next to Mando's bed. When Mando adjusted his eyes, the figure became his father. "You fuck up a lot," Colton said.

"How come every time I see you, I been beat to shit in some way?"

"Now that you ain't got running, what do you need?"

"Nothing you can give me."

"You need more money?"

"You already gave me a lot of money."

"I could try to give you some hope, but I wouldn't know what to say."

They looked at each other and didn't say words. "There's Jake Raven, an obnoxious sort. And what made him obnoxious was that he just couldn't let his past go. Just hung on to him, playing football with Odessa High School Bronchos. He played with me. Hell, we weren't even Permian, the team that won."

"You making a point about me?"

"I'm saying you ain't nothing like him. You changed your life three or four times already. Don't let this little bump get you stuck."

"I'm out of ideas."

Colton looked around him and peered into the dark. The words came out of his mouth but it was like those words weren't for Mando but for the dark. "I was like you the whole time I was in Odessa. I was playing scared. I could feel everything closing in on me. I *let* things happen instead of *making* them happen. Then I said, "fuck it.' I'm better now."

"Hell, you know what you do. How are you better?"

"I'm not scared."

"Tell me about your life now."

"Ain't much to tell. And there ain't much I'm gonna tell you. So, forget it."

"Then tell me about Odessa."

"I've told you."

"Well then, tell me more. Use different words. Go over it some more. Answer me some questions."

He started. Jake Raven's name came up again, and Bullet's, and Snake's, and Way Low's, and all the characters in his story. He told Mando about playing football, about finding Elena, about worrying about a future. Only this time, he told what he thought, what he felt, and what he should have done or could have done. And he laughed sometimes, and sometimes his voice halted, and he stammered, like the

251

story was getting stuck in his throat. And he let Mando stop him and ask to go back over, to get it just right, to get the right words, so Mando could remember it. And sometimes Mando asked him what he thought or what he was thinking to do such a thing. Mando even asked him about Elena, Arnie, and Way Low.

"I'm not sure if the fucked- up part just happened or if it was my fault. All I know is, I'd wish it different."

Finally Mando asked what happened with Danny Fowler's murder. "I told you. When the time is right, that story belongs to Way Low. And if you dare, you can ask Bullet. And there's this cop, maybe still a cop, named Justan Brady. I told you about him before. You're like him. He wanted to know things. Couldn't let things be. He wanted sense, justice, kitties, puppies, rainbows, and unicorn farts."

"Sounds like I'm like a lot of people in your stories." Mando said. "There's a few."

"But you stopped too soon. What have you been doing since? How do you come by what you come by?"

"By being quiet about what I done and how I came by what I got."

Mando stared back at Colton, and he, in return, stared back at his son. Mando finally breathed in enough courage to ask, "Have you killed people?"

Colton shook his head, "Answer ain't a part of the deal."

It was the most they ever talked. Colton talking to Mando made him feel truly grown up for the first time in his life.

It was the last time Mando saw Colton.

* * *

When the cast came off and Mando threw the crutches away and the foot came out misshapen and yet another size shorter but wider than the other foot, not knowing what to do, he asked Dolores to marry him.

She probably shouldn't have, but she did. And they graduated together. Desperate, needing some place to go, to just be, they took jobs with the Denver City ISD. She taught 5th grade P.E. and geography. Mando coached middle-school and taught basic health. As the years passed, Mando taught some English, the five-paragraph essay, phrases, clauses, and comma splices, the sure stuff that made sense. And sometimes, stuck in Denver City, with a starter home, and then one baby girl and then another one just a year and half later, Dolores and Mando would go out in the backyard while the girls took a nap and look up at the sky, hold hands, and start wishing and wanting. Over time Mando became truly married to Dolores and his girls, and he divorced his Odessa family.

Chapter 18

School was done, and Mando's family was getting older and established, so Mando was looking forward to a summer of boredom. The only relief was a small city pool, backyard barbeques, and foreign beer and wine from Lubbock. Now that the girls were older, they'd all end up in the backyard, staring up at the sky, just wishing and wanting for something to change, for something to do. Since it was a dry county and since Mando was a teacher upholding community values, he had to wrap his empty beer bottles in taped paper bags before he stuffed them into the garbage can for pick up. Couldn't have students see evidence of his drinking. These tiny details were taking a toll on his family life.

Mando was surrounded by women's things, hair dryers, tampons, mascara, eye-liner, skin abrasives and treatments. And sometimes he felt like the women just tolerated him, and so he missed the track and the boys, and he wished for some buddies at the bar, maybe some of his old Odessa life when he was living like his father did.

And so while he was in the kitchen and opening up a beer and looking outside at his family—red-head Dolores looking up at the stream left by a jet; his youngest, Lucy, with her head next to the spinning air conditioner, drying her red hair, wet from dousing herself with the hose; and the oldest, Audrey, jumping up and down on the trampoline, as she was prone to do all summer; Sebastian, their mutt dog, chasing all of them—Mando's pocket vibrated with his cell. It was Way Low. Mando wandered into the living room.

At first the years dragged by for Mando and Dolores, but then speeded up, and the faster they got, the less Mando kept in touch with his mother and Way Low. Then because he had this new, changeless life and because it was so much better than what he had known and seen as life in Odessa, he just kinda lost touch with his mother and

Way Low. And in this isolated world, Dolores lost touch with her family too. Mando knew only that Way Low was losing toes and then pieces of his feet due to diabetes and that Elena grew bored and that the men she ran with didn't satisfy her, so she grew mean and resentful. Age wise, it seemed like Way Low just stopped like he was, but Elena just kept getting older until she caught up with Way Low.

"Your father is dead," Way Low said. "And you got to bury him. And you got to be here 2 p.m., Tuesday. You got to be, no choice. A lawyer going to read his will to us."

"I need more info."

"It's all I got, but you gonna get some money. I know it. We all gonna get some money."

Way Low tried to explain what he knew or didn't know, but he kept circling in on himself. And when Mando asked how much money, Way Low said no one knew. Colton was private. Mando asked how his father died. Way Low didn't know or wouldn't say.

When Mando hung up, he sat in his recliner in front of the TV and clicked on the TV and surfed the hundreds of satellite channels, paying attention to none of them, hoping for some sound and a flash of color to get his attention. And then his wife came in.

"Mando," she said and sat on his lap. She was still a shapely woman, but she was tall, a lot of her, so to speak, so she was heavy in his lap. "We have to talk."

"I got to go," Mando said.

She grunted, patted his face, and squirmed in his lap, pressed the sharp angle of her butt into Mando. "See, there it is. That's what I mean."

"But I mean I got to. My father has died. Some lawyer is going to read his will on Tuesday."

She circled her arms around him and pressed her cheek next to his, filling his eyes with that red hair. "I am so bored," she said.

"Take a trip."

"See, look what you said, 'take a trip.' What about us?"

"Let me see what this will says. We may have a trip."

"We're like roommates."

"Yeah, well, that's true. It's hard to find a good roommate."

"No, we need to do something. We need to work on our marriage."

"Like what?"

"You need to get yourself out of that chair and notice me, us. You need to be involved with us. You're just so indifferent, so oblivious."

"That's how you got to live out here. What else can I do?"

"I want to take the girls and go somewhere. I want to be away from you and see if I like it more."

"I don't like the sound of this."

"We all have the summer off. I want to spend it away from you but with the girls. I want to see what that would be like."

"You're telling me this now? I have to bury my father."

Dolores pushed herself up and away from him but held his face between her palms. "Our marriage is on the rocks. It's crumbling. You never knew your father. You love us. Or so you say. And now, suddenly, you've got to run to him." Dolores let his face go and stood up to her full height.

"He's dead." Mando did not get up. He would rather look up at her from a chair, then with his feet planted in front of her.

"And you haven't cared if he was alive for longer than I've known you."

"I've got to go."

"Well then, go." Dolores walked away, but as she was about to get into the hall and go to their main bedroom, she stopped, reached up to grab the top of the door frame, and turned to face Mando. She looked like she was about to spike the volley ball. "You just made up my mind. The girls and I are going to my parents. I don't know if I'll come back."

"The dog, Sebastian? What will we do with him?"

She grunted again. "The neighbors can keep him. Their kids like him anyway. They can keep him."

"He's mine."

"Then] you figure it out." She turned and stomped down the hall. But she stopped and came back to face Mando. "You need a soulmate, not a roommate. And all you got is me."

Before Mando knew what was coming out of his mouth, he said, "I got a hard-enough time finding a *soul*, let alone a mate for it." From some time way in the past, Mando remembered Way Low saying that. Now Dolores turned her ass to Mando and went into their bedroom to pack.

Later, as Mando packed, his life unraveled. Dolores and Mando didn't say much to each other. Tuesday Morning, they sat across from each other at the breakfast table, avoided each others' eyes, and tried to think of something to say. If Lucy and Audrey noticed, they didn't let on. School was out, and they were busy being girls. Mando hoped for them that their lives wouldn't suddenly just shift. But he felt like his would for sure. Before he got into his truck, he limped out into the backyard, and Sebastian ran up to him. Mando held out his hand, and Sebastian rested his chin in it. Sebastian rarely stood still, and then only for Mando, maybe because, with a bum foot, Mando was the only one in his house not running around. He was easier to catch. He was quicker to admire the wiry-haired dog.

Mando left waving, then drove to Odessa. He had a couple of hours to think about being "oblivious," about being a "roommate" and not a "soulmate." He thought until his head hurt, and all he could come up with was that he chose Dolores, and then when they came along, he chose the girls. His life with them was better than the other choices he had, so he stuck with them and was determined to stay stuck with them. Now Dolores wanted to come unstuck.

In Odessa, he checked into a Motel 6 and drove around looking for the law office of T. Travis Griggs. The next day he was to inherit a piece of his father.

* * *

Mando drove to a changed but not different Odessa. The Odessa lawyer T. Travis Griggs had an office in a strip mall out by the new

Music City Mall. A couple of spindly maple trees were the only decorations, as was the habit in all of that dusty, make-do town, now in the middle of a boom, which people were already pissing away. With another boom, another building boom was going on, this time, though, it was franchise stores and shops and fast food joints. Mando could tell from just looking around, from the parking lot in that strip mall and watching the wind blow the trash and tumbleweeds through the parking lot and down 42nd Street, that this boom was different, not quite as wild and as unruly. But the town still just plowed, asphalted, and built, no little flowers or grass, not even a cactus. No decoration, no prettiness. That was for a weaker citizenry. And Mando knew, from listening to Snake and Bullet, that the town and the people would piss this boom away too.

Lawyer T. Travis Griggs' secretary told Mando to go down the hall and to the right. Mando stopped to get a drink from the water fountain next to the door, thinking he needed to wet his throat even though he planned to listen, not talk. He walked in to see lots of people, two in upholstered, fancy, lawyer-like chairs and others in folding chairs, all pulled up to a shiny wood desk. T. Travis Griggs sat behind it.

In an upholstered chair was Bullet Price. She looked up to Mando, and it looked like her scar had widened. And now her shoulders were curled forward. Two white plastic tubes stuck in each nostril and then passed over her ears. She took the tubes out of her nose, stood, and hugged Mando. She tapped her steel oxygen tank with her toe. "God damn emphysema," she said. She looked at least ten years older than she was, like she ought to be in a nursing home.

In the other upholstered chair was Elena. She let Bullet finish hugging Mando and then stood to hug him, not to be out done by Bullet, so as not to give mothership over to Bullet.

Next to her, in a folding chair, was Snake Popp, not looking a day older than back when Mando was a teenager. He got up, shook Mando's hand, and slapped his shoulder with the other one. He could not control himself. Tears were coming up. He dabbed at the thick hair combed back from his forehead and ran both hands along the sides of his head to straighten out those silver wings of hair.

Way Low could not get up because he wasn't in a folding chair. Mando had been mistaken; Way Low was in a wheelchair. He nodded. And when Mando's head dropped to look at him, it stayed down, and Mando couldn't bring it back up. Way Low had two empty pants legs curled up and hanging above the footrests of the wheel chair. His feet were gone.

Gray headed and cloudy-eyed Lionel Dexter got up to shake Mando's hand and then sat back down. And then, a man about Lionel's age got up. He seemed to sag, but he had a bright smile, like he was about to get something more than money. "Justan Brady," he said and shook Mando's hand.

They all waited a while longer, tried to make small talk, but none of them really had anything to say. Then, T. Travis Griggs checked his watch. "Well, let's all just sit down and make our way through these matters," T. Travis Griggs said. The rest sat, and Mando picked out a vacant metal folding chair. "Call me Travis." Then, Travis started, "This is the last will and testament of Colton Parker. Finding the *last* one was tough. He had several. And he had several names on them. But his attorney in Dallas and I and the probate court in Dallas chose this one. It's got his real name. And it's the newest. It must be the most accurate.

"Seems Colton Parker was generous and grateful to a lot of people. He left some of his money to a group of people just like you folks up in Dallas. And that part of him has been doled out. But there is this considerable left."

Snake put his elbows on his knees and leaned forward. Bullet leaned back. She looked like she was about to cry. Elena acted as though she was just indifferent to anything concerning Colton, even if it meant money. Lionel and Justan Brady looked confused. "Now, to get any money, you got to be here. And it appears that we have some folks missing. I see empty chairs. I'm going to do some doling out and do a roll call at the same time."

"Mr. Parker willed Bullet Price ten percent of this half of his money. Is Ms. Price here?" Bullet nodded and sucked in through the tubes in her nose. "Good, you win. A check mark goes by your name, and once all the particulars have been settled, you'll get your money."

"Just how much is that?" Bullet asked.

"Why don't you let me get through the whole roll call, then we'll see how it adds up."

Travis Griggs held his gaze on Bullet. "That your real name?"

"Yes," she said.

"Somebody's Momma named her baby girl 'Bullet'?"

"I had it legally changed."

Travis Griggs shook his head. "Ernest Popp?" Snake raised his hand like he was a school boy and smiled. "Well that sounds like a real name. We won't have any trouble disbursing your five percent." Snake looked at Bullet as if to ask why less. Everyone else leaned forward to listen for their names.

"Elena Parker?"

Elena said, "Me."

Travis said, "one percent." That percentage, Mando knew, as Colton had told him, was punishment for that affair—or affairs.

"Mina Fowler?"

"Who?" Mando's mother asked. And the rest were silent, like they knew who she was.

"She's dead," Bullet said.

Travis Griggs said, "Doesn't' excuse her. You got to be present to win. She would have gotten five percent."

"Why her, but he gives me nothing?" Elena said. Way Low reached to her and patted her leg to keep her from coming out of her chair.

"Justan Brady?" The sagging man raised his hand. "Ten percent." Justan Brady didn't raise a sagging part of his face, just stared ahead, caring less.

"Why does he get this money? Who is he?" Elena asked.

"Jennifer Peveto?"

"She's untraceable," Bullet said. She looked around at the rest of us. "I tried. I really tried. I did. I wish I could of found her." Bullet breathed deeply. "Poor girl. I can't afford a private detective. But if you want, depending on the money, I could try to find her."

"Poor girl," Snake said. Mando looked at Bullet and thought to himself and knew Bullet knew what he was thinking; whores ain't got no souls.

"Who is this 'poor girl?'" Elena asked.

"Four percent," Travis said.

"Lionel Dexter." Lionel looked around to see if there was another Lionel Dexter before he nodded. "Ten Percent."

"Arnie Parker?"

"He can't be here," Elena said. "He has good reasons."

But Way Low patted her knee again, "He should be here. Truth is, we don't know where he is. But he should be here. He is another soul lost to us." Bullet stiffened when Way Low said *soul*.

"Twenty percent."

"Raul Garcia?" Travis looked at Way Low, and Way Low nodded. "twenty percent." Elena gave her father a hard, cold stare.

"Amando Parker." All eyes turned to Mando.

"I guess that's you. Got to be you," Travis said. "Twenty percent."

"The people who aren't here?" Elena said.

Travis held up his hand. "If they are not here, their money goes to Amando Parker." Everyone turned to look at Mando.

"That's . . . ." Snake hesitated trying to figure.

"Another twenty nine percent," Bullet answered. "Congratulations. You done good. I guess you know what your daddy thought of you now."

"What if I wouldn't have been here?"

"Says nothing about that. I guess he just figured you would be here. If you wouldn't have come, you'd have left me in a sticky situation," lawyer Travis said.

"Now just to give everybody an idea about what's at stake here. After expenses Amando's initial twenty percent is about $180,000. Maybe y'all can help me with the math?"

The math hit Mando in the face. His hand started shaking. Lionel Dexter was smiling in front of him, "Let's go buy us a car, not repo it." But Mando was not happy. He was shaking his head. "Oh boy, you got a pocket of cash, and you look like you lost something."

Mando looked up at Lionel, but it was Bullet who answered. "He did lose something."

For all the words that Mando had read, he had trouble at times like this putting them together. "It's the way he got the money," he said while looking straight at Bullet.

Bullet took some hard breaths through her plastic tubes, "And what's probably hurting you is that he could make that much money at what he did."

"Well, now. Let's all relax. I'll do some figuring. And then on your way out make sure that you leave an address."

Mando walked out of Travis's office with the rest of *them*. Elena pushed Way Low in his wheelchair. Bullet pulled her iron tank and patted Mando's shoulder. Nobody talked. Snake eyed Lionel and tried to keep from smiling. By the time they got back outside, they were all counting their money, except for Justan Brady. His sagging look had turned into a smile. Mando looked at the one tree in the parking lot and the sand and trash blown against the curb. It looked beautiful. He could now buy his family a new life, where they wouldn't just stare up at the sky and wish and want. It was dirty money, but his father had gotten it to him.

* * *

Mando cancelled his reservation at Motel 6 and checked into the Elegante Hotel, which he remembered as the tallest, classiest place in

Odessa, the Hilton Hotel. Then he went up to his room on the sixth floor and stared down at Odessa. To the south and west, he saw where he grew up, and from that high point, those old streets and small houses didn't look so bad. He wanted to call his wife, but he wasn't sure what to say, though he had rehearsed several speeches; he just couldn't find the right words. So instead he called Lionel Dexter and asked him to meet him in the bar.

Two hours later, Mando was having a dark, foreign beer with Lionel. After three beers, He got to his point. "You told me about Gervin, but I gotta know more."

"Lionel stared at the mouth of his beer bottle. "I got no more."

"What about Danny Fowler?"

"I got to go. I ain't seen you in years, and now you asking me this kinda shit. I got to go."

He started to get up, but Mando put out a hand to stop him. "Mina Fowler was his mother. Why was she in the will?"

Lionel's smile and face drooped. "What the shit? That was all a long time ago. Me, I'm satisfied to know what little I know." He reached out for his beer. "You ought to be satisfied to know what little you do. Let some things rest."

"I got to know."

"Well then, know that I walked out. Mina hired us to find some boys that she thought killed her boy. That wasn't no problem for me. We was good detectives. Then she wanted us to kill them. That's when I dropped out. I just went away. Killing white folks just ain't the kind of business a young black man ought to be in. Not in them days. Not in these days."

"We been over that. So did my father kill these boys?"

"I got no idea. I don't want to know."

"Who knows?"

"Closest person to that news is Bullet."

When Lionel got up to go, Mando ordered him another beer. "I got to go."

"You came for the beer."

"And now I'm through with it."

"Drink another one." Lionel shook his head. "I'm short on story. I need to know some more."

"I got nothing."

"What you got for $2500?"

"That might loosen my memory."

"Sit down," Mando said.

And Lionel talked, and Mando bought him beers, and then Mando bought him dinner, and then more drinks, until Lionel could remember no more and Mando could think no more. When Lionel was worn out of story, time, and sobriety, he said, "Maybe you right. Maybe I should have started talking to you back when we was repoing together."

In truth Lionel didn't tell Mando anything new. He just told him more with different words. But Mando liked watching him tell it. Lionel felt good about telling and not just because he was getting money out of the telling. It was like he was working his way to being rid of it, of not being scared of it.

With repoing on his mind, Mando drove to the spread-out ranch house in Odessa's Country Club Estates that his father had bought for them. He had run through this neighborhood in high school cross-country. And his father had met him here. Colton must have looked around and liked what he saw. Colton put a sizeable chunk of his money into this house.

Elena answered the door, and Mando took her hand and pulled her through the living room and into the kitchen. He made her sit down. As Mando noticed and remembered, families discussed important things in the kitchen. "Why do you resent my father?"

"Cause he left us. That's why. Don't you know?"

"But what about him? How about him? As a man? As a human? What would you say about that?"

"Why you getting crazy about your father?"

Mando knelt in front of his short mother and put his hands on her knees. He saw in her face traces of his and recalled that she had given him his short body. "What you doing," Way Low yelled from the living room. "Is that Mando?"

"It's me. We're talking," Mando said, hoping that that was clue to Way Low to stay out of the conversation. Mando looked at his mother and squeezed her knees. "Why did you marry him? Wasn't there nothing good about him?"

"He tried, but he just couldn't do nothing."

"Tell me about how he tried and the nothing he couldn't do." Elena started slowly. And when she stumbled, Mando helped her with the words. She kept her chin jutted out, but when Mando squeezed her knee, she softened and dropped her head to think and almost cry. She told him, with more words than he could decipher, how she pulled away from his father as she realized what he was and what chased him. "He was scared," she said. "I shoulda seen that when I married him." She thought and rambled. "And he didn't know how to treat a woman or a family," she said toward the end of her story.

"What about love? Did you love him? At first even?"

"He did something for me, or to me, at first. It was touching, and you know, Mando, you know the thing that married people do, but there was more in it than just that. Then the more in it went away. It's got to.

"Did it go for him?"

"I don't know about him. It's just that when the *extra* was gone for me, there was no more *him* left for me."

"Even with all the money he sent you?"

"He got to be a better man, a better husband, once he left than when he was here."

"How could that be?"

"Mando, don't be stupid. Look around. He gave us this."

Mando got his thoughts and words wrapped around each other. "Is that all? I mean is that it? No more. I mean . . ."

His mother hesitated and put her hand on the side of his head. "You know, you sitting me down like this, asking me about this, makes you like your father."

"I'm nothing like him."

"We should have talked more, like this."

"Me or him?"

"Both you. And me too. You're like him. Don't be that way."

"What way is that?"

"It's not bad, not good. Just being him. Wanting answers where there is none." She rubbed the side of his head some more. "I'm telling you for your own good."

"Mando, that you?" Way Low yelled again as though he were trying to roll himself to them.

"Say something to your abuelo," Elena told her son.

Later that night, with his mother's words boring from his ears into the middle of his brain, Mando phoned Dolores in Abilene. They talked over and around things. He dared not ask if or when she was coming back, if or when their lives would be back on a track that he recognized. He didn't ask what went wrong. He wanted to know. But he couldn't' hear it yet. His heart thumped in his chest as he tried to think and concentrate in a way that he never had done in HIS life, maybe harder than he had ever done in his life. And he had to put the words together that said what he felt and what he had discovered. But words were getting tough, and he was afraid that he had failed them, and so when she asked for more words, he couldn't say them because he didn't trust himself to say the right ones. And he couldn't help but think that he was going to have to come up with those reasons and those words himself. And what else he didn't ask or say was that *he* or *they* were just a whole lot richer if they were together. He didn't tell her about the money he now had. After she hung up, he wanted to start running.

* * *

The next day, sweating into their black clothes, the people who remembered Colton gathered around the hole that was to be Colton's grave. There was no viewing, no service, no memorial, just a casket, arrived as freight from Dallas to a funeral home and then the planting at the cemetery. The casket was shut in Dallas and stayed closed. There were no flowers. There was a small, square grave stone, just a marker, not a tombstone, off to the side. The exact date of death was left off.

It was like Colton just to disappear, to erase himself from the earth and from people's memory, just a little postage-size stone imbedded on top of his grave. He required them to be at the lawyer's, but not at the burial. But all of them at the reading of the will showed up. They wanted to see the end of him. And they watched as the funeral director watched as the cemetery workers lowered the casket. The funeral director asked if anyone wanted to say anything. They looked at each other. No one said anything. Mando said, "Someone should say something."

"Perhaps we should take this as a celebration of life," the funeral director said.

"Not you," Mando said. "One of us." But no one had words. Mando had some but didn't trust them. He tried to force himself into thinking of some more, but as he was learning with his departed wife and his "dearly departed" father, he just didn't know words like he thought he did. Finally, all he could force out was a thought, "We just got to wonder if he was bad man. And then we got to wonder if we are bad people." Mando shouldn't have said that because everyone else looked at him like he had betrayed them.

The preacher asked if anyone wanted to say a prayer. Bullet finally spoke up, "Not a one of us feel like they have any right to prayer."

She looked at Mando, and so he dug some words out of his mind, "Hell, we flunked words, little alone words for God."

Smiling at Mando, Bullet said, "Colton didn't require us to be here. We could have just picked up our money and run. He didn't expect much of us when he wrote that will. I guess the money shows what he thought who gave him what and how much. So right now, we shouldn't expect more of us at his burial than he did."

As a blessing to them all, the preacher dismissed them and didn't ask them to watch as the workers shoveled dirt on to the casket.

They turned to leave. Bullet pulled her oxygen tank behind her. Snake held on to the elbow of her other hand trying to guide her. She needed no help. He would have been more help if he had picked up her tank for her.

Lionel twitched inside his suit. He didn't have to tell Mando that he didn't want to come. He was there because he had gotten some money.

Elena tried to push Way Low over the dried grass and gravel that made up the lawn of the cemetery. Way Low rattled in his chair. So Mando tried to help push, but the gravel and the roots and the weeds grabbed, shook, and bounced the chair. Tired of all this, Mando reached into the chair like Way Low was one of his daughters and pulled him out. Way Low didn't fight against Mando, but grabbed around his neck as Mando carried him to Elena's car. And Once Mando had Way Low stuffed into the car, Elena pushed the wheelchair over the rough ground and nearly shook the wheels off.

They all started back, but Mando went back to the graveside and stared at the casket. The men with the shovels looked at him, asking if he wanted them to go on. Mando wanted to help. He wanted to cover him up. He wanted to put an end to Colton Parker, and he felt like he got the most of Colton's money because Colton wanted Mando to put that end to Colton Parker. So Mando grabbed a shovel and scooped some dirt with the workers. But, as he was shoveling, he wanted some answers too, and here he was burying the answers—he should have been prying answers out of Colton when Colton was alive. And Mando said, "Go on. Go on, ahead. Bury his ass," as he pulled back and rested on his shovel, breathing heavy. And the Spanish-speaking working men talked amongst themselves, sometimes giggling, as they covered up Colton Parker and buried what Mando wanted to know.

Chapter 19

Mando remembered the way his jogging shoes stuck to the wood dance floor in Snake's cavernous Country-Western dancehall. Now, as he hobbled across Snake's dance floor in his suit, sweating in it, hobbled by his leather-soled dress shoes, he listened to the tap that hard leather makes on wood. When he let himself relax, his shoes almost scooted on the polished floor so that he was nearly dancing. So that was what dancing was all about.

The man behind the bar stumbled over and asked, "Can I help you?" a couple of times. But Mando kept walking, right past him, to Snake's door and then into his office.

When he opened it, Snake sat behind his desk and said, "There's the rich man." His smile spread his moustache. His winged white hair made him look like a kid-book illustration of an aging, silver-haired Greek God. Snake said, "You made out. You know, I always knew your Daddy was going to be one hell of a piss-cutter."

"Was he? Is that what he did for you? Is that what you thought of him?"

Mando sat down in the chair across from Snake's desk. Snake continued, "What you got to be pissed about? What would he have to be pissed about? I tried to help him every way I could."

Mando put his hands together then folded his fingers. He stared over the knuckles of his folded hands. Snake got a worried look. "I'm a little short on story and patience," Mando said.

"Don't dig in what's dead."

"I got to know."

"You don't got to know nothing. What makes you so special so as you get to put everything together? You get to be the one to figure it all out. You get answers. Try living your life like the rest of us, just not knowing shit."

"But you got some answers, ones I need. And I figure you owe me."

Snake hung his head, "I can't."

"How much of my money is it worth to you?"

Snake brought his head up. "It was in thinking right where your father had his problems. Now you need to think right."

"You not gonna let loose with story for me."

"I got nothing."

"Then how about opinion. Why couldn't my father think right?"

"Okay, for you, I'll give you opinion. And it's for free. For you, it's free."

Snake's opinion was honest—for him, that basically Colton just should have stayed busting heads for him, but his opinion wasn't worth much to Mando.

* * *

Still sweating into his new black suit, Mando opened the door to the Cactus Lounge, looked around to see what he had forgotten—mostly, nothing—and followed a sunbeam to the bar. The door closed behind him, blocking out that shaft of sun, and he sat on a barstool next to Bullet. She had on one of those forties-style hats with a lace veil hanging over her eyes. Mando couldn't see her scar. She looked to have been crying because some tracks of mascara rolled down to the plastic mask over her nose and mouth. She had replaced the two breathing tubes with a mask.

The air-conditioning was turned low, so the sweat under Mando's shirt and suit chilled and made him shiver. Bullet pulled her mask off. "They've got this genetic testing to see if you are prone to breast cancer. I am genetically pre-disposed. I got it once. I should have gotten it again. It should have killed me. With breast cancer gonna kill me, why not indulge in the pleasure of smoking? So now I've got this damn emphysema. It's kicking my ass."

"My grandfather's got no feet."

"You've gotten tougher."

"Hopefully smarter. Though Snake don't think so."

Bullet smiled at Mando and reached as though to touch his face, but her hand stopped just before it hit his face, like that whole gesture just wasn't true or real. Or maybe Bullet's eyes told him to stay away from her as though like she would bite him, hypnotize him, or put a spell on him. "First the whiskey bottle, then the cancer, now this. Seems something outside me, something not me, just wants me dead. And like your daddy, I got things to leave, but unlike your daddy, I got nobody to leave them to."

"I ain't asking for nothing."

"I ain't offering. . . yet."

"My marriage is falling apart." Mando didn't know where that statement came from. It was like he had pushed and tamped that fact way down in him and wanted to keep it hidden, but it wanted out. And it should have been told to somebody other than Bullet.

"I don't know nobody who is good at marriage. Well, maybe Snake, but then his wife must be either stupid or forgiving. Maybe those are the same." Mando squirmed on his stool. "You want a beer?" Mando stood on the stool, leaned over the bar, and was able to dig a cold beer out of the cooler. He twisted off the cap and felt that first good beer taste of the day. "You want to tell me about that marriage?"

"Nothing to say, really. No big story. I think she just got tired of me. Something I'm not giving her." Remembering his mother, Mando went on, "The something that was special, that was beyond just sex or beyond just being together, went away."

"If you ain't cheating on her, cheating her, or somehow abusing her, what's she complaining about?"

"Love's gone," he said. "She's looking for soul."

"Love always leaves. Souls are hard to find in the first place. You ever looked into a whore's eyes?"

"Well, I got no idea where my soul is or anybody else's, but love ain't left for me, not yet anyway. I said *it* was gone. But it wasn't like it was at first, but *it* still ain't gone for me, only for her."

"Well, sounds like she's spoiled." Mando looked at Bullet and rolled that thought around in his head. Bullet continued, "Why ain't you telling this to your momma? Why me?"

"It just came out now, and I am just now learning to talk to Momma and her to me."

"Shame on you."

"Yeah, shame on me, but I'm not here to talk about me and my problems but about my father. I figured I need some information."

"Reach over the bar and get another beer." Mando did as he was told, and Bullet produced a cigarette and a lighter. She lit the cigarette.

"Where the hell is your tank?" Bullet jerked her head. Her tank was setting below her, by her chair. "What the hell? You could blow us up."

"Ain't nothing gonna blow up." She inhaled and kept the smoke in her lungs, then slowly let it out. "We're at Colton's wake. I want a drink. And I figure, the condition I'm in, what's another cigarette gonna hurt? So back to your marriage."

"Back to Colton."

"Speaking of marriage, I could of loved your father." She sucked in on her cigarette and hung her head so she didn't have to look at Mando. "I like you." Mando felt air leaving him, so he had to catch some quick breaths. "I want to see you in a good life. I thought maybe you had it. Escaped, if that's the right word, like your daddy couldn't."

"I want to know about my father.

"I got to watch out for my own ass too, you know."

"I got money for story."

"It's not money I want."

"Why did my father leave? My mother was partially the reason. I remember what I saw. Colton gave me some clues. But he never quite told me all the way."

"You know why his casket was closed? You know what got him?" Mando shook his head. "He was retired, out-of-the-business. But somebody found out who he was and what he had done to somebody close to them, so they beat him and shot him all to pieces. He died not wanting anybody to know he was alive. And he died not wanting anybody to know he had ever lived. So, he planned. That was the reason for his monkey circus last will and testament reading." She sipped; she sucked the cigarette. Smoke swirled between them.

"What made him that way?"

"You're missing the point.

"I don't want to end up like him."

"You'd be lucky to end up like him." She waited for some reason, but seconds ticked into minutes. "You got a lot of money from him, didn't you?" Bullet didn't wait for Mando to answer. "And so did your family." Again, she didn't wait. "Y'all got all his money. Given his profession, he couldn't stay in one place too long, so he moved from one apartment to the next. Lease is up, he's gone. And I guess you saw the Lincoln he was driving, and he claimed he had several just like it?"

"He took me for a ride."

"Yeah, in a rented car. He drove old pieces of shit. His line of business, he couldn't have a permanent address or a recognizable car. He drove in old pieces of shit, lived in shitty apartments, and gave his money to his family."

"Don't try to tell me he was a saint."

"He wasn't. It was what he had to do. He had girlfriends. He bought whores. But he knew what was what. And ain't many men can claim to have done what he done for his family."

"He gave us money."

"And you took it every fucking time. You could've turned him down."

"He told me that his mamma was living with him."

"I bet that was a while ago. She did. But he couldn't be dragging his old mother around with him."

"He told me she died."

"She did."

Getting pissed off, Mando chugged his beer and turned his back to Bullet, ready to leave. "Get another beer and sit down. Don't get pissed off. You should have taken that money. It made him happy that you did. That's the point. He had it. He offered. You took it. It was never about the money."

Mando did as he was told and breathed in her smoke. "Danny Fowler was kinder to me than any man ever existed. But two boys killed him, not because he was queer, but because they knew he was queer and meant to steal from him. And they ended up killing him. And Mina Fowler, his momma, wanted the two boys dead."

"How do you know they just didn't go too far beating up a queer?"

"Because I know."

Bullet looked at Mando with a hard stare and made him think she might break her beer bottle across his face. She held her finger to her scar and pulled it along the length of that scar. "And because of this and because of the son-of-a-bitch who gave it to me and because of what and who Danny Fowler was, I wanted them two boys dead too. So, me and a skinny little whore with the real name of Jennifer Peveto killed one of them. And your father killed the other."

Then she started talking. And she didn't just tell Mando about his father but about her whole life. Mando listened hard, took notes in his mind, tried to memorize. She strained with the words like they were hurting her as much as the cigarette smoke. And her words and her truth weren't just for Mando. They were for her.

And when she finished, Mando was a little drunk, and he saw how a man could love Bullet but be scared of her nonetheless.

Mando held up his foot for Bullet to see, "I guess I'm a little like you. My foot is all fucked up."

Bullet chuckled, "You got a way to go to be truly fucked up."

Mando, listening to the beer that was now talking to him, said, "No, I fucked up. My father fucked up. There just must be something in us. Like this gene you were talking about."

Bullet looked through the smoke in front of her face to fix a stare on Mando, "You gotta learn to forgive yourself and your past. Or live with it."

"Like you."

Bullet chuckled again. "Better than me." She sucked in on the cigarette and took a long sip of beer. "There's this old West Texas joke. The county is prosecuting this guy for having indecent relations with a sheep, and the prosecutor is questioning an eye witness. 'What did you see,' he asks. And the witness said he saw the accused approach the sheep from behind, grab that sheep, and lower his pants, and just as he did, the sheep turned around and licked him in the face. Meanwhile, one juror says to the other, 'they'll do that, you know.' And the other juror says, 'I know.'"

"I heard that," Mando said. "I'm missing the moral about forgiveness."

"We're all sheep fuckers. We should be ashamed of it. Some of us are going to get caught. Some of us are going to get locked up for it. Some of us are going to pay for it over and over again. Some of us gonna be perfectly okay with it. But we need to let it go." Bullet turned from Mando to look at the mirror at the back of the bar. "Danny Fowler's fucking got him killed. Colton's killing got him exiled from you. You crashed a car and got a fucked-up foot and family. Arnie's in jail." Bullet gave a long, elaborate shrug. "Who ain't guilty?"

* * *

Elena opened the door to the long ranch house in Odessa's Country Club Estates. She was in her nightgown, ready for bed, and Mando was feeling the beer he had drunk with Bullet. "Don't you go to bed?" she asked Mando.

"I want to talk to Way Low."

"Why don't you just stay with us, instead of that hotel?"

"Because I've never been in a hotel that fancy, and now I got the money."

"I'm your mother, and your father just died."

"And I like my hotel room."

She motioned for Mando to come in, and he followed her through the living room to the den. Way Low sat in his wheelchair, his back to Mando, staring out the plate glass at the two scraggly mesquite trees in the dark backyard, lit by their flood light. "I bet that light pisses off the neighbors."

Way Low turned around smiling. "It keeps the robbers away. But I'm watching for them too."

"You want some dinner? I make you something," Elena said.

"Nothing," Mando said.

"A beer?" Way Low asked.

"A beer," Mando said and faced his mother. "I've got to talk to Way Low."

"So, talk."

"It's got to be private."

Way Low rolled his chair up to the plate glass door and pulled it open. Mando walked up behind him and rolled him out. Mando sat in a chair across from him and stared at his two empty pants cuffs dangling above his footrests. Way Low lifted his head to look at Mando's face. In the pleasant, cooling, dry air, they stared at each other, like they both knew what was coming. Elena brought them each a beer, then looked at each one for an explanation. But they held their stares, and she got the message and went back into the house.

"I hear you got foot problems too," Way Low said. "Is that what you want to talk about?"

Mando looked down and talked to the ground. "Lionel says my father got hired to find these boys that killed Bullet's queer friend. Then he tells me this dead queer's momma wants these boys dead. Then Bullet tells me she killed one and my father killed the other.

Then she mentions you. When he was alive, my father mentioned you had the story."

Way Low stared off into the darkness. He pulled his head around to look at Mando. Staring through the dark, trying to see Way Low's face, Mando couldn't tell if the old man was crying or not. "A man's job is to protect his family. Women want love, want to be treated right, want all kinds of women's shit. A man does what he has to. That's what your father always done."

"You and Bullet. Always defending him. All my father ever did for this family was to throw money at us. Money is all I ever got from him."

"That's cause money was all he had."

"Well, he didn't have to leave."

"You don't know. He had to live. And that's why you're here. You want to find out why he left."

"So why did he leave?"

Way Low looked down at his feet, like he had lost them and was wondering where they went. When he raised his head, some light caught on his face. He did have some tears running down his face. He began to nod his head. "Okay, okay, who knows how much more they going to cut off of me or how much longer I live when they do. So now you need to know what happened. Your father killed plenty of people after he left, but he never killed that boy."

Mando felt like he was back at Angelo State University and needed to take notes.

* * *

When Way Low finished his story, they saw a dim streak of orange across the dark sky. When Mando rolled him in, Elena had a pot of coffee going. Though she wasn't outside with them and wasn't listening to the story, she had stayed up with them. She told Mando that there were two extra rooms and that he could catch some sleep in one of them. Or, she said, he could stay in one of them. She was a short woman with gravity taking its effect on her aging body, but she held out against it. She held out against everything. She wanted, in the way she fought age and Mando's father, to stay as she was. Just as Way Low did. And Mando didn't want to hurt her, but he wanted to somehow, someway, for some misguided reason that Way Low had stuck in his head, to be true to his father.

After two cups of coffee, Mando went back to his hotel and stared out his sixth floor window until the sun came up. And then he called his wife. Dolores fussed at him for waking her up. And Mando said he just wanted to see how she and his girls were, and she fussed at him some more. And Mando told her that he had pieced his father's life together and would be going back home soon. He asked if she would be at home. She said that she didn't see herself coming back yet. Mando tried to tell her how he felt, but the thought of that empty house made it hard to talk. He could have told Colton's story. But those words got caught in his throat and just wouldn't let themselves get formed so that all that came out was a sob. Dolores listened to Mando trying to talk but just sucking in air until he said bye.

* * *

Mando lowered himself into the chilly saltwater of the pool and got eye-level with a floating, plastic frog with a thermometer attached to his belly. Neither Mando nor the frog blinked. The saltwater felt good around him, so he pulled his eyes away from the plastic frog and did a lap in Justan Brady's pool. Back at the steps, he raised himself out of the pool and felt chilled by the hot but dry weather. Funny, hot as it can get in West Texas, you can just add a little water to the dryness and you're cool. Trouble is, there is so little water. But Justan Brady had a pool. And when Mando called him and told him that he wanted to talk about Danny Fowler's killing, Justan invited Mando to his house. Come by in the afternoon, he told Mando, when no one would be around.

Justan Brady had gone from the Ector County Sherriff's Department to the Odessa Police, and then he retired. His second wife still worked, and he figured he deserved his afternoons splashing, swimming, and soaking in his new pool while he drank his chilled vodka straight up.

278

An hour before, Justan told Mando the story that Colton, Bullet, and him had imagined years ago. And then Mando told him what he knew. Mando figured they all owed Justan that story. He knew that was putting Bullet and Snake and Way Low in danger, but when he got in his house and sat down with Justan and told him the story, he knew Justan wasn't going to say nothing to nobody. The story was just for Justan.

Justan threw Mando a towel, and Mando dried off. He sat in the lawn chair beside him, and he reached for the bottle of Absolute in the bucket of ice. "Another little snort?"

"Sure," Mando said, and Justan poured another hit of high-dollar vodka into a plastic cup.

Justan was tanned. His belly bulged out in front of him. "Thirty pounds. Thirty goddamn pounds since I retired. I sure as hell don't want to be like those old oil field workers I knew when I was young. Drink and smoke themselves right to death soon as they retire." He stared out into the sun's glare bouncing off his pool. "I got me this pool. I got my kids grown up without fucking up too much. My second wife has a good job and still tolerates me." He choked. "Now I know what's ate at my soul for over thirty years. I thank you." Mando thought that Justan was going to cry.

"I ain't a lawman no more. Tell Bullet she's safe."

Mando nodded and shivered from the sun sucking the pool's saltwater off him and from his big gulp of chilled vodka. "I know that. And Bullet don't know I'm here. I'm paying you back for my father." Justan patted his stomach.

"What you thinking, now that you know?"

Justan looked at Mando. "Danny's murder was my last real case. West Texas is a good area for cops. Most cases are simple. You get a call from a woman screaming about her no good, two-timing, son-of-a-bitch husband. You drive to the crumbling house or trailer. There you find the husband dead and bleeding on the living room carpet and the woman holding a smoking gun, probably a birthday present he bought for her. That's the kind of crimes I solved from then on.

"After Danny's murder, the oil boom busted, and Odessa bars put signs on their windows that said, 'An oil field prayer: Please God, give us another oil boom, and I promise not to piss this one away.' Without oil money hiding the demand for whores, the city finally busted Bullet for good. I went by her motel to say goodbye. She said she was in good health.

"My marriage busted too. Michelle asked me what I was thinking, urged me to get a job, not a hobby, asked me what I wanted of myself. We kind of forgot why we picked each other to marry. We just didn't know what we were doing. As we got smarter, we divorced.

"I married again, had children, and I got on with the Odessa Police Department and more money, and then I got them children mostly grown. I didn't quit my job, but this time I worked harder and was more careful and scared. I arrested drunks, investigated simple murders. But the movie in my mind replays a lot. I'll bet Danny's surviving murderer plays movies in his mind about what he done to Danny. He's probably got grown children too, and I bet he can't stop thinking that he gave his grown kids that thing that made him murder Danny Fowler. All I am, all I gave my kids, is scared."

"I'm sure you gave your kids more than scared."

"Danny Fowler surely knew that he was in West Texas and knew what a dangerous game he was playing. But as surely as he knew West Texas, he just couldn't stop being himself. And the boys that killed him shouldn't of hit him, or should've stopped hitting him. I shouldn't of married Michelle. Should've listened to Bobby Cooksey and never investigated Danny Fowler's murder."

Justan wasn't looking at Mando. He was talking to his pool. "The boom is come back. It is tamer this time, and we're not all pissing our money away. But some things don't change. My children and Danny's murderer's children will make mistakes like ours. Those mistakes are taking place all over town. They say you can't prosecute stupidity. But as time goes on, I wish you could."

"Just let it be over."

"I thank you," Justan said. "But I want to go back to that story I made up with Colton and Bullet. What you told me is from all over and under Danny Fowler's death, but not about his death directly. There's three people know the exact truth of what happened with Danny's murder. And two of them, by what you say, are dead. So how are we . . . .how am *I* gonna know enough to cast judgment?"

Justan sat up in his chair and sloshed vodka, and his belly bulged out from him. "I still got a cop's mentality."

"Alls I got is my story, and I just told it to you. And it was hard to come by. And I ain't claiming it to be the exact truth. But it's something."

Justan started nodding his head. "Okay, I'm going with your story. And I'm saying things worked out as best they could."

"But you still gotta wonder?"

"I hope not."

Justan caught sight of Mando's foot, "What the hell you do to your foot?"

"Turns out, everything I could."

They sipped their vodkas and looked across the pool to the other side of Justan's backyard—like they were looking all the way across an ocean to another continent.

* * *

Talking to Justan Brady made Mando want his family, so he called his wife. He asked Dolores how she was doing. "My parents know a guy on the school board. They talked to him. I'm taking a big pay cut, starting out new, but I have a job for the fall."

"You're quitting?" Mando said into the cell phone. He heard no answer. "You think you're coming back to our house? To me?"

Without hesitation she said, "I can't see it." From there, the conversation got worse. The words Mando used didn't work. Neither of them could make a story that involved them, that gave Mando a break.

After talking to his wife, Mando tried to play like he was Colton Parker. He drove from one beer joint to the next in West Odessa. But the smoke and dust floating around his head choked him. So, he bought a bottle of bourbon and went back to his hotel room, went up to the sixth floor, mixed himself a drink, and stared below him at Odessa.

Mando had never drunk much, but he was seeing the delight in it. Diluted with a coke, the bourbon was sweet but stout. He could almost taste the charcoal. And that little burn working its way down his throat both warmed and cooled him. He wasn't drunk, and he wasn't going to be, but he sipped and waited to feel that first little kick that blurred thinking and took the edge off it. He got into the bed and slipped his jogging shoes off. He pulled off his socks to look at his feet, the mangled one a size too short but a size too wide, so that he had to wear shoes too big for both feet, making him feel like he was wearing clown shoes.

The foot and the bourbon couldn't keep his mind off his wife and family. He thought that, when this train hit him, he should have at least of heard it coming. He couldn't find any words to explain that train. There were no words to make it stand still so that Mando could make sense of it. And if, after the years, he couldn't count on Dolores and what they had made, then what could he count on? Running was gone for him. It had left him with a deformed foot and clown shoes. Words weren't helping. The only thing that had been consistent in his life—in moments spaced far apart—for better or worse, mostly worse—was his father.

* * *

The next morning, Mando got a call from Bullet. She asked to see him. At noon he drove to the Cactus Lounge. Bullet and Snake were eating burgers. They had one for Mando. Mando sat with them and ate the burger and dipped fries in ketchup. It seemed to be the best-tasting burger he had ever had.

Bullet had her tubes out of her nose and her tank pushed to one side. Snake was about Bullet's age but looked years younger. He was tanned but not wrinkled. He wore a starched Guyabara shirt and just as crisply starched cotton slacks and beige loafers with no socks on. He sipped from a Bloody Mary in a clear glass.

"You doing good?" Snake asked.

"Okay," Mando said.

"And what exactly is it you do?"

"I'm a coach for young kids."

They both shifted in their chairs and munched on the burgers. Mando took a bite of his and just savored. "How much is that coaching job paying you?" Snake asked.

"Not enough." With the sunbeams and dust drifting in from the cracks, the Cactus Lounge turned sort of golden. And Mando remembered it as sort of golden.

"Look, we owe your father. And we're sorry about your life," Bullet said.

"You mean my wife."

"Her too."

"I'm mostly retired now, but Bullet might be able to use somebody."

"I got people like your dad and what Lionel Dexter used to be working for me. They do what you did. But I need someone with some smarts. Someone to kind of take over some of the day-to-day affairs."

"To become you? To take over."

"And that would be such a bad thing?" Bullet said while chewing.

Mando shifted in his seat. Snake finished his burger, shifted in his seat, and ran his hands up the side of his head to give his head a pair of silver wings. "I'll leave you to it," he said to Bullet.

He pushed himself up and shook Mando's hand. His shoes squished as he crossed the wooden floor, and he let in a flood of sunlight when he opened the door. When he closed it, Mando's eyes adjusted on Bullet. "So is this a real job you're offering me?"

"Yes."

"Would I need a gun like when I was repoing cars and emptying vending machines?"

"Not unless you want one. But I'd recommend it." Mando stared over her shoulder and felt like he was back in Denver City in his backyard wishing. Bullet started talking again. "If you look at a whore real close, you can see she ain't got no soul. That's only part of the story. They aren't born without souls. Somewhere along the way they lose them."

"I know."

Bullet seemed to stare over his shoulder, but Mando looked at her eyes. Looking into his eyes, Bullet said, "The point is, you can lose your soul doing most anything."

"Like working for you." He was immediately sorry for being mean.

"Or being a coach in Denver City." Bullet nodded her head to herself. "Look, you may not believe it, but I'm trying to do something good here."

"What about my father? Did he lose his soul?" Bullet said nothing. "What about you?" Mando asked.

"I said you could tell with whores. I ain't a whore no more."

"Was my father?"

Bullet looked around and saw no one. She pushed herself up, went behind the bar, and came back with two bottles of beer. "Dessert."

"Don't you regret anything? Don't you just get pissed off at how stuff just seems to get worked out?"

"If you noticed, I'm not sucking air out of the tank today. So it's a good day. I don't want to ruin it by cussing my luck, or fate, or fuck ups."

"Pissed away," Mando said. "Can you give me a little while to think over your offer?"

"Take all the time you want. I'm not going anywhere."

"My wife said I needed a 'soul mate.' You said whores ain't got souls. You think maybe none of us got a soul, and we have to go out and find it, and some of us know where to look and some of us don't?"

"You looking, or are you one of the lucky fuckers who knows?"

"I don't know shit."

"My real name is Christina. The name even sounds funny coming out of my mouth. You may be the only person alive who knows that."

* * *

After saying good bye to his mother and Way Low, Mando drove to his house in Denver City. He went next door and got Sebastian, and Sebastian jumped nearly as high as Mando's shoulders when he saw Mando. Then, in Mando's neighbor's backyard, Mando sushed him, held his hand out flat, and Sebastian put his chin in Mando's hand.

Sebastian and Mando walked back to their house, and Sebastian twirled with excitement as Mando opened the front door. Then Sebastian ran through the house, happy to be back home. Mando wandered through it, looking at the woman and girl stuff. And even though he was looking at the hair curlers, and the cute paintings, and the flowers, he missed the stuff, which would soon be gone. Then he wandered out into the back yard, and Sebastian followed him, and he looked up at the sky. Up over him was the vapor from a jet. Mando wondered if some pilot was lost. Nobody flies over this collection of nothing.

Mando stared at the sky, wishing and wanting, until the sun set. As are most sunsets in West Texas, it was beautiful, but it wasn't enough. Mando stared at the stars coming out. Dolores used to tell him that he was a good husband. His school principal told him that he was a good coach. The church Mando went to told him that he was no longer a sinner. But his father's world told him that he had no choice. Hell, Arnie was likely to spend his life in prison. Mando figured he had a better idea of where to sniff out his soul than Arnie did. Hell, Mando used to have running, and now, though they failed him, he still had some words, even if not the right ones, even if he couldn't get them out.

And then he noticed, sitting beside him was Sebastian. Mando had him too.

It wasn't books Mando was after; it was words. He liked the way a thing could have two different words for it, and you use this word instead of the other word and change the way you thought about the thing. He saw this done all the time. And their words, the ones they chose, could make a person's story. The stories that we told ourselves and told others made us what we were. Colton had a story. And Mando, without wanting to, had inherited that story and made it a part of his story. And just as his father's story didn't much include Elena, so Mando's story didn't much include his wife and two girls, that house full of women in lonesome Denver City. His story included Bullet Price—and her offer to him. Unlike his wife, like those folks in Odessa, he knew you had to choose your story. Or your story chose you. There was not a right one, just the one given to you, or if you were lucky, the one you chose. And there's just no knowing whose words are ever the truth. All you can do is to hold on to *your words*, like Colton Parker did, like Danny Fowler must have done.

* * *

Several months later, Mando limped in from the night, like his father did, into where he lived, into the morning at his mother's four-bedroom house that sucked up electricity. His head was fuzzy from beer and coffee. The trunk of his car was full of coins and bills from vending machines. If all the machines started taking debit cards, he might be out of business. He had a pistol and tire tool tucked under the driver's seat. He had yet to shoot anyone—this time.

He limped through the house to the back yard, and there to twirl in circles and jump at him was Sebastian. And though his mother did not want Sebastian inside, Mando opened the backdoor and let Sebastian in with him.

Mando saw Way Low in his chair in front of the TV, smiling up at him, and from the hall with its four bedrooms lining it, his two daughters, still in their pajamas, appeared, and they screamed, "Daddy,

Daddy." Sebastian ran through the house because he was happy to be inside.

And they all reminded Mando of the life he used to have, and that memory burned against his eyes from inside his head. Then another memory burned, and he grabbed Lucy, the youngest, and hoisted her up, but the ceiling was too low, and she was too old and heavy to twirl above his head, but he blew air through his lips to make an airplane motor sound. Audrey looked at her father and slumped her body as young girls were prone to do. And that slump asked in disgust, "What are you doing, Daddy?" Way Low saw, and he remembered, and he smiled.

Mando put Lucy down, and both his daughters ran back to their bedrooms to play with their dolls. Mando sat down with Way Low and watched some of Sunday Morning. "We fed them pan dulce, and I let them take it to their rooms. They like their rooms," he said. Sebastian was at Mando's side, and though he was not supposed to be on the couch, Mando slapped his hands on his thighs, and Sebastian jumped into his lap.

Mando's girls were just visiting. Soon, they would return to Abilene and their real home, and Way-Low, Elena, and Mando would wander through the house that was too big for them.

People called him "Mando." But that word did not name him. "Bullet" and "Snake" and "Way Low" and even "father" gave you a better idea of a person.

Mando heard the garage door open and his mother coming into the kitchen, home from mass, a rustle of pots, pans, the refrigerator door, and plastic bags full of groceries. She smiled when she saw him and said, as she always did, that she was glad that they were all together. Then she saw Sebastian, even though he ducked his head to hide. "His place is not in here," she said.

Mando had tried to make words to describe how he was with his mother. What he knew was that he did not know his mother. He did not know his wife. So, he lost her. He *could know* Way Low and

287

Colton Parker and Arnie Parker. And he *could know* Bullet and Lionel and Danny Fowler and Danny Fowler's killers.

Instead of shooting it out over a debt in Gervin, instead of tracking down Danny Fowler's killers, instead of looking for love in the wrong way, instead of hiding from everybody because you killed that lost lover, Mando and Arnie had fucked up a crash-and-grab robbery at a Town and Country convenience store. Danny was just dead. A killer was still hiding. Colton Parker prospered and took to his new line of work but felt miserable. Lionel dropped a rung in the low-level crime world. Way Low just went on. Arnie went to prison. And Mando tried reading, running, and husbanding and fathering but never got unconfused.

His father was no more; Arnie was as good as gone, and the others that he knew, the ones around him—Way Low, Snake, and Bullet—they were older than Mando. And they would be gone soon, and Mando would be alone, like his father, with his children far away, maybe cussing him. So Mando hoped that he would be the last of them. But he was afraid that he would not be, like he was just looking at the sky wishing or praying for just one more boom and hoping not to piss it away.

CPSIA information can be obtained
at www.ICGtesting.com
Printed in the USA
LVHW111800150621
690286LV00008B/1360

9 781952 439049